RACHEL ARMSTRONG

Waltzing Maguire

**Pink Paws
Publishing**

First published 2024
ISBN 978-0-6453555-6-7

Published by
Pink Paws Publishing
Rachel Armstrong
Townsville QLD 4810
Australia

A catalogue record for this book is available from the National Library of Australia
www.librariesaustralia.nla.gov.au

For my nana
Maureen Hensley

In memory of my pop
William Eric Charles Hensley

About the Author

Rachel Armstrong has always loved making up stories and has never wanted to be anything but an author. She writes contemporary romantic fiction ranging from rural to suspense. Rachel enjoys creating epic feel-good stories and has a weakness for an adventurous holiday escape. Helping her characters find their happily-ever-after is her life's joy.

Rachel lives in Townsville, Queensland, with her border collie, Jacob, where she helps people live their best lives as an exercise physiologist. In her spare time, she is either reading on her treadmill or plotting out her next novel while grooving at Zumba. Rachel's a keen traveller and has enjoyed many holidays exploring historic London, flying through the Grand Canyon, and hiking volcanos in Bali.

Rachel enjoys connecting with readers on social media and through her website.

www.rachelarmstrongauthor.com.au

Dear Reader,

It is summer once again and heavy rain is saturating Elizadale as Cyclone Billy threatens the North Queensland coast. Newcomers Ana and Natalia are both stressing during their first cyclone warning but born and bred locals Meg and Jack are keeping their concerns close to their chests. Cyclones are unpredictable and at this point, who knows which way Cyclone Billy will go?

The skies might be grey, but I'm thrilled to welcome you back to Meg's sunshine town as she finally gets to share her story. Five months have passed since Ana and Liam married, and since Adam and Natalia agreed to tie their own knot. They made their vows during a small family ceremony at High Ridge and remain happily in love. But Adam's brother Jack has been falling deeper into his own despair. After all, he is the eldest and it's his responsibility to marry and ensure the farm is in safe hands for the next generation. But Jack is trapped in a deep, dark hole he hasn't been able to escape from since the accident that destroyed his future. And he can't tell anyone the truth about it, including the woman he's always loved.

People live with regrets, inner demons, and can lose their motivation when all seems lost. Facing these fears can be terrifying and feeling that you have little control over your own destiny leads to further hopelessness. I hope you understand both Jack's turmoil and Meg's patience in this story as they help each other emerge from the darkness and fight for their love and long-awaited happily ever after.

Like any Shadow Creek book, there is a danger lurking around the corner for Meg and Jack, but I hope you enjoy their story and share in the majestic North Queensland spirit as the Elizadale community bands together in the cyclone recovery efforts.

Happy reading,

Rachel

xoxo

Prologue

Meg Riley strummed the final note on her guitar, the music nourishing the hope inside her as it faded into the wind rustling the leaves of the jacaranda tree. She lifted her head, her hands tightening around the instrument as her best friend, Lucy, broke into applause.

'That was beautiful, Meg. Your show's going to be amazing.'

She smiled softly. 'Do you really think so?'

'Absolutely. This is the moment, I know it. For your music career, and for you and Jack.'

Meg's heart swooned. 'I hope so. I'm nervous, Luce.'

'Why? This is what you've always wanted. You and Jack will have a fantastic weekend, be married by Christmas, and have a bunch of rowdy kids you absolutely cannot dump on me.'

Meg bit down on her lower lip to suppress her grin. She couldn't believe it was happening. She could feel it in her soul, had seen the intention in Jack's eyes, and this weekend, her life would change forever. Her cousin, a rising star in country music, had arranged for her to open for his band at the

Gympie Music Muster and with the recent release of her EP, her big break was on the horizon. She'd get herself in front of writers, producers, and the people who would help her forge her career. It didn't need to be a stellar one. Meg loved singing, writing, and performing in her hometown, but she didn't have her sights set on international stardom. She longed for roots and stability. Love and family. She'd studied teaching so that she could settle down with a steady career. But Chaz had given her this chance, and she planned to seize it.

Then, Jack Maguire had offered to drive her the three-day trek to Gympie, and she hadn't missed the unspoken words in his eyes. She might have loved Jack since forever, but only recently had she realised that her desire wasn't one sided. In the eight months since she'd returned from university, they'd been tiptoeing around the chemistry that sizzled between them, and with this chance to escape their hometown and nosey friends, she and Jack could finally ignite that furnace.

Every cell in Meg's body tingled.

'I doubt it'll happen *that* quickly, Luce. It's already August.'

'Please, you've had the wedding planned for years. I know you only hang out with me to ogle my cousin.'

'I do not! We've been friends far longer than I've loved Jack.' Though it'd been their childhood friendship that had led to her schoolgirl crush. Shadow Creek was a second home to Meg, and the Maguires were like family. She'd had sleepovers with Lucy and had ridden horses through the bush with her. Then, when she was sixteen, she'd witnessed Jack Maguire lugging timber to build the new horse yards and had found her feet rooted to the earth. His dirty white singlet had moulded to his growing twenty-year-old chest, sweat had glistened his thickening arms, and when he'd shot her a wave and a smile, Meg had completely lost her heart.

Six years later, Jack still had it.

'True,' Lucy said. 'And I'm happy for you, Meg. I hope everything goes well in Gympie, with your music *and* Jack. Do you need me to drop hints about the ring?'

She shook her head. 'I don't want to scare him.'

'All right. But please, when I dress up as maid of honour, can you not put me in pink?!'

Meg sighed. 'I'll *consider* it.'

They shared a grin. It might sound foolish, but what was the harm in talking about it? Meg had always known what she wanted as every song she wrote was about Jack, and the future she desired revolved around the life they both envisioned. She had baked them a banana cake for the road, the secret recipe she shared only with him, and tomorrow morning, they would drive off into their future.

Meg could barely stop wriggling with glee. How she would sleep tonight, she didn't know.

* * *

A breeze blew through the open cab as Jack drove the tractor along the banks of Shadow Creek, the waterway which his ancestors had named the farm for. Or they'd named after the farm. He didn't know. The Maguires had ridden in to take up the land holding shortly after Stuart Riley had settled the town of Elizadale a hundred and fifty years ago. But while that truth had been lost to history, there Jack was, a seventh-generation farmer as rooted to the property as the treelined creek that ran through it. These bananas were his life. Everything he had in the world. He would die on this land.

After a long and fulfilled life, of course, and as a young man nearing his twenty-sixth birthday, Jack had many plans and dreams for the future. He and his brother would inherit Shadow Creek and maintain the banana farm their father had expanded since selling the last of the livestock thirty years ago. Henry Maguire and his brother Cliff had put their blood, sweat, and tears into building Shadow Creek into a profitable enterprise they could proudly pass on to their children.

Now it was Jack's job to take the farm to the next level. His father had given him some control when he'd turned twenty-one and, together, they'd immediately put Jack's dreams of diversifying into action. They'd had three successful seasons with the guavas and after a four-year labour of love, the lychee orchard would produce its first fruit this summer.

But Shadow Creek remained one farm, one business, and Jack wanted more. In the long term, he planned to expand the company across the Mareeba Shire and Atherton Tablelands by purchasing smaller farms to increase his family's landholdings.

Jack wanted to build an empire.

Grinning, hope filled his chest as he manoeuvred the tractor to avoid the unstable bank. The dream was so close he could almost taste it. But he had one more job remaining this afternoon before he headed home, packed the ute, and woke at dawn to collect his future and whisk her away for the weekend.

He was taking Megan Riley to the Gympie Music Muster. Meg, his charitable, vibrant friend who had stolen his heart so many years ago. The beautiful woman who had recently returned to town as a primary schoolteacher and who tormented him with her angelic voice when she sang at the pub with her cousin. He'd cherished their friendship while she'd been at university and had used that time to work, learn, and set his goals for the future. Now he was ready. He would drive her to Gympie so she could pave her way to becoming a country music star, and they could begin their lives together.

Which was a plan he'd had long before her grandfather, Victor O'Shea, had approached him. The aging farmer had made a mint in tobacco back in the day, until the industry had died and he'd made an early switch to avocados. Like most farmers, he'd hoped to pass his land to the next generation so it could continue to thrive in safe hands. Unfortunately, neither of his daughters nor three grandchildren wanted to take it on.

But Victor had casually mentioned that he could bestow Jade Farm to Meg if she were to marry a farmer willing to oversee it. He hadn't pressed, of course, and Jack had politely refrained from saying anything at all. What sizzled between him and Meg had nothing to do with business. He wanted to marry Meg because he loved her, not because she could help him expand his farming enterprise.

But even though Victor might have been jumping the gun, it was an issue Jack would address later. Right now, he just wanted to get this job done as he slowed the tractor and glanced over his shoulder. His father would be there any minute with their supplies and in a few hours, he could go home and—

A crack sounded, and Jack jolted. Spinning in his seat, he scanned the creek. That had sounded like a—

Bang!

A deafening explosion had his hands tightening around the wheel as air gushed out from beneath him. The world shifted. He reached for the brake, but it was too late. The machine groaned beneath him. Jack froze. Gravity beckoned.

A sickening crash thundered in his ears. The world darkened, then brightened again in one great flash. Breath heaved from his chest in short, sharp bursts as pain shot through his body and rasped from his throat in a yell.

He arched his back, but he couldn't move. Blinking, clarity beckoned as he glanced around him. The tractor lay on its side, the steel cab having done its job by preventing a complete rollover. But the engine body trapped his leg to the ground. His head fuzzed. Stomach roiled.

The roar of an engine cut through the air, followed by his father's voice screaming his name.

Chapter One

Five Years Later

Jack Maguire stood at the edge of the packing shed, rain flying at him sideways in the swirling wind as he gazed out over the dripping banana plants. It hadn't eased in days, saturating the farm, fouling his mood, and breaking his heart. This weekend, his life's work and everything he cared about—the bananas, the lychees, the guavas—could all be gone.

Thanks to Cyclone Billy threatening the North Queensland coast.

Beside Jack, his brother Adam shifted from foot to foot. 'Bastard will turn. He's days away from making landfall, but they always turn.'

It was late Wednesday afternoon, and the radar predicted the category four storm would cross the coast late Saturday near Cairns. Located only a little inland from the coastal city, Elizadale was preparing for a direct hit.

But Adam's confidence wasn't unfounded. Cyclones had never devastated Elizadale like they had other North Queensland towns. Hell, the whole reason banana farming had boomed around Mareeba was *because* of cyclones. Competing with Innisfail and Tully had been fruitless until 2006 when Cyclone Larry had destroyed the region and ninety percent of Australia's banana crop, hence Mareeba, Elizadale, and Lakeland had become some of the few remaining sources in the country. And they'd flourished.

Jack's arms tightened across his chest. He remembered the time vividly. He'd been thirteen and it'd been the first time he'd tackled hard work on the farm. They'd planted more fields and taken on many of Innisfail's workers to meet the demands. Innisfail and Tully had slowly recovered, sadly to be impacted again by Yasi in 2011, but the importance of banana farms this far north had been established. They were a contingency plan.

But this time, their luck might have run out.

'We need to prepare ourselves,' Jack muttered.

'Yeah, but we deleaf tomorrow, the bastard will turn and we'll have delayed the harvest by months.'

'And if we don't deleaf and are hit, we'll be set back a year.'

Hence the million-dollar question of whether to prepare the farm. A lot of research had gone into saving the banana crops from cyclones this past decade and deleafing was a viable option. Removing the canopy from the plant would delay fruit production, possibly help it survive the storm, and reduce their loss.

But if the cyclone didn't hit, they'd have sacrificed the current production income. And if they waited to know if the cyclone was imminent, they wouldn't have time to prepare. Not that deleafing would help them against a bastard as ferocious as Billy.

Nature. Farming's greatest enemy and the one variable

Jack couldn't control. He could wake up on Sunday with his farm flattened and no income for more than a year.

Jack tossed back his head and exhaled. 'Fuck.'

'Yeah,' Adam agreed. 'Fuck.'

Standing in silence, Jack and Adam watched the rain. Ultimately, their father and uncle would make the decision, but the four men operated Shadow Creek as a team. Their father had been on the Banana Growers Council for decades, and Jack had taken it upon himself to do most of the research and stay up to date with the latest ideas and techniques by attending nearly every conference and meeting he could. But should they take the risk and prepare for Billy?

Jack had no idea.

'It'll turn,' Adam said again, and Jack's teeth clenched. 'That's what I keep telling Nat, not that it stops the woman from driving me bloody mental. She's convinced the house will flood if the creek keeps rising.'

'Your house will be fine.'

'*I* know that. The flood would wipe out the town before it touched us, but it's Nat's first wet season and she's freaking out. We've got enough canned goods to last us years.'

'We may need them.'

'Hope not. I don't like canned peas.' Adam met Jack's gaze. 'Robbo get back to you?'

Jack nodded. There had been endless phone calls between himself and his farming mates these past few days as they all checked in to see how everyone was doing. Rob Wallace was one of Jack's closest friends in the industry and was running his farm south of Innisfail single handedly after losing his father less than a year ago.

'Robbo's preparing for the worst. Hoping the bastard does

a one-eighty and fizzles out in the ocean.' Although the likelihood of that happening was next to zero.

'Tried telling Nat that too, but she wouldn't hear of it.'

'Shouldn't you be getting home? Go and calm your wife?'

'Yeah, I'll go and put some chickpeas on the stove before she finishes work.' Adam shot Jack a grin. 'You know, it's good being married. Knowing someone's always there and that you won't sleep alone.'

Jack rolled his eyes. 'You're not the first bloke to get married.'

His brother hadn't stopped talking about it ever since he'd put a ring on Natalia's finger. Of course, Jack was happy for him. Adam was his brother, closest mate, and Jack only wanted what was best for him. But as he'd stood as Adam's best man, Jack hadn't been able to deny the dent in his older brother pride. Or the regret.

Adam never failed to notice. 'Jack's still jealous,' he teased, standing too far away for Jack to thump him. 'You could easily find out what marriage is like for yourself, you know.'

Jack's spine tensed, and he gazed back out into the rain. 'Shut up.'

'Seriously, mate. You're driving me nuts with this. Ever since my wedding, you've been a sad sack of shit every time I mention marriage. What the fuck's holding you back?'

Jack's jaw clenched. 'None of your fucking business. How many times do I need to tell you that before you let it go?'

'A million, 'cause I'm not letting it go.' Adam stepped around to face him. 'You love Meg, Jack. Always have. I know you didn't get your romantic weekend away because of the accident but come on! It's been five years!'

Inhaling, Jack looked past Adam into the miserable fields. If only his brother knew the truth about the tractor incident, but he couldn't tell him. If everyone else had said he was being stupid and overreacting, then Adam certainly would too.

'I know how long it's been.' Every day had been pure agony.

'Then sweep the girl off her feet and give Mum grandchildren before I beat you to it!'

Jack's fists clenched beneath his crossed arms. He wished he could sweep Meg into his arms and claim her as his own, but that chance had been shot to hell. Literally. There was no getting another.

'I thought you and Nat were waiting on the kid thing.'

Adam's eyes narrowed. 'You're avoiding the subject.'

'No shit.'

'Fuck, you piss me off.' Adam shoved his hand through his hair.

'Should be used to it by now,' Jack muttered. 'But seriously, are you and Nat going to give it a go?'

'Dunno. She's not sure she's ready, but I'm kind of keen, so she said we could try our luck for a few months.'

Jack wished he could smack the smug smile off Adam's face. Yep, his bloody brother had beaten him to it with his beautiful wife and a chance to have a family. He would fill his home with warmth and love, whereas Jack was destined to remain alone in his shack by the lychee trees forever. His parents could live out their days in the homestead because he'd never need it. He would work Shadow Creek and pass it on to his nephews or nieces. He'd never marry or have children of his own because if he did, he would marry Meg.

And that was something he could never do.

'I wish you luck, mate.' It took all of Jack's strength to reach up and clap Adam on the shoulder.

'Yeah. Fucking scary shit. Although if this cyclone hits …'

Adam's mouth twisted as he turned back towards the dripping banana plants. 'Might need to rethink things. Don't want a baby born in a disaster zone.'

'Yeah. If Billy hits …'

They couldn't vocalise it. Standing together, Jack and Adam glared at the pouring rain saturating everything they'd ever worked for.

Adam exhaled. 'It'll turn.'

Chapter Two

Meg Riley bustled about her kitchen, preparing for her friends' arrival with her Pomeranian, Lola, following at her heels. Every Friday night, Meg would meet her friends at the Royal Hotel for dinner, conversation, and fun after a long week at work. But tonight, the cyclone warning had forced all businesses to close.

Billy was still coming for them.

The next update from the Bureau of Meteorology was due in thirty minutes, and every second was a test of her nerves. She wanted to think positively, but while the Christian in her wouldn't allow her to pray for Billy to change projection only to devastate another town, she knew he would cross the coast somewhere. A community would pay the price and if that community was Elizadale, then so be it. Her town was strong. United. They would rebuild and stick together. Cyclone or no cyclone, Elizadale's spirit would live on.

Billy wouldn't break them.

But until that update came, she needed to remain busy, else risk fretting. Meg scooped Lola's dinner into her sparkling pink dish and the little dog's mouth dropped open as she danced backwards, her brown eyes alight among her wriggling caramel fur. 'Sit.'

Lola spun in an excited circle, then plopped her little bum down. Meg rubbed her soft head and placed the bowl on the feeding mat. Lola leapt at her dinner and Meg resumed making her own as she slipped the fishcakes into the oven and checked on her casserole in the slow cooker, the sweet apricot chicken aroma soothing her senses.

A tap sounded on the door and Lola abandoned her food as she raced down the hallway yapping her head off.

'Hey, Meggy!'

Meg glanced into the open-plan dining and living area, smiling as Adam and Natalia let themselves in. 'Hey! How are you two?'

'I'm trying not to freak out,' Natalia said as she slipped her covered dish into Meg's oven. 'Billy's now a category five!'

'I know.'

Noting the pitch in Natalia's voice, Meg reined in her fear and strove for calm. At least she'd been through this before, but it was Natalia's first summer in North Queensland and her first cyclone warning. She and her sister Ana had lived in Sydney until Ana had moved to Elizadale a year ago and married Liam Maguire. Shortly before their wedding, Natalia had moved to town to fill the position of junior general practitioner and had won the heart of Liam's cousin, Adam. Meg had claimed both women as her friends upon their arrival and had been over the moon to see them fall in love and find their happily-ever-afters.

Yet as Meg had stood beside each of the newcomers at their weddings, she'd barely managed to contain her frustration with life. There was a new Mrs Maguire working at the school and a Doctor Maguire who all the children adored.

Whereas she was still little Miss Riley, former show queen, failed country singer, and destined to spend her life alone.

Because her Maguire was a stubborn bastard whose words all those years ago continued to haunt her.

'I think it's best we just stay friends …'

'I want to start preparing,' Natalia said, 'but Adam won't let me tape the windows.'

'We don't need to tape them yet.'

'Ana and Liam have. They won't lose their house!'

'We won't lose our house either,' Adam said gently, placing beer in the fridge. 'I built it strong.'

'But what about the older homes? What about Riley House?'

Meg's throat tightened. Riley House was the Queenslander that her great-great-great-great-great grandfather, Stuart Riley, had built, and the oldest building still standing in Elizadale. The town, the house, and the relics in the two-room museum were her history, her legacy, and one day, the responsibility to ensure Elizadale continued to thrive would be hers. It was a task she held dear to her heart and what drove her to volunteer her time with many community organisations.

'It had some water damage from Yasi, but if we're in the direct path of Billy …' Meg couldn't finish that sentence. Swallowing, she nodded towards the oven. 'What you brought smells good.'

'Thanks. It's pumpkin curry.'

Meg's stomach rumbled. 'Yum. I've put the rice on and Isabella's bringing a salad.'

Lucy strode in with chocolate brownies and beer, then Isabella Brennan arrived. Meg greeted her at the door, relieving her friend of the large bowl of tossed salad as she struggled with it and her King Charles Cavalier.

'S-sorry, Meg.' Isabella placed Evie on the ground where Lola waited impatiently, yapping for her friend. 'I turned back because I forgot the salad and it started drizzling again—'

'It's okay, Iz.' Meg knew if she didn't reassure Isabella, she would continue rambling. 'We're all on edge with this cyclone. You're here now and I'll drive you home later if you need me too.'

Isabella smiled softly, turmoil rumbling in her eyes. 'Thank you.'

'Grab yourself a drink. I have chamomile tea.'

Meg began to follow her but stopped at the deep rumble of an engine. Glancing outside, she welcomed the familiar flutter around her heart as Jack Maguire shut the door of his Ford Ranger Raptor and strode up her driveway, sexy as ever with his dark hair damp from the drizzling rain. His grey polo stretched across his shoulders, clinging to every hard plane and groove of his muscular body, while his thighs strained against his dark chinos. Everything inside Meg heated, twisted, and sang. There was the man she'd loved for a decade, the man she'd missed while studying at university. The man she'd hoped to marry after their romantic weekend away in Gympie.

Until he'd almost died beneath that tractor.

She didn't know what had happened during his hospital stay that had made him change his mind about dating her, but patience was a virtue, and if friends was all he was offering, then she would take what she could get.

Meg held open the screen door. 'Hey!'

Jack kicked off his shoes while behind him, his younger brother Michael lifted his hand in a wave.

'Hey, darlin'.' Jack lifted the container he carried. 'Brought fruit salad.'

'Excellent. I have ice cream and Lucy brought brownies.'

'Mix all three and we have the perfect dessert,' Michael said, following Jack inside. 'Everyone else here?'

'Just waiting for Ana and Liam.'

She closed the door and followed the men into the kitchen, where everyone gathered and spread out into the living room at the back of the house. Lola raced around begging for attention while Evie curled up beneath Isabella's barstool. Placing the salad in the fridge, anxiety eased from Meg's spine. Disaster was coming for them, but at least all her friends were there, except for Cade, who was at a police seminar in Townsville.

'I could get used to this,' Lucy said, leaning against the bench with a beer in her hand. 'The pub's great, but I enjoy hanging at each other's houses.'

Isabella nodded. 'Food's certainly better.'

'Beer's cheaper too,' Adam said, handing one to each of his brothers.

Meg smiled softly. 'We could make a habit of it.'

'I'm keen,' Natalia said. 'We've got a big patio.'

'Yeah, we can always party at our house,' Adam agreed. 'Although Mike's the one we should be inviting ourselves over to.'

'I've already invited you over,' Michael said, leaning over the breakfast bar beside Isabella. 'Next month. I'm ready to go.'

A builder by trade, Michael had recently completed his grand home on Shadow Creek and was hosting a housewarming combined with his twenty-seventh birthday in April.

'I can't believe it's already finished,' Isabella said.

'Already?' Adam laughed. 'It's taken him forever!'

'It's taken the right amount of time, thank you.'

Lucy scoffed. 'And yet, it's not even finished.'

'It's liveable. I don't need to have the kids rooms painted and carpeted yet.'

'Need to get yourself a wife before you talk about having kids,' Adam said.

'Don't you start. The world hasn't righted itself since you got married. Don't knock it off its axis by having a baby.'

Meg's ovaries clenched as she helped herself to a glass of her favourite mango wine.

Adam laughed. 'You know how I like to shock you all.'

'Like it all you want,' Natalia said, 'I can assure everyone that Adam won't be having a baby any time soon.'

Jack slipped his hands into his pockets, and Meg's hormones sang louder. 'Boss has spoken, mate.'

'I think one baby around here is enough,' Lucy muttered as Ana and Liam called out from the door.

They *were* expecting the first Maguire baby in September, and Meg was not at all jealous.

'Sorry we're late,' Liam said, placing the potato salad and bean dip on the bench. 'Ana was—'

'I feel like crap.' Ana slumped onto the stool beside Isabella. 'Don't get pregnant, ladies. It's not worth it. You hear me, Adam? Keep your hands off my sister.'

Adam swigged his beer. 'I don't need my hands.'

Natalia wrapped her arm around Ana's shoulders. 'You'll feel better soon, I'm sure.'

'Would you like a cup of tea?' Meg might not like hearing her friend was ill, but she wouldn't heed her warning. She'd give anything to be where Ana was. At twenty-seven, the ache to start a family had evolved into downright torture. She should have started years ago. Except fate had had other ideas.

Gritting her teeth, Meg flicked the kettle on. Jack stood

beside Michael, paying idle attention to Ana as he swigged his beer. What was going through his stubborn head? What did he want out of life? Once, she'd thought she knew. He had a rambling homestead to inherit and a farm to pass down. Sure, he had a massive family and therefore didn't need to produce the heir himself, but didn't he want to pass Shadow Creek to his child like the generations before him?

How would he do that unless he broke his resistance and married her? There couldn't be anyone else. She might be confused, but she'd seen the way he'd looked at her when he'd offered to drive her to Gympie, and that look continued to fill his eyes today. He might have kept his distance, but Jack Maguire loved her. Deep in her heart, her soul, Meg knew that. He was always there for her. He cared about her and put her first. He drove the Raptor to Mareeba to collect furniture for her. He helped her build it. He'd lain her lawn and cleaned her gutters. He dropped everything to remove snakes from her house. He brought her soup when she was sick and had driven her around when she'd sprained her ankle.

He called her darlin'.

Jack was her best friend. She was his. So why the hell didn't he want more?

'What can I do to help?' Lucy asked, arriving at Meg's side. 'There's too much baby talk going on for me.'

'The rice is done, so let's serve the apricot chicken and get the food out. I'll grab some plates.'

'Good. I'm starving. And it might be our last chance to eat a hot meal.'

'Don't say that. We can still have barbeques.'

Lucy took Natalia's curry from the oven. 'Yeah, but honestly … I'm scared. Imagine everything we'll lose.'

Heart pounding, Meg wrapped her arm around her friend.

Lucy was right. Despite a lifetime of living in North Queensland, none of them had experienced the dramatic after effect of a cyclone. The destruction left by Yasi had been minimal in Elizadale, and Shadow Creek had lost only a small amount of crop. But this time …

'Shit!' Adam cried. 'It's seven-twenty!'

Drinks thudded onto benches as everyone leapt for their phones. Meg's fingers shook as she opened the Bureau of Meteorology app. The update had been due two minutes ago and surely …

A collective sigh echoed around Meg's kitchen. Natalia threw her arms around Adam while Jack slumped against the bench.

Pressing her lips together, Meg studied the updated tracking map. Billy had dipped south and would barely brush them as he headed inland.

Straight for Innisfail.

Chapter Three

Jack placed the last piece of his treasured banana cake in the microwave and poked his head out of the kitchen, unable to tear his eyes away from the devastating footage on the TV. Nausea roiled through his belly as relief and guilt continued to do battle inside his head. Billy had spared Elizadale. They'd had a bit of rain tonight, but it wouldn't destroy his farm or home.

Meanwhile, the banana capital of Australia and many of his friends were losing everything.

Again.

The reporters on TV talked their usual shit, exaggerating the drama as though they'd never seen a cyclone before. Not that anyone needed their commentary when the images spoke for themselves. Billy had crossed the coast shortly after eight pm this Saturday evening, and everyone from Cairns to Cardwell had battened down the hatches.

Pressure built inside Jack's chest as he watched trees blowing in the two hundred kilometre per hour winds. Fucking rotten luck. Innisfail didn't deserve another devastating storm. He thought about Robbo hunkered down at home. The Hodgsons, Mr Tucker, and the McNallys. His friends. Not only would they lose their crop, but the winds could damage or destroy their packing sheds, tractors, and fridges too. They could prepare as much as possible, shut everything down and lock up the equipment, but no one could predict the damage. All they could do was ride it out in the suffocating March heat with no power while the howling winds echoed around them and blew their livelihood away.

Jack felt their pain. He understood. He'd once lost everything too. It might not have been his farm, home, or income, but he'd almost lost his life and he'd certainly lost his future. And it could easily have been him facing Billy's wrath. His family and Shadow Creek. But instead—

The microwave beeped, and Jack retrieved the cake with a heavy heart. He wasn't sure when Meg would make him another, but it was delicious, their secret, and he always savoured the last piece. Hence why it'd been in the freezer for three weeks.

His kelpie, Jill, released a hopeful whine from his side, and Jack rubbed her head. Jill had been the one good thing to have come out of the tractor incident, despite having been forced upon him. He hated what had happened to her and her littermates, but Rebecca Taylor had rescued the abandoned, dying pups and no one could say no to Rebecca.

'Dogs are the best companions, Jack,' she'd told him, pressing the wriggling red pup into his chest. 'And I'm worried about you. You haven't been yourself since you came home.'

He'd been out of the hospital for six weeks and in a very dark place. The little red dog couldn't possibly chase away the big black one. A dog couldn't cure heartbreak or allow him to start a relationship with Meg. But he'd taken the pup and as he'd sat with her and unleashed all his woes and the truths he couldn't share with anyone else, she had listened. When he'd had nothing more to say, Jill had licked his hand to tell him she understood, and he'd been a goner.

She wasn't a replacement for Meg or family, but Jill was loyal and always there for him. He rarely let her inside, but the backyard resembled a mud pool and with the disaster currently unfolding, Jack felt it was a night for company.

Though if she thought he was sharing his banana cake, she was dreaming.

Rain pattered on the tin roof of his little house as Jack strode into the lounge room. The house wasn't much, but it'd served its purpose of getting him and his brothers—Liam included—out from beneath their parents' roofs. For many years, they had lived together and enjoyed their lives as single men. Adam had left three years ago when he'd built his house, Liam six months later. Michael had been back and forth this past year as he'd sometimes set up camp on his slab, but he too had officially moved out. Now, it was just him and Jill, and lonely as hell. But it was all Jack would ever have because even though he'd seen Meg's face last night when Ana had talked about babies, he knew he'd never be the man to give them to her. No matter how much he wanted to, he couldn't risk it.

But fuck, it was getting harder to resist the urge to hold her long, slender body in his arms. He longed to bury his face in her mango scented hair and press his mouth to hers. He wanted what his brother had. What Liam had. He wanted love and a future and something to enjoy other than work.

He wanted to be happy.

But Jack hadn't known happiness since he'd returned from Townsville with a sore leg, an anxious heart, and demons warring inside his head. Since he'd looked Meg in the eye and said those fateful words. *I think it's best we just stay friends.*

He hadn't wanted to, and guilt gnawed at his insides every day, but he didn't know what else to do. He was stuck in a bottomless pit from which he couldn't escape. If only he could leave Shadow Creek, Meg would no longer be a temptation. Perhaps he should? Adam could run the Shadow Creek operation while Jack found a new farm and expanded their company with something new. Maybe apples since that would mean leaving North Queensland for good.

He sank onto the lounge with a groan and, as usual, shoved the thoughts from his head. If only it were that easy to start a whole new life.

'We are keeping an eye on one creek that might rise and come into Innisfail … All you can hear is the wind and rain … We've already seen a lot of destruction … No one is on the streets—'

'No shit.' Rolling his eyes at the reporter, Jack bit into the cake. Fuck, that was good. No matter how many times Meg made it for him, it still tasted as fabulous as it had on his twenty-fifth birthday, when she'd surprised him by showing up from her university teaching placement in Atherton. It'd been a year before the tractor incident, he'd been head-over-boots in love with her, and the fact she'd driven the hour to wish him a happy birthday had meant more than he could say. But the cake … hell, Jack had known then he'd marry her for that cake alone.

It was the perfect comfort food while witnessing disaster.

'The power has gone off. There are no phones. As you can see, there is no underestimating the power of this cyclone—'

Jack muted the TV. It was hard enough thinking about his friends, he didn't need to listen to the crap city reporters were sprucing when the industry he worked for was being destroyed. So he watched, ate, and hoped like hell that Robbo and everyone else were all right.

***

The minister had cancelled Sunday church because of the cyclone, so Meg fed Lola apple slices while tears formed in her eyes at the devastation on the morning news. Some houses remained standing, but many more were missing walls or featured caved-in roofs. Powerlines dangled in the windy debris over fallen trees. Images of roofs peeling from sheds played over and over while other footage showed water gushing down streets around broken road signs. Trees crushed houses and sheds collapsed onto cars. The aerial shots captured too many devastating scenes of shattered communities and mud flooding the highways.

Every banana tree lay flat.

Meg sliced the apple and fed a piece to her impatient Pomeranian, unable to stop watching.

'The marina—a multimillion dollar junkyard … Coastal communities are in ruin … One hundred and eighty thousand homes and businesses are without power … Farmers are facing significant losses.'

It went on and on as they replayed the footage and reporters found more devastated people to interview. She didn't want to stop watching, but she was meeting Deborah Maguire for lunch to discuss the show queen contest. So, with a heavy heart, Meg switched off the TV.

Billy had wreaked havoc, but Innisfail had rebuilt before. They would do it again. It might have been over ten years since Yasi, but cyclones were a part of life in tropical North Queensland and the people were bred tough. The communities would join together and Meg would do whatever she could to help the people of Innisfail get back on their feet.

Right now, though, she had to focus on something

positive. The Elizadale Show was her favourite event of the year, and she was lucky they could go ahead with it and that they still had a show queen contest to organise. So Meg slipped on her shoes, placed Lola in her rainbow snuggle bed, and left the house.

Chapter Four

The skies had cleared, but the drive through Shadow Creek was a slow one as Meg navigated her soon-to-be muddy white Holden Astra around the potholes. Tension eased from her shoulders as she approached High Ridge Retreat. Show queen had always been Meg's favourite part of the local agricultural show, long before she'd had the opportunity to enter the contest herself. Each contestant organised fundraising events for the community to help local charities or those that supported the rural lifestyle, and she'd attended every trivia night, fashion show, and barn dance. She'd even played eighteen holes of golf one year, having never swung a golf club in her life. Her parents had bred community spirit into her, and Meg couldn't imagine missing out on any local event. When she was sixteen, she'd finally entered the contest herself and laid the foundations for her music career by hosting concerts to raise money for the Royal Flying Doctor Service. But she hadn't done it alone. Meg's uncle might have taught her to play guitar alongside her cousin, but she'd never been as talented as Chaz, and he'd jumped at the chance to form her backup band. The Charlie Boys had also sung their own songs at the concerts, along with any other local who wished to take part. She hadn't wanted the concerts to only be about her, but they'd certainly boosted her confidence. Her love of music had grown as she'd honed her talent and dreamed of becoming a star.

The Charlie Boys had realised that dream. But while Meg had missed her chance and music rarely spoke to her anymore, the show queen contest lived on, and Meg continued to support her community in her role as mentor. Helping other young women realise their dreams was as rewarding as participating herself.

She drove past the campground at the bottom of the hill, then started up the steep, winding road towards High Ridge, Shadow Creek's tourist retreat. Nestled on part of the mountain near the national park, it sat a hundred or so metres up on the rise and boasted a spectacular view. Meg parked and stepped out of her Astra into the warm air, soaking in the sight. The majestic bush landscape below the ridge bloomed with greenery, the raging creek separating it from the rows of leafy banana plants that continued to stand and spread into the distance towards the highway and the bulbous trees of Kelly Coffee Plantation.

Meg smiled. No wonder the place was so popular. She could enjoy this view every day. Lucy sure did.

Turning, Meg strode towards the lodge. As the live-in manager, Lucy kept an apartment above the dining hall and kitchen. A verandah stretched along the elevated ground floor before opening onto a large undercover deck featuring wooden tables and heat lamps for the winter. Party lights hung from the awning, but Meg hadn't seen Lucy use them in years, which was a shame as they looked great from a distance.

Meg stepped into reception, where Lucy and her aunt Wendy sold their boutique line of jams, chutneys, and other foodstuffs, then entered Wendy Maguire's magnificent dining hall. There, Meg found Deborah waiting at one of the beautiful wooden tables Adam had handcrafted many years ago. Meg had always loved his work and while Adam might have been reluctant at the time, he was a talented woodworker and she'd been delighted when he'd decided to utilise his skills and start a business last year.

'Morning, Meg!'

'Hey!' She greeted Deborah with a hug as they exchanged pleasantries. Deborah and Meg had always been close. She'd practically been another parent considering the many nights Meg had slept over her house with Lucy. Now, Deborah was Meg's boss as principal of Elizadale State School and together, they'd run the show queen contest for five years.

'We have six young ladies entered,' Deborah said, 'and some amazing mentors. I'm glad Natalia agreed to help Brittany.'

'They're a good match. Nat loves being involved in the community, but I think Brittany choosing to raise funds for that animal sanctuary helped.'

'She'll be quite the contender. I've put you with Samantha Burgess.'

Meg smiled. Samantha had plenty of potential with her go-getter attitude, creative soul, and popularity.

'The other contestants look promising and will represent Elizadale well,' Deborah continued, handing Meg the list of young ladies, mentors, and charities. She nodded with approval. They were all good causes. Rural aid, Farm Animal Rescue, the Royal Flying Doctor …

Biting down on her lower lip, Meg frowned. This was a fundraising event and one the community felt passionate about. Could they—

'Hi, Meg!' She glanced up as Wendy poked her head out of the kitchen. 'Are you staying for lunch?'

'I would love to. Thanks.'

As if she could ever pass up lunch from Wendy, Jack's mother and the world-class chef who had moved to Elizadale after falling head over heels for Henry Maguire. But even though she'd given up her culinary career in Brisbane, she'd continued to pursue her dreams and after her youngest child, Lily, had started school, she'd opened High Ridge. Back then, it had just been a kitchen in a small donga on this site and the campground at the bottom of the hill, but it hadn't taken long for word to spread about Wendy's mouth-watering food. Reviews had flourished, the view had added to their fame, and in the fifteen years since, Wendy had built the lodge and added cabins onto the hill. Lucy had come on board to start horse riding tours, they'd formed their boutique food business, and the resort had won various tourism awards.

'What are you making, Wendy?' Deborah asked.

'Just a variety of rolls. Nothing special.'

Meg swallowed a laugh, highly doubting that. Even Wendy's simplest foods were mouth-wateringly decadent, and the tourists knew it, hence the retreat was popular all year round. Though right now, Billy's presence had left the campground empty.

The reception door tingled and Jack called out. Meg's heart leapt and she turned, sending him a smile as he strode into the dining hall, shirt sleeves rolled up and the hems of his jeans wet over his socked feet. She could imagine the state of his boots since he'd left them at the front door.

'Hey, Aunty Deb. Meg, darlin'. What brings you here?'

His hand fell to her shoulder, his calloused thumb sending a shockwave of heat through her body as he stroked her soft skin.

Like a good friend, she shrugged. 'Show queen meeting. What about you?'

'Need to speak to Mum. You think she has lunch ready?'

'Yep. She's making "just rolls."'

'Yum. Good thing I stopped by.'

Jack strode into the kitchen. Meg tore her gaze from his denim backside, exhaling as she glanced at the list she'd been reading. She might have been in love with the man her whole life, but her heart still waltzed every time he walked into the room. Everything was right with the world when Jack was present. Everything inside her felt complete and whole, which was a feeling that had never vanished in all these years of being 'just friends.'

'Are you happy with the interview questions, Meg?'

She nodded and handed the list back to Deborah. 'And everyone's chosen worthwhile charities, but I was thinking …'

The kitchen doors swung open, and Jack returned carrying a plate of sandwiches. 'Mum thought you'd like the ham and cheese with her special mustard,' he said, handing Deborah the partially wrapped roll.

'Thank you.'

'And Meg, I thought you'd like the chicken and coleslaw.'

Meg's stomach rumbled as she gratefully accepted her lunch. He hadn't been wrong. 'Thanks,' she said as he slipped into the seat beside her with what looked like a barbeque chicken roll for himself.

'No worries, darlin'. How's the contest going?'

'Good. We have some strong contenders this year.'

Jack nodded, the muscles in his tanned throat working as he swallowed. 'You always do. Are you raising money for the RFDS again?'

'Yep. Although …' Meg paused and picked up a piece of carrot that had fallen out of her roll.

Deborah frowned. 'What is it?'

'Maybe we could do something different this year. Disaster recovery is going to need funds, so why don't we pool the proceeds from show queen for cyclone relief?'

Deborah's eyebrows shot up. 'I think that's an excellent idea, Meg. There will be a call for relief soon.'

'Absolutely,' Jack agreed.

'You don't think the girls will mind?'

Deborah shook her head. 'Nope.'

'And working for a common cause will help build camaraderie,' Jack said. 'Both with the contestants and the community.'

Meg grinned, glad they thought so as they finished their sandwiches. Jack was right. Working together would boost morale among the contestants, and it was a cause the community would certainly rally behind.

'Any plans this afternoon, Jack?' Deborah asked.

'Going to help Mike tile the main bathroom.'

Meg frowned. 'I thought you didn't do tiling.' In fact, she remembered the task causing him great frustration when they'd been building Adam's house.

'I do what needs to be done. Tiling's easy, I just hate it when they won't align neatly. But Mike's probably expecting me, so I should go.' He stood, then offered her a small smile. 'Walk with me, Meg?'

'Sure.' Meg slipped off the bench seat, her spine tingling when Jack placed his hand on her back. Taking a deep breath, she fought for her renowned composure as they left the dining hall. 'Have you had any issues with the rain?'

'Nah.' He opened the front door, allowing her to precede him. 'We've had a few bogged vehicles, but nothing to complain about. Bloody glad we didn't deleaf though, so the harvest is still on track.'

'That was a brave and tough decision.'

Jack sat on the bench outside and tugged on his muddy boots. 'I just hope some guys down south managed it. Did you watch the news?'

'I couldn't stop watching. Innisfail's practically destroyed and the farms ...' She shook her head, her heart breaking as she recalled the images. 'How are your friends?'

Grunting, Jack lifted his hat from the verandah post. 'Some are worse than others. I spoke to the McNallys but haven't got through to Robbo yet. No one's hurt that we know of, but they're all bloody devastated. Mr Tucker couldn't bring himself to go out and assess the damage.'

'Yeah ...' Meg grimaced, wringing her hands as their gazes strayed out over the view of Shadow Creek.

'I only wish I could be grateful,' Jack muttered. 'And I am, but ... I think your plan for show queen is good.' His eyes returned to hers. 'The more we can help, the quicker they'll recover.'

'I think it'll be nice to band together this year.'

'It'll mean a lot. And now that Billy's gone, hopefully this damn weather will clear up and we'll have some sunny days ahead. Might go riding.'

Meg's heart swooned. 'I haven't been riding in ages,' she said as they strode towards his sexy red Raptor.

'Dante and I went out earlier this week to check the fences along the national park.'

'He'd have liked that.' Meg glanced around. 'Where's Jill?'

'She'll be somewhere.' Jack whistled, called his dog, and a moment later, Jill came running down the path from the cabins. With her tail wagging and tongue hanging out, she raced towards them and rose to place her wet paws on Meg's belly.

Grinning, Meg rubbed her red ears with enthusiasm. 'Hey, girl! How are you? Did you have fun exploring?'

Jill might not be the little, cute, and fluffy dog that Meg usually preferred, but she loved the Australian kelpie just the same. And since the smart girl recognised Meg as a dog-crazy person who would spoil her rotten, Jill adored her. She didn't receive the same indulgence from Jack. Meg might love him, but they certainly had different opinions on how they should treat their dogs. Lola knew it too, which was why she never gave Jack the time of day.

'She has to make sure everything's in order,' Jack said, opening the passenger door. 'Come on, girl. We've got tiling to do.'

Jill leapt into the cab. Jack closed the door, then turned back to Meg. 'What are you doing later?'

'Not much since Liam cancelled agility training. The park is too wet for the dogs to jump hurdles. But I'm meeting Elanora later as she's agreed to be a mentor, so I'll see what she thinks about pooling our fundraising efforts.'

'I think she'll like the idea.' Jack climbed into his ute and wound the window down before closing the door. 'But if you need any help, Meg, let me know, okay?'

She resisted a smile. 'Thanks, Jack.'

'Good. Catch you later, darlin'.'

* * *

Jack spent the afternoon on his hands and knees in Michael's ensuite bathroom setting spacers, aligning tiles, and cursing as they measured and cut the delicate porcelain to the correct size. Meg was right, tiling wasn't his favourite job. He much preferred nailing the plasterboard, bricklaying, or installing kitchen cabinets. But this was the third house he'd helped his brother build and while Michael and his mentor, Graham, had the official qualifications and licences in construction, Jack had never shied away from lending a hand in plumbing, flooring, or installation as it appeared he was capable of doing pretty much anything. Except painting. That was Liam's forte.

When they'd finished, Jack stood with Michael in the doorway and admired their handiwork. 'It'll look good once you remove the spacers.'

'Yeah. The colours look good too.'

'Well, you picked them,' Jack said, eyeing the chocolate feature tiles among the cream.

'I didn't, really. I had help.'

That was true. Michael had seemed incapable of making any decisions regarding his dream home without bringing brochures to the pub and asking for opinions about everything from the floorplan to the light fixtures. The ladies seemed to have enjoyed helping him and even though it'd taken him almost two years, Jack was glad to see the place finished. Fresh paint graced the walls, the granite bench tops in the bathrooms and kitchen glistened, and they had some stylish light fittings to install before the housewarming party.

'I tell you though,' Michael said. 'I'm bloody glad I spent that extra time reinforcing the walls and nailing down the roof. We don't often build much that doesn't hold up to category five standards, but still. These last few days reminded me it's worth the effort.'

'Sure is.' Jack's stomach sank as he thought about the houses he'd seen destroyed on TV this morning. Of course, those that sustained the most damage had been the fibro houses built decades ago, but it didn't matter. Every one of them had been someone's home. 'We were bloody lucky.'

'Yep. Have you spoken to Robbo?'

Jack shook his head. 'Tried calling this morning, but it went straight to voicemail. Probably turned his phone off to save the battery. I'll try again later.'

'Well, let me know how he is when you reach him.'

'Will do.'

They washed out the grout buckets, tossed the tile shards, then Jack left his brother to it as he coerced Jill away from Michael's cattle dog, Sally, and climbed into his ute. It wasn't a long drive from Michael's back to his place, but as he navigated the Raptor around the potholes, his mind wandered to Meg's plans for show queen.

He doubted the committee would deny her idea to pool the funds for cyclone relief. The recovery process would require time and patience, but everyone would come together to help those affected by Cyclone Billy. It's what communities did. The state and the country. The Premier of Queensland was flying in tomorrow and had already announced a few million dollars would be donated to the region. The Elizadale Show Committee might offer little in comparison, but every bit would help the Innisfail community.

Right now, though, all Jack wanted was to make sure his mate was okay, so pulling up outside the house, he let Jill into the backyard and phoned Robbo again.

This time, he answered. 'Jack.'

'Hey, mate.' Releasing a deep breath, Jack shot his hand

through his hair, unsure of what to say. 'I just wanted to check in. Are you okay?'

Jack had met Robbo thirteen years ago when they'd been studying agriculture at TAFE in Toowoomba. They'd been two young blokes straight out of high school on their own for the first time and, having been the only two boys from banana farms, they'd formed an instant friendship and helped each other through their studies.

'Oh, mate …' Robbo's exhale whistled in Jack's ear. 'It was a rough night. I couldn't sleep. Lay on the mattress in the bathroom staring at the ceiling waiting for the roof to fly off. It didn't, thank fuck. But there was nothing I could fucking do except worry and sweat like a bloody pig.'

Jack could only imagine. No power meant no fans or air conditioning in a house with all the windows closed.

'You're okay though?'

'Yeah. Physically fine. So is everyone else I've checked up on.' Cyclones might cause a lot of damage, but with the education and preparedness of North Queenslanders, fatalities were rare. 'The house survived. Packing shed looks okay.' The sheds were in clear view of Robbo's house. 'My pergola didn't make it and there's shit everywhere. Trees and pieces of buildings and junk that people didn't clean up.'

Jack winced. 'Shit, man.'

'Crop's gone,' he said matter-of-factly, but Jack didn't miss the anguish in his friend's voice.

'I'm sorry, Robbo.'

'Yeah. Thanks, Jack. And thanks for calling.'

'Of course, mate. And if you need anything, let me know.'

'I will. But I should go. Need to save battery and generator power. Who knows when we'll get back on the grid.'

They said their goodbyes and Jack hung up. He'd never heard his friend more gutted. Never felt more helpless. He couldn't even imagine what Robbo and the other blokes he knew down there were going through and if there was anything he could do to help, he'd do it in a heartbeat. Especially since now that banana supply was down, there would be increased demand on Shadow Creek, and they'd be run off their feet busy.

But what could they do?

Sighing, Jack sank into a chair. Well, for one, they could take some workers from down Innisfail way. The regular banana pickers would be out of work, but if they were willing to relocate for a short time, the operating farms would need some extra help. That's what they'd done last time, although it wouldn't be as bad as it had been after Cyclone Larry. Shadow Creek had been planning to plant a new field this month and Jack was used to working long hours. The only benefit was that they'd get a decent price for the crop for once.

If only guilt didn't churn in his gut when he thought of the profit they would make from the misfortune of others. Sure, he could take on workers to help carry the extra load, but Robbo had just as much work to do and no one to help him do it.

So maybe …

Jack frowned, glancing at Jill as she rested her head on his knee. 'Maybe if I can sort some things out, girl, I might have an idea.'

Chapter Five

Meg sat in the booth at the Royal Hotel sipping chardonnay as the beat of the bass drum and strum of guitar echoed from the neighbouring room. The Charlie Boys were setting up for a night of entertainment and while they rarely held gigs on a Sunday, Chaz, Chuck, and Eric Charles had wanted to lift everyone's spirits. Despite their success, The Charlie Boys' hearts would always belong to Elizadale, and Meg was grateful for that. They might have multiple Golden Guitar Awards and a name in Nashville, but she delighted in their achievements and would kick anyone's arse who dared call themselves the band's biggest fan. She'd earned that title long ago when she'd encouraged them to form in the first place.

On the other side of the booth, her fellow schoolteacher, Elanora Kelly, sipped her own wine. Elanora had wanted to keep her commitment to the show queen contest, and Meg had been relieved to hear it. Elanora had been a shell of herself since kicking her cheating husband out six months ago, and Meg had only just begun to see her friend stitch herself back together.

'Mum visited Jordan today,' Elanora said, tears glistening

in her eyes as she selected a chip from the bowl they shared. 'I know it's hard for her. She doesn't condone Jordan's actions and I can't blame Mum for not cutting Jordan out of her life. But still …'

'It must hurt.'

'It really does.'

Meg still couldn't believe the events that shattered the Kelly family had happened. Elanora was Jack's age and the eldest in the family, and Meg had been in the same class as her younger sister Jordan. Their brothers Paul and Harrison were the middle siblings and while their parents were lifelong friends of Jack's parents, Jack and Adam had been fighting with Paul and Harrison for most of their lives.

Then Jordan had fallen pregnant with Elanora's husband, Shane; had accidentally drugged Paul while intentionally spiking Adam; and had tried to convince Adam that he was the father of her baby. It had broken the family apart and Meg's compassionate heart ached for them. Especially Elanora.

'I just don't know where to go from here, Meg. Work's good and I'm happy to help with show queen. Mum also suggested I help run the show jumping.'

'You'll enjoy that.' Liz Kelly was a devoted horse lover, breeder, and Elanora had been a show jumper herself back in the day. 'Will you enter the flower competitions?'

'Of course. I'll even throw something into the baking comp, but … the thought of starting all over again …' Elanora groaned and dropped her head into her hands. 'How am I ever going to be okay?'

Meg reached across the table and squeezed Elanora's forearm. She couldn't imagine being in Elanora's position—thirty-one, divorced, and starting the dating game from the beginning. Elanora had known from the age of sixteen that Shane was the man she wanted to love forever, just like Meg had known about Jack. Meg had always been envious of Elanora's luck, but now, she didn't know what was worse. To have loved and lost, or never to have loved at all.

'Starting afresh might seem scary, El, but you'll be ready to try one day. Many people have second or third loves in their lives and any man will be lucky to have you.'

'Not when I cry every day. It's hopeless, Meg. And by the time I find a man, I'll be too old to have children.'

Meg smiled sadly. She might not have experienced the agony of trying to get pregnant like Elanora had, but Meg shared her longing and feared she too would remain childless if she didn't help Jack release the restraints around his heart.

'Anyway.' Elanora reached for another chip. 'Let's just … What are your plans for show queen? You've got Samantha, right?'

Meg scooped a chip through the gravy. She wanted to be there for Elanora, but she'd always let her friend lead their chats and when she wanted to stop talking, they stopped. 'Yep.'

'And you're fundraising for the RFDS?'

'I have to run it past the committee, but I wondered if this year we could try something different and pool our fundraising efforts for cyclone relief.'

'That's a fantastic idea!'

'I thought so. After seeing all those images …' Meg shuddered.

'I know. I'm so glad we were spared. It's not bad to say that, right?'

'No, we're allowed to be grateful.'

'Just gracious as well because I do feel for them. I don't

think I'd have been able to bear it if it'd been Mum and Dad. I heard all of Innisfail's bananas are gone, not to mention the sugar cane and mangos. I wonder how Paronella Park held up?'

'Fingers crossed it hasn't sustained terrible damage.' The famous castle hidden among the rainforest had lost an historic wall in Cyclone Larry. 'It'll take a while to tally up the total loss and cost.'

'It'll be close to a billion dollars, so I'm keen to do anything to help. We'll need some fresh ideas for the contest, though.'

'I think Natalia and Brittany were discussing a fun run.'

'That sounds like them. I'll do it.'

'Me too,' Meg agreed, her legs aching just thinking about it. She liked walking but wasn't a jogger. 'Maybe we can raise more than just money too? A clothes drive is always helpful.'

'I'll do some research and come up with some ideas.'

Meg nodded as they finished their chips, glad to see a spark had lit inside Elanora. But then Elanora groaned, and the light vanished again.

'Great. Paul's here.'

Meg glanced over her shoulder. Paul Kelly slipped onto a barstool and lifted his hand in a hesitant wave. Meg turned in time to see Elanora shoot him a small smile before lowering her gaze.

'You know he cares about you,' Meg said gently.

'He's smothering me. I know he's hurting too and that he wants to make sure I'm okay. He doesn't have Jordan to worry about anymore, so he needs to fuss over someone. Doesn't help either that Harry's angry with him.'

Meg resisted a grimace. Paul had been on the fence about pressing charges against Jordan for drink spiking, but he'd gone through with it after watching Elanora's downward spiral. Harrison and his anger issues hadn't been able to accept that.

'Hopefully everything will work out for the best,' Meg said. 'But anyway … Have we got judges for all the competitions?'

'Yep. The regular rides are coming, and we're getting the big Ferris wheel back this year.'

Meg grinned. 'I love Ferris wheels!'

Elanora shuddered. 'You can keep them. I don't care how qualified those people are, those things are dodgy.'

The ladies ordered another glass of wine as The Charlie Boys started to play. The music reverberated through the colonial building, echoing the nostalgia in Meg's heart. She might be proud of her cousin, but no matter how much she enjoyed listening to him play, regret was a powerful monster. And if she allowed her mind to wander then the 'what ifs' would plague her until she could barely breathe.

What if she had opened for The Boys in Gympie? What if she'd gone to Tamworth with them the following year? What if she'd taken Chaz up on one of his many offers to record with them?

She tossed back a gulp of chardonnay.

But as she hummed the sweet tune of 'Jane' and tapped her foot to the rocking beat of 'Life in the North', pride wriggled its way up her spine. She'd written those chart toppers, the royalties kept her in killer clothes, and after watching the news this morning, a song had been niggling at the back of her head. It was the first one in a while, but Meg had welcomed the words as she'd jotted them on a napkin while waiting for Elanora. Passion often spurred inspiration and many feelings currently conflicted inside her.

But would anything become of those few lines?

She doubted it.

* * *

Elanora left at eight o'clock, but Meg decided to stay until The Boys finished playing. Slipping onto a stool at the bar, she ordered a Diet Coke and chatted to Georgina, the owner of the Royal. Like most people in town, Georgina was one of Meg's many friends and they were also distantly related, sharing great-great-great grandparents. When Georgina moved to serve other customers, Meg sipped her drink and enjoyed the music she knew by heart. She couldn't see The Boys from the bar, but applauded anyway when they finished rocking out to 'Shooting the Shots.'

'Hey, Meg.' Paul Kelly slipped onto the stool beside her and leaned his tanned forearms on the bar, a bottle of Great Northern clutched in his hands.

Meg suppressed a grimace. It wasn't in her nature to be rude and honestly, Paul had never done anything to hurt or upset her, except for the times he'd punched Jack. But when Paul wasn't arguing with her friends, he'd always been polite to her, and his fellow horse breeders, coffee growers, and members of the gun club seemed to like him.

But Meg was a Maguire in everything but name, and therefore, he was her enemy.

'Hey, Paul.'

'How are you?'

Meg frowned at the spark in his blue-grey eyes. 'Fine. Did you want something or …'

'Well, I'm happy to get straight to the point if you are.' He swigged his beer, his gaze never leaving hers. 'I have a proposition for you.'

She resisted a wince. 'I'm not interested.'

'No, hear me out.' He touched his fingers to her forearm,

then quickly withdrew his hand, shifting awkwardly on the barstool. 'Please.'

His eyes clouded and curiosity took hold as Meg turned to face him better. 'What is it?'

He stared at her for a moment, then said, 'I think you and I should have dinner tomorrow.'

Meg almost fell off her stool. 'What?' Had she heard right? Was *Paul Kelly* asking her out? Did he … did she …

'I said hear me out.' He leaned closer but maintained a comfortable distance. 'I don't … it's not what you think. You're a nice woman, Meg, but … I think it might benefit us both if you and I have dinner. Casually.'

Meg blinked as she tried to shake away the shock. What did he mean it would benefit them both? He didn't fancy her, but wanted to have dinner because … 'How?'

'Look, I know we've had our differences, but don't you think it's time we overcome that?'

'Ahh … do you mean between you and me? Because we have nothing, Paul. Jack and Adam—'

'I don't care what Jack and Adam think. I'm only thinking about what I want. And need. And you, of course.'

Meg frowned. 'What's in this for you?'

'That's my business. But you see …' He shook his head.

Confused, Meg resisted doing the same. When he didn't continue, she cleared her throat. 'Paul, thank you, but I don't think you and I having dinner is a good idea.' Meg slid off her stool, deciding it would be best to leave. 'I don't think my friends would understand.'

Smiling softly, she turned towards the door.

'Go to dinner with me and you'll get Jack.'

Meg stilled, then turned. 'What?'

'Think about it.' His eyes gleamed as he swigged his beer.

'If you go out with me, Maguire will realise just how much he has to lose. He'll see how big a tool he's been for stringing you along all these years. If you make him think you've cut him loose, you might finally get him.'

Speechless, Meg stared at Paul. Was he *crazy*? 'You want me to make Jack jealous? Why would I do that?'

Paul shrugged. 'Anyone with eyes can see that Maguire adores you, yet he hasn't made a move. Why?'

'I … I don't … that's none of your business!' Paul didn't need to know that she longed to know the answer to that very question.

'And I don't plan to make it my business. But think about it, Meg. You'll never be part of the Maguire clan until he wakes up to himself.'

Meg exhaled through her teeth. 'I am part of the Maguire clan because of Lucy. She's been my best friend for over twenty years.'

Paul smirked. 'Exactly. Which practically makes you her sister.' He placed the empty bottle down. 'So, think about it, Meg. It doesn't have to be tomorrow, but whenever you're ready, I'll buy you dinner.'

'Oh, I've thought about it.' Clenching her fists, Meg stepped towards him. 'And my answer is no. I have no intention of making Jack jealous. If I had dinner with you, he'd probably never talk to me again. Not to mention I'd also lose my friendship with Lucy. I'm not crossing that line, Paul. So, sorry, but you'll need to find another way to get whatever it is you want because I'm not interested.'

She hurried towards the door, but Paul's words followed her anyway.

'Or Maguire will realise the true pain of losing the person he loves.'

Meg didn't bite. She strode out of the pub and into the humid night. Heart pounding, she unlocked her Astra. What had happened back there? What could Paul possibly get out of having dinner with her? It was ridiculous!

She shoved her car into gear and sped up Stuart Road. As for making Jack jealous, she'd never agree to that. Because yes, going out with Paul Kelly would be a sure-fire way to achieve that. Meg had witnessed the greenness of Jack Maguire's jealousy last year when she'd dated Scott Mansfield. Dinner with Paul … Meg shuddered. It would be awful. Jack would never speak to her again. Or blow his top. Or he would realise that he could lose her, so he'd sweep her into his arms and—

Meg shook her head. No. The way to a man's heart wasn't by hurting him. She loved Jack, so why would she even consider going on a date with a man he loathed? It would cut Jack deeper than she'd ever wish to, no matter how much of a stubborn bastard he was. No matter how much she hated Jack's 'just friends' nonsense, Meg considered herself his with every fibre of her being, and she would never intentionally break his heart.

So why was he breaking hers?

Her hands tightened around the wheel as she stopped at the end of Stuart Road, indicating to turn right for home, though she longed to go left and tear onto Shadow Creek.

She should talk to Jack. But what was the point? She'd dated other men and until Scott, he hadn't batted an eye. And she would not create a scene. A woman needed to maintain her dignity. So, like always, she grappled with her inner calm until her pulse settled. By the time she parked in her driveway, a dead weight filled the space her heart should be.

It was better to have Jack as a friend than not have him at all.

Chapter Six

'It'll take at least eight months until Innisfail and Tully produce bananas again,' Henry Maguire said. 'That's for the fields that are completely flattened. Some farmers might produce sooner. But either way, we need to increase our production to meet the supply demand.'

Jack sat across the desk from his father in the office at the packing sheds. Uncle Cliff sat beside him while Adam leaned against the wall. There wasn't much work happening while the skies remained dark and thunder rumbled in the distance, but farming was just as much business management as it was hard physical labour.

'Good thing we planted two new fields last year,' Adam said. 'That should help.'

'It will. So, we're going to have a busy year ahead as I doubt we'll see much fruit coming out of the Cassowary Coast before Christmas.'

Cliff nodded. 'We'll manage it.'

They'd done it before. Biosecurity prevented overseas import of bananas, as disease wasn't worth the risk to the agricultural industry. They farmed under strict quarantine measures to prevent the spread of Panama Disease Race 4. Therefore, Shadow Creek, Tropic Sun, and the farms in Mareeba, Darwin, Coffs Harbour, and the Kimberly region had a big task ahead of them. More than eighty percent of Australia's bananas came out of Innisfail and Tully. And the farmers were picking them up out of a swamp.

'I've spoken to some representatives from the Banana Growers Council,' Henry said, 'but most of them have been impacted and the corporate blokes in Brisbane haven't got a clue what's going on. And I'm still waiting to hear from the Department of Agriculture. It's too early to determine the extent of the damage in Innisfail, but we'll be receiving new contracts soon and there'll be piles of paperwork to go through.'

Cliff blew out his breath. 'Well, we have no right to complain.'

'No, we don't.' Clearing his throat, Jack sat up straighter. 'I spoke to Robbo yesterday.'

His father winced. 'How's he holding up?'

'Not great. He's physically fine, but he can't bring himself to go look at the whole farm yet.'

'Don't blame him,' Cliff muttered.

'But he's all on his own there to clean up, so I reckon Adam and I should go down to help him.'

'What?' Adam's eyebrows shot up as he straightened from the wall.

'You want to go to Innisfail?' Henry asked.

Jack nodded. 'Not straight away, but sometime in the next two or three weeks. When the power's back, maybe, and the roads are clear.' Flooding had cut certain areas off and the Palmerston Highway had snapped in half due to heavy landslides on the range. 'There's a lot of work to be done to repair the fields and clean up the debris. The sheds need fixing and there'll be damage to fences and irrigation. Robbo can't pay workers to help when he'll have no income and we know contractors will be flat out busy over the next few months. So, I want to help.'

'I can't argue with that,' Cliff said, glancing at his brother.

Henry shook his head. 'No. That's good of you, son.'

'Do I get a say in this?' Adam asked.

'No,' Jack said.

Adam sank back against the wall. 'Okay.'

Henry sat forward and rested his forearms on the desk. 'We can spare you. It won't be easy, but we'll work it out if that's what you want to do.'

Jack's gut clenched. 'I need to do something, Dad. We were bloody lucky. I'd want someone to do the same for us if things had been different.'

'Damn, that's true.' Sighing, Adam rubbed his jaw. 'How long you want to go for?'

'We'll probably need two weeks. I'll talk to Robbo first, but I'm sure he won't object.'

'At least you give *him* that courtesy.'

Jack rolled his eyes. 'Stop whining. You agreed to go.'

'I didn't agree. I won't say no, but I don't just have myself to consider. What about Nat?'

'Nat won't stop you.'

'No, but I still have to discuss it with her. I can't just up and leave my wife for two weeks. We're trying to have a baby, you know.'

'I really don't think you are.'

Adam blew out his breath. 'Whatever. But yeah, you know I'll go. Nat won't mind.'

Jack glanced at his father. 'I'll stay longer if he needs me to, but two weeks should be enough time to help clear his fields. I'll see what Robbo says and ask Mike if he can come.'

'If you're dragging me into it, he's coming too.'

'I'm sure Michael will happily lend a hand.' Henry smiled. 'I'm proud of you, Jack.'

A ball of warmth rose in Jack's chest. 'Thanks.'

'Hey, I'm going too!'

'I'm proud of you both,' Henry said. 'And Michael.'

Jack managed a smile. He might never get to be with Meg, but she'd always inspired him to be a better man. This disaster had affected thousands of people and it was at times like this that communities needed to band together. The State Emergency Service was hard at work, the Rural Fire Service was doing their part, and if the Prime Minister gave the order, the army would be deployed on relief duties too. Dozens of organisations would volunteer their time and services, and the State Government would fund what they could.

But that was big picture stuff. All Jack wanted to do was help his mate.

Adam, being Adam, continued to complain as they left the packing shed, thunder rumbling in the grey skies. 'I mean, it's a bloody good idea and I'm keen to go. It's just harder now that I'm married.'

Jack gritted his teeth. 'Nat will be glad to get rid of you for a fortnight.'

'Piss off. But I'm fucking glad it wasn't us, so I'll pitch in and help Robbo out. We'll get him back on his feet. Might have to take the camping equipment though.'

'His house is still standing, but we'll take the generator and plenty of fuel if he's still without power.'

Adam clapped Jack on the back as the rain returned in a light drizzle. 'Let me know what Mike says and we'll sort it out. Not that he gets a choice about going if I didn't.'

* * *

Jack reminded himself that he preferred rain over drought as the clouds broke and wept over Elizadale mid-afternoon. He might be up to his knees in mud with his shirt sticking to his skin and hair dripping in his eyes, but bananas loved water. They needed water.

But the bloody feral pigs didn't need to knock over his fence. Dirty, rotten, stinking creatures they were. He wasn't one for pig hunting—there were other locals who took care of that—but he cursed the swine to high heaven as he unloaded the wire from the back of the aging farm ute. His boots squelched through the mud as he approached the broken fence. Quarantine required he fix it as soon as possible as the last thing he needed were feral pigs trampling through his farm. But he was already late for his afternoon beer.

Every Monday, Jack and his friends met at the Royal Hotel for a weekly get together in addition to their Friday nights. It was his favourite part of the week. Sure, he saw Adam every day and Michael when banana harvesting was in higher demand than building jobs. But the pub was the only time he caught up with Liam, Lucy, and Meg.

The twice weekly drinks with Meg were Jack's reason for breathing. So, he completed the job as quickly as he could, ensuring the fence was secure enough in this atrocious weather and the soft, ever-shifting ground.

'It'll have to do.' He gathered his tools and trudged back to the ute, mud halfway up his shins. He tossed everything into the back and climbed behind the wheel. Five-thirty had been and gone, and he couldn't go to the Royal like this. He needed to get home, change, then see if he could catch his friends.

Tearing off his shirt, he blasted the heater, then shoved the ute into gear. His skin dried as he drove through the farm and a small smile tugged at his mouth at the thought of the cool beer awaiting him at the Royal. He longed to tell Meg about his plan to go to Innisfail, to see her face light up and her eyes glitter with pride. Meg was as selfless as they came and always gave back without expecting anything in return. She was like her grandmother that way. Margaret Riley had been an asset to Elizadale for over fifty years as an active member of the local church and the Country Women's Association.

Jack couldn't help respect people like them. Charity had never been his thing. He was happy to help people, but heading committees and leading campaigns took a certain type of person. He could be a good boss and leader on the farm, and believed he had a sound head to expand the company, but otherwise, he'd rather be the supportive type. The man who bought more biscuits than he could eat at the bake sale, who attended the charity concert, and bought tickets in raffles he had no desire to win.

This time though, he'd found something that lit a fire inside him. Something he knew he could do and that he had the skills for. Giving up two weeks of work to volunteer his time was the least he could do.

But he wanted Meg's support. So, he parked the farm ute at the fence, left the controlled zone, and climbed into the Raptor to race home and shower, all the while knowing he'd be too late.

Chapter Seven

Rain ricocheted off the Royal Hotel's tin roof, rattled down the drainpipes, and gushed into the deep gutters along Stuart Road. Meg had to raise her voice to be heard as she farewelled Lucy, Adam, and Natalia, who'd decided to head home to Shadow Creek before the weather worsened.

'Drive safely!' she called, before hurrying back inside to Ana and Liam.

'I still can't get used to this crazy weather,' Ana said, staring out the window even though they couldn't see past their own reflections. 'It's worse than last year.'

Meg nodded. 'Just be glad we didn't get the cyclone.'

'Oh, I am.'

Liam downed the last of his beer. 'We might head off in a moment too. I'm getting hungry.'

Ana placed her hand on her belly and groaned. 'I could eat a whole cow.'

Meg laughed. 'You're vegetarian!'

'Well … a whole wheatfield. I don't know. But we better go see what state Steph and Louis are in.'

'They're probably playing zoomies in the mud.' Meg

wouldn't put it past those border collies. 'Lola will be curled up in her snuggle bed.'

'At least you have a good dog.' Ana finished her drink and nodded at Meg's full glass. 'Do you want us to wait?'

'No, I want to chat to Georgina about some show business.' Though she wouldn't stay long as her belly was rumbling too, and she wanted to fine-tune the lyrics that had distracted her all day.

She waved Ana and Liam off, then relaxed into the booth and pulled her notebook from her bag. Georgina was busy serving a couple of ladies at the end of the bar, so Meg sipped her drink and reviewed the second chorus she'd jotted down after work.

Deep inside, my soul I know—

The air exhaled from the cushion across from her, and Meg glanced up to find Paul sliding into the booth.

'Hey.' He flashed her an awkward smile and folded his forearms over the table, his red polo wrapping snug around his shoulders. He seemed more relaxed than usual, but secrets flickered in his eyes, and Meg closed her notebook.

'Okay, what's your motive?'

He raised an eyebrow. Just the one. 'Do I need a motive to have dinner with a pretty lady?'

'We're not having dinner. But seriously, Paul. You've said you're not interested in me like that, so … why?'

'I've already told you.'

'No, you haven't. You just said it'll benefit us both.'

'Exactly.'

Meg's hand tightened around her glass. 'I know you think it'll benefit me, which is ridiculous, but I don't know what you'll get out of it.'

'You don't have to. Just think of it as a free meal.'

'I'll think of it as no meal because—'

'The grilled mackerel?'

Meg's mouth fell open as Cassie arrived at the booth with two steaming plates in her hands.

'That would be Meg's,' Paul said.

'You *ordered*?' The audacity of this man! No wonder she and her friends hated him.

'I was hungry,' Paul said, shrugging as Cassie placed a steak before him.

Meg shook her head. 'I'm not eating with you unless you give me a reason.'

'I can't tell you.' His gaze lowered as he selected a chip. 'My reason would kill me and I don't want to face that wrath.'

Her eyebrows shot up. 'This is about someone?'

'Can't you just think about what *you'll* get out of it? Why do you care about my reason?'

'Because I don't like being dragged into things when I don't know why!'

'You don't need to know. You do like mackerel, right?'

It was her usual order, but she didn't want to know how he knew that. Stomach rumbling, Meg glanced at her plate. She either ate now or in another half hour by the time she got home and cooked something.

Screw it. She'd take five minutes to eat, then leave. 'I'll reimburse you for this.'

'If it makes you happy.'

'And if this goes badly for me, I hope whatever it is you want crumbles around you.'

Paul shrugged. 'My world has already crumbled, Meg. I'm just trying to rebuild it. And yeah, I'll probably fail. I'm good at that. But I'm still going to try.'

Frowning, Meg's pulse slowed as she studied the man across from her. She'd known Paul all her life, but he was three years older than her and, honestly, remained quite a mystery. He was just the man she'd sworn to hate because Jack did, and life hadn't been easy for him these past six months. His family had fallen apart, he worried about Elanora, and Meg rarely saw him with his brother anymore. So, was that vulnerability in his eyes? Loss? Pain?

Her foolish, caring heart clenched. 'Paul—'

'Stop asking questions, Meg.' His face hardened as he cut into his steak. 'If you want to talk, we'll talk about you.'

'Fine.' Exhaling, she snatched up a chip and forced her concern aside. 'Why do you care if Jack and I are together or not?'

'I don't.' Paul paused as he chewed. 'I mean, I think you should be. He might stop being such a moody bastard if he had you. But anyway. What are you entering into the show?'

Meg resisted rolling her eyes. He really wasn't going to tell her anything. 'I don't enter the show, Paul. I run it.'

'Didn't you enter flowers once?'

'Only because I happened to have marigolds that year. I'd grow more, but I don't have gardens at my place.'

'Gardening is hard work,' Paul agreed. 'But at least it keeps Elanora occupied.'

'She has beautiful gardens and will win many categories, I'm sure.'

'She's been on a gardening binge, so she better. She's planted pansies and petunias and is trying to grow snapdragons. Every time I visit her, all I can get her to talk about are her bloody flowers. It's like they're her—'

Meg raised her eyebrows. 'Like her babies? Cut her some slack, Paul.'

His eyes darkened as he rested his forearms on the table, clutching his knife and fork. 'I do. Every day I worry about Elanora. And I don't mean to sound like her obsession with flowers is a bad thing. I'm happy to hear about her latest favourite bloom as it beats finding her curled up on the floor unable to bloody move.'

Anger, regret, and pain flashed through Paul's eyes. Again, that foolish concern spread through Meg's chest. 'I'm sorry. I know it's been tough on both of you.'

Paul resumed his dinner. 'Like I said, my life's screwed up. But this really isn't dinner talk. Looks like we're both out of practice.'

'I'm not out of practice!'

'You don't date.'

'Neither do you.' She couldn't recall seeing him out with many girls, not recently anyway. Although … why not? It's not like Paul wasn't attractive with his dark hair, blue-grey eyes, and his lean, muscular, farmer's body. He might not be as broad and sexy as Jack, but he was tall and handsome enough when his nose wasn't bleeding. She might not know him well but put aside his overprotectiveness of Jordan—which no longer existed—and his anger issues towards Jack and Adam, Paul couldn't be too bad. Meg refused to believe that of people.

Most people.

'Dating's not the problem,' he muttered, staring at his food. After a moment, he shook his head and lifted his gaze. 'Anyway, why don't you enter the show? Do you knit or crochet like your mum at all? There's a quilting comp, isn't there?'

'Mum might be crafty, but it's not my thing.' Meg had been asked that question many times before. Her mother and aunt

Heather owned and operated Elizadale Homewares where they sold local craft including their own blankets, tea-towels, and crochet work. 'I can sew, but only to alter my clothes or fix things.'

'What about the cooking contests?'

'I don't like stepping on Lucy's toes. I have a big enough job running show queen.' She paused to eat. 'How many horses are you entering?'

'One in nearly every category. Diego is going to win thoroughbred stallion four years running.'

Meg's lips quirked. 'Is he, now?'

'Have you seen a horse more stunning than Diego?' Paul's eyes lit up and Meg couldn't help it. She laughed.

'I can't say I have. He sure is one nice looking man.'

* * *

Jack pulled up outside the Royal Hotel, his windscreen wipers losing the battle against the hammering rain. It'd taken him far longer than planned to get there. He'd arrived home to find Jill soaked and shivering, so he'd had to dry her off before setting her up in the laundry. As the walloping on the tin roof had echoed over the shower, he'd known it was foolish to head back out. He should just stay home where it was dry and have left over chicken cacciatore from High Ridge.

But Meg might still be at the Royal, and he wanted to buy her a drink so they could talk. Just the two of them. No storm would stop him.

Leaping out of the ute, he slammed the door and dashed for cover beneath the verandah. One beer, a quick chat with Meg to get his dose of her sweet scent for the week, then he'd head home. But since it was already late, maybe he could buy her dinner. No big deal. They'd eaten dinner plenty of times before. Even alone.

Stomach rumbling, he stepped inside the pub. He could do with some food after the shithouse of a day he'd had. Just something small as he'd be bound to finish Meg's fish like usual. She never ate the entire over-portioned meal.

Then his gaze landed on their booth, and Jack slammed to a halt. His breath caught hot inside his chest. Meg was there, all right. Dining. With Paul Kelly.

Jack's feet rooted to the spot. The world shut down around him. The music droned and conversations slurred. Fridges flickered off and the rain ceased until there was nothing but Meg, Paul, and the pounding of his own heart bruising against his ribs.

What the fuck? What was Kelly doing? What was *Meg* doing? Did she … was she … on a date?

Jack's jaw clenched. Stomach plummeted. He didn't want to know.

Turning on his heel, he strode out into the storm and shut himself back in the Raptor. Shoving the ute in gear, he sped off down Abbott Street at a speed only anger could control, his knuckles white around the wheel as he took a deep breath and blew it out through his nose. Then another. And another.

He had no claim on Meg. He knew that. He'd told himself on countless occasions that she could never be his. She was his friend. He wanted her to forget about him, date, and find love with another man.

But Paul Kelly?

'Fuck!'

He thumped the wheel. Clenched his teeth. Fury washed through his veins in a blazing rage. His heart pounded until it shattered.

It was all his fault. He shouldn't have let this happen. But he'd made this decision when he'd been lying in that hospital room with the letter clutched in his hands.

The letter that had changed everything.

It hadn't been easy. He might have been broken and doped up on a cocktail of meds, but with the explosion echoing inside his head, the threat had been clear. He'd done what needed to be done. No one else had understood or agreed with his decision. Apart from the police, only two people knew about the letter and the reason he couldn't be with Meg. One of them was his father, and they'd both told Jack the same thing.

You're overreacting. There's no evidence to your claim.

But even though he felt like a bastard, a threat was a threat. And while others might think he was being stupid, it made sense in his head. He wouldn't let Meg get hurt. Or worse. It would end him. He had to abide by the sinister words and avoid anything romantic between them. Thankfully, whoever had sent that letter hadn't had a problem with them being friends and, for the most part, Jack liked how easy their relationship was. If that's all he could have, he'd cherish it.

Sure, that meant she'd marry someone else one day. But Paul Kelly? Over his dead body!

Jack careened into an angle park outside the Smithfield Hotel, the only other pub in town. He'd wanted a beer and he was going to fucking get one. Rain pissed down, but Jack didn't care about getting wet as he sauntered inside. A couple of old guys played pool and a few young blokes sat at the bar, but other than that, the place was dead. Jack slid on a stool, thumped his elbows onto the polished wood, and dropped his face into his hands.

What had Meg been thinking? What was Paul's game? That

bastard had given Jack and Adam enough grief over the years. They'd never been friends, but they'd tolerated each other as children for the sake of their parents. Then Liz Kelly's father had died and Harrison's bullying had spiralled out of control. Stan had been a rock for Henry and Cliff growing up. He'd been a grandfather to them all. But despite their parents' interventions, Jack and Adam had never got along with Paul and Harrison again. Adam had crossed enemy lines when he'd started hooking up with Jordan, and many fistfights had ignited between the brothers. Jack was fucking glad that was over as he'd never trusted that woman and his brother had been lucky to escape her clutches virtually unscathed. When Paul had discovered he'd been a victim of Jordan's party prank too, it seemed to have eased the rift between the families. Jack had hoped the feud would die.

But Kelly had pulled another ace from his sleeve. Fucking bastard.

'Hey, Maguire.' Jack glanced up as Luke Smithfield approached. The bloke was about his age and basically managed Smithy's these days while his parents enjoyed semi-retirement travelling around Queensland. 'You and Kelly have another blow?'

It was usually the greeting reserved for Adam since the Maguires only frequented Smithy's when Georgina kicked them out of the Royal for fighting.

'Should have knocked his block off. But no. Just need a beer. Great Northern, thanks, Smithfield.'

Luke nodded and grabbed a bottle from the fridge. After downing half of it, Jack's pulse began to slow, but his disbelief lingered. He didn't understand it. He wasn't blind. Every day apart from Meg was as torturous for her as it was for him.

She'd loved him probably long before he'd first noticed her as a woman. She'd been sixteen and had just won her first show queen crown after a stellar concert. He'd been almost twenty and dating her cousin Rebecca, who'd dragged him to the performance. Not that he wouldn't have attended anyway, as Meg was Lucy's friend and he'd always thought she was a nice girl. But that day, he'd looked up at her on stage and seen something exquisite.

Megan Riley was beautiful with golden hair cascading over delicate shoulders, her lithe body swaying as she moved about the stage in a glittery blue dress and sexy cowgirl boots. Her voice might have been sweet and melodic, but dammit, she could also belt out a tune in a way that made a man's insides quiver.

Deeming himself too old for her though, he'd shoved those feelings aside. She'd left for university eighteen months later and he'd breathed easier. But every time she returned home for the four years following, his feelings had grown until there had been no doubt in his mind.

Megan Elizabeth Riley was the one.

The moment she returned home as a teacher, he'd formed a foundation. He'd started hanging out with her and Lucy, their Friday night ritual was born, and they'd flirted over drinks and shooting pool.

Then he'd offered to drive her to Gympie and had almost lost his life.

'Shit.' He took another swig of his beer. He'd broken her heart when he'd told her they should just be friends. Even though she'd accepted it, he'd seen the hurt in her eyes. Every time she flirted, every time Adam teased him, his heart crushed even more. He was surprised it still beat as rubble inside his chest. He'd hoped that as time passed, she would realise they could never be more than friends and would move on.

She almost had last year, but Scott Mansfield hadn't been the right man for her. Jack wouldn't want anyone he cared about to be associated with that family and if he had to watch Meg fall in love with someone else, then that man had to be worthy.

Paul Kelly was not.

Jack finished his beer and ordered another.

'Something troubling you, Maguire?' Luke placed the fresh beer on the bar.

Jack blew out his breath. 'World's fucked up, Smithfield.' But surely nothing was going on between Meg and Paul. The wanker was just fucking with him because he had nothing else better to do.

'All right. Take it easy on the beer, okay?'

Luke moved on and Jack ground his teeth. The worst part was, Meg had seemed to be enjoying herself. So what if she did like Paul? Stranger things had occurred.

Which brought him back to the bigger question, the one that plagued his heart and tore at his soul.

Who didn't want him to be with Meg? Who had sent him that letter? Did they still feel the same way? Would they still stop their union? Would he be putting Meg at risk if he stormed into the Royal and stole her back from Kelly?

Was it worth finding out?

He had to sweet talk Luke into letting him have another beer. He wished it could be rum.

'One more, but I'm calling someone to come get you. You can pick.'

'Liam will do.' He couldn't bear to face Adam and his cousin only lived around the corner.

Liam didn't hurry, but he was there by the time Jack finished the beer. He rarely drank that quickly so wasn't surprised his head resembled a leaf tumbling down the stormwater drain as he left with Liam.

'You want to tell me why you were at Smithy's on a Monday drinking yourself blind?'

'Only had three beers.'

'In about twenty minutes, I'm told. Even Adam never downed them that quick. Have you eaten?'

'Nope.' Jack closed his eyes, the windscreen wipers making his stomach churn.

'Ana cooked pasta, so you can have some of that. It'll soak up the booze. Then you can crash in the spare room, but only if you tell me what put you in this mood.'

Jack exhaled. No one could hide anything from Liam. The man had a sixth sense and didn't need to find Jack on-his-way-to-drunk to know something was wrong.

'Maybe in the morning. I just want to sleep.'

'Fine.' Liam turned into the driveway of his sprawling Queenslander. 'But food first.'

Jack ate the pasta and black beans without complaint. It was bloody delicious. Then he muttered a hearty thank you before collapsing onto the spare bed.

He wouldn't blame Meg. She was faultless and always would be. Meg would never go out of her way to hurt him, and she had every right to date. He wanted her to. She deserved a life filled with love, family, and a man who adored her.

But that man could never be him. Everyone around him

would move on, marry, and have babies, while Jack continued to grow old to die a lonely man surrounded by his fucking bananas.

* * *

Sleep didn't ease his pain. Jack woke and after an agonising minute of reliving last night, dragged himself into the kitchen and ate the strawberry porridge Ana prepared even though he wasn't hungry.

'At least I can stomach sweet porridge again,' Ana said. 'I was getting sick of dry toast.'

'Shouldn't you start showing soon?' Jack asked, doing his best to make conversation as Ana and Liam's baby was perhaps the only light in this dark, fucked up world.

'Yep. I'm eleven weeks today, so give me two or three.'

When they finished breakfast, Jack and Liam farewelled Ana and climbed into Liam's LandCruiser. Jack glanced out the window, hoping for a silent drive. He didn't get it.

'You going to tell me, or what?'

Jack's jaw tightened. He didn't want to talk about it, but if he had to, then Liam would be the person he chose. Liam was the good sort, the one who understood and encouraged. He didn't give him shit like Adam did.

'You go to the Royal last night?' Jack asked.

'Yeah.'

'Meg there?'

'Of course. She stayed to chat to Georgina.'

Jack's fist clenched. 'You sure? She didn't mention …' He stopped himself before he said anything stupid.

Liam turned onto the highway. 'I'm guessing by your mood, she didn't.'

'No.'

Silence filled the car until Liam parked outside Smithy's. 'Spit it out, Jack.'

'Meg had dinner with Kelly.'

'What?' Liam's eyebrows shot up. 'Paul Kelly?'

'Fucking bastard. Lucky I didn't punch his lights out.'

'What the hell is Kelly doing making a move on Meg?'

'That's what I'd like to know! Couldn't believe my bloody eyes. I thought I'd catch up with her, share some news, but I walked in to find her eating with Kelly and laughing. *Laughing*! Fuck me …'

Exhaling, Liam tapped his fingers on the wheel. 'Huh.'

'He better not be fucking with us again. And if he does anything to hurt Meg …'

'Kelly might be a tool, but I doubt he'd hurt Meg. Although it is strange. Kelly goes for the more earthy, country girls. Meg might have grown up running around Shadow Creek, but she's too much of a townie for him.'

Jack frowned. 'You think that's Kelly's type?'

'From what I hear. Though I don't think he's dated anyone for a while.'

'I don't take any notice.' But Liam always seemed to know what people were up to, whether or not he was interested.

'Anyway. What are you going to do about it?'

Jack turned his gaze out the windscreen. 'Nothin'.'

Liam's hands dropped from the wheel with a slap. 'Seriously?'

'What do you expect me to do?'

'Tell the woman you love her!' Liam's eyebrows shot up as though it were that easy. 'Seriously, mate. If you don't do it soon, you'll lose her!'

Jack's mouth twisted as he glared at the Smithfield Hotel. He had no response.

'This is getting ridiculous. Everyone knows you're in love with Meg. The whole town expects the two of you to get married and she's chomping at the bit waiting for you to make your move. So, what's stopping you?'

Jack ground his teeth. That was the problem, everyone *did* expect it. And someone had gone to great lengths to stop their union.

But he couldn't tell Liam that. His cousin might understand seeing that he'd tried to keep Ana safe when her ex-fiancé had sought revenge on her last year. But even so, he'd tell Jack what everyone else had. That he was wrong to keep his troubles to himself and that Meg was worth the risk.

And she was. She absolutely was. But Jack wasn't prepared to pay the price.

'Meg's better off with someone else, mate,' Jack said, opening the car door. 'I'm no good for her.'

'That's bullshit, Jack.' Liam's tone could cut glass as Jack climbed out of the LandCruiser. 'You think she'd be happier with Kelly?'

'That's for her to decide. We underestimated that bastard, though. He still has ways to drive us bloody mental.'

'Only because you're letting him! Go get your girl, Jack. She won't pass you over for Kelly.'

Jack's chest tightened. 'Thanks for the ride, mate.'

He closed the door and strode to his ute.

Chapter Eight

Meg sent Jack a few messages on Tuesday, but he didn't reply. Biting down on her lower lip, she stared at her phone as she strolled out of the school gate. It wasn't like him not to answer her. He rarely checked his phone when working in the fields, but he'd reply if he was supervising or in the office. Either way, it was four o'clock and he should have received her message by now. So why hadn't he replied?

Exhaling, she shoved her phone in her bag and began her walk home. She'd had enough of this. The not knowing. The confusion. Last night with Paul had been pleasant, and she'd rather enjoyed her evening as he'd been friendly and not at all hard to talk to. Closed and guarded at first, but he'd opened up once they'd started talking about horses and the coffee plantation. He hadn't gone into detail, but apparently his father had plans to grow the business. And Meg had enjoyed talking to a man over dinner without the rest of her friends. Just the two of them with the undivided attention had made her feel special.

But she didn't want *Paul* to make her feel that way. She wanted Jack to single her out, to buy her dinner and fill her with the warm and fuzzies. Thankfully, dinner with Paul hadn't given her any of the 'feelings', but the evening had reminded her of everything she wanted in life. Romance. Love. And while she treasured her friendship with Jack, he was wasting her bloody time.

Arriving home, she dumped her work things and prepared Lola for their afternoon outing.

'Seriously, Lola,' she said, clipping the Pomeranian into her sparkly pink harness. 'I love you and all, but I can't keep talking to you, cuddling you at night, and buying you toys and clothes. Mummy needs a husband and a real—a human baby.'

Lola didn't listen as she used her whole three kilos to drag Meg to the door. The only word Lola understood once the lead was on was 'walkies!' Meg grabbed her hat and locked the screen door behind her before Lola led her to the dog park. With the sun out for the first time in weeks, Meg and her friends had decided to take their dogs for a playdate.

She and Lola crossed Station Drive and joined the footpath that ran alongside Shadow Creek, Lola making sure she splashed in every puddle along the way. Meg rolled her eyes and reminded herself that a child would behave no better. They arrived at the dog park on the corner of Station Drive and Riley Road, where bushes lined one fence and a large ficus shaded the new mud pool. Isabella and Evie were already there, sitting on the park bench.

'Hey, Iz.' Meg sat and rubbed Evie's floppy black ears, leaving Lola to explore.

'Hey.' Isabella smiled and brushed her platinum blonde hair behind her shoulder. 'Sorry I didn't come to the pub last night.'

'That's okay. They're not predicting much more rain though, so hopefully it'll start to dry up.'

'I hope so. I'm over it, and not just because I hate the rain. I'm sick of getting wet and tourists don't come when it's raining.' Isabella worked at Liam's tourist centre, The Bent Banana, and had recently been promoted from casual staff to assistant manager now that the business was booming with the café that had opened last year.

'No, it's not the best time of year for tourists,' Meg agreed. 'But it must give you more time to source books.'

Isabella's face lit up. 'There are just so many good ones out there, I want to promote and sell them all. But Liam would kill me if I did that.'

As a passionate booklover, Isabella had recently suggested sourcing and selling rural fiction at The Bent Banana, and Liam had happily given her the go ahead. But like any new product, it wouldn't be wise to overindulge, and books were Isabella's weakness.

'Just choose a few that you really love. And those from the authors on the Tablelands because they're local.'

'Yeah, I know. And I can control myself. Maybe.' She blew out her breath. 'I've also started my quilting for the show. I'm testing myself on this one, but just wait. It's going to be adorable. I'm making a blanket for Ana and Liam's baby.'

'I'm sure it'll be gorgeous.' But Meg didn't get a chance to ask more about it as the gate tingled open and Steph and Louis raced into the park. 'Hey, Ana!'

Ana waved. Lola spotted the border collies and took chase, sprinting after them as fast as her little legs could carry her. Meg laughed.

'Afternoon.' Ana scooped Evie up and sat, cuddling the precious cavalier who refused to get her paws dirty and be a 'dog.'

After exchanging pleasantries and idle chatter about the

improving weather and their fur babies, Meg took a deep breath. 'So, I have something weird to tell you. I ... kind of had dinner with Paul Kelly last night.'

Ana jerked in shock. 'You did what?'

'Why?' Isabella cried.

'I didn't *plan* to.' Meg tore her gaze from the dogs and glanced at her friends. She'd been bursting to tell someone about her unexpected evening with Paul and wouldn't dare have spoken to Lucy about it as her Maguire blood would undoubtedly boil. But Isabella remained impartial and Ana's newness to town kept her neutral. 'He asked me on Sunday, and I declined. I mean, I don't think he wanted a *date* exactly, which is what's so weird. He just wanted to have dinner for reasons he wouldn't share.'

'Typical.' Ana rolled her eyes. 'Probably only trying to stir trouble. Jack would flip his lid.'

Sighing, Meg watched Lola sniff the fig tree. Out of all her friends, Ana was the one who gave her the hardest time about Jack. Lucy had let it go a year after the accident, but Ana had only endured twelve months of Meg refusing to talk about it.

'Then again ...' Ana grinned as she rubbed Evie's ears. 'You going out with Paul might make Jack realise what he has to lose.'

'But I don't want to make him jealous. I'd hurt him and that's just cruel.'

'Yeah, but ... honestly, Meg. I've been here a year now and you never talk about it. I see how much you adore Jack, and he you. So why is it such a hopeless case? Why aren't you two together?'

Meg exhaled, waves of frustration and regret washing through her and crashing one after the other. She hated talking about it. Refused to. But that was because— 'I don't know!'

Her cry made Evie's ears twitch as Lola head-tilted her from the tree. 'That's the thing, Ana. We almost were together.'

Ana's eyebrows lifted. 'You were?'

'Yeah. Or at least we were going to be. Then the tractor accident happened.'

'Oh.' Ana's eyes dulled. 'I see.'

'We all thought it was going to happen,' Isabella said sadly. 'But you weren't here then, Ana.'

Ana shook her head. 'Liam told me about the accident, but I didn't …' She glanced at Meg. 'What happened?'

Meg slumped back against the park bench as the vice around her heart loosened. 'Jack and I … we were going to go to the Gympie Music Muster. Chaz got me a gig and it would be my big break. I was so excited. Then Jack offered to drive me down and there was this … vibe, I guess.' Shivers coursed through her at the memory. 'I could sense it. We had an understanding. The time was right and we'd been battling these feelings while I'd been back and forth from uni. Then that tyre burst on the tractor and next thing I knew, Jack was fighting for his life in Townsville. I never went to Gympie.'

Isabella nodded, remembering the time too, and Ana's eyes clouded. 'Is that why you never pursued your music career?'

'Kind of. I spent so long worried about Jack. We spoke every day on the phone and even though we'd always been friends, that was when a deeper connection formed. It was hard to jump from friends to more, which was why going to Gympie was so important. We could be away from everyone else and figure it out. I thought we'd have our chance when he came home, but he returned a different man.'

'He sure did,' Isabella agreed sadly. 'He used to be so much happier.'

'Yep. But he was quieter. Broodier. And I tried, ladies.'

Meg's voice broke. 'I asked him if he wanted to get away for a while, but he said it'd be best if we just stayed friends.'

Ana shook her head, the disbelief in her eyes echoing that in Meg's heart. 'Why?'

'I don't know. That's the mystery.'

'Hmm …' Ana's gaze dropped back to Evie. 'I'm sorry, Meg. That's disappointing.'

'Disappointing is one word for it. But I don't want to hurt Jack by having dinner with a man he hates as much as Paul.'

'I don't understand why he'd ask you,' Isabella said.

'He has a motive, but what it is, I wouldn't know. I probably don't want to. But the thing is, I want to date.' Meg's chest swelled with longing. 'I want to be married. I'm sick of being alone and single and wasting away my days. I'm ready, you know?'

'I've known that since the day I met you,' Ana said.

'So why don't you ask Jack?'

Meg glanced at Isabella. 'Ask Jack what?'

'Why he only wants to be friends. He must have a reason, especially since we all know he loves you too.'

'Absolutely,' Ana agreed. 'The man worships the ground you walk on. So, tell him how you feel.'

'But he knows!'

'Does he?' Ana raised her eyebrow. 'I mean, Jack's a great guy, Meg. He's not stupid. But I think he needs to be told.'

'But Jack's my friend. The last thing I want to do is fight him on this and lose him forever.'

'That makes sense,' Ana muttered. 'But sitting back and waiting to be swept off your feet hasn't worked for you either.'

Exhaling, Meg shoved her hand through her hair. 'But … I just …'

'You want to be swept off your feet,' Isabella said.

'Yes! What's wrong with that? I'm an old-fashioned girl and *he* should be the one to ask me on a date. He should pick me up and woo and surprise me. It doesn't need to be anything big, and I know it'll be hard since we're such good friends. But deep down, I think it'll be the easiest thing in the world. We're meant to be together. I know it. Jack's just being stubborn.'

'Yes, he is,' Ana agreed. 'I've always wondered why he doesn't take you into his arms and declare his love for you. But you don't get what you want without fighting for it, Meg. Maybe Jack needs a little push.'

Meg's mouth twisted. Jack didn't need a push. He needed an avalanche. 'Yeah, which is exactly what Paul said. He thought that us having dinner together might spur Jack into action.'

Isabella shook her head. 'Maybe, but I still don't get Paul. Why would he want to have dinner with you?'

'He wouldn't tell me. But he seemed kind of … down? Lost maybe.' Meg wasn't sure what it was, but something was going on with Paul, more so than the dissolution of his family. She'd sensed pain inside him, deep and dark. She doubted she'd find out what bothered him or what he wanted, but she hated seeing anyone so shattered.

Ana frowned. 'That doesn't sound good.'

'No. And I felt kind of … sorry for him.'

'So you went on a date with him?' Isabella asked, raising her eyebrows.

'It wasn't a date. I probably wouldn't have eaten with him if he hadn't already ordered. Dinner just showed up. I was hungry, so I ate. But you are right, I shouldn't wait around for Jack to make the first move.' She glanced between her friends. 'I don't want to be with anyone but him. But I've been trying to contact him all day and he won't respond to my messages. I don't want him hearing about me and Paul on the grapevine in case he gets—'

Ana gasped, her eyes widening as her hands flew to her mouth.

Meg frowned. 'What?'

'I can't believe I didn't think about this before! Jack spent last night at our place. Liam had to pick him up from Smithy's because he was drunk and moody about something and—'

Meg's heart rate hit a crescendo. 'What was he doing at Smithy's?'

Ana shrugged. 'It's not like Jack to miss drinks. Do you think he arrived at the Royal and—'

Groaning, Meg dropped her head into her hands. 'No. Please don't tell me …' He couldn't have. Jack hadn't arrived late and seen her eating with Paul. Life couldn't be that cruel.

Except Ana was right. Jack never missed drinks. If he couldn't make it, he'd have messaged her. He could easily have arrived late and—

Shit!

Meg peered up at her friends. 'Do you think that's what happened?'

'I don't know, but he seemed really down. And angry.'

Meg clutched her knees, nausea swarming in her belly. 'Did he say anything?'

'No, but that's not unusual.'

The gate opened, and Natalia entered the park.

'You didn't bring Rusty?' Ana called.

'No, I came straight from work. Hello, Louis.' She patted the border collie who'd run to greet her. 'Lola! You're filthy!'

Meg wasn't sure how she'd find her dog beneath the mud, but Lola was the least of her worries.

'Meg, has Jack spoken to you?'

She glanced at Natalia. 'No. Why?'

'Adam said he wanted to talk to you.'

'About what? Did Adam say something?' Her pulse spiked. 'Does Jack know?'

Standing in front of them, Natalia frowned. 'Does Jack know about what?'

'Meg had dinner with Paul Kelly last night—'

Natalia gasped. 'You what?'

'I didn't mean to!' Meg cried, her hands covering her face again. 'He tricked me and it's not what Jack thinks! But that mustn't be what you were talking about …'

'No, Jack has a plan to help with cyclone relief, but that's no longer important.' Natalia waved that subject away with her hand. 'What do you mean you had dinner with Paul?'

Sighing, Meg quickly filled Natalia in.

'Wow … that's quite a mess.' Slipping her hands into the pockets of her black work pants, Natalia nodded slowly. 'But I agree. You should tell Jack how you feel. He needs some sense knocked into him.'

'Tell him and he'll forget about this Paul nonsense,' Ana said.

'Because he's probably confused,' Isabella added. 'And angry.'

Their comments snowballed, rattling inside Meg until she snapped. She shot to her feet. 'Dammit! This wasn't how this was meant to happen! I don't want him to be angry! Or confused or hurt or thinking that I went on a date with Paul. Or that I like him. Last night wasn't horrible, but still! Damn, Paul Kelly! He got what he wanted, didn't he?'

Meg pressed her clenched fists to her eyes as anger pulsed through her body. She could see how it would have all unfolded. Jack had arrived at the Royal hoping she'd still be there. He'd seen her with Paul and gone to Smithy's to drown his sorrows. All because Paul had some personal vendetta.

No wonder they hated him.

'I should have left the mackerel to rot and gone home.' But the foolish Christian inside her had wanted to help Paul, to know his secret and uncover why his eyes were so hollow. 'And then Jack …'

Jack would what? Still be keeping her at arm's length? Pulling his 'just friends' nonsense? If he really wanted to be just friends, then he shouldn't care about who she dated.

Dammit. What had she done to deserve such a mess?

A ball dropped at her feet and Meg glanced down as Louis shuffled back and lay his belly in the mud, eyes focused as he waited for her to throw it. Reaching down, she grabbed the old slobbery thing he'd clearly found in the bushes and heaved it across the park. Meg watched Louis as he darted after it, her chest heaving until Natalia's hand rested on her shoulder.

'It'll be okay, Meg. Jack will come around.'

That's what she'd always thought too, but she couldn't continue to hold on to hope. It hurt too much. Her friends were right. She needed to take the risk, talk to Jack, and shove her love in his face.

Their friendship was strong and would survive anything. Except him not talking to her. That, Meg could not bear.

Chapter Nine

The closed door did nothing to drown out the chaos of the packing shed as Jack sat in the office scanning news articles and emails, anxiously awaiting updates from the government and the Banana Growers Council. The statistics didn't differ from the devastation left by Larry and Yasi as three hundred million dollars worth of fruit had been destroyed. Thousands of people were out of work as not only had the pickers and packers lost their jobs, but the transport operators had too. Yet the news never seemed to improve and unable to read anymore, Jack left the office.

The mechanical whirr of the winch echoed through the shed as it lifted bunches of bananas off the trailer. The contraption halted, and the workers pulled the bags off before hosing the bright green fruit down to wash away the pesticide. Further along the packing line, conveyor belts carried bananas towards the packers, who split them into hands no bigger than five before laying them into boxes branded with the Shadow Creek logo.

At least none of their employees had been impacted. They all had their jobs and could keep a roof over their heads and food in their bellies. Jack was grateful for that, but he'd be out on Robbo's farm tomorrow if he could. Maybe then, Meg would stop asking if he wanted to catch up and he wouldn't want to hurl the phone against the wall every time it pinged with a text. He could escape Elizadale and tackle hard labour while he re-evaluated his life and figured out how he would cope seeing Meg with Paul Kelly.

Grimacing, he pressed his hand to his chest, but the ache lingered as he strode towards the packing line. 'All good here, Amanda?'

'Yep. Got a lot of doubles today.' She nodded towards the growing pile of double bananas and Jack resisted a groan. 'And more are damaged than usual.'

'The wind wouldn't have helped there,' he muttered, picking up a banana with dark scratches marking one side. There was nothing wrong with the blasted thing, but commercialism dictated it wasn't pretty enough to sell. 'The bag only provides a small degree of protection, but we'll see how much we have left at the end of the day and check what Mum and Liam need.'

Guidelines set by the consumer market meant Shadow Creek couldn't sell bananas that were too big, too small, or too ugly. Even the doubles or triples—bananas that hadn't split properly—were considered imperfect, which was ridiculous since tourists who passed through The Bent Banana found them fascinating and would happily pay normal prices. But until supermarkets added bananas to initiatives like The Odd Bunch, farmers had to take the loss or eat the fruit themselves. Jack liked a good banana, but even he couldn't eat kilos of them every week.

Thankfully, Shadow Creek sold their imperfect fruit to High Ridge and The Bent Banana, who used them in baked goods and ice cream. But wastage was unavoidable in farming, especially in industries that had experienced a recent boom and now faced oversupply issues. Like avocados. Jade Farm had suffered significant losses and reduced their production when everyone else jumped on the bandwagon a few years ago. It's what made the exotic fruit market appealing, and Shadow Creek did well with their lychees. Natalia had mentioned something about growing black sapote once, and Jack wouldn't say no to chocolate pudding fruit. It was a wonder Adam hadn't already planted her an orchard.

Leaving the packers to their job, Jack strolled towards the end of the shed as the next tractor pulled in. 'How is it out there, Ed?'

'Bloody wet, mate.' Ed hopped off the tractor as the pickers connected the bananas to the hoist. Ed was his father's age and had been working on Shadow Creek since Jack was a boy. 'But the fruit's in good nick. Will have more ready by next week when the red stringed fruit is ready.'

Every time they tied new bunches down, they used different colour strings to establish a timeline to help determine when the fruit was ready for harvest.

'Good.' Jack slipped his hands into his pockets. 'We'll have more workers by then, but did Dad tell you? Adam and I are heading to Innisfail in about a fortnight. Going to help a mate.'

Ed slapped Jack on the shoulder. 'Good on you, Jack. I can't imagine the damage. You and Adam are top blokes.'

Jack shrugged. 'I try.'

Ed hopped back behind the wheel and started the engine. 'Better get down there. You staying in the sheds today?'

'Yeah, Dad and Uncle Cliff are getting ready for the Department's visit next week.' Agricultural officials visited every two weeks to test the soil and examine the crop to advise on spraying, fertiliser, and disease control. The Maguires didn't need to make those decisions considering how tightly the government regulated banana farming. Not that Jack couldn't run those tests and interpret the data himself, but to remain in the commercial game, they needed to record the numbers and prepare the paperwork for the scientists.

'Righto.' Ed tipped his hat. 'Be back later with another load.'

'Bye, mate.'

Ed drove out of the shed with the young humpers—banana pickers—sitting on the trailer, and Jack turned back to the production line as his phone buzzed. Gritting his teeth, he extracted the blasted thing from his chest pocket, knowing it was Meg again even before he saw her name on the screen.

I hope everything's okay with the farm. I know you must be busy. I have a show committee meeting tonight, but if you want to catch up for a drink, let me know.

Jack shook his head. Her messages weren't out of the ordinary, but what the hell did she mean? Did she want to see him for a drink? Why? Was Paul busy?

Exhaling, Jack watched the bananas float through the wash towards the packers. Why couldn't she just be straight with him? If she wanted to get a drink, why didn't she just ask? He didn't need this confusion. How was he supposed to chat with her and be friendly when all he wanted to do was grab her around her slender waist and tell her she should be his?

Fuck.

Opening his messages, he began typing. But not to Meg.

Camping Friday night. No excuses.

He sent the message to his brothers, then went to meet the truck that had just pulled in. Problem solved.

***

'What do you mean they've gone camping?' Meg asked, lugging groceries inside with Natalia on speaker phone. 'It's wet out there.'

'Which is what I told my crazy husband, but he laughed and said it makes for a softer sleep.'

Placing the bags on the bench, Meg untucked the phone from her bra. 'But it's Friday night.'

'I know.'

'Can't they go camping tomorrow?'

'I don't know why they have to go at all. We have a perfectly good bed here. And walls. And plumbing.'

'At least you can spread out in the bed without Adam there.'

'True. And let Rusty sleep with me. Adam always kicks the poor little dog out.'

Meg laughed as she placed her frozen vegetables in the freezer. 'Lola doesn't sleep in her own bed either. But do you think Jack's avoiding me?'

'I don't know. Adam's been working in the guava orchards all week, so he hasn't seen Jack much. But I spoke to him, and he promised to grill Jack tonight.'

'Won't do any good,' Meg muttered. She'd let things simmer between her and Jack, despite her desperation to talk to him. After sending him messages on Tuesday and failing to get a response from her invitation to drinks on Wednesday, she hadn't bothered again. These things couldn't be resolved via text, which was why she'd wanted to see him tonight.

'We'll see,' Natalia said. 'Adam's apparently fed up with Jack too. He thinks you two should be together.'

'Yeah, I know. I'm so over this, Nat. If Jack wants to avoid me, then fine. Let him think I'm interested in Paul Kelly. He deserves it.'

'I thought you didn't want to hurt Jack.'

Meg shoved Lola's apples in the fridge. 'I don't, but I won't chase the man. He can be too stubborn for his own good.'

'So true. Now, I've just arrived home, so I'll get ready and see you at the Royal soon.'

'Dress up and we'll call it a girl's night. I'll text the others.'

'Excellent. I love dressing up.'

After saying goodbye, Meg texted her friends, then continued to fume as she unloaded the groceries. It was such typical behaviour of Jack. He was the master of avoidance and not speaking about the things that hurt him. He hadn't always been. Once, he'd been more open. Happier. Almost as cheeky as Adam.

Until the tractor accident.

Sighing, Meg pressed her hand against the ache in her chest. She understood, of course. The accident had been traumatic for everyone. The Maguires, their friends, and many people in the community. Meg would never forget standing with Lucy in the comfort of Deborah's arms as tears streamed down their faces, watching a hysterical Wendy cradle the head of her trapped son while stoic-as-stone Henry had barely held it together. The tractor may have had the roll over protection requirements installed, but the shredded tyre and angle of the bank had altered the physics, pinning Jack's leg beneath the engine body. Premature grief had filled their hearts as rarely did someone survive being trapped beneath machinery. They'd feared for Jack's leg and downright panicked when his lung had collapsed. Only Cliff had maintained control as he'd stayed on the phone with the paramedics. Even after they'd extracted Jack and the rescue chopper had been nothing but a memory in the bright blue sky, there had been no relief. It had been hours before Meg had accepted that Jack was still alive and even then, his stay in hospital with the blood clotting complications had kept everyone on edge.

What had been going through his head remained a mystery though. He'd never talked about it. Fear and avoidance had become part of his life and even though he might deny it, anxiety lingered. He still didn't drive the tractors despite Shadow Creek only owning those with the highest safety ratings, and he'd thrown himself into promotion of farm safety. For the most part, she understood. She just wished he'd face some of his other fears, like why a relationship with her terrified him.

Sighing, Meg stepped into the shower. The fact Jack would rather run off to the bush than come to the Royal tonight confirmed that. But while she longed to see him take a chance to be happy, right now, it hurt Meg too much to care. So, she would put on her sexiest dress, do her hair, strap on her favourite heels, and have herself a damn good time with the girls.

Wrapping a towel around herself, she was telling Lola not to lick the water from her ankles when the front door opened and slammed.

'Meg!' Lucy's voice ricocheted through the house as her footsteps stomped down the hall.

Meg hurried into the hallway, her hair dripping as she clutched the towel to her chest. She drew up short at the sight of Lucy. Her friend had clearly received the message about dressing up. She usually moaned and groaned about putting an effort into her appearance, but tonight, Lucy looked *hot*. The short red dress clung to her hips and generous breasts, highlighting her shapely thighs. Her long dark hair swung in a high ponytail and strappy black heels graced her feet. Meg would have asked how Lucy even owned such a dress if it wasn't for the fury burning in her blue eyes.

'Luce? What's wrong?'

'What. The hell. Are you doing going out with Paul Kelly?'

Meg ran her hand through her wet hair. 'Luce, it's not—'

'Are you insane?' Lucy's hands flew into the air, her voice pitching. 'What were you thinking? He's only trying to … Probably wants … What about Jack? You're in love with him! I know he's a fucking idiot for mucking you about and I get why you date other guys. But Paul? Really?'

Whoa, Lucy may have been her best friend since childhood, but Meg had never seen her this angry. Recoiling, she raised her hand in a calming gesture. 'Luce, it's not what you think. I did not choose to go out with Paul. We *didn't* go out. The sneaky bastard all but tricked me into having dinner with him.'

Lucy's lips thinned, her chest heaving as she rested her hands on her defined hips. After a moment, the glower in her eyes simmered. 'Well, I didn't know the whole story, did I?' She blew out her breath. 'Bloody typical though. What was Paul thinking?'

'Apparently, he thought the date would benefit us both.'

'Oh, did he now?'

Meg shrugged. 'I don't know what was in it for him, but he thought I might want to make Jack jealous.'

'Idiot,' she muttered. 'So, how did this happen?'

'Let me get dressed and I'll tell you. Grab a drink.' *And calm down.*

Lucy turned to the fridge as Meg hurried into her bedroom. She pulled on her underwear and zipped up her pale pink bodycon dress. Returning to the living room at the back of the house, she found Lucy nursing a glass of water.

'I've been meaning to talk to you all week,' Lucy said as Meg sat beside her, 'but I wasn't sure I'd keep my cool. I couldn't believe that you'd had dinner with him.'

'Yeah, it took me by surprise too.' Meg filled Lucy in on everything, from Paul's initial suggestion to his sneaky pre-ordering. 'But honestly, it wasn't that bad. He was interesting to talk to.'

Lucy rolled her eyes and sipped her water.

'But I am worried about him,' Meg confessed. 'It seems like something's bothering him and I think he's really hurting.'

'That's because no one's talking to him.'

'No, it's more than that. He wanted to make it look like we were dating for some purpose, but he refused to say what.'

'Dunno why you care,' Lucy muttered, before meeting Meg's gaze. 'But honestly, why don't we focus on fixing you and Jack? That's what's important here.'

Meg glanced down at her hands. 'He probably hates me.'

'Hell no!' Lucy grabbed Meg's forearm. 'Jack could never hate you. And we can't let a insane plot of Paul's destroy what was always meant to be.'

Pain tore through Meg's chest. 'We're not meant to be else we'd be together by now!'

'No, you just picked a stubborn man.'

'And that's my problem. I always thought it would just happen. Like in a movie, you know? He'd ask me out, we'd date, get married, and live happily ever after.'

'If only life worked out like that.'

'But it doesn't.' Pressing her lips together, Meg fought the tears threatening to brew. 'Something's stopping him, Luce. I don't know what it is, but I can't keep waiting.'

'No, you can't. You two need to sort out whatever it is between you.'

'I'm going to tell him. I haven't wanted to rock the boat, but I'm going to tell him we should be together. That I want him and no one else.'

Lucy grinned. 'Yes! Be strong and confident. He won't turn you down.'

'I hope not. He can't avoid me forever, so tomorrow, that's what I'm going to do. He'll be back from camping tomorrow, right?'

'Bastards didn't even invite me, so I wouldn't know. But I wouldn't tell him tomorrow, Meg. Let him stew. Make him realise what he's missing out on.'

Meg frowned. 'But what if he gets angrier?'

'What if he does? He needs to know how good a thing you are, Meg. Make him chase you a little.'

Exhaling, Meg sank into the lounge. Lucy's advice wasn't the same as Ana's. She should tell Jack the truth and finish these ridiculous games.

Although Lucy also had a point. Why did she have to do the chasing?

'I'll think about it. Thanks, Luce.'

'No worries.' She drained her glass of water. 'I'm glad we had that chat though because for a moment there, I actually thought you were interested in Paul.'

Meg smiled. 'No. I mean, I don't like that his "make Jack jealous" plan worked, and I'm keen to know his secret, but I don't want to date him.'

'Doubt he has secrets worth knowing.'

'Well, he certainly had more than one reason to mess with me and Jack. But I'm glad we talked, Luce. Anything you want to share with me?'

'Nope.' Lucy stood and strode into the kitchen.

Sighing, Meg followed her. 'But we were having a nice time

confiding in each other about our love lives. How are things going with Sam?'

Lucy had met Sam at the pub most Friday nights for the past few weeks, but while Meg thought they looked good together, she hadn't managed to convince Lucy to take him seriously.

'They're okay. Nothing special.'

'So, he's not the reason you've dressed up looking like you've walked off the catwalk?'

'I'm not that dressed up.' Lucy glanced down at her devilish dress. 'I just … threw this on.'

'I didn't know you even *had* such a dress.'

'I have things for special occasions.'

Meg raised her eyebrows. 'And this is a special occasion because …?'

'You're the one who said to dress up!'

'But you look like you're out to cause trouble.'

'No, I'm just going to the pub.'

Meg shook her head and turned towards her bedroom. It was like talking to a brick wall. 'Fine. Let me do my hair and makeup, then we'll get going. And if Paul's there, we'll show him he can't mess with us.'

'Sounds like my kind of night.'

* * *

Confidence shot up Meg's spine as they strode into the Royal Hotel and caught the eye of a few men. Dressing up on Friday night had only become a regular occurrence since Ana had arrived in town, and Meg didn't know why she hadn't started it sooner. She didn't buy pretty dresses and killer heels for them to sit in her closet for the rare special occasion. Every week was a cause to celebrate. To be beautiful, bold, and brazen.

Meg and Lucy approached Georgina at the bar.

'Hello, ladies. Meg, we didn't chat on Monday.'

'Sorry, I know. And by the way, I wasn't out with Paul. That was a misunderstanding.'

Georgina's shoulders relaxed. 'I did find that odd.'

'We were just chatting. And eating. But are you still okay to do some judging at the show?'

'Always, Meg. No one knows their home brew or their flowers like I do. What are you ladies drinking tonight?'

'Vodka Cruiser, please,' Meg said. 'Strawberry.'

'Coke, thanks,' Lucy said, and Meg frowned.

'No beer?'

'Nah. Not in the mood for alcohol.'

Natalia, Ana, and Isabella arrived, ordered, then the ladies settled into the booth.

'I still don't understand why they like sleeping in the bush,' Natalia said, her blonde hair shimmering as she shook her head. 'I gave in and camped with Adam by the creek before Christmas and it's pointless!'

'That's because you were by the creek with a picnic dinner you'd prepared in the house,' Lucy said. 'Camping is all about the experience.'

'I'm with you Nat,' Ana said.

Meg nodded. 'Me too. Although camping can be fun when you're in the right spot with good equipment.'

'Exactly.' Lucy glanced across the room. 'Hey, there's Sam. Do I get kicked out of ladies night if I go say hello?'

'No, but you do if you don't give us the goss.' Ana smiled around her straw. 'It's been two months, Luce. Is it getting serious?'

Lucy shook her head. 'He's nice, but he's not "the one."'

Meg rolled her eyes. Lucy said that about every man she dated. 'Do you think you'll ever find "the one?"'

'Dunno. Thought I did once, but—' She cut herself off as pink streaked across her cheeks.

Ana gasped. 'Who? The secret one? You're not still hung up on him, are you?'

Lucy's nose wrinkled. 'Why would I be? That was *ages* ago.'

'Yeah, six years,' Meg said. 'So why does it matter if you tell us?'

'Because. It's ancient history and not important. Besides, he's like … I don't know. Married now or something.'

Lucy downed a mouthful of Coke, and Meg raised her eyebrows. That was probably the first information she'd ever received about Lucy's secret lover all those years ago. 'Well, that narrows it down.'

'Yeah,' Ana agreed. 'So, can we order dinner? I'm starving.'

Natalia nodded. 'You stay here, and I'll order for you.'

'You're a good aunty,' Ana said.

Lucy laughed. 'We have the best job, Nat. Ana's always sick or hungry and has to go through childbirth, whereas we just get to spoil.'

'Which is what I keep telling Adam, but he still wants one. Then he'll take *my* baby and teach it crazy things like how to catch snakes!'

Meg sipped her vodka, but it did nothing to ease her envy. She'd reconciled with the fact that Jack would do the same with her babies. If they ever had them.

'They have to learn though,' she said, slipping out of the booth.

The ladies handed over their debit cards, then Lucy followed them to her feet. 'I'll back you up. Paul's just arrived.'

Meg glanced over her shoulder as Paul slid onto a stool at the end of the bar. He nodded in their direction and offered her a small smile. Meg found herself smiling back.

'What is going on with him?' Natalia frowned. 'Are you sure he doesn't like you?'

'Of course he doesn't. It was just a game to him.' Sighing, Meg shook her head. 'Come on, let's order.'

Lucy tossed her hair over her shoulder and straightened her tight skirt. 'Let's. And I'll say hi to Sam.'

They strode around the bar and into the bistro. Meg and Natalia waited in line while Lucy chatted and laughed with Sam at one of the high tables. Despite her claim it wasn't serious, at least Lucy had someone to talk to and spend time with.

Meg and Natalia ordered their food, then returned to their booth. Paul sat hunched over the bar, staring into his beer as though hoping it would solve all of life's problems. Meg's heart clenched.

What was with these men who wouldn't talk about their feelings? First Jack, now Paul. Both had problems they didn't want to talk about, but at least Paul had tried to reach out. Jack … God, Meg didn't know what she was going to do about Jack.

Chapter Ten

Wind whistled through the coolabah trees as Jack stoked the campfire. It wasn't cold enough for one and they had the gas stove to heat their stew, but camping wasn't the same without toasting damper over a fire.

Jack swigged his Great Northern as he stared into the flames. The ladies would have gathered at the Royal by now, wrapped in their sexy dresses with their hair styled and makeup setting their eyes aglow. Meg had always been beautiful. It didn't matter what she wore or how she did her stunning hair, she never failed to take his breath away. But when she put in an effort or showed her toned legs beneath a short skirt, Jack had a hard time concentrating on anything else.

How long had Paul been appreciating her?

Lip curling, Jack drained his beer and crushed the can in his fist. Lounging back in his camp chair, he glanced at Michael. 'What's the next job on the house, mate?'

Michael shrugged. He hadn't wanted to come out tonight, but Jack hadn't been taking no for an answer. 'It's just the back bedrooms now. I'll install the fittings after Liam does the painting, then I'll lay the carpet.'

'Getting yourself a dining table?'

'As soon as Adam makes me one.'

'Make your own!' Adam called, swigging his beer from where he manned the camp stove. 'If you can build a house, you can build a bloody table.'

'But tables are your thing.'

'Elizadale Homewares just sold my golden ash one for fifteen hundred bucks. You got fifteen hundred bucks?'

'You made Liam's at The Bent Banana for free.'

'That was before I went into business. I have a wife to feed now.'

Jack rolled his eyes. 'You grow half your own veggies and she makes more money than you.'

'Beside the point. I need to earn a living.'

'But Mike's got that bloody big dining room,' Jack said. 'You going to make him buy commercialised crap to feature in it?'

'I built your house at cost,' Michael reminded Adam. 'And I'll buy the wood.'

Adam rolled his eyes as he stirred the stew. 'If you don't have anything for me to use, why ask? Get me the wood and I'll build whatever you want. Nat's good at designing, you know.'

Jack chuckled. 'Yeah, but her imagination is too creative for you. Have you started on the banana carvings she wants in those new dining chairs?'

'I've made the chairs, but I'm no artist. I told her I'd only do it if I can make a highchair to match.'

'Maybe you should make the highchair first,' Michael suggested.

'I already have wood for a crib.'

'Your wife's told you that you're not having a baby!' Jack cried.

'Not tonight we're not 'cause you had to go camping.' Adam pointed the wooden spoon at Jack. 'See what your girl problems get me into.'

Jack ran his hand down his face. 'I don't have girl problems.'

'Right. We're just out here because we love the bush.'

'We do love the bush,' Michael pointed out.

'We love Friday nights at the Royal too, but Jack can't handle the thought of Kelly chatting up Meg.'

'And you can?' Jack snapped. 'You think that bastard is good enough for Meg? He saves your arse with the drink spiking and now you're friends?'

'Hell no! It's fucked that I'm grateful to him, but we're not friends. Just thought after Jordan left town, we'd have ended the feud too.' Adam grabbed a camp bowl and ladled stew into it. 'Although Jordan was hardly the reason for it, was she?'

'We were fighting long before you started fooling around with her,' Michael agreed.

Adam's eyes darkened. 'And if he messes with Meg, he might get another bloody nose.'

'It is strange,' Michael said, pushing to his feet. 'I mean, Meg's great and I get why anyone would be into her. But Kelly?'

Adam handed him a bowl and Michael grabbed one of their mother's freshly baked bread rolls. 'He's only doing it to mess with Jack.'

Jack gritted his teeth. 'Shut up.'

'Trouble is,' Michael said, handing Jack the bowl and bread, 'you're letting Kelly win.'

Jack dropped the bread into his lap and snatched the stew. 'This isn't a bloody game.'

'Oh, I think it is,' Adam said.

'If Meg wants to date Kelly, that's her business.' Jack shoved a spoonful of stew into his mouth and sputtered, his tongue burning. 'Fuck me!'

Adam chuckled. 'It's hot, mate. But you're fucking delusional if you think Meg's interested in Kelly. And I've told you a million times to just tell the woman you love her.'

'If you had, she wouldn't have dated Kelly.' Michael settled into his chair with his dinner. Gritting his teeth, Jack threw his bread roll at him. It hit Michael square in the chest and bounced into his stew. Michael lifted it out and nodded. 'Thanks, mate.'

'You're not getting another one,' Adam told Jack, switching off the stove and joining them around the fire.

'Why do we have to talk about this crap?' Jack muttered.

'Isn't that why we're out here?' Adam asked.

Jack grunted. Why had he thought bringing these two wankers was a good idea? He fucking hated it when his brothers started on him about Meg. They didn't understand. And he couldn't talk about it, so around and around they went in the endless shitty cycle that was his life.

'Nah, Jack just likes the no running water,' Michael said, biting into Jack's bread roll. 'And lack of power.'

Jack narrowed his eyes. 'Don't you complain. You moved into your house with neither.'

'While still living with you.'

'Whatever. Give me your bread.'

Michael tossed back the same bread roll with a large bite taken out of it. Jack didn't argue.

'But seriously, mate.' Adam lowered his bowl. 'We've had

this conversation a million bloody times and nothing changes. I don't get it. You love Meg, right?'

Jack rolled his eyes and shoved more food into his mouth.

Adam raised his eyebrows. 'Right?'

'Drop it.'

'Just admit it!'

'He's right, Jack,' Michael said. 'This has gone on long enough.'

Jack's throat tightened, his heart pounding as his brothers stared at him, waiting for an answer. Yep, he should have come alone. These bastards weren't going to let it go. Not this time.

'Jack.'

'Fine!' His bowl tumbled into his lap, thankfully not spilling. 'I love her! I always fucking have and you know it!'

'Yeah, I do. We all do. It's as obvious as dogs' balls. So come on.' Adam leaned forward. 'Tell us. What's holding you back?'

'Yeah.' Michael's tone softened too. 'When she got back from uni, you were so keen. Adam and I thought you were nuts taking all those months to make your move, then you were going to take her to Gympie—'

'We know why the Gympie thing didn't happen,' Adam said. 'And I know being in hospital sucked. But when you came home …'

Jack's heart beat so fast he was afraid he'd hyperventilate. Pain rose and spread through his chest. His grip tightened around his bowl. Throat clogged. Lips pressed together. He didn't want to fucking talk about it. He didn't want to share. They'd tell him he was crazy. Foolish. Or would his brothers finally understand? Would they stop pestering him? Support his decision to stay away from Meg and stop giving him grief?

Would he finally be able to move on if they knew the truth?

Adam cleared his throat. 'Was it the accident?'

His words echoed around the campsite as the fire crackled and leaves rustled in the wind. Bugs and birds filled the air with the sounds of the bush that had always brought Jack comfort.

But not tonight. Tonight, he was ready to explode. Lifting his gaze, he expelled his breath and nodded. 'Yeah. Kind of. Yes. I don't bloody well know.' Jack ran his hand down his face.

'Okay …' Frowning, Adam dipped bread into his stew. 'That makes no sense at all.'

Michael shook his head. 'Come on, mate. I'm sure we'll understand.'

Jack swallowed a laugh. They might understand what stopped him from sweeping Meg off her feet and into his arms, but he'd never know whether they supported his decision unless he told them. And his brothers were right. Enough was enough. Everyone was moving on with their lives and he needed to too, lest he be stuck behind in his bitter past.

'After that day with the tractor …' Jack glanced at Adam, then Michael, then back at his dinner. Somehow, he forced the words out of his aching throat. 'I was told to stay away from Meg. Or else.'

The fire crackled. After a moment, Adam said, 'Or else?'

Jack nodded. 'Like a threat.'

'Who threatened you?' Michael asked softly.

Jack shrugged, his pulse slowing as he ate. 'Dunno.'

'Did you talk to the police?' Adam asked.

'Brett and Jim looked into it.' The sergeants had taken the threat seriously. At first. 'But there wasn't much to go on. A letter arrived while I was in hospital and that's all it said.'

'To stay away from Meg?'

'Yep.'

'So you did? For years? Just because a letter told you to?'

Jack's hand fisted around his spoon at Adam's tone of disbelief. 'It was a threat against Meg. Someone would hurt her. Wouldn't you have done the same?'

'I could have stopped Jordan's vendetta against Natalia if I'd dumped her. But I didn't. I loved Nat and fought for her because if I hadn't, Jordan would have won.'

Michael nodded. 'Exactly. You're letting someone you don't even know keep you from being with the woman you love.'

'You don't even know if the threat is credible!'

But he did, and Jack had the scars to prove it. Any time he remembered the pain, the agony, it reminded him of what this person was capable of to keep him and Meg apart.

Jack glared at Adam. 'What if it was Nat?'

Adam's eyes darkened. 'If someone threatened Natalia, I'd make it my mission to hunt them down and make some fucking threats of my own. No one would ever dare harm my woman.'

Jack's chest expanded until his heart burned. 'And that's what I did, mate. I told Meg we could only be friends to hold her at bay while I had the threat investigated. Brett did everything he could. He spent months chasing every lead, but he could never close the case. He found nothing. After that, I thought about asking Meg out, but …'

Images of lying beneath the tractor flashed before his eyes. The numbing pain, the pressure in his chest as his lung collapsed. His mother sobbing, begging him not to leave her, to hold on and that help was on the way. His anguish, his terror. Wanting to give up and slip into nothingness. In the end, the accident hadn't even been the worst part. The severe bruising had caused problems with his circulation, and a deep vein thrombosis had developed in his lower leg. Before it could reduce, pieces had broken off to move into his lungs. They'd surgically removed the DVT and continued to monitor him as medications worked to break down the pulmonary emboli. He knew he'd been fucking lucky considering the circumstances, but it wasn't an experience he wished to repeat.

Or inflict upon Meg.

'I couldn't bear it if anything happened to her. If this bastard hurt Meg … If he threatened her or harmed a single hair on her head, I wouldn't be able to live with myself. I can't lose her.'

Adam's face softened. 'Mate, that would never happen. We'd all be there to protect her.'

Jack's jaw tightened. 'That's what Liam said about Ana and look what happened to her. We banded together, protected her, kept a look out, and that bastard still got her.'

Adam winced. 'Yeah, but … these mongrels who threaten and hurt people might stop at nothing to get what they want, but that doesn't mean we stop living our lives. Isn't that what Ana said? She didn't run when Rick arrived in town because she wanted to put roots down here. And I'd hate to think of anyone hurting Meg, but Jack … *you're* hurting her. You're hurting yourself. The two of you are miserable while that bastard who threatened you is probably grinning with fucking glee!'

Adam's words pierced through Jack's heart and splintered. He knew all of that. He'd told himself the same thing many times and knew he was self-inflicting this pain. But the thought of his enemy grinning with glee? Rage rose inside Jack until he feared he'd snap his stew bowl in half. Fuck, his brother had him there. What was this unknown bastard thinking? Did he relish in his success? In Jack's grief? In Meg's heartache?

Nausea churned in Jack's gut until he feared he'd be sick. He'd always regretted the way he'd treated Meg. She didn't deserve it. She deserved to be cherished and treasured and spoiled. Megan Riley was the golden girl, the crowning jewel, everything he had ever wanted. She was worth the risk, even if only for a moment. And if that bastard had threatened just him, Jack would have told Meg he loved her without hesitation.

'You don't need to carry this burden alone, Jack,' Michael said. 'We'll all protect her. It's *Meg*. Why would someone want to threaten her anyway?'

Adam frowned. 'She's beloved by all.'

'Exactly,' Jack said. 'Who the fuck wants to hurt her? Why do they care if we're together? How will it hurt them? It makes no sense.'

Michael shoved his hand through his hair. 'You're meant to be together.'

'And I want to be.' Jack glared into the fire, his shoulders sinking. Longing rose from his chest to clog his throat. 'Fuck, it's all I want.'

'Then fight for her!' Adam cried. 'Don't let this bastard with an agenda hold you back! Who knows? They could be over it by now.'

Jack lifted his gaze. 'And if they aren't?'

'I still say fight for her,' Michael said. 'Fight for what you want, Jack. No one would tell me what to do or how to live or who to love.'

'Or who not to love,' Adam said. 'Come on, mate. You've been a martyr long enough.'

Jack's hands tightened over his knees. He longed to give in, to take his brothers' advice and be strong. To fight for Meg. But … 'Look, I know it sounds like I'm running scared. That I'm a fucking fool. But … I am, guys. I'm fucking terrified of what this person is capable of. They'll do anything to stop us from being together and I won't risk Meg getting hurt.'

'She won't be.'

Jack's jaw tightened. 'You don't know that.'

'I don't,' Adam agreed, 'but if you take a chance and date, this person threatening you might come out of the woodworks.'

Jack's eyebrows shot up. 'You want me to take a chance on Meg's life?'

'No, but at least give the police a chance to catch the guy!'

'Then you can live happily ever after.' Michael had the audacity to grin.

Adam nodded. 'Exactly. Then our kids can grow up together and we can start marrying off Michael. Take a chance, mate!'

Jack forced his shoulders to relax as he stared into the dancing flames, watching as the embers consumed the log. Torn, he didn't have a clue what to do. Adam and Michael made it sound so easy. Talk to Meg. Take a risk. Let everyone band together and catch the bad guy.

But at what cost? He'd been there when Rick had abducted Ana. He'd witnessed Liam's fear and seen her return batted and bruised. He'd watched Isabella suffer trauma. He'd almost been killed himself and the terror …

Jack's chest squeezed until he could barely breathe. He couldn't do it. Meg might be tough and if she knew the truth, she would fight for them.

But Jack would rather see her living happily ever after with

Paul Kelly than hurt, bleeding, or dead. And that's all a future with him held for her.

He owed her something though as he couldn't keep stringing her along and seeing hope in her eyes. Because even after all this time, he knew she still believed in them.

'I'll talk to her.' It would be the hardest conversation he'd ever had, but he'd do it. 'For now, let's drop it. I've heard what you said, but I want to have damper, honey, and beer now. And talk about marrying Mike off.'

Adam exhaled. 'Fine. Although I don't know how Mike's ever going to find a wife for that house of his. When was the last time you asked a woman out?'

Chapter Eleven

He loaded his rifle. The gun club had reopened now that the rain had bloody cleared, though it was fucking unfortunate that the cyclone had turned. He'd have rather enjoyed seeing the monstrous storm flatten the crops around here. It'd have served all those fucking farmers right. None of them were his friends.

But once again, luck wasn't on his side.

Assuming his stance, power shivered through his muscles as he shot bullets through the bullseye one after the other. Saturdays at the gun club were his favourite time of the week, the time he could escape his wretched farm, wife, and relieve his never-ending frustrations with a gun in his hands. Though he probably shouldn't be complaining about Billy. It'd have been bloody devastating for the region, but he wouldn't have lost much. Not like those useless pricks who'd betrayed his family all those years ago. This time, they would have known what it was like to lose everything.

It'd have taken Bernard Kelly three years to re-establish his coffee plantation. Ron Riley would have had his work cut out for him to get his precious town back on its feet. And as for Henry and Cliff Maguire … he'd flatten their banana fields himself if he could blow hard enough.

He reloaded the rifle, pissed that mother nature had spared the fuckers. Even more so that Billy had taken his wrath out on the Innisfail banana farms, which would only put more fucking coin into Henry Maguire's fat pocket. Last time that had happened, the bastard had revelled in the profit that had allowed his precious wife to open her overpriced retreat and spoil their kids rotten. Pony club, horse shows, TAFE, brand new houses. They'd given their brats everything, while Henry had secured the business for his son, Jack. And that boy knew how to farm. When he and his sleaze of a brother took over, Shadow Creek would continue to thrive.

Gritting his teeth, he shot another round. Yeah, it pissed him off. But not as much as the fact that Jack had always had his sights set on the crowning jewel of Elizadale. Megan Riley, the woman who would inherit most of her backstabbing father's property and possibly her mother's family farm. The farm that should have bloody well been his. So, the thought of it ending up in the Maguires' hands … well, he had put a stop to that happening.

He rolled his shoulders, then reloaded the gun. He drew strength from the weaponry, the thrill of the shot. He came every week without fail to remind himself that he was a man in control. But today, he had another agenda.

He eyed Paul Kelly down the line-up. He didn't know what it was about guns that had drawn Paul to the club, but the younger man had been shooting for most of his adult life. He supposed the boy's father had rubbed off on him there. While the Kellys had given up cattle decades ago, the stockman lived on inside Bernard Kelly. No wonder his sons were a wonder with horses and shooting, as Harrison, too, was quite the marksman.

But he wasn't as good as his brother. Paul had skills with a rifle, and the ladies too, it seemed.

Exhaling, he aimed at the target. He didn't know what to make of Paul weaving his way onto his playing board and throwing a spanner in the works. Asking Meg Riley on a date? What had the boy been thinking?

He wasn't leaving here until he found out.

They were packing up when he slid up beside the young man. 'Don't see your brother round here much.'

Paul eyed him shrewdly. 'Thought you knew Harry's up at Cape Trib.'

'He's been there a while. Must be lonely without him.'

Paul snapped his gun case closed. 'I'm getting by.'

'I heard you took Meg Riley to dinner.'

'Can always rely on the old bush telegraph.'

'Didn't take you for the townie type.'

Paul's pale eyes blazed. 'What would you know about my type?'

'You've always liked the farm girls, haven't you?'

'Why do you care?'

Shrugging, he strove for nonchalance. 'Just curious. Always thought Meg would hook up with Jack Maguire.'

'I'm sure she will because I promise you, I have no interest in Meg Riley.'

He frowned, fists tightening around his gun case. 'Then why'd you take her to dinner?'

'Thought it might spur Maguire into action.'

He stilled. 'You want them together?'

Shrugging, Paul slung his gun case over his shoulder. 'I honestly don't give a shit, but it's inevitable.'

'Nothing's for certain.'

'Some things aren't,' Paul muttered, casting his eyes down. 'But others are.'

'If you think Meg belongs with Maguire, why'd you take her out?'

'That's my business.' Paul nodded at him. 'See you next week.'

Glaring daggers into Paul's back, he tapped his fingers on the table. Strange. Paul didn't seem like a threat, but the thought of the Riley bitch joining the Kelly clan?

He didn't like that either.

Chapter Twelve

Meg met Samantha Burgess at The Bent Banana on Saturday afternoon and bought them both a mango sorbet before settling in the alfresco dining area overlooking the thriving parkland. Lola sat at Meg's feet, enjoying a pumpkin pupcake and getting peanut butter 'icing' all over her cute black nose.

'This place makes the best sorbets,' Samantha said. 'Liam's done well for himself.'

'He sure has. And this is the best sorbet because it's one hundred percent mango. With a touch of lime juice, I think.'

'Just like the banana ice cream, right?'

'Yep.' Meg spooned more of the frozen treat into her mouth, letting it melt over her tongue as she studied the young woman across from her. Having just turned seventeen, Samantha was in grade twelve at Mareeba High and wanted to study business and have a career in event planning. 'This is your first time running for show queen, right?'

Samantha nodded. 'I thought it would be fun and a great way to help the community.'

'It will be. Have you decided what sort of fundraiser you'd like to host?'

'Well …' Samantha paused as she mixed her sorbet. 'I was hoping we could do some kind of bachelor auction.'

'Really?' Meg blinked. That would be different. She couldn't recall them ever having a bachelor auction before.

'Yeah. I see it all the time in TV shows and it looks like fun.'

Meg considered that as she ate her sorbet. 'It could be fun, but … we'll need to find men who are willing to do that.'

'A few boys from school are keen.'

'Oh, so you want an auction for teens?'

'I thought we could do both, for teens and adults.'

'Hmm …' Her interest sparked, Meg took the empty plate off Lola, who was trying to lick the taste of peanut butter off the paper. 'We'll need to do it in a way that keeps everyone safe. We can't risk putting men or women in a position where they feel uncomfortable.'

'I thought about that. On TV, they usually pack a picnic, bid on a man, and then have lunch together.'

Well, that was a much better idea than the auctions Meg had read about in fiction. 'That sounds doable. We can host a lunch event, and I'm sure that could be appealing to the men.' She smiled at Samantha. 'Do you have a certain someone in mind?'

Samantha laughed. 'No. Plus, it's my event, so I wouldn't be able to bid. I'll be too busy hosting.'

'That's true. We'll need to find a location that's both attractive and big enough.'

'We could do it at the park or by the river.'

'But where would you hold the auction? You'll need a hall or something.'

'Could we use the community hall?'

'Maybe.' Scooping the last of her sorbet, Meg considered

the possibilities. The golf course had lovely gardens, but picnicking there wouldn't go down well with the club. 'What about High Ridge? I'm sure Wendy would be happy to help. There's plenty of parking and it's a beautiful setting. We could host the auction at the lodge and then everyone can go on a picnic.'

'Sounds great!' Samantha grinned. 'I'll call Wendy and ask. I'll do the promotion too as I have so many ideas.'

'Excellent. If you do that and find other teens, I'll source some men.' Excitement wriggled its way up Meg's spine. She could already think of a few men to ask as not only would the event be interesting, but it could be beneficial for people looking for love. Her colleague Joe might be interested, and she'd ask Michael. But she'd need to recruit Cade since he was undoubtedly the sexiest man in town and single again. After a year of procrastinating, he'd finally asked Jessica Smithfield as his date to Adam's wedding, but their relationship had sizzled out after a few months.

'And you know what?' Meg said. 'I think it should be the men who pack the picnic. It's only fair if the women are paying. Then we can auction them off *with* the food.'

Samantha clapped her hands together. 'That's brilliant!'

* * *

Meg kept herself calm over the weekend with housework, church, and trying to get Lola to do the obstacles at agility training on Sunday afternoon. But when Natalia arrived at Monday afternoon drinks with the news Adam and Jack were stuck on the farm doing paperwork for their new employees, Meg's frustrations hit a whole new level. The longer this avoidance went on, the worse things with Jack would get.

She'd given up on texting him. He barely replied and when he did, his one-word responses were hardly reassuring.

Somehow, she moved through the rest of the week using the show, work, and grooming Lola as distractions. But when Friday night rolled around, Meg readied her attack, styling her hair until curls hung long and loose over her shoulders. She slipped a black headband on to match her strapless little black dress, the bodice hugging her figure tight until falling into a swishy skirt that ended above her knee. She slipped her feet into a pair of pink kitten heels, added lippy and mascara, and sprayed a dab of perfume just as Lucy arrived.

'Wow, you'll leave Jack tongue tied.'

Meg managed a laugh as her belly knotted. 'Jack's always tongue tied. He hardly speaks a word. You look great too.' Lucy wore tight jeans that hugged her slender legs and a canary yellow top that accented her cleavage. 'Are we still trying to make Sam eat his heart out?'

Lucy rolled her made-up eyes. 'Sam doesn't need to eat his heart out. I don't even know if he's coming tonight. But while men can be complex creatures, they're also simple-minded when it comes to appearances. Look drop dead sexy and they know they cannot have you.'

Meg frowned. 'Have things gone wrong with Sam?'

'No. But I just …' Lucy's eyes clouded.

Meg reached for her hand. 'Luce, is everything okay?'

'Yeah,' she muttered, pulling at the hem of her top. 'I just … it doesn't matter. We both look hot and you're going to leave Jack drooling.'

Meg pressed her lips together as she glanced down at the dress she'd paid too much money for because of how stunning and desirable she felt wearing it. 'What does it matter? Jack could drool a river, the stubborn man still wouldn't want me.'

Lucy shook her head. 'Men. They don't know what they want or how to get it. Now, let's go. I'm dying for a drink.'

On the short walk to the pub, Lucy chatted about the tourists who were currently staying at High Ridge, but Meg paid little attention as she tried to settle the butterflies having a rave party in her belly. She hadn't seen Jack since that day at High Ridge and hadn't a clue what he was thinking. Natalia had been Meg's advocate, telling Jack that her dinner with Paul hadn't been a date, and apparently Jack and Adam had had a heart to heart during their camping trip, but Natalia hadn't known the details.

Meg couldn't go on like this though, aching with hope, longing, and confusion. It had to stop. She couldn't be Jack's friend and have him fly into a silent rage whenever another man took an interest in her. One way or the other, they needed to talk.

Taking a deep breath, Meg strode into the crowded pub.

'Ladies!' Georgina grinned as they approached the bar. Meg's gaze darted to their booth, but none of their friends had arrived yet. 'What can I get you?'

'Sav Blanc, please,' Meg said.

'Just a beer, thanks.'

'You're out of your alcohol-free phase again?' Meg asked.

Lucy shrugged. 'You know me.'

Meg did, but she'd yet to figure out why Lucy went on and off the grog for no apparent reason. Georgina poured Meg's glass of wine as Paul arrived beside them.

Lucy's eyes narrowed. 'You here to cause more trouble?'

Paul grinned, and Meg's eyebrows shot up. 'Just hoping to have a chat with Meg, Luce. If that's all right with you.'

'Sure.' Lucy handed Georgina her card and snatched the beer off the bar. 'Meg can handle herself.'

She turned on her heel and walked away. Meg shook her head as she took Lucy's card from Georgina and handed over her own.

'Have you got what you wanted out of our dinner?' Meg asked.

Paul leaned his forearm on the bar. 'Nope. How about you?'

'No. Jack hates me.'

'I doubt that very much, Meg.' Paul's eyes softened. 'Maguire's an idiot if he lets you go.'

'He can't let me go if he never had me in the first place,' she muttered.

'Then have dinner with me again.'

She jerked. 'Don't you think you've caused enough trouble?'

'Maybe, but I haven't got what I want.'

'And what is that?'

'Nothing you need to be concerned about.' His shoulders slumped and he blew out his breath. 'Look, it doesn't need to be dinner. Let's have a drink and chat. We can talk about anything you want.'

'I don't know …' Meg picked up her drink. 'Can you give me a hint about why it's important to you?'

Paul's gaze darted over Meg's shoulder, lingered, then he glanced over his own. His throat worked as he swallowed and turned back, his eyes shuttered. 'It's best I don't. So just … let me know, okay? I'll buy you a drink any time.'

Paul turned, leaving Meg frowning at his back as he disappeared into the crowd. What was going on with him?

Sighing, Meg shook her head. She shouldn't concern herself. She left the bar and went to join Lucy in the booth.

'You having dinner with him again?'

'He asked, but I said no. I don't know what he's up to, but I won't play his game.'

'Good.' Lucy took a swig of her beer. 'I'm still willing to punch him though if he messes things up for you and Jack.'

Meg managed a weak smile. 'Thanks. But tell me, why isn't Sam coming tonight?'

Lucy shrugged. 'He's probably over me.'

'What? Why?'

'Maybe because I haven't slept with him.'

'You haven't?' Meg frowned. 'Has he pressured you?'

'Not really. He invited me home a few times, but I just …' Lucy dropped her gaze. 'Not feeling it, you know?'

Meg nodded and sipped her wine. She was on Lucy's side, of course. Just because you danced, ate, and flirted with a man for two months didn't mean you needed to have sex with him.

Ana and Liam arrived and slid into the booth beside Lucy.

'I have a baby bump! You want to see?' Ana addressed the question to Lucy since Meg had already seen the bump earlier at work.

'Oh my God, yes!' Grinning, Lucy's hands dropped to Ana's belly. 'Wow. It's really there …'

Meg blinked as tears pooled in Lucy's eyes. 'Luce?'

'Is that waterproof mascara?' Ana asked.

'No.' Withdrawing her hands, Lucy blinked rapidly. 'Dammit, I don't know what's wrong with me. I'm sorry, Ana.'

Liam reached across his wife and squeezed his sister's hand. 'It's okay, Luce. I was all "shit, it's real" too.'

Lucy choked out a laugh. 'Yeah. But seriously, that's awesome that you have a baby bump, Ana. I can't wait until my little niece or nephew is born.'

Ana wrapped Lucy in a sisterly embrace. 'The baby will be lucky to have you.'

'Just remember to share,' Meg said. 'I'll need honorary aunt cuddles too.'

Envy might have hold of her heart, but Meg couldn't wait until the little Maguire was born. It had been a long time since she'd been around babies now that her own nephew was four, and unless she could discover why Jack denied his feelings for her, she wouldn't be having her own babies any time soon.

'Hey, friends!' Cade Wilson slid into the booth beside Liam.

'Hey! How was Townsville?'

'Good. Caught up with Lily a bit.' Jack's younger sister Lily studied veterinary science in Townsville and would graduate at the end of the year. 'I tell you, that girl has a serious sugar addiction. She always wanted to meet up for ice cream.' He rolled his eyes, then glanced at Meg. 'But I heard you've given Jack more of a reason to kill Paul Kelly. What's that about?'

'Nothing.' Meg dismissed it with a wave of her hand. 'Jack's angry and hasn't spoken to me in two weeks, but I doubt you'll be arresting him for murder.'

'Good, because I'd hate to do that. I'd probably have to take Adam too as an accomplice. Then I'd have no friends.'

'You'd have me and Mike,' Liam said.

'And me,' Meg added. 'But I'm glad you're here, Cade, because I have a tiny favour to ask.'

Cade's mouth twisted as he swigged his beer. 'I don't know about you and your favours. Usually, you want me to do something.'

'That's what a favour is,' Lucy said.

'And it's for charity. I need some handsome young men to help my show queen candidate with her fundraiser.'

'Are you trying to flatter me?'

'Only because it works.'

'Does Liam need to do it?'

Meg shook her head. 'We want to host a bachelor auction at High Ridge.'

Raising his eyebrows, Cade lowered his beer. 'A bachelor auction?'

'Yep.' Meg flashed him her best smile. 'I need a few bachelors to put together a picnic and then ladies will bid to go on a date with you. Nothing scary, just a little bit of fun. So, will you do it?'

'Don't see why not. Can I pick who wins me?'

'I'm not sure that's the point.'

'Why not? There are some scary women out there, Meg. And I think most bachelor auctions are rigged.'

She supposed it really made no difference. 'As long as someone bids on you, I don't care if you've prearranged it.'

'Deal. How about you, Luce?'

Lucy pressed her hand to her chest. 'Me?'

'You leave my sister alone,' Liam said, his eyes narrowing. Meg wasn't sure if he was being playful or serious.

But it didn't deter Cade. 'It's not a real date. I'd rather her than some random person. And Luce and I get along, don't we?'

Lucy shrugged. 'I guess. But what if I want to win myself a date with another bachelor?'

'Do you?'

'I haven't seen the options yet. But sure. I'll win you if it comes to it.'

Cade grinned. 'Thanks. You're a mate.'

'Did you really just arrange a date with my sister?' Liam asked.

'It's not a real date,' Lucy reminded him.

'And it's for charity,' Meg added. 'It's only supposed to be fun. But you never know, it could also be a chance for new love to bloom.'

'In that case, I'll ask Darren too.' Darren Hudson was the local mechanic and one of Cade's best mates. 'That guy needs to fiddle with something other than engines.'

Meg smiled. 'Thanks, Cade. I'd appreciate that.'

'And may as well throw Jack and Mike into the mix, hey?'

Cade's eyes gleamed with suggestion, and Meg's pulse spiked. She'd thought about asking Michael, but Jack? 'I don't know …'

'Well, here they are, so let's ask them.'

Chapter Thirteen

Every bone in Jack's body ached as he dragged his feet into the Royal. He'd spent the week agonising over what his brothers had said. He wasn't an idiot. He knew he was letting this mysterious bastard win. But the thought of taking the risk rendered Jack immobile with fear. He couldn't handle it. He'd roll another tractor over himself before he ever let Meg get hurt. Which only left him with one choice. He'd been a bloody bastard all these years keeping her close, dancing with her, buying her drinks, and rescuing her from snakes. He'd entered a relationship with her without the physical intimacies and while it might have been what he'd needed, he'd also been selfish. He'd given Meg false hope and allowed her to hold out for something that could never happen.

So, he had to tell her the truth. If that meant breaking her heart, so be it. He would mourn their friendship, but he'd get over it with time.

He would never get over her death.

Steeling his spine, Jack ordered drinks with his brothers while Natalia joined their friends, but the beer hardly gave him strength as he sauntered towards the booth. Foolish as he was, he slid in beside Meg and bore the torment of her sweet scent assaulting his nasal passages and wreaking havoc on his heart. It didn't help that her sleeveless dress highlighted her slender neck and shoulders, the places Jack longed to brush his mouth over and kiss. Taste. Worship. His knuckles whitened around his beer as he took a deep swig.

'Jack, Mike, you need to join me in Meg's bachelor auction.'

Jack frowned at Cade. 'What auction?'

'Why not me?' Adam asked.

'You went and got yourself married, so you aren't a bachelor anymore.'

Michael raised his eyebrows. 'What's this for?'

'Show queen,' Meg said. 'Samantha wants to do it and I need to find some men willing to take part.'

She continued to explain the process and Jack nodded along as he picked at a coaster, keeping his gaze on the table.

'It'll be fun,' she concluded.

Michael glanced at Cade. 'You're doing this?'

'Only if Lucy wins me.'

Michael jerked. 'Keep your hands off my cousin!'

'You guys are unbelievable!' Lucy shook her head. 'Would it matter if I *did* want to date Cade?'

'Yeah, what have you guys got against me? I'm your friend!'

'Exactly.' Adam pointed his beer at Cade. 'I know the things you've done, mate. You're getting nowhere near Luce.'

'Ooh, you make him sound so enticing.' Wriggling her shoulders, Lucy sent Cade a flirtatious wink.

Adam narrowed his eyes. 'Not going to happen.'

Cade nudged Luce with his elbow. 'We could have a forbidden romance, Luce.'

Meg blew out her breath. 'So, what do you think, Mike?'

'Why not? I won't even rig it.' Michael raised his eyebrows at Jack. 'Are you game?'

While he'd always enjoyed supporting Meg's fundraisers, the idea didn't interest Jack in the slightest. Then again, it could be his chance to start over. He could take a woman on a picnic for cyclone relief. Jack rarely dated and whenever he had, it hadn't been for long and he wouldn't usually let Meg know about it since he'd always carried a torch for her. But he needed to extinguish that flame and remind himself that there were other women out there.

He ripped the coaster in half. 'Why not? It's for a good cause.'

Grinning, Cade lifted his beer in salute. 'There you go, Meg.'

Sipping her wine, she didn't reply, but Jack didn't miss the glare she sent Cade. Or the hint in his mate's eyes.

Shit, what had he done? Did she plan on buying him? He couldn't have that. He'd have to rig the bloody thing too.

'Well, it sounds like a fun event,' Natalia said after a moment, breaking the silence. 'I caught up with Brittany this week and we've set a date for our fun run.'

'I'm looking forward to that,' Isabella said.

'I can't wait,' Natalia agreed. 'And I'm excited about the show. I've never been part of something like this before, so I'm going to enter the vegetable competitions.'

Meg straightened so quickly her shoulder brushed Jack's arm. 'That's a great idea!'

Adam had done many things to woo the city-born doctor, but nothing had topped his offer to build her a vegetable garden. Natalia had swooned at the gesture and ever since, she'd maintained and loved her garden like any country woman would.

'Yes, but growing produce is so hard! I have the perfect capsicum on the vine now, but the show's months away! What if I don't have anything when the time comes?'

Jack managed a small smile. 'Welcome to farming, Nat.'

She groaned. 'I don't know how you guys do it. I'm competitive by nature and I want to be known to grow the best something in town.'

'You'll have something fabulous to enter, I'm sure,' Meg said kindly.

Jack nodded. 'But remember, many people grow their own veggies out here, especially on the farms, so it's a tight comp.'

'I'd have a veggie garden if I lived on the land,' Meg said. 'All I can manage now are herbs.'

Jack swigged his beer before he could say anything foolish. He'd always imagined revitalising the gardens at the homestead, which his mother had neglected since moving hers to High Ridge. She grew some herbs at home and kept the lemon trees productive, but with a little tender loving care, those gardens could thrive again.

Not that it would ever happen as Jack would stay in the shack if he never married. He, Jill, and all the dogs that would come after her didn't need the sprawling five-bedroom house. Maybe he'd leave it for Lily.

'I love growing veggies,' Natalia said. 'I'm also going to enter the baking.'

Meg laughed. 'You've become quite the country woman, haven't you?'

'I'm a farmer's wife! I might also enter some flowers now that they're thriving. And they certainly keep the pests away.' Natalia had discovered that tip after delving into scientific articles about growing vegetables, which had almost put Jack and Adam to shame when they'd admitted they'd overlooked the advantages of coupling vegetables with flowers. But since they were commercial farmers and rarely gave home gardens a thought, Natalia had forgiven them and happily planted various flowers to attract pollinators and improve soil quality.

Meg smiled. 'That's great, Nat. You do have some lovely zinnias. But what are you going to bake?'

'A banana cake, obviously. As the wife of a banana farmer, I'd love to be known to make the best banana cake.'

Jack stilled.

'You'd have to beat Millie Taylor,' Adam said. 'But you'll certainly give Luce a run for her money.'

Lucy shrugged. 'I don't need to win every year, which is what I keep telling Meg. But she refuses to enter despite being a wonderful baker.'

'I don't need to enter the show. I'm too busy organising it.'

'Just enter one thing,' Adam suggested.

'Bake a cake or bickies,' Natalia said. 'Or enter your herbs.'

'My herbs aren't that good.'

Jack's hand clenched around his beer. His throat tightened. Stomach churned. This was his golden opportunity and if he wanted to let Meg go, he had to start somewhere. 'You could enter your banana cake.'

Meg froze. Jack stared at his beer as her breath caught, icy gales of disbelief radiating from her. He couldn't look at her. Didn't want to.

Silence fell until the only sound was that of Jack's pounding heart. And Meg's soft whisper of, 'Are you serious?'

Jack lifted his heavy shoulders and strived for nonchalance. He had to push her away. It was for her own good. 'Why not?'

'B-but … it's *your* cake,' she whispered, the hurt in her tone squeezing his insides. 'You want me to enter it into the show where people judge and taste it?'

Fuck, he was a bastard. Of course, he didn't want that. That was his bloody cake. His and Meg's. He'd refused to let anyone else try it and she'd joked it'd be their special cake. And until now, it had been. But sacrifices had to be made.

'It's just a cake, Meg.'

No one spoke. Ana and Natalia exchanged confused glances while everyone else stared into their drinks. Adam shook his head and stamped on Jack's foot. Hard. Jack didn't grunt at the pain. He deserved it.

Eventually, Lucy broke the silence. 'Enter whatever you guys want, no one's going to beat my jam drops. Now, let's order dinner.'

* * *

Meg loaded her online shopping cart with pretty dresses, added her debit card information, and hit confirm. Four hundred dollars. Gone. Screw it. They were pretty and she needed something to make herself feel better.

Although nothing would release the vice squeezing her heart.

Groaning, she laid her head on the table. What was happening? What had she done wrong? After all these years, Jack Maguire was pushing her away as though everything that had been brewing between them had meant nothing to him. Like he could erase it from their history. Add it to the compost heap. Wash it down the creek.

But why? What had changed? He might have closed himself off before, but this time was different. He'd put himself up for auction at the event she shouldn't bid at. There had been no special sparkle reserved only for her in his eyes last night. No smile. No tease, fun, or banter.

He hadn't called her 'darlin'.

And then he'd said her banana cake was 'just a cake.'

If she was the type of woman to curl up and cry, she would. She'd bake her special banana cake and eat the whole damn thing while bawling her eyes out. But no matter how much she wanted to, Meg couldn't do that. It wouldn't solve anything. Neither would shopping, but at least she'd have pretty dresses.

She would blame Paul Kelly, but that wasn't fair. None of this was his fault as it shouldn't matter if they'd had dinner together. She'd had dinner with other men before. But as expected, Jack had viewed dinner with Paul as the ultimate betrayal and was determined to carve her heart out in retribution.

Which wasn't like him. Jack wasn't the vengeful type. Jealous, definitely, but not angry. He brooded and turned silent, but he wasn't mean.

So why would he go out of his way to hurt her?

Exhaling, Meg shoved away from the table and stood. She couldn't keep thinking about it. Nothing would subdue her heartache, but Chaz had returned from Tamworth yesterday and while she was in no mood to discuss music, it was better than driving out to Shadow Creek and begging Jack Maguire to love her. So, shoving her feet into shoes, Meg walked the two streets down to Chaz's house.

From the outside, it didn't look like the home of a country music star with its white cladding and simple gardens, but he'd renovated the inside to within an inch of its life with hardwood floors, crystal chandeliers, and all the latest high-tech kitchen and bathroom appliances.

Meg knocked on the screen door. 'Hey, Chaz!'

He appeared in the hallway. 'Hey, Megan. I've just put the

kettle on.' Flicking the lock, he let her in. 'You want tea or coffee?'

'Tea, thanks.' They stepped into the kitchen where white stone benchtops gleamed beneath the downlights. Meg slipped onto a plush stool while Chaz worked his beloved espresso machine, his long hair falling over his eyes. He'd grown it out again and had most of it tucked back in a tiny manbun. Some days, Chaz oozed 'rockstar.'

Meg ran her finger over the glass fruit in the Waterford crystal bowl. 'How's the album going?'

'Good. We've got some party songs scratched and hope to have something out by the end of the year.' The machine hissed as Chaz steamed milk. 'The new single will be out next week and the label's been breathing down our necks.'

'Do you need more songs?'

He raised his eyebrows. 'You got one?'

Tucking her hair behind her ear, she shrugged. 'I was inspired, thinking about community spirit and how we can help the cyclone victims. The song is about banding together, and I thought you might like it.'

Grinning, Chaz switched off the machine and set the jug down. 'It's been a while, Megan. I thought you'd given up on me.'

'You don't need me,' she muttered. 'I dabble from time to time but don't write anything decent anymore.'

'That's where you're wrong,' Chaz said, pausing as he ground coffee. '"Jane" is still one of our biggest hits. I always said we could use you on the team. Or you could … you know … release some singles and write your own album.'

The kettle clicked and Meg jumped to her feet, her heart pounding as she reached into the cupboard for a mug. 'Do you want to see the song or not?'

'Of course. Is it just lyrics or did you fiddle with some tunes too?'

'Just lyrics.' She made her tea, then took the notebook from her handbag. 'I imagined it more as a duet and I know you don't do them often, but it'll add to the theme of community spirit and joining forces.'

'Hmm …' His eye skimmed the words. 'Yeah, I see it.'

Meg settled onto her stool, smiling softly as she blew on her tea.

'This is deep, Megan.'

'I hope so. There are some wonderful artists I think you should consider too.' She named three top female Australian country singers she thought would suit. The first one had been in contact with Chaz about a duet before, the second Meg desperately wanted to meet, and she suggested the third because Meg honestly thought her voice would blend well with Chaz's. 'Personally, I think you should ask Hayley, but that's just me.'

Chaz eyed her over his coffee mug. 'And you know what I reckon?'

Meg stilled. 'Don't say it.'

'Come on, Megan! You'd be perfect.'

Meg shook her head. How many times did she have to tell him no? '*Hayley* would be perfect. Or anyone with a name and a hit single. You don't want me.'

His eyes darkened. 'You know that's not true. You should write and sing again. That had always been the dream. When Dad was teaching us to play guitar, you were the one who always talked about singing on stage to a crowd of roaring fans and dancing the night away. You can still do it, you know? You loved hosting concerts for show queen. You can go far.'

Nostalgia roiled in Meg's belly as she lifted the tea bag

from the mug. It had been her dream once. She'd wanted to write songs, sing, and travel a little. She didn't need the grandeur; a moderate career would suffice so that she could also keep her dream of living on Shadow Creek and bearing Jack's babies.

Her heart sank. 'The concerts were fun.'

'So, record the song with us,' Chaz suggested as though it was that easy to do. 'It's not a love duet, so it won't feel weird. This song is about everything that means the most to you. Community spirit and friendship. In fact …' Chaz's forehead wrinkled as he glanced back at the lyrics.

'What?'

'Hmm … never mind. Leave it with me. But you haven't missed your chance, Megan.' His gaze returned to hers. 'Gympie was a loss, but you know I'm always happy to help you. So, sing your song with us.'

Meg stirred her tea. Strangely enough, she almost wanted to. She'd declined his offers for so long and denied her dreams. But why? What was she afraid of? If anyone supported her pursuing a music career after all these years, it was Chaz. And her previous work hadn't gone unnoticed. Her four singles occasionally played on the radio and, based on her success at writing for The Charlie Boys, artists had contacted her once or twice with offers to work with them.

So why not give it a try? It might have been easier to stay in Elizadale and embrace her teaching career, but that was when she'd hoped she and Jack would get married.

Meg swallowed a laugh. That wasn't going to happen any time soon. If ever. So maybe she *could* see if she could find a place in the music world.

'You can still have the simple life you want, Megan. You don't need to tour all the time and go to Nashville. You can live here, teach the kiddies, and have a family of your own.'

'Yeah, right,' she muttered, sipping her tea. 'But … I'll think about it. I mean, I did like putting songs out there.'

Remembering the excitement, the joy, seeing the number of downloads increase and reading positive reviews, Meg's heart swelled. Her music had been an accomplishment like no other.

'You did enjoy it. But I do like this song.' Chaz tapped her notebook. 'I'll talk to Eric and Chuck and put some music together. You're welcome to join us if you want input, but time might be of the essence because I have an idea.'

Meg raised her eyebrows. 'What idea?'

Chaz grinned, cheeky in his eyes. 'I'll let you know.'

Chapter Fourteen

Jack swung the axe into the wood beneath his feet and leapt onto the ground as the log split a second before Adam's. 'Three in a row.'

'Piss off,' Adam said, resting his axe over his shoulder. 'Some of us don't have a raging temper behind us.'

Jack propped his axe against the fence, guilt churning in his gut over how he'd behaved last night and the things he'd said. Meg had remained unusually quiet for the rest of the evening with a slouch in her shoulders and hurt in her eyes.

He'd hardly slept a wink.

'Don't pester me, Adam.' Jack snatched his water bottle off the fence. 'Just because you're married, doesn't make you an expert.'

'Ah, yeah, it kind of does. I've been, I've won, I have my life sorted. You, you're thirty and alone and will be forever if you let Meg go. Come on, mate. "It's just a cake." What the fuck was that!' Adam took a swig from the pink shit he drank—hibiscus tea. 'None of us have ever been allowed to taste Meg's special banana cake. And believe me, I tried! The bloody thing's always been for you and you only, and now you tell her to feed it to the whole town? You're breaking the poor woman's heart! What happened to talking to her?'

Jack slammed the water bottle closed. 'What good will it do? We can't be together and that's that. Besides …' His words died as he spotted their father approaching the yard.

Henry tipped back his old Akubra. 'How's the chopping going, boys?'

'Jack's a machine. Might even beat Kelly this time.'

Jack frowned. 'When was the last time Kelly beat me?'

'Last night.' Adam snapped, and Jack's jaw clenched. He'd never punched Adam before, but—

'Boys, be nice,' Henry said, and Jack forced his fist to uncurl. 'Adam, Natalia has lunch waiting for you inside. She's made the most colourful pasta salad I've ever seen.'

'Yum.' Adam lay his axe down. 'See, Jack? It's wonderful having a wife.'

'Enough.' Henry's tone tightened, but Adam merely grinned as he clapped their father on the back, then strode towards the house. Henry waited until Adam was out of earshot before placing his hand on Jack's shoulder. 'Let's take a walk, son.'

Knowing better than to argue, Jack blew out his breath and fell into step with his father as they crossed the end of the looping road central to Shadow Creek's living quarters. His parents' house dominated one end, his aunt and uncle's sat to its right, and the stables sprawled along the left. Henry and Cliff had built their houses shortly after they'd both married, but the stables dated back to the time Shadow Creek had been a cattle station. The love of horses was the only thing Henry had brought with him in the transition from stockman to banana farmer, a love that he'd passed on to Jack and his siblings as he'd taught them to ride, care for, and enjoy horses.

In the centre of everything was an old wooden playground and a swing set shaded by a jacaranda tree.

Henry led Jack towards the bench which, in spring, would be littered with purple flowers. But it wasn't the season for the jacarandas to bloom.

'Sit down, mate. We need to chat.'

His soul weary, Jack sat beside his father and leaned his elbows on his knees, watching the old swing rattle in the light breeze. 'What has Nat said?'

'Enough.' Henry exhaled. 'What are you doing, Jack? Are you really going to let Meg's dinner with Paul Kelly get to you like this? You don't even know if it meant anything.'

'Nat said it meant nothing.'

'Of course, it didn't. Meg would never intentionally hurt you. So, what's the problem?'

Jack glanced at his clasped fingers, pain gripping his chest. 'I need to let her go, Dad. We can't be together.'

'Not this again.' Henry clasped Jack's shoulder. Hard. 'Mate, it. Was. An. *Accident*. A bloody awful and terrifying accident. Do you think I'd have let Brett stop investigating if I'd thought someone wanted to hurt you?'

'No, but—'

'There are no buts about it. We exhausted every possibility, and Brett questioned many people. But there was no evidence that anyone caused the accident, Jack, and you might find it easier to move on if you accept that. The tyre blew. We will never know how. We just need to be bloody grateful that we were lucky.' Henry's grip tightened as he leaned in close. 'I didn't lose my boy. I didn't lose my heart that day, but it kills me you lost yours.'

Jack squeezed his eyes shut. Rarely did his father speak about emotions. They were similar in that way. But if anything had knocked Henry Maguire out of his quiet self, it had been that day by the creek.

'I am grateful,' Jack whispered. 'I know I'm bloody lucky and that's why we do all that stuff on farm safety. And I know it would be easier to write it off as an accident, but what if the threat *was* tied to it? I can't take that chance and I can't keep holding onto something I can never have. I need to let Meg go.'

Henry straightened. 'Jeez, boy. Don't you get it? Meg's not going anywhere. She loves you. You can tell her all you want that you're not right for her, not good enough. That you'll hurt her. Whatever your excuse is, it'll never work. Meg will make up her own mind.'

Jack glanced at his father. 'It's not the same as you and Mum.'

'Maybe not, but I'm grateful every bloody day that she didn't listen to me. What would have happened if she had gone? I wouldn't have you! I wouldn't have Adam or Mike or that little Lily. I wouldn't have all of this!' He threw his arms out, gesturing around them. 'I'd be a lonely old man pining for the woman he lost and avoiding your aunt and uncle. Is that what you want? Could you spend the rest of your life in Elizadale without Meg?'

'I'd rather watch her live without me than have her dead and buried.'

His father's eyes softened. 'Come on, Jack. It won't come to that. I've been where you are and I can't bear the thought of you being so unhappy. Take a chance. Don't you want what Adam and Liam have?'

Jack's lip curled. 'Adam pisses me off. Just because he beat me to it, he thinks he can lecture me about marriage.'

'I've seen you since his wedding. You've been more down

than usual. But don't let what happened after that accident hold you back anymore, Jack. I don't want you to be alone. And if you get with Meg and someone tries to hurt either of you, we'll deal with it. I promise.'

Jack exhaled. 'I don't know why everyone's so keen to put Meg at risk.'

'I'm not. I'm just keen for you to live your life. And so is her father.' Henry raised his eyebrows as he stood. 'Remember that.'

Jack's heart twisted until he could barely breathe. Brett, Ron, his father … were they right? Was he being a stubborn fool?

'Come on.' Henry tapped Jack on the shoulder, and he stood. 'I know it's difficult, but you'll do the right thing. Now, let's go check out this salad Nat's made. She's put bloody strawberries in it!'

* * *

Meg didn't know where the music had come from, but after returning home from church, she'd curled up on the lounge with her guitar in her lap and a melody tingling in her fingers. It wasn't anything special, and moody more than upbeat, reflecting her current emotions. But Meg longed to set it free, to express what she felt and hopefully settle the turmoil inside her. She might have suppressed her music, but she needed something in life to ground her, to aspire to, and a reason to continue going on if she wasn't able to fill the bedrooms of Shadow Creek's homestead with little Jack look-a-likes.

Slapping her hand over the strings, she gazed heavenward. Lord, give her strength. How would she ever let go of that dream?

Her phone rang and jerked her out of her sorrow. Seeing Elanora's name on the screen, she answered. Elanora asked if she wanted to meet for drink and with nothing on her schedule but time to wallow, Meg agreed.

She and Lola arrived at The Bent Banana ten minutes later, ordered a guava and mint smoothie, then sat with Elanora in the undercover dog-friendly section. Meg smiled when she noticed the book resting by her friend's elbow. 'I loved that story.'

'Oh, good. I thought it sounded interesting.' Her fingers brushed over the laughing couple on the cover with the red-dirt background. 'I haven't read in so long, so I thought I'd get back into it. And I like the range Isabella has as I love rural stories.'

'It's a great thing she's doing and it helps her explore her passion.'

'Indeed. When I called, you said you were playing music.' Elanora smiled softly, curiosity sparkling in her eyes. 'Is the spark coming back, Meg?'

'It does occasionally. I've had a lot on my mind lately as men are driving me insane.'

'Including my brother, I hear. Though I asked him about it, and he said nothing is happening between you two.'

'There isn't. But do you know why he thinks that having dinner with me will benefit him?'

Elanora shook her head. 'I don't know what he thinks half the time. But I am worried about Paul. Something seems to have really got him down lately. At first, I thought he was hovering over me, but now, I'm not so sure.'

'He seems lonely.'

Elanora sipped her coffee. 'Yes, but he won't talk about it. Bit hard to help him.'

Meg rolled her eyes. 'What is with these men keeping everything to themselves?'

'Pride?' Elanora shrugged. 'I don't know. He's agreed to help me with the trivia night though, so that'll be good for him. I think we have a great variety of fundraisers this year.'

They talked about show queen until they finished their drinks, then stood, farewelling and thanking each other for the chat before going their separate ways. But as Meg settled Lola into her car seat and drove home, her mind wasn't on Jack. Elanora was right. Paul was hurting. And whether or not he'd admit it, he'd come to her for help.

Meg pulled into her driveway, her heart pounding as she glanced into the back seat. 'Lola, what's Mummy going to do?'

Lola had no words of wisdom as Meg climbed out of her Astra and unbuckled the little dog. Heading inside, she settled onto the lounge and cursed the Good Samaritan inside her. She didn't want to cause Jack any further grief, but she couldn't shake her concern either. And it's not like Jack had bothered to talk to her about that dinner with Paul, so what did it matter if she caught up with him again? Paul might have his own agenda, but he'd reached out to her for a reason. He'd been sincere on Friday night so he couldn't be the villain everyone made him out to be. And if she helped him get what he wanted, maybe he might leave the Maguires alone. The feud could finally end. So, in the interest of protecting her friends, Meg pressed the call button.

'Hello?'

'Paul, it's Meg. I've been thinking and if you want to talk, let's catch up tomorrow.'

Chapter Fifteen

'Wow. You're sure dressed up for a Monday night.' Lucy's eyebrows lifted as Meg emerged from her bedroom. 'That's a damn sexy dress.'

Meg glanced down at the fuscia bodycon dress that highlighted her yoga-toned hips, thighs, and flat belly. 'It's just a dress.'

'Please. I know what you're doing. You look hot. Jack might be all "share my secret cake recipe" but no way is he going to let you get away.' Lucy's eyes narrowed. 'You *are* going to talk to him tonight, right?'

Meg swallowed. 'That will depend on his mood.'

'Then, you might as well go all out. Put on some heels. Jack likes you in heels.'

Jack didn't deserve anything he liked, but a girl needed her weapons. And a confidence boost. Besides, he might be driving her bloody mental, but Meg still had no interest in hurting him. She would talk to Jack tonight and sort everything out, but it'd be damn hard if he didn't let down the reinforced titanium wall that he'd erected around himself.

Meg strode into her room. 'What makes you say that?'

'I notice these things. Jack's always checking out your legs.'

She slipped on her white platform heels. 'How is it you notice these things about others but haven't got a man yourself?'

'I don't want one.'

'So, you cry at Ana and Natalia's weddings, but don't want your own special day?'

Lucy shrugged as her gaze lingered on the floor. 'One day, maybe. But right now, I'm far more concerned about you and Jack. We need to fix that, so grab your bag and let's go.'

Meg gathered her things, fed Lola, and followed Lucy out the door. She'd had all weekend to prepare for tonight and she wouldn't back down. Jack wore stubborn like a second skin, but she could wriggle her way beneath that. She had to, for her sanity, his, and that of their friends.

Which was also why she needed to settle this situation with Paul Kelly.

'Just don't let Jack push you away, Meg,' Lucy said as they strolled down Stuart Road. 'Have a quiet talk away from the booth and explain that you didn't mean anything by having dinner with Paul. That it was all just Paul's bullshit.'

Meg nodded. 'And I will, as soon as I find out what that bullshit is.'

'What do you mean?'

'I'm meeting Paul at the pub.'

Lucy halted and threw her arms in the air. 'What the hell's the matter with you?'

'Relax, Luce.' Meg grabbed her hand. 'I'm not trying to cause more trouble, but aren't you curious about what Paul's up to?'

Lucy's chest heaved as she shook her head from side to side. 'Paul's motives are purely selfish, Meg. He's done nothing but cause a rift between you and Jack. Why are you falling for it?'

'Because I don't think that was his plan. He's hurting and I want to help him if I can. Besides, after all the grief he's caused, I think I deserve to know what he had to gain out of us having dinner.'

'Fine.' Lucy stalked past Meg. 'Whatever. Don't listen to me.'

Wincing, Meg started after her. 'Luce, don't be like that.'

'I can't believe you even care about Kelly!' Lucy's longer legs kept her ahead of Meg. 'After everything he's done to Adam and Jack, to … You're an honorary Maguire, Meg! Which means you don't talk to the Kellys.'

'I don't think that's ever been a rule.'

Lucy spun around. 'What?'

'What about Adam and Jordan?'

'That was different. *They* were the problem.'

'I think it was more than that,' Meg said, recalling Harrison's bullying nature and Paul's competitiveness throughout their lives. Not to mention they were overprotective brothers who hadn't seen the vindictiveness of their little sister until she'd shattered their entire family. 'But either way, the feud should be over by now.'

'You'd think.' Lucy spun on her heel and walked off.

Sighing, Meg followed her, letting the subject drop as they arrived at the Royal Hotel. All their friends were there except for Jack, Adam, and Natalia. Spotting Paul at the bar, Meg offered to grab drinks while Lucy joined their friends in the booth. Meg's heart hammered as she approached him. He smiled politely, but it didn't reach his grey eyes.

'You look nice, Meg.'

She leaned her elbow on the bar. 'Thank you.'

'Why the change of mind? Last week you were dead set against helping me.'

His expression remained shuttered, and Meg's belly knotted as she studied the man she'd always considered her enemy. Why though? For the reasons Lucy had said? Because she was an honorary Maguire? She couldn't justify that. Personalities clashed, sure, and Harrison was a tosser. But God expected her to treat all people equally, and Paul had never directly hurt her.

'I was, but you know me.' She frowned. 'I think. We've never been friendly, but you must have asked for my help for a reason. I'd like to know what that reason is, Paul, but I also understand it's not my right. I care about people though, and after everything you and your family have been through, I can see that something is troubling you. So, if there's anything I can do …'

Paul's gaze remained fixed on his beer. 'The family thing hasn't been easy.'

'I wouldn't expect it to be.'

Georgina approached and Meg ordered drinks.

'Put them on my card, Georgina,' Paul said, before glancing at Meg. 'I said I'd buy you a drink.'

'The beer's for Lucy.'

Paul shrugged. 'The least I can do. And I like that you want to help, but I really don't think you can.'

Meg blinked. 'You were adamant about talking to me last week.'

'Yeah, but I think I'm going about it the wrong way.' He took a swig of his beer, muttering, 'As usual,' beneath his breath. 'Let's just forget it.'

Meg's chest tightened. 'Are you sure? It's just … you seem lonely. Is that it?'

'Does it matter? No one gives a shit about me.'

'That's not true.' She wanted to lay her hand on his shoulder, but she resisted. 'Elanora cares. She's concerned about you too.'

'Yeah ...' Paul slid off his stool. 'I know. But please forget about it, Meg. I'll work something out.'

Before she could say anything else, he turned and wove through the crowd into the next room.

***

'I can't fucking do this.' Jack's fists clenched as he paced outside the Royal Hotel. 'I thought I could, but seeing her ...'

Natalia placed her hand on his shoulder while Adam stood behind her, his arms crossed and biceps twitching with the urge to slug him.

'You don't know why she was talking to Paul unless you ask her,' Natalia said in her easy, calm manner. 'Remember, Meg's just a pawn in Paul's stupid game. She *isn't* interested in him. I've told you that.'

'What does it matter if you won't be with her anyway?' Adam asked.

'Adam, be quiet,' Natalia said. 'But Jack, Meg can't help it if someone talks to her at the bar.'

Jack shoved his fingers through his hair as chatter and laughter drifted from inside the pub. It shouldn't be this hard. He should be able to go in there, sit beside Meg, and enjoy his Friday evening like he always had. To enjoy her smiles, hear about her week, to ...

Sweep her into my arms and tell her I love her, tell the world, and never let any bastard near her again.

FUCK!

'We could punch him,' Adam said, 'but I doubt that'll solve your problems with Meg.'

'You will *not* punch him.' Natalia's eyes flashed. 'You are both going to calm down. Adam, stop goading Jack and Jack, stop torturing yourself. Go inside, get yourselves a beer, and act like civilised grown men. And if you want any happiness in your life, Jack, you will swallow your pride and *talk to Meg*!'

Natalia turned in a swish of golden hair and stalked inside.

Jack's mouth twisted. 'Why'd you have to marry someone who's always right?'

'Annoying, isn't it?'

Jack blew out his breath. 'Shit, mate. What am I going to do?'

'I've told you what I think.' Adam clapped his hand on Jack's shoulder. 'But right now, let's get a beer.'

Needing one, Jack dragged his feet inside, his gaze wandering as he approached the bar. Meg sat in the booth with her attention on Ana, who was telling a story with her hands. And dammit, she'd dressed up more than usual. Her pink halterneck dress hugged her slender throat, leaving her shoulders bare as it clung to her torso and accentuated her breasts. Her laugh was the only thing he heard among the crowd chattering around him, the sound as melodic as her songs.

He slouched against the bar. Fuck, he wanted to fight for her. He wanted the life he'd pictured all those years ago before the tractor had squashed it. A home with Meg on Shadow Creek, where he could give her the gardens she desired, the sprawling homestead, and a family. The old playground would once again hear the delight of children's laughter. He couldn't imagine any other future, except for the gut-wrenching thought of watching Meg have that life with another man.

Jack ripped his gaze from his beloved as Adam ordered them each a beer. Spotting the stool, Jack sat.

He could almost hear Adam's teeth grind. 'You're not serious.'

'I can't go over there, mate. I can't keep pretending.'

'Then don't.'

'I can't be her friend. I can't be more. It's over. I should go home. Move away and farm mangos.'

Blowing a gale of a breath, Adam eased onto the stool beside Jack. 'You are really pissing me off.'

Jack lifted the beer and took a swig. 'I'm pissing myself off too.'

***

Meg's hands tightened around her glass. 'Are you kidding? He won't even sit with me now?'

'Don't start.' Weariness filled Natalia's eyes as she relaxed into her seat. 'He saw you talking to Paul and got all cranky.'

'Oh, for …' Meg tore her gaze from Jack's ridiculous position at the bar and tossed back a mouthful of wine. This was unbelievable. How could he be so pigheaded? So angry? How could he keep pushing her away? They were friends. Best friends. She wouldn't stand for it.

Meg slammed her glass down and nudged Lucy. 'Let me out.'

Her friend leapt out of the booth, shooting Meg a grin that Meg didn't return as she stood. Without hesitation, she strode through the crowd, slid herself between Adam and Jack, and rested her elbow on the bar.

'We need to talk.'

Adam's presence vanished. To Jack's credit, he held her gaze as he took a long swig of his beer. Her heart ached at the pain and frustration that filled his dark, chocolatey eyes. His tanned throat worked as he swallowed, then he let out a breath. 'Meg—'

'We're friends, Jack,' she said, forcing frustration out of her tone. She didn't want to argue or make this any harder. 'And you're sitting here glaring at me from across the room. I had one impromptu, platonic, absolutely-couldn't-care-less dinner with Paul Kelly. That's it. Now you want to sacrifice our banana cake and you won't even sit with me. Why?'

She twisted her fingers as clouds passed through his eyes. His jaw tightened. Shoulders tensed. Jealousy? Rage? She couldn't figure it out.

'It doesn't matter,' he muttered, glaring at his feet. 'You can eat with whoever you want.'

'I know! But I feel you don't even want to be friends anymore and Jack—' she grasped his forearm '—we can't do that. I can't lose you.'

He stayed silent. A heartbeat passed. It took all of Meg's strength not to dig her fingernails into his warm, hard flesh and shake him.

Then on a whisper she could barely hear above the chatter, he said, 'We shouldn't be friends, Meg.'

She froze. 'Wh-what?'

'Fuck.' He downed the last of his beer, then pushed to his feet. 'We can't talk about this here.'

Her hand loosened and Jack walked away. Meg's breath caught in her throat. What did he mean? Dammit, why wouldn't he talk to her?

She hurried after him, passing the booth and entering the

hallway that led towards the beer garden. 'Jack, you can't say we shouldn't be friends. That's what you wanted all those years ago when you know that I—'

Jack spun around, grabbed Meg around her waist, and hauled her against his body. She gasped. Her hands fell to his chest and tightened around his shirt as he lifted her onto her toes. His head lowered and the world stopped. His breath mingled with hers, and her lips parted. Everything inside her burned. A heartbeat passed. Two. But Jack's eyes only darkened as his face remained inches from hers.

'What I want doesn't matter, Meg. You can date, love, and marry whoever you want, but over my dead body will that man be Paul Kelly. Choose someone else.'

Then he was gone. The heat vanished as Meg stumbled and sank against the wall. Her head spun, the skin on her back burning from where his large hand had held her. It took all her effort to catch her breath.

Can't be friends? Choose someone else? She chose him!

But he didn't want her. Why? For God's sake, why?

She pushed off the wall and hurried through the pub, weaving through the crowd before rushing out into the sunset. Her heel stumbled on the footpath as she looked left and right. An engine rumbled, and she caught sight of Jack's Raptor as it disappeared up Stuart Road.

Hands fisting, Meg pressed them to her mouth, unsure whether she wanted to cry or scream.

Chapter Sixteen

Jack paced a ditch on the back verandah, Jill's head following his pounding footsteps back and forth as he spoke to Robbo the next morning.

'Most of Innisfail has power restored, so I'm staying with my cousin for a few days. At least I can charge my phone, have a hot shower, and a meal. She's been great.'

Jack was glad to hear it, though his mate hardly sounded any more upbeat than the day the clouds had cleared. 'But some parts of the grid are still badly damaged, hey?'

'Yeah, and South Johnstone's one of them. The lines to my house seem fine, but they need to fix the connections. Reckon it might be up and running within the fortnight, but you can still come down this weekend and we can get started.' Robbo's tone deflated. 'Farm's a mess, mate. Just be glad it wasn't you.'

Jack kicked Jill's ball into the yard. She bolted after it. He was glad, but he'd never admit it. In retrospect, he'd rather be cleaning up the farm and losing income than losing Meg.

'We'll be there, mate. I'll bring more gas, fuel, and we're okay roughing it. Just send Mike some pics of any damage you want fixed so he can bring the right supplies.'

'Will do. Thanks, Jack. I mean it. Really.'

'No worries, mate.'

He spoke to Robbo for a few minutes about anything other than the cyclone, then hung up. Jill dropped her ball at his feet, looking up at him with pleading brown eyes. Jack retrieved the dirty, slobbery thing and threw it across the yard.

The trip to Innisfail couldn't come soon enough. Returning home last night, he'd pounded the walkway through the lychee trees in fury. With himself, with the world. Jam on toast for dinner hadn't sat well and he'd hardly slept a wink, ashamed at how he'd treated Meg. At how he'd grabbed her with every intention of kissing the bloody breath out of her, until a miracle had occurred and he'd stopped himself.

He didn't want that. He couldn't risk it. But he'd come so close to telling her how he felt, either that he loved her or he never wanted to see her again. He still wasn't sure which would be better. Holding her had told him the first was true, while coming home to pack up the ute and head to Innisfail had proved the second.

But running away wasn't the answer. He'd been a coward, still was a coward, and he hated it. He couldn't bear to hurt Meg any longer. Seeing the pain and confusion fill her eyes had broken him. She deserved to know the truth. She would understand. He'd never met a more reasonable woman.

But after holding her closer than he'd ever dared before, Jack barely trusted himself around her.

'Fucking screwed up big time, girl.'

Jill didn't care as he picked up the ball. She just wanted to play. He obliged, watching as she gave chase. His yard was mown five meters beyond the four-foot metal fence where the bush created a barrier between him and the neatly structured rows of lychee trees. The sun shone bright in the sky and the wind whistled in the scrub, green and thriving from the wet season.

He wasn't proud of how he'd told Meg to marry someone else before walking away. He'd fucked up and wished more than anything that things could return to normal. Everything had been fine the way it was. He wanted his friend back, the lively woman with the golden hair who he could always rely on to make him smile. The woman who played pool with him just so that she could be on the winning team. The hysterical girl who called him when a gigantic spider was in the house, and the sweet talker who needed her leaking tap fixed. The friend who brought him dinner simply because she longed for company.

They might have been friends, but deep down, they were two lonely souls who longed for companionship.

For love.

Jack slumped against the verandah post as pain ripped through his chest. He wanted to find the bastard who'd written that letter and tear him to shreds. What the hell had been his problem? What was so terrible about him and Meg falling in love? What business was it of his if they married? How would their union threaten anyone enough to cause him or Meg harm? Sure, he would inherit the farm one day, but he'd share it with Adam. Meg's parents' assets would also split between her and her sister.

Who out there stood to lose from that?

Jack dropped his head into his hands. If he knew the answer to that, he'd have solved the mystery years ago.

***

Meg threw her pen against the wall, leaned back in her desk chair, and spun in a fast circle. Writing her feelings down in lyrics didn't ease her heartache, which was weird considering it always had before. Ever since the age of twelve, poetry had been her creative outlet.

But creativity couldn't overcome the turmoil inside her head. *Marry someone else?* Screw Jack Maguire. She would marry him or die an old maid. And since she didn't plan to do the latter, she needed Jack to overcome his resistance and accept that he was the man she chose. There was no one else.

But she'd seen the clouds in Jack's eyes last night. They'd been stormier than Cyclone Billy and filled with more than pain, more than jealousy and rage. Jack desired her, but something stronger than gale force winds held him back.

And it was time she knew what it was.

But that had to be tomorrow's task because Chaz had invited her over to hear the demo of her new song. As usual, The Boys hadn't wasted time in putting music to her lyrics, and the prospect soothed her frustrations with a combination of excitement and nerves. It would be best she and Jack had time to cool off, so as dusk approached, Meg grabbed her contribution to their shared dinner to celebrate both her new song and their single that had been released yesterday and was already soaring to the top of the charts. Not that she was surprised. 'Not my Boots' was as catchy and clever as all their previous chart toppers, and in the spirit of the evening, she set it to play on Spotify and tapped her fingers on the wheel as she drove to Chuck's large house on the highway north.

The Boys greeted her enthusiastically as Chaz accepted her potato salad and slipped it into the fridge.

'Congrats on the new song, guys.'

Chaz smiled. 'Thanks, Megan.'

'It's been awesome.' Eric threw his arm around her shoulder and led her into their studio-worthy garage. 'But just wait until you hear what we've done with yours.'

'It's a ripper, Megan,' Chuck said, settling beside his prized drum kit. 'It's gonna blow everyone away. No pun intended.'

Meg grinned as she settled on a swivel chair. 'I'm glad you like it.'

'Bloody love it. And so will the crowd when we perform it at—'

'Hey!' Chaz cut his friend off. 'I told you, that's not definite.'

Meg frowned as she and Chuck glanced at Chaz. 'What's going on?'

'I'll tell you when it's finalised,' Chaz replied, plugging in his guitar. 'But for now, just relax and tell us what you think.'

Exhaling, Meg twirled slowly from side to side, her heart pounding as The Boys readied their equipment. She trusted that they would have written fantastic music to accompany her words, but anxiety continued to niggle alongside her excitement as Chaz opened with a delicate melody. He sang her words in his deep, slow baritone, then hit a crescendo to transform her fun duet into a bloody anthem.

As the final note died, Meg had stopped swivelling, her ears ringing and mouth hanging open as Chaz's voice echoed on the panelled walls.

Her cousin grinned as he lowered his guitar and glanced at his friends. 'I think she's impressed.'

Meg picked up her jaw and swallowed. 'Impressed? That's just … wow. Demo that and artists will be hassling you with calls begging to do the duet.'

'We could.' Chaz lifted his eyebrows. 'Or you could do it.'

She resisted a groan. 'Please don't start.'

'Come on, Megan.' Eric's smile was far too cocky as he set his bass guitar onto a stand. 'You know you want to.'

Meg's chest tightened until she could barely breathe. She wanted to, all right. Her soul ached at the very thought of her voice blending with Chaz's and streaming over the airways with the best song—sorry, *anthem*—she'd ever written.

'It's your song. You deserve to sing it,' Chuck said.

'I wrote "Jane" too, but I didn't sing that.'

His nose wrinkled. 'But that's about love for a girl. And last I checked, they're not your type.'

Meg bit her tongue. Yes, 'Jane' might be a song about undying love for a woman, but it hadn't always been. All she'd done was change the pronouns and 'Jack' to 'Jane'. Strangely enough, no one except Lucy had made the connection. If they had, they hadn't mentioned it.

'The offer's there, Megan, so please think about it.' Chaz lowered himself onto a stool and rolled up beside her. 'But you approve?'

Grinning, Meg wrapped her arms around him and kissed his cheek. 'It's perfect, Chaz. Thank you.'

'I need a hug!' Chuck leapt out from behind the drums, his arms outstretched. 'Good work, Riley.'

Meg stood as Chuck wrapped his bulging drummer arms around her and squeezed her tight. 'You wrote a good beat.'

He grinned. 'Always.'

'You really are a star.' Eric hugged her too. 'And please, do consider recording with us.'

'You guys …' Meg glanced between them, her heart swelling. These three had always supported her, and they wanted her for this. She could see it in their eyes. 'I'll think about it.'

Chapter Seventeen

Too many times Meg found herself humming The Boys' catchy tune on Wednesday as she began lesson plans on complex sentences and distributed new reading books. She couldn't get the song out of her head, or their offer. But as the afternoon wore on and she farewelled her class of cheerful faces, Meg shoved all thoughts of music aside and focused on the more important matter.

Tonight was her best opportunity to talk to Jack without letting Friday night drinks get in their way, and she wouldn't let the chance pass them by. So when she returned home, she showered, changed into her good jeans, thew on a cute T-shirt, and brushed her hair until it glistened. Meg fed Lola, then left the house.

She forced her hands to relax around the wheel as she turned onto the dirt road and drove beneath the overhanging Shadow Creek sign. She needed to approach this conversation with patience as they'd been carrying this emotional burden between them for a long time. She was more than ready to get it off her chest, but Jack wasn't the kind of man who opened up easily. The best way to get him talking was with a soft touch and gentle probing.

And if that didn't work, she'd yank out the crowbar because she wasn't leaving tonight without answers.

Guava orchards spread along her right while lychee trees sat in neat rows to her left as she drove towards the homestead. Jack's house was about halfway between the intersection and the central living quarters. She turned into his drive, rounded the patch of scrub, and arrived outside his cabin-like house. His ute wasn't there, but Meg was prepared to wait. She cut the engine, climbed out of her Astra, and settled herself onto the foot-high stoop of the verandah. Crossing her arms over her knees, a calm settled over her as she observed the beautiful landscape and watched the paperbarks blow in the dying breeze. She didn't mind how long she waited as she had nowhere else to be and nothing had ever been more important. They were going to talk, calmly and rationally, like the two friends that they were.

Fifteen minutes later, the rumble of an engine cut through her serenity and her pulse spiked when Jack's Raptor muscled around the trees and pulled to a stop outside his tin shed. The engine idled, then died, leaving their world in peace again. Meg sat up straighter but kept her arms on her knees as the door opened and Jack stepped out. His eyes met hers over the bonnet, and he nodded in greeting. Meg managed a small smile in return as he strolled towards her, hands in the pockets of his dirty jeans, shirt sleeves rolled up to reveal his strong, tanned forearms as he sank onto the verandah beside her. Warmth rushed over her skin, but Meg kept her gaze forward. Despite her earlier courage, she hadn't the first clue where to start the conversation.

Jack reached down and plucked a weed from the grass.

Meg watched as he twisted it between his large, long fingers, the callouses squishing the weed to pulp before he tossed it away.

'I'm sorry, darlin'.'

Meg crumpled, that one word unravelling every insecurity and frustration inside her. Shifting closer, she leaned her shoulder against his.

'No more pretending, Jack. I don't like what is happening between us. You're keeping something from me and bottling it up isn't good for you. So, please. Talk to me.'

His breath released on a whoosh, tension easing from his shoulders as his knees fell open and his denim clad leg brushed hers. 'Where do you want me to start?'

'What's troubling you?' she asked softly, watching as he plucked another weed.

'Today?'

'Today. Now. This past fortnight since Paul tricked me into having dinner with him.'

'Tricked you, did he?'

'He ordered dinner, joined me, then started talking. Before I knew it, food had arrived. I was hungry and didn't want to be rude to the Royal and waste it, so I ate.'

He rested his forearms over his knees, copying her position. 'You were laughing.'

'He must have said something funny. I can't apologise for that, Jack. And I won't lie, I didn't hate talking to Paul. But I talk to everyone. I like people and I want to help them. Something is bothering Paul and he reached out to me. I was curious.'

'It's your bleeding heart, darlin'.'

Meg's mouth curved. 'Exactly. You know that about me, Jack. But I'm sorry that my dinner with him hurt you.' She grasped his forearm. 'I never meant to do that. Never have, never will. Because if I care about anyone in this world, Jack, it's you. Which is why I know you have not been yourself. Something is hurting you. So please.' She squeezed his arm tightly, desperately. 'Talk to me.'

His stubbly jaw hardened as his dark gaze remained on the yard. Meg's heart pounded as indecision, pain, and longing flashed through his eyes.

Eventually, he mumbled, 'I guess I finally realised what it'd be like to lose you.'

She smiled softly. 'Does it look like I'm going anywhere?'

'No, but—'

'Did you really think I was interested in Paul?'

His mouth twisted. 'Natalia said you weren't, but … I couldn't bear it, Meg. You're my friend, my *best* friend, and the thought of that wanker taking you away from me …'

Jack shook his head. It took all of Meg's effort to keep from grinning. 'Don't you see, Jack? I go where I want to go. Be with who I want to be with. And while you might have only wanted to be friends, I've never wanted to be with anyone but you.' She leaned closer. 'I am yours.'

Jack's forearm corded beneath her hand, but Meg didn't tear her gaze from his profile as he stared into the bush. It cost her nothing to say it as the words had longed to escape her for years. So, she watched as his lips thinned and eyes shadowed. Then his breath escaped, and his gaze finally met hers. The utter defeat in them shattered her soul.

'I never wanted to be just friends.'

She quirked her eyebrows. 'But that's what you said. Before the accident, I thought we were going to be together. We were going to go to Gympie and everything would fall into place.'

His arm moved from beneath her touch, and he grasped her hand in his. 'It would have, Meg. I'd been prepared to lay it all on the line and tell you how I felt. That's why I wanted to take you to Gympie.'

Her breath caught. Everything faded around her except for the regret in Jack's eyes. 'But we never went.'

'No.' His gaze dropped back to the ground.

She squeezed his hand. 'Nothing has changed for me, Jack. I waited for you while you were in hospital. I was ready. When you came home and took me on that picnic, I'd hoped we'd call that our first date.'

'But instead, I told you we should just be friends.'

Her heart broke, an echo of the devastation that had assaulted her that day they'd been lounging on her new picnic rug by the banks of Shadow Creek. She'd bought a genuine wicker basket and had driven all the way to Cairns to buy the perfect summer dress. She'd wanted the day to be special. Memorable. And it had been, but for all the wrong reasons.

'And I accepted that, thinking you still needed time to recover from the accident. So, I waited. I was your friend. But I can't keep waiting.' She brushed her thumb over the back of his hand. 'We still feel the same way about each other. I know we do.'

'That'll never change.' He blew out his breath, his shoulders slouching. 'But we can't be together, Meg.'

Meg forced herself to remain gentle. 'Why not? We were going to date once, so what changed? Was it the accident?'

'Yes.'

Meg blinked, surprised by his lack of hesitation. His honesty. 'Okay … but why? Did—'

His gaze locked onto hers, his jaw hardening. His eyes flashed as fingers squeezed hers, and Meg's throat closed over.

'It wasn't an accident, Meg. Someone tried to kill me.'

* * *

Meg's perfectly pink mouth formed a small O, her long lashes blinking slowly over her wide blue eyes. The battle had raged inside him and, despite wanting to tell her the truth, Jack had resisted saying those words. But now they were out there, lingering between them and leaving him wondering whether sharing the burden had been the right thing to do.

After what felt like an age, she sputtered, 'Wh-what do you mean?'

Jack glanced at their clenched hands, unable to look her in the eye and break her heart at the same time. 'That day on the tractor, the tyre didn't blow from a stick, nail, or wear and tear. Someone shot it.'

Meg jolted, her shoulder moving from his and leaving him cold. 'Did you go to the police?'

'Of course.' What sort of question was that? 'Brett investigated, but there was nothing for him to go on. He believed I heard a shot for the most part, but there was no evidence for him to work with. The rip in the tyre could have been caused by many things and since there were no further attempts to harm me, he suggested I let it go. But I couldn't, Meg. Someone wanted me gone so that ...' He shoved his hand through his hair. Shit, this was harder than he'd thought.

'What, Jack?'

Gritting his teeth, Jack swallowed a groan. Best he get it over with. He turned back and met her calm, concerned eyes. 'There was a note. Someone sent me a letter in hospital saying that I had a lucky escape. That I should stay away from you or else.'

She blinked again. 'What?'

'That's it. So, don't you see? Someone doesn't want us to be together. You and I going to Gympie would be the beginning of a relationship between us, and someone tried to kill me to stop it. That same someone would be prepared to kill you.'

Meg shook her head. 'No. Jack, that's—'

'Don't tell me it's ridiculous,' he said, his jaw clenching. 'I'm not overreacting.'

'But why?' Her pretty mouth twisted. 'Who would care?'

'That's what we tried to figure out, but we couldn't identify any suspects. Not Brett or Dad or your ...' He trailed off, but it was too late.

Meg blinked. 'My what?'

Wincing, Jack confessed his greatest sin. 'Your father.'

She jerked back, dropping his hand. 'My father knows about this?'

'Brett had to speak to him. We were trying to establish a connection. A reason someone would be opposed to a union between us.'

'It's none of their business!'

'I know that. But together, we will inherit many assets and—'

'So what?'

He grabbed her hands as shock radiated from her stiff posture. 'Calm down, Meg. I'm not saying it makes sense.'

'I've never heard anything more ridiculous in my life!' She tore her hand out of his to shove his shoulder. 'Why didn't you tell me?'

Because he knew she'd react this way. 'I wanted to sort it out. To find out who tried to kill me and put him away so we could be together without worrying.'

Her eyes blazed. 'But you didn't find him.'

'No.' He took her hand again and squeezed gently. 'So, I thought it'd be best—'

'To remain friends? To keep me at arm's length and deny us the one thing we both wanted most?'

Bile rose in his throat. 'I didn't want to see you get hurt.'

Rolling her eyes, her breath escaped on a *pfft*. His heart lurched at the tears that welled. 'I'm so mad at you right now.'

'And you have every right to be. I've been mad at myself, at *him*, for years. But I couldn't …' Shaking his head, he longed to draw her close, to hold her and comfort her as she grieved the truth. 'The thought of anyone harming you tore me to shreds, Meg.'

'So you, Henry, and Dad thought it'd be best to keep me in the dark, break my heart, and pretend that you didn't love me? Is that it?'

His chest tightened. 'No, I decided that. After the investigation, Brett determined that the tractor incident may have been nothing more than an opportunity to threaten me. That if he'd wanted to shoot me, he would have. Our fathers believed him and felt that I should disregard the threat and move on.'

'But you didn't.'

'No.'

'Because you think someone wants to harm you?'

'I don't care about me.' His jaw clenched. 'But I do think they'll harm you.'

'Me?' Her gaze narrowed. 'Why?'

He shrugged. 'Does it matter? Either way, we'd be gambling with our lives.'

'So, you'd rather us be miserable and alone?'

Jack exhaled. 'No. I'd rather you be happy.'

'Then problem solved!' She tossed her hands into the air before dropping them onto his shoulders. Frustration eased from her eyes until they sparkled, her mouth curving softly. 'The one thing that will make me happy is to be with you.'

Her hand brushed down his chest, and Jack drew in a sharp breath. 'Meg, don't—'

'No. You've said your piece. Now it's my turn.' She leaned closer, assaulting him with her fruity scent. 'I love you, Jack Maguire. Your stubbornness, your pride. Your broodiness and kindness. I may be thoroughly annoyed with you right now, but nothing will ever change the fact that you are the man I want to spend my life with. You always have been, always will be. And it's about time you accepted that.'

Jack didn't move. Couldn't. Her words weren't anything he hadn't known but hearing them brought warmth to his chest unlike anything he'd ever felt. His structurally reinforced walls cracked. Her hand lying over his pounding heart knocked them down further, as did the softness in her eyes, the smile curving her mouth, and her golden hair whipping in the wind. Everything he wanted lay within his grasp.

With strength he couldn't control, Jack wrapped his arm around her beautiful waist and drew her close. Then inhibition vanished all together, resistance died, and he kissed her.

Chapter Eighteen

Fireworks erupted in Meg's chest as her lips parted to welcome Jack's. His hand lifted to caress her cheek, and she fell into his touch. The reeling in her head disappeared and her pulse steadied into a comfortable rhythm as she kissed the man she loved.

Telling him that had been easy. Frustration continued to wind her up and she could barely believe what he'd told her, but right now, nothing else existed but her and Jack sitting on the verandah, isolated in their own little world, and Meg wasn't prepared to let his moment of surrender slip by. Her hand curled around his shirt as his pressed against her spine, urging her closer. His mouth was everything she'd ever imagined, warm, strong, and inviting as he kissed her with tenderness and enough heat to fuel her loins and curl her toes into her sandals. His fingers brushed her bare skin at the small of her back and she shivered as his other hand drove into her hair and held her still.

Jack deepened the kiss. His tongue brushed over hers, and a moan escaped her throat. With one gentle tug and her need to be closer, Meg tossed her leg over his thighs and straddled him. Chest to chest, she looped her arms around his neck and pressed her body against the hard planes of his while a mix of lips, tongue, and teeth emptied her mind and ignited her desire.

Inhaling, she changed angles. 'Don't push me away anymore, Jack.'

His arms tightened around her, and he stood as though she weighed nothing. Meg locked her legs around his waist and melted as he pressed her against the verandah post.

'Meg …' Cursing under his breath, his mouth dipped to her throat. 'We shouldn't do this. We—'

Her fingers dug into the hard flesh of his back. 'No. Don't send me away. Not tonight.'

Jack's hold tightened as he breathed her in. Tension radiated from his every pore, but Meg wouldn't back down. Not now. She ran her hands across his back and held him closer, angling her face to brush her lips over his hair in silent reassurance.

After an age, he whispered, 'Stay.'

Meg grinned so big it hurt. Slowly, Jack lifted his head to meet her gaze, and she neutralised her expression.

'We'll have dinner,' he continued, 'and we can talk. But first, I need to shower. I stink.'

'I hadn't noticed.' Unable to resist, she buried her nose into the open collar of his shirt and inhaled his earthy, manly scent. Her brain fuzzed. Good Lord … 'You smell the same as usual. Like sweat and hard work.' And something else that wasn't entirely pleasant, but she wouldn't admit it.

'I've been shovelling compost.' Jack loosened his grip around her until Meg had no choice but to drop her feet to the ground. His height diminished hers and she missed his warmth already. 'How about you see what's in the fridge. Mum gave me leftovers.'

'Okay,' she said as Jack opened the door and gestured her inside.

'Make yourself at home, darlin'. I'll be right back.'

He strode down the hallway, unbuttoning his shirt as he went. Gazing around the open-planned living area, Meg resisted the urge to dance a jig. Make herself at home? She already was.

It'd been weeks since she'd been to Jack's house and while everyone affectionally referred to it as 'the shack', there was nothing simple or shabby about it. The two dark grey lounges had been in residence since they'd built the place and Adam had scored them at a bargain in Mareeba. The square dining table was one of Adam and Jack's first efforts at making furniture and a sliver of wood still sat beneath one leg to stop it from wobbling. A large TV sat against one wall and a bookshelf holding anything but books stretched along another. All the furniture reflected the time Jack had spent there with his brothers.

But on the wall facing the front door was the canvas print she'd bought him of puppy Jill sitting on Dante's back. The café curtains she'd sewn with banana patterned lace hung over the kitchen window, and the horseshoe printed rug she'd found in an op-shop in Townsville during her university days still graced the living room floor. Her mother had made the crochet blanket over the back of one lounge, a gift from Meg to Jack one Christmas, and a succulent sat on the table, which she'd bought him this Christmas just gone.

A whimper came from the back door and Meg bounced through the house to greet Jill.

'Hey, girl!' Squatting, she rubbed Jill's reddish-brown ears as the sound of the shower drifted from the other end of the house. Tingles shot through her at the mental image of Jack standing naked beneath the running water. Heat pooled in her belly, and she straightened, shaking the enticing picture away. 'Let's see what's for dinner.'

The kelpie raced ahead of Meg into the kitchen. Opening the fridge, she found vegetables, double bananas, and clear plastic containers. Meg lifted one and prised off the lid. It looked like lemon chicken. She examined another and found pasta bake. Either would be tasty, but if things went well tonight, and they built on that kiss, then pasta would be a clear winner to replenish their energy.

Slipping the food back, she closed the fridge and bit down on her lower lip. Jack was right, they needed to talk. She couldn't comprehend what he'd said. Someone shooting at him? Attempted murder? She'd considered many reasonable and farfetched reasons of to why Jack didn't want to date her over the years, but she'd never have expected a threat upon their lives. It seemed like an extreme length to go for someone to keep them apart. Things like that didn't happen in her sunshine town of Elizadale. Why would someone go to so much effort?

Meg glanced at Jill. She understood why he hadn't told her but wished to God he had. To have received that threat while recovering in hospital and suffering from pulmonary embolus wouldn't have been easy. But what about after Brett had run out of leads? At least she'd have known why Jack had suddenly lost romantic interest in her. She wouldn't have spent all those months hurt, confused, and torturing herself by thinking she'd imagined his feelings before accepting their friends-only status.

She could have told him not to be ridiculous and that she didn't need a protector.

Meg sank onto the lounge, kicked off her shoes, and tucked her feet beneath her. It didn't matter anymore. He might not have said the words, but Jack Maguire loved her and that's all she needed to know. He'd tell her in time, once his fears ebbed away and he realised no one could stop them from being together. Let this mysterious villain try. Meg would fight for them. Especially now that she'd got this far, curled up on his lounge with his kiss lingering on her lips.

The shower turned off, and her pulse spiked. A moment later, footsteps padded down the hall and she glanced up as Jack strode towards her, pulling a white T-shirt down over his hard, toned belly.

Meg didn't hide her smile as he sank onto the lounge beside her and placed his hand on her knee, smelling better with his scent of plain soap.

'What you been up to lately, darlin'?'

It'd been far too long since they'd talked, so she had plenty to fill him in on. But she could barely concentrate as his thumb ran circles over her denim-clad thigh.

'Show committee and work. I also wrote Chaz a song.'

His eyebrows shot up. 'Yeah?'

She smiled softly. 'Billy inspired me. It's a song about community spirit, hope, and fighting back after disaster.'

'Sounds like your thing. You didn't want to keep it for yourself?'

Stifling a laugh, she dropped her gaze to where his hand was slowly torturing her thigh. 'What's the point? I can't give it the justice it deserves.'

He nudged her shoulder with his. 'I'm sure you could.'

'Chaz liked it, and that's all that matters. I heard the demo yesterday. I'd imagined it as a soulful, heartfelt duet with a blend of male and female voices, but they've turned it into a hit.'

'As they usually do.' He quirked his eyebrow. 'And the female voice?'

'Of course, they asked me.' The words escaped her before she could stop them, and her chest tightened as Jack's hand lifted to her shoulder.

'You should do it.'

'I knew you'd say that.' Meg ran her fingers through her hair and exhaled. Yes, her music might be emerging from the dark crevice she'd shoved it into long ago, but Jack had always been a massive supporter of her singing career. It'd been his idea—fault—that she record her demo in the first place. He'd inspired her to hope, motivated her, and she'd been ready to take on the world.

Until she hadn't.

Dropping her hand, she lifted her gaze back to his. 'But it'd be foolish. I'm a little nobody, and who wants to hear a nobody sing with The Charlie Boys?'

'How does a nobody become a somebody?' Jack quirked his eyebrow in a way she usually found sexy. But right now, it was just annoying.

'Yeah, I know. I guess it's just … I'm not sure if …' Toying with the hem of her jeans, Meg pressed her lips together. She didn't know how to explain it.

After a moment of silence, Jack wrapped his arm around her shoulders and drew her against him. 'Come here, darlin'.'

Meg went without hesitation, switching her weight through her hips and tucking her legs to her other side as she nestled her head against his shoulder. His hand settled into a strong, steady stroke down her arm, and she drew comfort from his embrace.

Jack pressed his lips to her hair. Meg couldn't contain her smile, loving the intimate gesture. 'I think it's great you've written another song for Chaz. The last two were hits.'

'Yeah …'

'But tell me. Do you want a music career?'

Her hand hardened against his chest. 'I don't know. Sometimes it feels like it was just a dream. That I'm better off with the simple life of being a teacher and, hopefully one day, a wife and a mum.'

'You can be all of those things and still sing.'

'Can I, though?' It wasn't a deep question, more like a general wondering. Since allowing her dream to take a back seat, she'd been thankful for the fact she didn't have to juggle music, teaching, and life. But now …

'You can have it all, Meg.'

Meg stared at the horseshoe patterned rug. She knew where this was going. 'It's too late for me, Jack.'

'You could have gone to Gympie.'

She closed her eyes and forced down her frustration. 'And like I've told you before, it wasn't possible. I couldn't get in the car and drive. Not when we were all worried about you.' And she'd been in no state to perform. If she'd driven anywhere, she wouldn't have made it further than Townsville and the hospital Jack was in. 'I missed my chance and that was that.'

'We don't only get one chance, Meg.' His hand stroked up and down her arm, easing her rapid pulse. 'Do you still want it?'

Inhaling, Meg breathed him in, then lifted her head to meet

his gaze. He'd told her his truth, finally, so she needed to tell him hers. 'I don't know if I can. I lost it, Jack. After the accident, I couldn't write anymore.'

His brow furrowed. 'But … what about …?'

'I dabbled a little. "Jane" doesn't count as I wrote that during uni, but I couldn't produce the words that I used to. The words that came from me. I was too shattered.'

Understanding dulled his eyes and he stroked his hand down her cheek. 'I'm sorry, darlin'.'

'It's not your fault. I'm the one who lost my inspiration.'

'Because I broke your heart.' He gripped her knee again, his jaw tightening. 'I should have tried harder. To find him. To find out who sent me that letter.'

'I'm sure you did your best.'

'We thought we did. But Meg …' His eyes softened as he inched towards her. 'It's not too late for you. You're a beautiful singer and a talented songwriter. You deserve a chance.'

She smiled softly. 'And if I have my muse back …'

Jack stilled. 'Meg, we—'

'No.' She pressed her finger to his lips. 'No excuses. You can't kiss me like you did and expect us to go back to the way things were. The only way in life is forward and we will face whatever comes.'

His eyes steeled. 'But—'

'No! At least …' She lowered her finger and pressed her body to the side of his, lifting her head until they were only a breath apart. 'Not tonight, okay? Tonight, nothing exists outside this house. And no one will know what happens inside it.'

Jack stared at her for what felt like an eternity. Heat flashed through his eyes, ousting the fear and uncertainty until finally, longing pooled in a swirl of chocolate brown she'd spent her life waiting to witness.

'Okay,' he breathed. 'Tonight.'

Suppressing her grin, Meg touched her mouth to his. She'd let him pretend it would just be tonight if that pleased him, but if they really did only get this one chance, then she would make the most of it. Savouring his taste, she threaded her fingers into his soft, damp hair. Jack kissed her back like a man who'd been starved, sending thrills through her body. She straddled him again and deepened their kiss. He gripped her hips, his thumbs brushing her hipbones as his fingers snaked beneath the hem of her T-shirt. Meg's blood heated. Her thighs ached. With nothing to lose, she dropped her hands and lifted her T-shirt off over her head. Her pink lace bra accentuated her breasts, which Jack seemed to appreciate.

'Oh, darlin' …'

'Jack, I'm not all that hungry. Are you?'

His gaze shot to hers and a smile she'd never seen before curved his gorgeous mouth. 'Starving. For you.'

Triumph surged inside her, bursting from her chest. 'Take me to the bedroom, Jack.'

In one smooth movement, his arm looped behind her knees and he stood, lifting her into his arms. His lips smothered her smile as he carried her down the hallway and into his room. Her heart pounded, thighs burned. She welcomed the sensations, aching as Jack placed her back on her feet.

His large wooden bed with the blue-and-white striped bedspread sat central in the room, neatly made and flanked by two wooden bedside tables. But that's all Meg cared to notice as she gripped the hem of his shirt and lifted the cotton up Jack's broad, strong torso. He slid his arms out and dropped it to the floor. Meg's hands splayed on the perfect squares of his pectorals. Her breath caught.

This was really happening. She was in Jack Maguire's bedroom and they were about to make love.

Finally.

Chapter Nineteen

He shouldn't be doing this. Letting Meg in was a mistake. Foolish. But as she stood before him partially naked and brushed her soft, tantalising hands down his body, Jack didn't have it in him to stop. A man could only hold out for so long and he'd been a fucking saint.

She hooked her fingers beneath the waistband of his shorts, drew him closer, and his resolve crumbled. His breath caught and heat rushed through him unlike anything he'd felt before. Nothing else mattered except for Meg. She was right. No one would know what went on inside these walls tonight, so he would take the opportunity as the gift it was. One special night.

Swooping down to capture her beautiful mouth, Jack backed her towards the bed, lowering her gently onto the mattress as he knelt over her. Her beautiful golden hair spread over his bedspread and everything else vanished. He was a goner. Lost. He brushed a loose curl off her face and watched as her eyes sparkled and clouded with desire.

He kissed her again, slowly, softly, before diving into the depths of her. A decade's worth of repressed feelings soared.

He gripped her hips and she gasped, her fingers digging into his shoulders as he moved his mouth down her creamy, throbbing throat to capture her nibblie collarbone.

'Whatever you do,' she breathed, 'don't stop.'

'Never, darlin'.' He wanted her, needed her, and she him. Relishing the two perfect mounds of her breasts, Jack brushed his nose over her soft skin and inhaled. He slipped his hand behind her back and loosened the pink lace. Making quick work of freeing herself, Meg threw her arms back and lifted herself to him.

'Beautiful …' He kissed her sternum, tasted the swelling curve of her body, then took her breast into his mouth as her heart pounded beneath his lips. Her hands thumped against his shoulders and gripped. Hard. Grinning, Jack gave her what she wanted, delighting in her sharp breaths that whispered his name.

An age later, he moved to her other breast, unsure how he managed to restrain himself. But he wanted to experience, kiss, and memorise every inch of her. If he only had one night, he'd make it last forever.

He continued to move down, her belly sinking below her ribs and creating more arches to kiss and caress before racing his tongue around her belly button. Meg quivered. When he arrived at her low-riding jeans, he found himself on his feet, leaning over her as his hands brushed down her thighs. Her fingers slipped through his hair as he reached for the clasp at her hips. Then he stopped.

A horrifying thought shuddered through him as his gaze shot to hers. 'Meg …'

She lifted onto her elbows, her eyes wild. 'Don't you dare stop.'

Fuck. 'We have to.'

'No!' She bolted upright, grabbed his shoulders, and shook him. 'Not now, Jack. You—'

'Meg, I'm not prepared for this. I have no protection.'

'Oh.' The fire vanished from her eyes as she flopped back onto the bed and waved her hand in the air. 'Whatever.'

He blinked. 'Whatever?'

'It's you and me, Jack.' She lifted back onto her elbows and quirked her eyebrow. 'Do I have a reason to worry?'

'No.'

'Right. So quit wasting time talking about it.'

Then her hands were on his shorts, pushing them down. Having just showered, he hadn't bothered with anything underneath and free, he realised Meg was right. It was him and her, so he unclasped her jeans and slid them down her strong, slender legs. As he tossed them aside, she scooted herself up and positioned her head on the pillows.

'Don't think, Jack.' She reached for his hand and tugged. 'Love me.'

Then he was on top of her. 'I will, darlin'.' He pressed his mouth to hers, capturing this moment of no return. 'Now, look at me.'

* * *

Meg didn't dare look anywhere else as Jack's dark chocolate gaze bore into hers. His hand caressed her hip while the other dipped into her hair. Bending her knee, she brushed her thigh against his hard, warm torso while his body caressed hers. She dug her fingers into his back. She was ready.

Lifting herself to him, she breathed his name. Then together, they were one. Meg gasped, keeping her gaze glued to his as they absorbed the moment. Savoured it. His lips brushed hers ever so lightly and she melted into nothingness.

'Oh, darlin' …'

'Jack.' Her breath caught as she sank into his hold, pulling him closer. Her body angled to his and his calloused fingers dug into her hip. Everything was right. Perfect. He filled her— her body, her heart, her head. It was more than she'd ever imagined as they moved in a rhythm so easily found. Harmonious. Natural. Her toes curled, thighs burned, and he loved her slowly as they rocked towards their crescendo.

She came apart, crying out and blinded from the relief, but still watching as Jack's gorgeous face etched with the same glorious sensation. The pieces of her shattered heart glowed back together.

Later, as she lay tucked into Jack's warm, comforting chest, she never wanted to move. Never wanted to leave. Never wanted the sun to rise again so that tonight could last forever. One night would never be enough.

'I'm glad you came over, Meg.'

'Me too. And not just because of this.' She snuggled closer, squeezing his hip with her thigh. 'I'm glad I know what's been holding you back.'

His fingers trailed lazy strokes up and down her spine. 'You wore me down, darlin'. I vowed never to tell you. But this past week or so, I realised I had to so that you'd realise why we couldn't be together—'

'Too late now.' Lifting her gaze, she met his hooded eyes. 'No going back, Jack. You love me. Your jealousy proved that.'

'I wasn't jealous,' he muttered, his jaw tightening. 'I was bloody wretched. Wanting you. Knowing I can't have you.

Yeah, it was my own stupid decision, but ... seeing you with Kelly ...'

'I didn't mean for that to happen. It's always been you, Jack. And you *can* have me. You do.'

His hand stilled. 'It's always been you too, Meg. But—'

'No excuses!'

His head fell back against the pillow as he blew out his breath. 'You won't let this go now, will you?'

'I don't want to rush you.' Softening her tone, she grasped his shoulders. 'But you haven't been happy, Jack, and I want you to be. We can do this. I promise.'

His fears would settle eventually, she was sure.

'This was why I never told you,' he muttered, pinching the bridge of his nose. 'And I hope I have no reason to worry, Meg, but ...'

She waited for him to finish that sentence, but he didn't. 'We can keep it quiet. Although, we'll have to tell our friends because we'd never be able to hide it from them.'

'Adam will know the moment he looks at us,' Jack said, rolling his eyes. 'But for now, can we just enjoy tonight? I'll think about it next week.'

She frowned as he rolled onto his side and glanced down at her. 'Why next week?'

'I've been meaning to tell you. I'm going to Innisfail on Saturday. To help Robbo for a few weeks.'

Meg's eyebrows shot up. 'Really?'

'Yeah. I thought you'd be proud—'

'I am.' Grinning, she kissed him. 'That's amazing, Jack. Very generous of you. So you're going to help clean up? Get the farm back on its feet?'

'Something like that. Taking Adam and Mike with me.

Repairs are needed for the house and sheds, and he's still without power.'

Meg's heart swelled at the pride in his eyes, at his eagerness to help. Beneath his hard, broody exterior, her man had a heart of gold.

She just needed to show him he could trust her with it.

'You're a good man, Jack.'

'I'm glad you're pleased, darlin'. I plan to come back on Thursday to avoid Good Friday traffic. Should probably get most things back on track by then and I can't stay away from here for much longer. The farm gets busier every week.'

'Well, I'll miss you, but what you're doing is wonderful. Maybe I could come visit you on the weekend?'

His shoulders slouched. 'Meg—'

'No one will know. Surely there's something I could bring down or a way I could help. The church is organising a bunch of donations to send down, so that would save them from finding a way to get them there.' Actually, that sounded like a good idea. She'd talk to the ladies at church about it.

'Well … I can't argue with that. But we might still be roughing it with just the generator.'

She shrugged. 'I can tolerate camping.'

'All right.' He inched away. 'But if I don't eat soon, I'll starve to death. You hungry, darlin?'

'I'm always hungry when your mum's pumpkin pasta bake is in the fridge.'

Jack tossed back the covers. 'Let's eat, then I'm tucking you back into bed.'

'I won't say no to that.' She reached for her jeans. 'But first, would it be much trouble to go get Lola? I don't like leaving her alone.'

Jack tugged on his shorts. 'No trouble at all. And you know what else we can get in town?'

She slipped his shirt over her head, her heart fluttering as the soft material fell halfway down her thighs, just like she'd always hoped. 'What?'

Grinning, Jack pulled her close. 'Ice cream.'

<h1 style="text-align:center">Chapter Twenty</h1>

Jack woke on Thursday morning with Meg's warm, naked body tucked against his. Burying his smile in her soft golden hair, he breathed in her fruity scent and shivered as she wriggled against him. His blood ignited and arms loosened around her as she turned and blinked open her sapphire eyes.

'Morning, darlin'.'

'Hey.'

Her mouth curved, pink rising in her unblemished cheeks. Jack watched as her eyes sparkled, resisting a groan as her leg lifted and toes rubbed against his calf. Capturing her mouth with his, he eased into the kiss as her arms tightened around his shoulders and pulled him closer. Fuck, he could get used to this. He couldn't get enough of her and as he moved his mouth down her creamy neck, he knew he never would. But as her leg hooked around his hips, he lost himself in her taste and relished in the delight of making love with Meg. He wouldn't deny that's what it was between them. He loved this woman with every essence of his soul, hence the years of torment. But last night, she'd broken through his resistance and his heart had cracked through its restraints.

How would he ever put it back?

He didn't want to contemplate it as they lay sated in each other's arms. Scratches sounded on the door and Jack glanced over his shoulder at the soft, '*Yap, yap, yap.*'

Meg placed her hand on his chest. 'We should get up.'

'*Yap, yap, yap.*'

'Why?'

'We have to go to work.'

Jack groaned. He couldn't argue with her, but he wasn't ready to let her go. Wasn't ready for things to go back to the way they had been.

'Aren't you hungry?' she asked.

'*Yap, yap, yap.*'

Jack's breath hissed through his teeth. 'I'd say Lola is.'

'Jill too, probably.'

'But at least she has manners.' After kissing Meg once more, Jack reluctantly sat up. All good things had to come to an end. Meg had to be at school in an hour and he would usually be on the farm by now. 'Lola's got attitude.'

'She's used to getting what she wants. And I oblige because she's so adorable.'

Jack threw back the covers without comment. Meg tugged on her blue sleep shorts and pulled a singlet over her head before opening the bedroom door and scooping the fluffball into her arms.

'Morning, Lols. How did you sleep? I know you missed Mummy, but you were such a good girl not barking at the door all night.'

Jack tugged on his boxers and resisted rolling his eyes. He'd never understand people who treated their dogs like children. Sure, he cared about Jill. After the poor start she'd had in life, he'd taken pity on the girl and had given her everything she needed to survive. Good food, fresh water, a warm bed, toys, and daily affection. He bathed her and took her to the vet. She was a good dog and he'd be a little lost without her.

But last night, he'd pulled up at Meg house to pick up Lola and after waiting five minutes, he'd gone inside to find out what was taking so long. The little dog had been strapped into a sparkling pink harness with a matching lead and Meg had been tossing an overnight bag by the door. Neither action had been surprising until she'd added a second bag.

'Are you staying for a week?'

'I wouldn't object, but the pink one is Lola's. I need to grab her spare seatbelt, then we'll go.'

He hadn't said a word as he'd fetched Meg's and Lola's bags, and the fluffy Pomeranian had sat in the middle seat panting the whole drive home. Of course, he knew dogs needed their own things. Meg had brought Lola food, a ridiculously fluffy rainbow bed, and a toy to make sure she was comfortable for a night in a strange house, which had been a good call as Lola had *not* appreciated being locked out of the bedroom. But Jack had drawn the line, not prepared to let the fluffball get in the way of his one night with Meg.

She had been good by not disturbing them though, so he reached out and rubbed the little dog's head. It was the only time he could pat her when she was secure in Meg's arms as the cheeky Pom refused to come near him.

'Are you okay with toast for breakfast?' he asked Meg.

'Yep. Do you have jam?'

'I always have jam.'

They left the bedroom and Meg placed Lola outside where Jill greeted them spinning in excited circles. Jill and Lola had never spent much time together, but they seemed to get along well enough. He'd have to fix up the fence though to make sure Lola wouldn't be able to escape. Not that she was staying.

Chest tightening, Jack popped bread into the toaster. One night with Meg wasn't fair or what he wanted, but he couldn't risk anything more. Her safety was too important. He might wish things were different, but he couldn't have everything. So he made her toast and asked what she was teaching her class today, distracting himself with chatter about spelling words and grade two science.

'I get to hand the kids over to Joe for PE this afternoon though, which means I have time to catch up on marking. I'm always out early on Thursdays.' She fed her last piece of toast to Lola. 'But I won't go to yoga tonight.'

Jack stood and gathered their plates. 'Why not?'

'Because you're going away on Saturday, so I thought I could come over and—'

'Meg.' Placing the plates in the sink, he turned. 'I don't—'

His words died as she quirked her eyebrow and moved towards him. 'Don't what?'

He blew out his breath. Fuck, he couldn't do it. He'd hurt her enough, hurt himself.

'Don't do this, Jack.' She laid her hands on his forearms. 'We can't go back now. And I know you say someone wants to keep us apart, but shouldn't we want to find him?'

His belly knotted. 'Yes, but—'

'There are no buts about it! We find him, put an end to the threat, and then we can be happy.'

She rose onto her toes and wrapped her arms around his neck. Jack's heart pounded at the dark determination in her eyes.

'I know it sounds easy, Meg. But ...' He blew out his breath. 'We'll discuss it when I get back from Innisfail.'

She pondered that, then nodded. 'If that's what you want. But I'm still coming over tonight. Okay?'

She brushed her lips over his to prevent him from arguing. Or convince him. Jack wasn't sure which, but it worked. 'Okay, darlin'.'

Two nights couldn't carry greater risk than one.

* * *

Driving through Shadow Creek, Meg wriggled with glee. Last night had exceeded every one of her fantasies, and she'd had many. Even his resistance hadn't deterred her as kissing Jack had set her world alight, and the sex still had her toes tingling. Everything had been perfect. He might not have said the little four-letter word, but he would. Jack never rushed these things.

But now that she'd spent those long, glorious hours warm and safe in his arms, she wouldn't let her future go any other way. They would be together. He might feel his fears were justified, but she would help him overcome them. If that meant they couldn't flaunt their love, then she could do that. She would do whatever he needed.

But she was still a woman and couldn't keep the fact her dreams were coming true to herself. Dropping Lola off at home, she almost messaged Lucy, but Meg didn't want to share the news with her best friend over text. Lucy would be back from the dressage club tomorrow and had been waiting for this almost as long as Meg had. Her friend deserved to hear it face to face, and Meg would rather tell her that way.

But that didn't mean she still couldn't unleash her excitement as she arrived at work and strode into Ana's classroom.

'I spent the night with Jack.'

Ana spun around from her desk. 'You what?'

Grinning, Meg practically skipped across the room. 'It was amazing, Ana. I went to talk to him and he opened up about everything that had held him back all these years. And it makes sense, but … actually, never mind.' She didn't want to talk about the threat, at least not until she and Jack discussed how much they were going to share with their friends. 'But we worked things out.'

Ana squealed and threw her arms around Meg. 'Oh my God, I'm so happy for you!'

'Thank you! But please, we're still working things out, so I don't want to spread the word, okay? At least not outside our circle of friends.'

Ana frowned, but quickly shrugged it off. 'Well, that's fantastic, Meg. I'm sure that now you and Jack are over that first hurdle, you will work out the rest.'

'Let's hope so.' Meg couldn't bear it if his walls went back up, but she decided not to think about it and focus on the positives as she headed across the walkway to her classroom.

Soon enough, the children raced, skipped, or dragged their feet inside and with six weeks left until the show, Meg needed to ensure she had her grade twos prepared.

'All right, everyone. Who can tell me what the Elizadale Show is about? Bryan?'

'Fairy floss!' the little boy cried.

Meg smiled. 'Fairy floss is fun, but it's not the reason we have the show. What's its purpose?' She selected another raised hand. 'Bree?'

'To show off our horses.'

'Horses are one thing we show, yes. Does anyone want to elaborate on that? Amanda?'

'It is to show many things about the community.'

Meg nodded. 'Yes. The show is an *agricultural* show that gives the people of Elizadale the opportunity to display and showcase their talents. That can be in many different areas. We might enter something we have prepared into a competition, or we might compete in an event. Is anyone here going to enter the show?'

Holly raised her hand. 'I help Mummy with the baking competition.'

'That's very good. Anyone else?'

'We put our chickens in the show,' Jason said.

Meg smiled at her class. 'Well, you're *all* going to enter the show.' This shouldn't be news to them as the show always involved school participation. 'This year, you all get to enter two competitions. The first one is the grade twos' animal photography competition, which you can work on from home. We will learn about photography over the next few weeks, and you can take your best photo of a pet or animal. The second competition will be a clay pot, which we will make closer to the show. Who likes the sound of that?'

Eleven little hands shot into the air along with wriggles, giggles, and grins. Meg clapped her hands together. 'Excellent! I'm excited too.'

Not that it took much since every aspect of the show sent thrills shooting through her veins, but what Meg enjoyed most was getting others involved, especially the children. Encouraging them in their artwork inspired creativity and helped them learn new skills. Opening the children's minds, developing their interests, and discovering their passions was the whole reason she'd become a teacher. And while she might not know a lot about photography herself, she could teach them about angles, light, and framing their subject to help them capture a beautiful image. Kids loved taking photos and with smartphones, they could take hundreds every day. They weren't limited to a roll of film like she'd been. They didn't know about capturing a good image in one click, waiting for the roll to develop, and hoping that the photos turned out well. Learning the skill of taking a great photo was important, so that's what she and the other teachers had chosen to showcase across the school, with each grade given a different subject to focus on.

When the bell rang for lunch, Meg joined Ana and Elanora to supervise their students in the undercover area by their classrooms.

'My kids are excited to begin their birdhouses,' Ana said, that being the grade ones' art project.

'Mine can't stop talking about which of their favourite toys to photograph,' Elanora said. She taught the prep class. 'I think one plush Olaf is going on an adventure to the beach.'

Meg grinned. 'Olaf will love that!'

* * *

Jack sat beside Adam in their father's study at the homestead and forced himself to concentrate on farm business. They were expecting a spike in the harvest come mid-April but overall, production was busy, steady, and Jack wouldn't be complaining about the price of bananas any time soon. With luck, purchasing a new farm in the coming year might actually be possible.

But no matter how much he tried to shake the tension rising inside him, his worries wouldn't ease. Bottling up his feelings had done nothing but cloud his mood and he didn't want that anymore. He needed to get things off his chest and if he was going to talk to anyone, it would be these two men.

His father knew all about his fears and even though the last thing Jack wanted was to add to Adam's ego, he needed his brother's advice.

'If you two have nothing else to talk about,' Henry said, 'let's go see what your mother's made us for lunch.'

Jack took a deep breath and let it out slowly. 'I may have sorted things out with Meg.'

His father and brother stilled.

'In a good way, I hope,' Adam said. 'Don't bloody tell me you made things worse.'

'I may have. I told her the truth and just as I feared, she wasn't deterred.'

Adam smiled. 'I never doubted it. Meg knows what she wants, Jack. Most of the time, I can't believe she let you get away with your nonsense all these years. I bet she told you to stop being a stubborn fool and that she loves you.'

'Yeah.' He swallowed the knot in his throat. 'She did.'

Laughing, Adam leaned over and slapped him on the back. 'Excellent! Good on you, mate. Fucking happy for you.'

'Yes,' Henry agreed, smiling softly. 'I'm glad to hear it, Jack. You two should be together.'

'You *are* going to be together.' Adam raised his eyebrows. 'Right?'

Adjusting himself in his chair, Jack winced. 'Yeah, but … I'm not sure I can do this. She's all "if someone threatens us, we'll catch them and lock them up," but I know it's not that easy.' He glanced at his father. 'We tried that last time, and this bastard is too good. He can cover his tracks and no one seems to match the profile we created. What if he remains untraceable?'

Sighing, Henry leaned forward and placed his clasped hands on the desk. 'Jack, if the threat does resurrect itself, we will do everything we can to make sure neither of you gets hurt.'

Adam's eyes sobered. 'Sure will, mate. Last time, it was just a letter. It wasn't a lot for the cops to go with, I'm sure. This time, you might get lucky.'

'It's easy to say that, but—'

'Take some time,' Henry said, standing and striding around the desk. 'Enjoy the moment, Jack. Keep it quiet, let Meg support you, and ease your way out of the darkness. Trust me, it's the best way.'

Jack nodded as his father's hand clamped over his shoulder. 'All right, Dad. I'll try.'

'Good, because I want to see you happy.'

'Me too. It's about time, mate. Bloody thrilled for ya.'

Jack managed a smile. 'Thanks, mate.'

'And I'm thinking that maybe you don't want to pursue one of those farms down south?' Henry asked.

Jack shrugged. He was no longer interested in running away, though if the threat did resurrect itself, he might reconsider. 'Perhaps not. But we could keep an eye out for something local. You do think expanding is a good idea, right?' He glanced up at his father. 'Once we get through these few months of increased banana demand, we should consider it?'

Henry nodded. 'The lychees and guavas do us well and even though we could cultivate more of the southern land, spreading further afield sounds like a solid idea.'

'Buying something established would be a better investment,' Adam said. 'Though I tell you, I'm keen for this black sapote. Never knew chocolate pudding could taste so good. Or we could grow dragon fruit because Nat buys too much of that shit too.'

'We could look into dragon fruit,' Jack considered. 'Or papaya. I like papaya.'

'There's already a substantial market for papaya,' Henry said. 'But we'll keep our ears to the ground, boys. We'll make a fair offer, but a good deal will come around.'

Hope rose in Jack's chest as he pushed to his feet. 'Thanks, Dad.'

'No worries, Jack.' Henry wrapped his arm around Jack's shoulders. 'We'll make it happen, son. I want you to have your dreams.'

Chapter Twenty-One

A bounce filled Meg's step as she and Jack strode briskly by the lychee orchard, enjoying an afternoon walk as he shared his plans to expand Shadow Creek. She'd always known he was keen to diversify and that he loved learning about new produce and farming techniques, but his passion spoke volumes as his eyes filled with a light she'd missed all these years.

'I wouldn't mind planting a few small orchards of exotics. Nothing as big as the lychee and guava enterprise, but a dozen or two trees would work. I do like the idea of black sapote as the chocolate pudding Nat made with it at Christmas was bloody delicious.'

'I'll have to ask her to make me some.' Meg, of course, hadn't been part of the Maguires' Christmas celebrations, but with any luck, that would change this year. 'And if she likes it so much, Adam will throw his heart into growing it.'

'Exactly.' He cleared his throat. 'You know why I planted the lychees, right?'

Meg's heart fluttered. 'I had a feeling …'

Jack had planted the orchard while she'd been away at

university, and since lychees had always been her favourite seasonal fruit, the gesture had been the first sign that perhaps he might have feelings for her.

Taking her hand, he squeezed gently as he shared in her smile. 'So, if you have any other ideas, let me know. There are a few fruits I'd like to try, but most of them are more suitable for the rainforest climate. Might have to look at purchasing some land up near Cape Tribulation.'

'That's not far away. What else would you like to grow?'

'I like the idea of canistel. Mum could make a lot with that.'

'That's the egg yolk-like fruit, isn't it?'

'Yep. Mum made a delicious canistel pie once. I also like the idea of rambutans and star fruit. All would be good choices for boutique farming.'

'They would be,' she agreed as she gazed out over the lychee trees and bit down on her lower lip. 'What about avocados?'

Jack exhaled, his gaze dropping to his feet. 'Yeah, I've read a lot about avocados.'

Meg frowned at the tension in his shoulders. 'But …?'

The silence was longer than she'd expected, their feet pounding the dirt road for a few strides before he lifted his head. 'You know your grandfather approached me once.'

She nodded. It was an awkward topic and had embarrassed her at first, but it wasn't a secret that her grandparents wanted to retire. Or that they wanted to keep the farm in the family. Meg had always thought she could help them with that.

'It was just before the tractor incident.'

Meg's aerobically fuelled heart rate spiked. 'So …?'

Jack expelled another deep breath. 'At one point, your father suggested that the person who threatened me might have a problem with that.'

Meg drew to a stop. 'What?'

Jack turned. 'I know. It's—'

'It's absurd!'

'Which is exactly what I said!' Shoving his hands through his hair, Jack shook his head. 'And even though your dad had a point, I just can't ...'

He dropped his hands to his side, her heart breaking at the helplessness in his eyes.

'Don't attempt to understand it, darlin'.' He moved beside her, his arm coming around her waist as he dropped a kiss to her hair. 'I've tried.'

Her gaze on the ground, Meg wrestled with disbelief and wonder as they continued walking. 'You really think someone wanted to kill you to stop us being together? To stop me from bringing an inheritance to Shadow Creek?' One that would bolster his dream and help him expand?

'There is no other explanation.'

She gritted her teeth. 'Well, it's stupid.'

'I know.' He kissed her hair again before releasing her waist. 'But I don't want to talk about it right now. Let's just enjoy tonight.'

Meg nodded. Even though she longed to talk about it, deep down, she wanted to sweep it all under the rug too. Especially if this time before he left for Innisfail was all they could have. Part of her had been worried when she'd left work and driven back to his house, as she'd been pushing her luck asking for another night together, but Jack had greeted her with a sparkle in his eyes and a kiss that had melted every bone in her body. Suggesting that they go for an afternoon walk wasn't what she'd expected, but she hadn't been prepared to say no as it seemed to be one of Jack's regular habits and she enjoyed exercise herself.

'It is nice walking along here.' She'd driven the road plenty of times before from Jack's place to the homestead but had never had the time to appreciate the serenity or shade of the bushland. 'Quiet and breezy. You can hear the birds too.'

He grinned. 'That is a willie wagtail. They're always around. I also get a few kookaburras at dusk, and I see many honeyeaters out here.' Since the Elizadale region was home to over two hundred different bird species, Jack had always been quite knowledgeable about the wildlife. 'The galahs often hang out at the homestead. I know they're your favourite.'

'They are,' she agreed, having always loved the grey-winged parrots with their proud rose-pink chests. 'So, how often do you go walking?'

'Any day I get away from the farm early. Why?'

'I just didn't realise you enjoyed a brisk walk. Or that you did it regularly.'

'It was all part of rehab after I got out of hospital. Had to keep my circulatory system healthy. And I found it the best way to clear my head.'

'Yes, it certainly is good for that.' Walking was when she usually thought best too. 'Will you do the fun run with me, then?'

'Of course.'

She glanced up at him. 'Run?'

'How else do you do a fun run?'

'You can walk it. Ana and Liam plan to.'

'But Ana's pregnant, and I'm not walking a fun run. I jog this road occasionally.'

Her eyebrows shot up. 'Really?'

'Yeah. More so now that Adam's taken up jogging with Natalia of an afternoon. She's really rubbing off on him, though he has this crazy idea that he'll beat her in the fun run.'

Meg shook her head. 'Those two can get very competitive. But I'm glad he found her as she's been good for him.'

'She's too good for him.'

Meg laughed. 'Probably. But it's nice to see Adam settled and Nat's become such a passionate country girl. She can't stop talking about her vegetables for the show.'

'She's putting my gardening knowledge to shame.'

'Scientists like to research.'

He chuckled. 'I know. But I still think you should enter the show, darlin'. You're a passionate country woman too with many skills.'

'Yeah, I'm coming around to it. Though I tell you now.' She narrowed her eyes. 'I am *not* entering our banana cake into the show.'

Exhaling, Jack ran his hand down his face before reaching over and tugging her into his side, barely slowing his pace. 'Good. Because that's my cake and I don't want you to share it.'

Her spine loosened as she placed her hand over his racing heart, her gaze on their synchronised feet. 'I know you only said it to push me away, Jack. But it did hurt me.'

'I'm sorry, darlin'.'

'It's okay.' She straightened out of his hold to walk easier, smiling softly as she met his dark eyes. 'But I think I will enter something into the baking contest, because why not?'

'You could enter your carrot cake.'

'Yes, you do like that one. I might even try making an apple pie.'

'Anything you enter will be delicious, darlin'. Just be sure to let me taste test it first.'

After a brisk hour, they returned to the house. Jill barked at them from the fence, unimpressed that they'd left her behind, while Lola welcomed them with excited wriggles. Until Jack reached for her and Lola scurried away.

Meg shook her head. 'One day she'll come to you.'

He shrugged. 'Only if I have food.'

'Yeah, probably.' Sighing, Meg moved to the back door to let Lola outside. Jill lowered her front legs and wagged her tail in the air, wanting to play. Meg kicked off her shoes without undoing the laces as she watched the girls race around into the yard.

'Who's taking care of Jill while you're away?'

'Mum's taking her up to the homestead.'

'Oh.' Her shoulders sank. 'I guess she'll be happy there.'

'She'll be fine.' Silence fell as Jack sipped a glass of water. 'You want to look after her, don't you?'

Meg clapped her hands together, beaming as she turned to him. 'Yes!'

A ghost of a smile passed through his eyes as he slipped his arm around her waist. 'I think Jill would like that.'

It might sound feeble, but looking after Jill was just one more step towards helping Jack overcome his fears and shake him out of his protective we-can-never-be-together mindset. He'd spent far too long in self-imposed darkness, she in heartache and confusion, and neither of them deserved to live like that. They would be happy.

* * *

Meg and Natalia waited patiently at the bar as the crowd filling the Royal had Georgina and her staff run off their feet.

'I've never seen it this busy when The Charlie Boys aren't playing,' Natalia said.

'I know. It's crazy.' But it was easier to resist leaning against

Jack in the booth when they didn't know who could be watching. Not that the secretive smiles passing between their friends would help much. Adam had told Natalia, and Ana had told Liam. Meg had swung by Isabella's place on her way to the pub to let her know about the development between her and Jack too, and now everyone was positively bursting with excitement.

Meg wondered if it'd been a mistake to tell them at all, especially since Jack hadn't made her any promises. But even so, there was no way they'd have been able to keep the truth from their friends and if it wasn't a secret among them, then she might stand a better chance at convincing Jack that there was safety in numbers.

'Yeah. So only one more week of term left. Do you have plans for the holidays?'

'Just to relax.' Meg was looking forward to it. 'I'm going to drive some donations from the church down to Innisfail. And to—' she lowered her voice '—visit Jack and the guys.'

'God, that's going to be a big job for them, isn't it?'

'I can't imagine.'

'But I'm glad Adam's going. He was worried I'd be upset when he told me about it, but it's not like I'd stop him. Rusty and I are going to have a great time all by ourselves.'

Meg laughed. 'You'll miss Adam.'

'Totally,' Natalia agreed, just as Meg heard her name called.

She spun around, grinning as Lucy squeezed her way through the crowd. 'Hey! You made it.'

'Yeah, sorry, I left later than planned.' Lucy reached them and slumped her elbow on the bar. 'Jeez, who's having the party?'

'It's certainly crowded,' Meg said. 'So, how was the workshop?'

'Great. I learned some new things. But some of the show jumpers I can't stand are coming to the retreat at High Ridge this month, so that sucks.' Lucy sighed, irritated. 'Anyway. You look great, Meg. As usual. Still showing Jack what he can't have?'

'Bit late for that,' Natalia muttered with a laugh, and Lucy blinked.

'What?'

Meg's grin widened. 'I told him.'

Lucy squealed as her hands flew to her mouth. 'Told him what?'

'Shh …' Heart pounding, Meg leaned forward and lowered her voice. 'We need to keep it quiet.'

'Keep *what* quiet?' Bouncing on her toes, Lucy grasped Meg's hand. 'Are you two …?'

Meg bit down on her lower lip, but it did nothing to suppress her smile as she nodded. Lucy squealed again as she flung her arms around Meg and knocked the breath from her body. But Meg didn't care. Ignoring the prickle at the back of her neck, she hugged her friend as they rocked from side to side.

'Oh my God, this is fantastic! How? When? Tell me—'

Meg squeezed her. 'I'll tell you later. Just don't say anything.'

'Why?' Lucy drew away, frowning. 'What's going on?'

Meg's heart began to pound. 'Later, Luce. Right now, just pretend that nothing has changed.'

Lucy's frown deepened. 'Okay. But I—'

'Ladies, what can I get you?'

Meg welcomed Georgina's interruption as she turned to the bar and ordered drinks. Lucy jiggled beside her and once served, led the way through the crowd, excusing herself loudly until they reached the booth. Meg handed Jack his beer, but before she could slide in beside him, Lucy grabbed her forearm.

'Come with me, you can't leave me hanging.' Grinning, she playfully punched Jack in the shoulder. 'Seems Meg has exciting news to share, cuz.'

He nodded silently, and Lucy dragged Meg out the back of the pub.

'Luce, I know you want to know, but—'

'Oh, you cannot hold out on me. The beer garden's busy too. Wait, come here.'

Lucy pushed open the door to the handicapped toilet and pulled Meg inside. After twisting the lock, she turned, wide eyed. 'Okay. Spill.'

Meg smiled. 'Do you want the good part or the bad part?'

'Bad part. Wait. Why is there a bad part?'

'Maybe I should just tell you from the start.' Sighing, Meg tucked loose hair behind her ears. 'I told him I loved him.'

Lucy squeaked and gave a little jump. But her smile slowly vanished and her feet stopped dancing as Meg told her about the threat Jack had received, his fear, and the reason he'd resisted their love all these years.

'I can't believe him.' Lucy whispered, sinking back against the door. 'Doing that. He's incredibly strong. And stupid. I mean if you love someone …'

Meg nodded. 'I guess I understand his reasons, however foolish they might seem.'

'Hmm …' Lucy's gaze dropped for a moment before she sighed and straightened. 'Anyway. What's the good part?'

'Well, despite his resistance, I think I can bring him around. We're talking again and we've had two wonderful nights together. I'm so happy, Luce.'

Her friend danced another jig, then threw her arms around Meg. 'That's fantastic. God, I'm happy for you too.'

'Thanks. It has been amazing, and a relief. I just hope that his two weeks away won't change his mind.'

'I don't think you have to worry about that. Jack loves you. It might not be easy for him to set aside his belief he would put you in danger, but time away might help him overcome that.'

'I hope so. And if someone emerges to hurt us, we'll ensure they're put in jail.' *That* was how the world was supposed to work.

'And you won't be alone in that. We'll all be there to keep you safe and fight for you guys.'

'Thanks, Luce.'

'Of course.' Lucy smiled softly. 'That's what friends and family are for. And with any luck, we'll soon be cousins-in-law. Just let me know if you want me to drop hints about the ring because if he knows what he's doing, he'll want to take you by surprise.'

Meg's left hand tingled as her mind drifted into the fantasy. Jack on one knee with her dream ring taking her completely off guard. Declaring that he loved her and wanted to spend the rest of his life with her.

It was all Meg wanted.

But she doubted it would happen any time soon, so shaking away the silly images, she smiled at her friend. 'I will.'

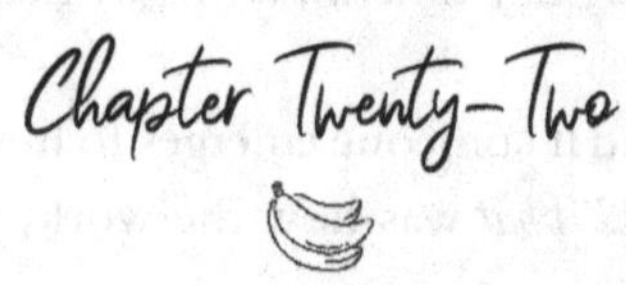

Chapter Twenty-Two

Meg stood on the verandah on Saturday morning, dragging out the farewell as she ran her hands down Jack's chest and lost herself in their kiss. He didn't seem keen to leave either as he tightened his grip around her waist. Jack's tender mouth moulded with hers, passion fuelling the moment as a breeze blew across the verandah. Meg never wanted it to end. But eventually, she gathered her inner strength and pulled away.

'You better get going.' Patting his chest, she eased out of his arms. 'Adam will tease you if you're late.'

'That's if I can tear him away from Natalia.' He took Meg's hand and led her off the verandah towards the Raptor.

'Just drive safely and let me know when you get there. The girls and I will be okay.'

Jack climbed into the ute, started the engine, and wound down the window before closing the door. His eyes narrowed. 'Don't spoil my dog.'

Meg placed her hand on her chest. 'Me? Never.'

'Yeah right.' He crooked his finger. 'Come here, darlin'.'

She bounced over to the ute and met him in one last kiss. 'I'll drive down on the weekend.'

'Meg …' The shutters came down over his eyes. 'You know I've enjoyed these past few nights with you. They've been the best of my life. But when I get back …'

Heart pounding, she waited for him to finish his sentence, giving him the opportunity to make another excuse. But it never came.

'Take the time, Jack. Think about it. I'm willing to take the risk if you are.'

His gaze held hers, but he didn't say anything. After a moment, he nodded briefly and swept a quick kiss over her lips. 'I gotta go.'

She stepped back, ignoring the clench in her belly as she waved him off. Time healed all wounds and if nothing else, she needed to hold on to faith.

Once the dust settled in the driveway, Meg returned to the house and scooped Lola into her arms. 'What do you say, Lols? Should we spoil Jill and turn her into a girly-girl? I bet she'll look great in pink.'

Meg packed up her things, then prepared to move Jill to her house. Jack might think her frivolous when it came to Lola, but despite Jill's sturdy kennel and tennis ball, Meg thought the kelpie had been quite neglected in the 'pampered pooch' department. Of course, she didn't expect Jack to be the type to give his dog manicures, but Jill deserved more than the dirty red collar around her neck and old towels in her kennel. Did Jack even wash them? Meg didn't want to know.

'I'll get you a pretty collar, Jilly,' Meg promised, rubbing the smiling girl's head. 'And maybe I'll call Rebecca and see if we can set you up a playdate with Banjo.'

Did Jill ever see her siblings? She'd been one of three pups Meg's cousin Rebecca had rescued. She'd kept Banjo, given Jill to Jack, and her sister-in-law Claire owned Maggie.

But Rebecca and Jason were taking Lisa away for school holidays next week, so Meg would keep it in mind for another time as she gathered Jill's food, dish, and ball. After securing the girls in the car, she drove back to Elizadale and settled Jill into her house. Once they were happy and she'd spoiled them with too many hugs and treats, Meg left to meet Samantha Burgess for lunch.

'Guess what?' Samantha slid into the seat opposite Meg at The Bent Banana, a wide smile on her face. 'Wendy said she'd host a lunch after the auction. For helpers, friends, and people who don't win themselves a date.'

'That's fantastic! What a great idea.'

'Admittedly, it was hers. She'll put together a fifteen-dollar menu to cover the costs and leave enough profit to contribute to disaster relief.'

'We'll need to promote it as people will come just to watch and have lunch.'

Samantha nodded eagerly. 'I will.'

'And have you secured some bachelor teens?'

'I have seven!'

'Good job! We'll have to set a lower starting limit for the teenage girls, but we'll start the adults for fifty and so far, I have six very eligible men.'

Meg rattled off their names and Samantha's eyes widened. 'Cade's doing it? Oh my God, he's so dreamy.'

The young girl's eyes glazed over, and Meg stifled a laugh. 'Yeah, he is a bit. But he's lined Lucy up to win him.'

Samantha frowned. 'Are they dating?'

'No.' Meg paused, frowned, then shook away that thought. 'There are a few other guys I want to ask because I'd like an even ten. But right now, let's order lunch and we'll talk about advertising.'

They ordered two pasta salads, then Samantha showed Meg the flyers she'd created. The girl sure had a flair for advertising.

'I think people will enjoy the event. Although …' She ate her pasta, frowning as her mind began ticking again. 'Why don't we take it a step further? We could auction off more than just a picnic lunch with a bachelor and widen our audience. This is about community spirit and lending a hand, so why don't we see what skills and services people might want to offer? For example, I could auction off … an hour of tutoring or something?'

'I could ask my mum if she'd offer a free dog groom!'

Inspired, Meg grabbed her pen and jotted down the ideas. She could ask Grace White if she'd do a one-on-one yoga session, and her uncle might give a guitar lesson. Her mother and aunt could offer a wide variety of sewing and crafty skills. The possibilities were endless, so she'd spread the word and see what people would contribute.

Samantha practically skipped out of the café. 'Thank you so much, Meg! I'm so excited.'

'You've done a fantastic job, and it's my pleasure to help. I look forward to the auction too.'

It was quickly becoming her favourite show queen event ever.

* * *

Mother Nature was a cruel, sadistic bitch. After Jack and his brothers left Mareeba, the signs of Billy's wrath grew worse and more desperate. It'd been three weeks, so people had cleaned up most of the debris, but forests lay bare with their ecosystems damaged by wind, rain, and trees that had been brought down, changing the landscape of the rainforest south of Atherton forever. After navigating through the roadworks down the range and arriving on the outskirts of Innisfail, their cheerful chatter had been rendered silent. The damage was heartbreaking. Houses awaited repair, roofs were missing, and gardens remained unkept. Sheds had fallen and debris was piled in yards. Evidence of minor landslides and flooding was abundant.

Banana trees lay on their sides.

Billy had caused this destruction in less than twenty-four hours, but the clean-up would take months. Repairs longer. Recovery would go on for years.

'Shit, man.' Michael broke the silence in the back seat. 'I barely remember Yasi, but this is just …'

Adam blew out his breath. 'Bloody devastating, all right.'

The sight of the destroyed banana farms tore Jack to shreds as they bypassed Innisfail on the way to South Johnstone. All that work, gone. The money, lost. The fruit ruined and turning into its own special kind of compost.

Adam called Robbo when they neared the farm and he met them at the gate. The moment Jack was through the foot wash, he greeted his friend in a backslapping hug. 'Good to see you, mate.'

Robbo greeted Adam and Michael too, then lifted his hat to run his hand through his hair. 'Thank you for coming. I know I've said it before, but it means a lot. Really.'

'That's what friends are for,' Adam said, clapping Robbo on the shoulder. 'So, let's go see what's what.'

They climbed into Robbo's ute, planning to take the Raptor through the decontamination procedures later, and drove past the hundreds of horizontal banana trees towards Robbo's brick home. Shadow Creek was unique in the way the residential properties remained separate to the banana operation, designed that way because of their history as a cattle station and the basic geography of the farm. Robbo, however, lived right next door to his crop and across the road from his packing sheds.

'The shed held up okay,' Robbo said as they drove past. 'Dad built it to category five standards, so that was a blessing. The bloody compost went everywhere though, and the irrigation needs fixing. I've started on the fences, which toppled in the flooding. But I just haven't got into the farm yet. Help's been …'

Jack's jaw tightened, unable to tear his gaze from the ruined crop. 'That's why we're here, mate. We've heard how hard it's been.'

'Yeah, but at least the big mobs could keep on staff to help. Being by myself, I had no choice but to let mine go.'

Jack placed his hand on Robbo's shoulder. 'We've got this,' he said as they rounded the bend in the road. His heart warmed at the sight of the young crop still standing. 'This is the field you deleafed?'

'Yeah. Worked out pretty well. It was a tough decision, but the moment Billy started turning, I had nothing to lose. I'd have done more if I'd had the time and manpower, but this field took us all of Saturday afternoon as it was.'

Deleafing was not a quick or easy job to do right.

'But at least you'll have some crop in a few months.'

'Exactly. Dad experimented during Yasi and it helped us then. That field should give me bananas in about four months. They'll be small bunches, but better than nothing.'

'Gotta look on the bright side,' Jack said. After all, there was nothing else one could do when faced with such heartbreak. 'Now, where are we going to start this afternoon?'

Chapter Twenty-Three

Meg arrived at church on Sunday and waved polite hellos to fellow members as she searched for her parents. Her mother was probably helping in the kitchen, but she found her father sitting in their usual pew and curiosity unravelled in her belly. She hadn't spoken with him yet as he'd been in Atherton these past few days, taking care of a few things at the courthouse and visiting her sister. But she needed answers, so she wove her way through the congregation and sat beside him.

'Morning, Dad.'

'Hey, Meg. You look lovely this morning.'

'Thank you.' Heart pounding, Meg tucked her hair behind her ear. 'Dad?'

Ron glanced up from the program. 'Hmm?'

'I know about Jack.' His brow furrowed. 'About the accident. The threat. He told me everything.'

Ron blinked, stared at her, then sighed. Resting his elbow on the back of the pew, he angled to face her. 'He did?'

She nodded. 'I'm not angry, Dad. I know you knew.'

'I answered questions for Brett,' he said, keeping his voice quiet. 'And I offered Jack and Henry legal advice.'

As he would being the local solicitor. Her father only worked part-time these days, but he remained a managing partner at his firm in Mareeba. 'And I know that's why you couldn't tell me. Confidentiality and all. But … did you believe, Brett? When he said there might not be a threat?'

Ron gripped her shoulder. 'It was a tough call to make. I didn't support Jack in keeping you in the dark, especially as I knew how much you cared about him. But I'd hoped with time he would come to his senses. I saw how much he cared about you and no man can resist those feelings for long. Trust me, Jack did everything he could to find out who sent that threat, who might have tried to kill him. But Brett had no choice, he had to let it go. There was no evidence.'

Meg's shoulders slumped. 'It all sounds absurd to me.'

'It does. But on paper?' Ron quirked his eyebrows. 'You're an heiress, Meg. You and your sister will get everything I own, and you know the value of the estate. Add to that the legacy of this town and your influence …' He shrugged. 'People have killed for less.'

Meg stared at her father, her heart pounding hard and low. 'But there's no money in farming, Dad. Why does it matter if I were to marry Jack?'

'Shadow Creek has prestige, and the Maguires do all right for themselves. Add in Jade Farm, and their value increases.'

Meg shook her head. 'This is crazy!'

Ron caught her flying hand. 'I know. Trust me, that's exactly what I thought. And I was angry for you, which is why I did everything I could to help. But we couldn't understand who would lose if you and Jack were to marry. We considered the farmers. The Kellys are Henry and Cliff's best friends. And your cousins are married onto Tropic Sun and White Peaks. We're all family, Meg.'

'So, who would care, then?'

'I don't know. But tell me.' He squeezed her hand. 'Has the time come where this might become a problem? Are you and Jack together?'

Meg couldn't have stopped her mouth from curving even if she'd wanted to. 'Yeah ...'

At least she hoped they would be as joy burst through Meg's heart when her father grinned. He wrapped his arm around her shoulders and kissed her forehead.

'I'm glad, Meg. It's about damn time.'

'I'll say!' Susan Riley squealed, and Meg glanced over her shoulder as her mum slid into the pew. 'Oh, Meg. I'm so happy for you!'

Squeezed between her parents, Meg laughed. 'Yeah. Me too.'

* * *

'Megan!' Eric greeted her from the doorway, holding a steaming cup of coffee in one hand and waving with the other. 'In your Sunday best, I see.'

'Always.' She returned his hug and stepped inside Chaz's house. 'Must be big news if you're here too.'

'Sure is.'

Meg's belly clenched. 'I'm not going to like this, am I?'

Laughing, Eric strode down the hallway. 'You'll love it.'

'Just come in, Megan,' Chaz said from the kitchen. 'I'll make you a cuppa.'

Keeping her wild imagination at bay, Meg slipped onto a stool beside Eric and greeted Chuck while Chaz placed a cup of tea in front of her. She gripped it tight as wicked gleams flickered in The Boys' eyes.

'Can you guys not drag this out? What have you done with my song?' Her eyebrows shot up. 'Did you get Hayley?'

'Forget Hayley,' Chaz said, dismissing her hope with a wave of his hand. 'This isn't about that.'

'Then what's it about?'

'We're headlining a charity concert in Mareeba,' Chaz said, and Meg's spine straightened. 'The council's hosting it and it's going to be quite a big do.'

'The moment they asked our man here,' Chuck said, nodding at Chaz, 'he took the bull by the horns and now it's a massive event.'

'Artists are coming from all over,' Eric added, and The Boys rattled off a few big names in Australian country music. 'It'll be like any other one day, one stage festival. We'll have acts during the afternoon, then the main show at night. All proceeds go to disaster relief.'

Meg glanced between them. 'Wow, guys. That sounds incredible. Makes my bachelor auction look ridiculous.'

'Hey, that's cool too,' Chaz said. 'But yeah, charity concerts do well.'

'And you've got a stellar line-up.' Meg sipped her tea. 'When's it on?'

'The weekend before the show.' A smile tugged the corner of Chaz's mouth as he leaned his hip on the counter. 'And you're going to sing your song with us.'

Meg stilled. Damn. She'd been so impressed with the concert she hadn't even seen that coming.

She set her mug down. 'You want to sing that song there?'

'It's perfect. You wrote it because of the disaster, so it's going to be our feature song.'

Meg could barely breathe. 'You want me to sing the *feature* song with you?'

Chaz grinned. 'Don't be silly. I want you to sing it with everyone. All of the feature artists.'

Meg almost fell off her stool. Her cousin had finally lost his mind. He wanted her, a nobody, to sing with him and the two other amazingly talented, insanely famous headline acts? To perform a song that, if done properly, could soar to the top of the charts in the name of cyclone relief? She'd merely hoped he'd feature it on the next album, maybe release it as a single.

Eric chuckled. 'You've done it this time, Chaz. You've stunned her into complete silence.'

Gathering herself, Meg cleared her throat. 'You can't be serious?'

'Megan, you know I'm always serious when it comes to your music career. And this is an opportunity too good to miss. We're going to perform your song either way. We'd just prefer if you stood beside us.'

Chuck grinned. 'You haven't even told her the best bit.'

'Oh God, there's more?' Meg didn't think she could take another blow.

'The name of the concert.' Eric nodded. 'Tell her, Chaz.'

'We've called it *Our Spirit Can't Blow Away*,' he said, and Meg's breath escaped in a whoosh.

'Oh, guys …' She didn't know what to say. She'd given Chaz the song to do with as he pleased, but she'd never expected he'd name a whole concert after it. 'It's too much.'

The three of them chuckled. They were backing her into a corner, and they knew it. Because this event had her name written all over it.

'You know it's fitting,' Eric said, and Meg nodded.

'So come on, Megan. Sing with us in Mareeba.'

Heart racing, Meg glanced between her cousin and his

friends. Her friends too, really. They'd backed her up all those years ago when she'd hosted her show queen concerts, then had gone off to become stars. She'd never begrudged them that and loved how successful they'd become. They deserved every piece of it, and she deserved her regrets.

But now, her dreams were awakening. The desire to sing and her love for music flowed through her veins. She'd been afraid, and still was, but what had Jack said the other night? *It's not too late. You're a beautiful singer and songwriter.*

Meg exhaled. Jack would tell her to do it. He'd drive her to Mareeba and push her onto that stage if he had to. And she'd never get another opportunity like this. Not one that meant so much to her. She didn't care for fame and glory, but writing the feature song for a charity concert and singing it with her friends? Missing out on that was a regret she didn't need.

She lowered her mug onto the bench. 'Okay. I'll do it.'

'All right!' Eric cried as Chuck let out a whoop. Two sets of arms came around her as The Boys squeezed her tight. On the other side of the bench, Chaz smiled, the light in his eyes filling her heart.

'Thank you, Megan. I promise, this is going to be great.' As his bandmates let her go, Chaz rounded the island counter and drew her into his arms. 'We can also give you a set in the opening act. You could sing "Country Girls Gone Wild."'

'That's a damn good song,' Chuck said. 'If it wasn't so girly, we'd cover it.'

Meg laughed. It was a good song and fun to perform with its dance beat and catchy tune. But her own set? Was she ready for that?

The words escaped her lips before she could stop them. 'You know what? Sign me up.'

Chapter Twenty-Four

He slumped against the ute, stuck the fuel nozzle in, and pumped petrol that was far too fucking expensive into the ageing tank. Dunno how a bloke was meant to make a living when it cost him a shitload just to drive to the pub. Might have had too much to drink too, but the blasted young copper was probably too busy warming some whore's bed tonight to uphold his stand on road safety, so he should make it home without getting caught.

And he'd need the pub now that fucking Maguire had given into weakness and was pretending not to date Meg Riley.

His hand tightened around the nozzle. Right place, right time, he'd heard the dolled-up women at the pub on Friday night. The Maguire bitch's squeal had been loud enough to make a man's ears bleed.

'We need to keep it quiet,' Meg had said, but her friend had been too excited.

'Keep what quiet?'

Then there'd been secretive whispers, sickening smiles, and more ridiculous shrieking before Meg had placated her friend.

'Just pretend that nothing has changed.'

But it had. He'd watched them from the bar after the ladies had returned to the booth, and there had been no mistaking the stars in Meg's eyes. They were the same stars he'd seen long ago in eyes so similar. The woman was hopelessly in love. It made him sick. At least Maguire had managed to act out his indifference.

But he'd followed Maguire's flashy Ford Raptor when he'd left the pub with Meg and Isabella Brennan, and after he'd dropped the young bookworm home, he and Meg had left for Shadow Creek.

There was no mistaking it. Maguire might have been holed up on his farm scared bloody shitless for years, but time had loosened his hold on the man. His threat had been forgotten and hormones had taken over.

The bowser clicked off and he slammed the money-drainer back into place. Fucking Maguire. Fucking Shadow Creek. He hated them. Hated them all. Even Kelly hadn't been able to throw a spanner in the works, the useless bastard.

He stomped into the roadhouse and paid an outrageous amount of money for a basic necessity. It pissed him off, but he'd never get away with stealing fuel. Bloody cameras.

Slamming back into his geriatric ute, he grabbed the bottle of rum from the passenger seat and took a long swig. Something had to be done. That girl would *not* marry Jack Maguire. It was not 'meant to be.' Ron Riley's money would *not* go to Shadow Creek and over his dead body would he let the Maguires have Jade Farm.

Well, maybe not *his* dead body.

Chapter Twenty-Five

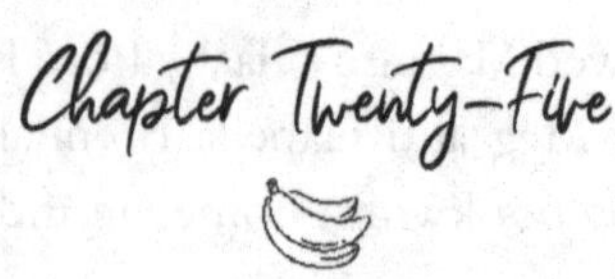

Any doubts lingering in Meg's mind about singing at the charity concert vanished at the pride in Jack's voice when she spoke to him on Sunday night.

'That's fantastic!' he said, the grin in his tone crackling through the phone. 'And it's not foolish, darlin'. You deserve this chance. I'm thrilled for you.'

Meg smiled as she fed sliced apple to Lola and Jill. Lola didn't quite understand the concept of sharing her favourite snack or waiting her turn, but Meg had offered the kelpie a slice and she'd gobbled it up with gusto.

'Thanks, Jack. I am nervous though.'

'Don't be. You can't let this opportunity go by, and we'll all be there to support you. You won't be able to keep Adam away. The fool thinks he's your biggest fan.'

Meg laughed. 'He's certainly one of them. But I'd love to have you all there. It's been so long since I performed. Like, really performed. The Christmas carols don't count.'

'Yet, you still put on a great show. No one sings "Silent Night" like you do, darlin'.'

Meg grimaced as she began slicing the last apple quarter.

The Christmas carols were all she'd had these past few years and she only sang because she couldn't let the community down. She loved Christmas and enjoyed spreading the cheer. But the charity concert would be different. She would sing her own songs, feel the rush, and share her music with people who wanted to hear it. Music filled her heart and until these past few days, she'd forgotten how much she longed to have it in her life.

'I just can't believe Chaz wants me in the stellar line-up to sing my song. They're amazing artists, Jack.'

'Sure are. You'll love it though and it'll feel like it was only yesterday. You're a natural, darlin'. Take this chance and build your music career. It's always been your dream.'

Meg fed Lola a piece of apple. 'You think it'll be that easy?'

'All depends what sort of career you want. There are thousands of artists out there, Meg, and most release music for the love of it and perform at a schedule that suits them. But if nothing else, you'll be combining two things that you love with this concert, music and charity. And honestly, these people down here need it.'

'Yeah, I can't believe Robbo's still without power,' she said with more wonder than actual disbelief. After Yasi, rural areas had remained without power for months while Ergon restored six hundred kilometres of cable and over two thousand power poles to get them back on the grid. 'Are you sure you guys have everything you need?'

'We have plenty of fuel for the generator to charge our phones, run the microwave, and keep the fridge going, so the beer's cold.'

She laughed. 'Good to know.'

'Can't get through this without beer. It's hot enough that a cold shower isn't a big deal, and we've got torches for nighttime. Robbo said it might be restored this week, but honestly, nobody knows.'

Meg fed the girls another slice of apple. 'That's okay. You've got gas for a barbeque, right?'

'Yeah. Though I tell you, I'm not afraid of hard work, but this is a bloody big job.'

She didn't doubt it, which was why she loved him even more for volunteering.

She spoke to Jack for a little longer, but since she didn't want to keep him from his friends, Meg soon wished him luck and hung up. With the apple gone, she and the girls resumed watching *The Secret Life of Pets* as Lola loved watching dogs on TV. When Jill realised that the figures on the screen were animated pups, she hopped off the lounge and stared at the TV too, her reddish-brown tail whipping slowly from side to side. Meg took a photo and sent it to Jack.

See? Treating her like a dog.

His reply came through within seconds. **Why? Because she's not on the lounge?**

Grinning, she glanced at the spot Jill had just vacated. **Of course not. That would be spoiling her.**

He replied with an eye roll and smiley face emoji.

The week passed in a blur of work, phone calls with the show committee, and text messages from Jack. On Friday, she slipped into the booth for a night of gossip with her friends. But while she might be missing Jack, it was nothing compared to how much Natalia longed to see Adam.

Though Meg doubted Adam would want to see her. Natalia's eyes flashed as she crossed her arms over the table, radiating irritation. 'I can't wait until he gets home. I need to talk to him now.'

Meg smiled. 'They do have working phones down there.'

'I know. But I need to *see* him.'

Ana frowned. 'Did Adam do something wrong?'

'Oh, he'll know what he did. Trust me.'

'Why don't you come with me tomorrow, then?' Meg asked. 'The car's full of donations from the church that I need to drop off in Innisfail, but I can make room. Especially if it's that urgent.'

Natalia's eyebrows lifted. 'Can I? We can take my Rav-4 if it's easier.'

'Sure. But remember, they have no power. Or hot water.'

Natalia's lip curled. 'They have Adam, and he's all I need right now.'

Concern etched Liam's brow. 'Is he still going to be alive after you get to him?'

'Don't worry, I won't be killing him.' Although it seemed like Natalia wanted to as she blew out her breath, then glanced at Meg. 'What time do you want to leave?'

* * *

They left Elizadale late morning for the two-hour drive to Innisfail.

'Jack told me the cleanup's going well,' Meg said, glancing out the window of the passenger seat. 'Robbo may actually have bananas in a few months.'

'I'm glad. Adam said the shed only needed minor repairs.'

'They've come a long way since Larry in learning how to prepare for cyclones and every time, they get better. Of course, we're never going to save the plants, but every step forward helps reduce the losses.'

'I'm glad they had that cyclone prep meeting with the Banana Growers Council in November.'

'The Council does a good job,' Meg agreed. 'So, what are you mad at Adam about?'

'What do you mean?'

'Last night, you seemed like you're coming to tell him off. What did he do?'

Natalia exhaled, her shoulders slouching as she adjusted her hands on the wheel. 'I'm not mad, just irritated. And I figured it wouldn't hurt to get past my fear of roughing it for the night. If it'd been us devastated by Billy, I wouldn't be enjoying my lights, oven, and TV.'

'Very true. As long as Adam's not in trouble.'

'Oh, he's in trouble all right.' Natalia's laugh held no humour. 'That wood he wants me to pick up tomorrow better be nice because he owes me something pretty.'

Meg's suspicions rose, but she didn't probe Natalia as her friend clearly wasn't going to share. 'Jack said that wood is to help with the table they're building for Michael. But Adam's talent sure has grown since he's been woodturning more often. The business seems to be doing well.'

The gleam returned to Natalia's eyes. 'He's doing great.'

They drove through Mareeba, Atherton, then the rolling green hills of the Tablelands, where they began to catch sight of the damage left by Billy. Roadworks on the Palmerston Highway set them back half an hour, but when they arrived on the outskirts of Innisfail, Meg's heart broke.

Natalia drove with her eyes wide and her hand pressed to her mouth. 'Oh my God. Oh my—look at that house!'

The 1940s fibro home stood with no roof, beams exposed, and external walls crumbled. Meg nodded sadly. 'Yep.'

'It'll take forever to recover. The builders won't be able to keep up. Maybe Michael could get work here for the next few months.'

'They don't take well to outsiders coming in and taking jobs. The local guys will get to it as soon as insurance comes through.'

'Which will be a struggle itself. I hope the companies don't rip these people off.'

'They will, and premiums will go up again. Soon, no one in this region will be able to afford insurance, and some companies refuse to cover this area.'

'I know. I couldn't believe it when I saw the premium on our house. I thought Adam had made a mistake or was getting seriously ripped off. But that's what he had to pay, even though cyclones and floods have destroyed other cities.' Natalia gasped. 'Oh God, that house is even worse!'

The damage grew more severe as they passed through Innisfail, and Natalia's shock left her speechless. Posts that had once held shade sails in the Coles car park stood empty and patch jobs had begun on some businesses while missing signs and gutters exposed the beams and the interior construction one rarely saw. Meg barely knew where to look as she directed Natalia to the church. Evidence of disaster might remain, but at least some businesses were operating again.

'I'm so glad our show queen efforts are going towards cyclone relief,' Natalia said. 'Shouldn't we pick one project though? Maybe donate the funds to the school or something?'

'Schools all around the state are having free dress days and discos to help the Innisfail schools.' Elizadale already had theirs scheduled. 'But I'll talk to the committee and see what we can do.'

They dropped the donations of clothes and household items off to the minister and his wife, who were sincerely grateful. Then Meg took the wheel of the Rav-4 to drive to

Robbo's farm. Beside her, Natalia tapped her fingers on her thigh and bit down on her lower lip. Her gaze never left the destroyed farms.

'I wonder how the sugar cane held up.'

'It doesn't fall over like bananas, but growth will be slower from the excess rain. At least the farmers who grow both will have a sugar income for the year, and a lot of them around here do.'

'All I have to say is you and I have amazingly generous husbands. And a Michael.'

Longing filled Meg's chest as she nodded. 'We do.'

'You and Jack are going to get married, right?' Natalia asked, tearing her gaze from the window.

Meg adjusted her hands on the wheel and glanced at her bare left hand. 'I hope so. I just need to wait until he's ready.'

'Yeah.' Natalia consulted the map on her phone. 'Almost there, Meg. You know … Adam told me what happened. To Jack.'

'You knew?'

'No, he told me once you got together. I knew about the accident, but Adam hadn't known what was making Jack hesitate until that night they went camping. And even though I can't believe someone would threaten Jack, I can see where it would have been hard for him. He loves you. I knew that before I even moved here. So, give him some time. Fears are hard to let go of.'

Meg's shoulders slumped, and the ache that had eased this past week returned to fill her heart. 'I know.'

Chapter Twenty-Six

A few minutes later, Natalia told her to take the next right as they passed what Meg suspected to be Robbo's place. The paddocks were clear with organic debris lying in the rows of young banana plants. Meg slowed and turned off the highway.

Natalia shook her head. 'They had to cut all those plants down ...'

'Yep.' Meg ached just thinking about it. Banana farming was already labour intensive, but this was a whole new level. 'They'll be exhausted when they get home.'

She pulled up on the grass beside the driveway, phoned Jack to tell him they'd arrived, then they grabbed their bags and stepped out into the sunshine. Rather than take Natalia's car through the decontamination process, they'd leave it outside overnight. Within moments, the Raptor curved around the driveway and Meg grinned, waving like a loon as Jack pulled up on the other side of the fence.

'Hey, darlin'.' He climbed out of the ute. 'Nat! Didn't know you were coming.'

Meg glanced at Natalia. 'You didn't tell anyone?' she asked, holding her arms open to embrace Jack over the fence. He drew her close and she sank against him, ignoring the wire pressing into her belly.

Natalia crossed her arms. 'Adam didn't need a warning,' she said, bitterness lacing her tone.

Jack exhaled as he and Meg drew apart. 'What did he do?'

'Never you mind.'

Meg eyed Jack as she handed him her bag. 'She's not mad, apparently.'

'He'll be glad to see you though.' Jack took Natalia's bag too and popped them into the ute. 'Now, Robbo said we'll take your shoes through the wash and give them a good scrub up at the house.'

Jack set up the foot wash and after Meg had walked through the water tray, he lifted her chin with his finger and kissed her softly. Splaying her hands over his chest, she relished the warmth that flooded through her. He smelled of sweat, hard work, and bananas.

'Missed you,' he whispered.

'I missed you too. I see you've been working hard.'

'It's been gruelling, but I'm glad you came.' He kissed her again, then let her go as Natalia opened the car door and climbed in. 'Is Nat really going to kill my brother?'

Meg shook her head. 'She needs him alive.'

'Let's get up to the house, then. We were waiting for you to have lunch.'

They climbed into the ute and Jack drove them up to Robbo's brick home. Robbo and Michael sat in the roofless pergola beside the house while Adam strolled over from the empty packing sheds. Natalia was out of the ute before Jack had even cut the engine, slamming the door behind her. Meg jumped out, not wanting to miss the show.

Adam halted. 'Nat! Holy shit, I didn't expect to see you!'

'Don't you smile at me, Adam Maguire!' His grin vanished as she stormed towards him.

Jack came up beside Meg. 'What's Nat upset about?'

'Dunno.' Meg leaned into Jack as he wrapped his arm around her waist. 'Although I have a sneaking feeling that—'

Adam let out a whoop that could be heard back in Elizadale as he whisked Natalia into his arms and spun her around. Grinning, Meg pressed her hands to her mouth.

'He can't be in that much trouble.'

Meg laughed. 'Oh, I think he is. But the good sort of trouble.'

'Hey, guys!' Adam called, Natalia still in his arms. 'You're going to be uncles!'

Shrieking, Meg skipped out of Jack's embrace and ran to Natalia. Adam had no choice but to put her down.

'Congratulations!' Meg squeezed her tight. 'Oh my God, I can't believe you kept that to yourself!'

'It was so hard! But I had to tell him first.'

Jack came up beside her and took Adam's hand. 'Congrats, mate.' He pulled his brother into a hug, slapping him on the back.

'Thanks, Jack.'

'Knew she hadn't come just to see your ugly mug.'

Adam laughed. 'Shut up.'

Blinking back tears, Meg glanced at the happy couple as Adam wrapped his arm around Natalia. She'd had her suspicions on the drive and was delighted for her friends. But as Jack took her hand, Meg couldn't deny the touch of envy that niggled in her belly.

Hopefully next time, it would be her turn to make such a delightful announcement.

* * *

Jack ignored the prickle around his heart as they celebrated Adam and Natalia's news with hugs and hearty congratulations, then Jack introduced the ladies to Robbo.

'I think we've met before,' Meg said. 'A few years ago, when you were in Elizadale.'

'I remember. I couldn't understand why Jack wasn't with a pretty girl like you.'

She laughed. 'Me either.'

Jack managed a small smile, but the knots in his gut refused to unravel. The endless work this past week had provided a physical outlet for his frustration, but as they kicked back of an evening, all he'd been able to think about was Meg. She'd turned their one amazing night into three of the most glorious afternoons and evenings of his life as they'd walked, talked, and dined. If he had one wish, it would be to return to Elizadale, take her into his arms, and seize the life he'd envisioned all those years ago.

Except how could he do that when he couldn't guarantee her safety? Part of him hadn't wanted her coming today, but he was selfish and hadn't had the heart to fight her on it. The only thing that eased his fear was the fact they were away from prying eyes.

They made sandwiches, then sat in the pergola talking general nonsense before taking Meg and Natalia for a drive around the farm. As the sun set, they lit the firepit and gathered around the dancing flames while Robbo fired up the barbeque. Jack drank his beer, enjoying the warmth of Meg's body as she snuggled beside him on the log.

But Jack couldn't tear his gaze from Adam and Natalia. His smug brother held his wife close, unable to wipe the smile from his face while Natalia whispered, giggled, and positively glowed in the firelight.

An ache burned inside Jack's chest. Adam had bloody well done it again. One upped him and was moving on in the game of life. Whereas he, despite recent events, remained stuck.

Tension corded his spine as Jack glanced at Meg, the light flickering over her delicate face. She was everything he'd ever wanted. With her, he could have it all. He knew Meg's hopes and dreams. She longed for marriage and children. He knew she'd named them already and that she probably had the wedding planned too. Some men might have run for the hills at that knowledge, but it hadn't scared him. Life with Meg was all he could think about when he'd been pinned beneath that blasted tractor. Letting go of the dream had marred his soul. Yet even after he'd broken her heart, she'd never given up on them. And now, he still wanted to deny her the love, wedding, and family she wanted with his nonsense of 'one night only.'

Jack swigged his beer and stared into the fire. He'd be foolish to think he could walk away, but how could he give her what she wanted and keep her safe?

Adam's laughter cut through the air as Natalia rolled her eyes and he kissed her temple. Jack's gut clenched. Their road to love might not have been a walk in the park, but they'd fought for each other. No one had threatened their lives, but Natalia had stood beside Adam, and he'd have slain anyone who dared hurt her.

Why couldn't he do the same for Meg? Was he not as strong as Adam? Did he not love Meg as much as Adam loved Natalia?

Jack's hand tightened around his beer. He did love her. He loved her more than anyone or anything in this world. It's why he'd tortured himself all these years. Why he'd sacrificed his heart. He'd thought he'd done the right thing and that the pain would be worth it. But he'd been wrong. All he'd achieved was a life of misery, a broodiness he couldn't shake, and jealousy of those who weren't afraid to chase their dreams. He hadn't even expanded the farm. And why? Because he'd lost the opportunity to operate Jade Farm when he'd lost Meg?

If he could thump himself, he would. But like Meg had said, they couldn't live with regret. He still had a future, and he wanted that future with her. He'd had a taste of happiness and he couldn't let it go. Jack wanted everything he'd been dreaming of that day on the tractor. He was the eldest, dammit, and therefore, it was *his* responsibility to take Shadow Creek into the future. Not Adam's. He needed to expand the property, secure it, and have children to pass it on to.

He'd never get that if he didn't take a chance. And maybe Brett, Henry, and Ron had been right. There was no telling what had caused that tractor tyre to blow. He would swear he'd heard gunshots until his dying day, but while he doubted the person who'd threatened them had moved on, he had to believe that he and Meg could overcome any hurdles they faced. All he had to do was stay vigilant. Hold her close and protect her. Be prepared.

Exhaling, he wrapped his arm around her slender shoulders. Her head lifted and she smiled softly. 'You okay?'

That was a good question. He wasn't sure. But he did know one thing. 'Yeah, Meg. I'm just glad you're here.'

'Me too. And after seeing the destruction today, I'm glad we're doing all we can to help.'

'Absolutely. Have you been practising for the concert?'

'Yeah, Jill and Lola have been a captive audience. And I've thought a bit about what you said, about the career I want. I always knew I didn't want to be a star and seek international tours and such. I want to stay in Elizadale, continue to teach, and have a life suitable for bringing up a family, you know?'

A knot lodged in his throat as he nodded.

'I want to write, sing, and share what's in my soul. Downloads would be nice, and the country radio network is extremely supportive. I can find myself some airtime and gather the fans I need. But I can't let this opportunity go because I've had enough regrets and I don't need any more.'

'Yeah. It's awful to live with regret, darlin'. Chews you up inside.'

'So, let's not.' She angled her body towards his, her blue eyes soft and hopeful. 'We can't change the past, Jack, but give us a chance. Please? You can't tell me you don't want to try.'

He lifted his hand to her face, brushing a piece of ash from her creamy cheek. 'I dread what will happen if we're together, Meg. I can't shake the fear.'

She wrapped her arm around his waist. 'I know it's hard, Jack. But don't fear loving me. Please.'

'I don't fear that.'

'Good.' Her eyes softened. 'Because if I'm going to do this singing thing, I need you there in the crowd. Cheering me on.'

He smiled softly. 'I don't think cheering's my thing, darlin', but I'll be there. You can count on that.'

Chapter Twenty-Seven

Meg sat on the lounge and settled her guitar over her thighs. With the convenience of school holidays, she planned to spend her time singing scales and playing for her devoted canine audience. It'd been so long since she'd performed. Standing before her hometown singing 'Joy to the World' didn't count as it was just something she did to celebrate the festive season. But it'd been almost two years since she'd sung with her cousin at the Royal Hotel and whenever she had graced the stage at the show, she'd only sung covers. 'Country Girls Gone Wild' had occasionally broken free, but that's only because the crowd had demanded it. Or Adam had.

But those performances were for her home. For the crowd who knew and loved her. The concert in Mareeba was going to be massive, and her song could skyrocket to the top of the charts, as songs for charity often did. So, while she had maintained her vocal training over the years with exercises and singing at church, she needed the practise to build her confidence before she stepped onstage in Mareeba with those amazing artists.

Meg slapped her hand over the strings. 'I'm being ridiculous, aren't I, girls? It's not that scary.'

Lola panted happily while Jill tilted her head. Meg ran her hand through her hair, let out a deep breath, and focused. She could do this. She *wanted* to do this. After seeing the destruction of the Cassowary Coast and the heartbreak in the locals' eyes, she needed to be part of everything she could to help them. So, since 'Country Girls Gone Wild' was the song she was most comfortable with, she strummed the upbeat opening and sang.

The days up to Easter flew by as she continued to practise. On Thursday, Meg headed to the post office, then raced home with her parcel.

'Girls, look what came for you!' Just in time too since Jack was on his way home. He'd messaged her when they'd left Innisfail, so he'd likely be back any minute now, and she needed to have the girls ready.

Grinning, she tore open the parcel. She'd gone a little overboard with the bandanas, but Lola loved them and the little dog wriggled with delight as Meg fastened the polka-dot cloth around her neck. Then she tied a matching one around Jill's and positioned the girls for photos.

'You two look so pretty,' she said as an engine rumbled in the driveway. Scampering to her feet, Meg raced to the door, paws pattering behind her. And there he was, Jack Maguire in his boots and rugged jeans coming home to her. Joy outweighed all other emotions as she swayed on her feet and pushed open the door. 'Welcome back!'

He glanced up, his eyes dark and shoulders rigid. Meg's heart sank. Oh God, she could hear his excuses already. They'd had a lovely night in Innisfail, but she hadn't a clue what his current thoughts were about their relationship. Had he rebuilt his walls? Was he about to burst her happy bubble? His text messages had grown shorter and shorter these past few days and clouds continued to haunt his eyes.

But before she could call herself a fool, his mouth curved. His stride quickened and, stepping inside, Jack pulled her against him. Meg gasped as her body collided with his and her hands fell to his chest. The screen door crashed closed with a metallic clang.

'Hey, darlin'.'

She blinked. 'Wow. You're energetic.'

Jack's grin broadened, then his mouth captured hers. He moved her one step backwards, then two, until Meg found herself pressed against the wall. His hands brushed her hips and snaked up her sides, pushing her T-shirt up around her ribs. A longing radiated from him that had filled every one of her fantasies as she sank into the kiss. She dug her fingers into his shoulders, unwilling to draw away even though she couldn't breathe.

After an age, he softened the kiss until his lips barely brushed hers and Meg noticed Jill was trying to force her head between them. They drew apart to find the kelpie looking up at them with her whole body wagging in delight.

Jack shook his head. 'Jill, what are you wearing?'

Meg grinned. 'I bought her a bandana.'

Mouth open, Jill jumped up to place her paws on Jack's belly and he rubbed her head. 'Why?'

'Because they're cute.' She scooped Lola up. 'See? They match.'

'Yes …' Jack guided Jill down, amusement flashing through his eyes. 'I knew you'd spoil my dog.'

'I didn't *spoil* her, but all girls need to feel good about themselves, and doesn't Jill look pretty in her new collar?'

Jack fingered the sparkling pink collar around Jill's neck. 'I guess hers was getting old.'

'Exactly!'

Smiling, he rubbed Jill's head. 'You do look pretty, don't you?'

Jill spun in an excited circle and even though Meg knew Jack had only said it to please her, warmth filled her chest. If that greeting before was any indication, it didn't seem like he'd rebuilt his walls, but did that mean …?

Jack straightened and drew her back into his arms. The light faded from his eyes and everything inside her twisted as dread rendered her still.

'I'm sorry, Meg.'

'S-sorry?'

'For treating you like I did. For pushing you away. For saying we could only have one night.'

She swallowed. 'We had three …'

'Because you fought for it. For us. I've been stubborn, but you wore me down. And now …' He shook his head and she clung to Lola tighter. 'I'm done with that. I'm done with being a moody bastard and hating life. I want to be happy. You make me happy, darlin', so I'm all in.' He inched closer and dropped his voice as he said, 'I love you, Meg.'

Time stopped. Lola even stopped wriggling as Meg stared into Jack's dark, determined eyes. Had she heard him correctly? Was he going to give into his fear and take a chance?

Her shoulders deflated and her breath caught in her throat. He'd said everything she'd ever wanted to hear. Biting her lower lip, tears welled in Meg's eyes.

'Shit.' Jack plucked Lola from Meg's hold and placed her on the floor. 'Darlin', please—'

Meg threw her arms around him, grinning as she rose onto her toes and pressed her mouth to his. 'I know you do, Jack Maguire. Gosh, you sure know how to overwhelm a girl.'

Smiling softly, he rested his forehead against hers. 'I'm not good with words, Meg. But I thought the "I love you" wouldn't be enough.'

'It's enough. It's all I've ever wanted to hear.'

He touched his mouth back to hers. 'I know. And I'm sorry I made you wait so long.'

'You were just trying to protect me.'

'And we'll still have to be careful, but I've realised that I can protect you and love you at the same time.'

Everything fluttered inside her as she gazed into his dark, soulful eyes. 'We can love and protect each other, Jack. I know you're worried, but we will be okay.'

'I hope so, Meg.' He kissed her again and drew her close until she had no choice but to rise back up onto her toes. He started soft and slow, then their lips parted, and she didn't hold back.

* * *

Jack woke on Saturday to the sweet melody of Meg's voice drifting from the kitchen. Breathing in the soft scent of peaches and cream, his chest expanded until he feared it would burst. They'd had a fantastic Good Friday together, although he hadn't joined her at church. Not because he'd never particularly thought about God as he'd long ago accepted that the church would be in his future if he wanted to be with Meg. But if he were to go with her, gossip would spread and could alert whoever didn't want them to be together, and Jack would prefer they stay in their happy bubble for as long as possible. So, he'd made breakfast instead and loved her for the rest of the day.

Grinning, Jack rolled out of bed, stretching out muscles he hadn't used in years before tugging on his jeans. He zipped but didn't button as he left the bedroom and drew to a halt. Meg stood at the stove with his shirt hanging off her creamy shoulder and swaying around her wriggling hips. Golden hair tumbled down her back as she turned her head and grinned.

'Good morning.'

'Morning, darlin'.' He crossed the room, gathered her from behind, and placed a kiss deep in her neck. She sank against him, setting the knife down and leaving the blueberries uncut. 'You're chipper today.'

Her hands fell over his at her waist. She'd left most of the buttons on his shirt undone, allowing him a glimpse of her perfectly round breast. 'Always am when I wake up with you.'

He kissed the exposed skin of her shoulder and resisted the urge to seduce her on the kitchen floor. But while he'd never satisfy his appetite for her, he was bloody hungry. 'What are you making?'

'Pancakes.'

'Yum. I'll make the tea.' He stepped away and reached for the electric kettle. 'What were you singing?'

'Something I made up earlier this week. It's not any good.'

'Try me.'

Her gaze fell back to the blueberries. Jack caught the familiar shade of self-doubt in her eyes, but she sang as he watched her and waited for the kettle to boil.

'Your eyes light up because you depend on me. You give your love so easily. I will hold you for eternity. Because you, my baby, are all I need.'

She sang a few more verses. When she finished, her gaze flittered to his.

He smiled. 'That's a sweet song, Meg.'

She scraped blueberries into the pancake batter. 'It's silly, Jack. I wrote it about Lola.'

The laugh escaped him before he could stop himself. 'Shit, I'm sorry.' He crossed the kitchen and placed his hand on her shoulder. 'I see it now, but that doesn't mean it's silly. I liked it.'

She raised her eyebrows. 'Really?'

'Yeah, it has a maternal sense to it. Like a mum singing about her baby, and people will relate to that. Who cares if Lola inspired you?'

Her mouth curved. 'Thanks. It needs some work, but I'll need more songs if I'm going to release an album.'

'True.' The kettle clicked and Jack crossed the kitchen.

'And it's been fun writing again, but don't go thinking about me hitting the big time, okay? I just want to get back into the rhythm of things, write what's in my heart, and practise for this concert.'

'I won't.' The last thing he would do was push her. Besides, right now, all Jack could think about was how quickly they could eat their breakfast and he could liberate her from his shirt. At least the wholemeal blueberry pancakes would provide him with hours of energy because with the buttons only done up to her navel, the temptation to carry her back to bed corded through his body. He could honestly think of no better way to spend the long weekend than making up for lost time.

He was a gentleman though, so they ate. She updated him on all things show queen while he ignored Lola staring up at him. The damn dog could look all she wanted. She wouldn't wear him down with her ridiculously adorable oversized black eyes.

'You really should stop trying,' he told Lola as he helped Meg take the plates back to the sink. He placed the glasses down, then moved behind her to slip his hands through his shirt over her belly. 'I think it's time we return to bed.'

Her phone rang as she sank against him. 'I wouldn't mind a shower first.'

'We can shower.' Spinning her around, he caught her mouth with his and with a few twists of buttons, he had her naked.

Meg pulled herself close, her bare skin pressing against his as her hands slid into his hair. Heart pounding, he trailed kisses down her neck, shoulders, then claimed her breast with his mouth. Her gasp filled the silence, then the ringing resumed. She arched into him, not that he needed the encouragement. No one tasted better than Meg. He'd never get enough of her creamy skin, scent, or how she felt beneath his hands as she responded to his touch.

He should have done this years ago.

'Jack …'

'I gotcha, darlin'.' His hands slid over her bare butt, and he was about to hoist her up when that incessant ringing resumed. 'For fuck's sake.'

'Give me a sec.' Huffing out a breath, she stepped around him to grab her phone. He would have argued, but after three attempts, he doubted the caller would give up. Moving behind her, he brushed Meg's soft hair off her neck.

'Who is this?'

The pitch in her voice halted his kiss as Jack's spine stiffened. Meg lowered her phone and turned to him. She didn't say anything. She didn't need to. Her wide eyes, the tone of her voice, Jack didn't need to hear the words. His insides turned to ice.

'Jack ... he ... someone ... he told me to stay away from you. Or else.'

Jack's jaw clenched until he feared he'd crack teeth. He knew it. He'd fucking known it. They'd told him he was overreacting, that he had nothing to fear, but now—

He gathered Meg into his arms and crushed her to his body. Her face buried into his chest as her hands clutched at his bare back. Jack bit back a curse as she shivered.

He hadn't been crazy. Hadn't been wrong. He hadn't lain beneath the tractor and suffered all those injuries for no fucking reason. He'd been justified in keeping Meg at bay.

But now, he'd given into temptation. And had put her at risk.

Drawing a deep breath, Jack pressed his lips to her hair. 'Get dressed, darlin'. I'll call Brett.'

Chapter Twenty-Eight

After hanging up the pay phone at Riley Road shops, he adjusted his Akubra and strode across the car park. Irritation prickled his skin as he entered the supermarket. If Maguire had any sense, he'd dump Meg's fine arse and his plan to take up avocado farming and stick to what he knew. He'd given the boy two weeks to let his guard down while he devised his own plans. Bad luck for Maguire that he'd been away playing hero.

But he doubted that evoking fear would work this time. He'd have to get his hands dirty. He needed to blow up their relationship to save himself from ruin. To protect his family and future. And there was only one way to ensure Meg and Jack's union never happened.

He needed to remove one of them permanently.

Clenching his teeth, he snatched a bottle of milk from the fridge. He'd failed taking Jack out last time, but that's because he'd hoped to make it look like an accident. How the bastard had survived he still didn't know, but this time, he wouldn't fuck it up. A clean shot to the head was all he needed. Bloody useless cops around here wouldn't trace it back to him, and he'd fix all his problems with one bullet. Hurt all of those who had done him wrong. He had no care for the Maguire or Riley families. Maybe once they lost one of their own, they would know what real life was like outside their rosy picture of success, charity, and sunshine.

But who would he take out? Scratching his chin, he considered the options as carefully as he did the ice cream choices. Getting rid of Maguire would leave his brother in charge. He could handle that. Adam had no care to expand and create an empire. He knew his place in the world, despite punching above his weight with the hot doctor wife. Getting rid of Jack would serve the backstabbing Maguires right and leave Meg heartbroken. Maybe enough so that she would never marry and her influence would shrivel up.

Or he could just blow her pretty dumb brains out and never see her face again.

He grabbed a tub of Neapolitan and slammed the freezer door shut. Yeah, if he wanted to hurt anyone it would be Ronald Fucking Riley. Screw the Maguires. They might have pissed him off, hurt him, and destroyed his family, but golden boy Riley had taken something worse.

That bastard had taken his future.

It was only fair that he returned the favour by taking out the daughter Ron should never have had.

Chapter Twenty-Nine

Everything blurred around Meg as she sat across from Senior Sergeant Brett Wilson at the Elizadale Police Station. Her fingers and toes numbed. She could barely swallow. The voice in her ear sounded over and over.

Break up with Jack Maguire. Or else. This is your only warning.

Or else.

Or else …

'The call came through at nine o'clock.' Jack's hard tone drew Meg back to the present. 'We were finishing breakfast and the phone kept ringing. She answered and …'

Brett turned his dark gaze to her. 'What exactly were you told?'

She took a deep breath, but it didn't slow her racing heart. She couldn't believe this was happening. That the words had been real. That Jack had been right. 'He called me Megan Riley. "Megan Riley, break up with Jack Maguire. Or else. This is your only warning." That was it.'

Brett's tapping pen paused. 'Who calls you Megan?'

'No one. Well, The Charlie Boys do because that's the name I sing under. Sometimes my parents do. And my grandmother, Margaret, always does. That's just her way. But while it is my name, no one calls me Megan.'

'It's the name you sing under …' Jack frowned. 'Do you think that has anything to do with it? You were about to get a big break the first time and now with Mareeba coming up …'

Meg's eyes widened. 'Do you think? I mean, it sounds crazy, but this whole thing is just insane.'

Jack took her hand and squeezed softly. 'I know, darlin'. And I'm not saying I don't agree, but we need to take this seriously.'

Meg took a deep breath, then let it out slowly. She had to gather herself. Shake off the shock. Focus. But why was this happening? Who wouldn't want them to be together? What threat did their union impose upon anybody else?

'I don't see how my singing career has anything to do with this, but if it's a lead you want to pursue, I'll help you out.'

'I'll consider it,' Brett said, 'but I still think this threat's coming from an old connection. Could even be a former love interest since they have a problem with your relationship. That's usually the first place we start with things like this. Jealousy makes people do unspeakable things, but it would have to be someone from a while back.'

'This is the same person who threatened Jack, right?'

'We can assume so.'

'But I don't have love interests from back then! I've dated since, and there were two guys at uni, but they could be anywhere now. And Jack …'

She frowned. Who had he dated? Certainly no one serious in the past few years. More than a decade had passed since he'd dated Rebecca, who was now happily married to Jason Taylor.

'I've dated no one important,' he muttered.

Brett leaned back in his chair. 'I have to say, I'm sorry this has resurfaced, Jack.'

His jaw tightened. 'Me too.'

'I'll review the old case file and make some enquiries. I'll probably have to bring Cade in on it this time, though. Fresh eyes might be helpful.'

'Do what you have to do.'

'Cade didn't work the first case?' Meg asked.

Jack shook his head. 'I didn't want him to.'

'Jim and I kept it to ourselves,' Brett said, referring to the police sergeant. 'This time though, we'll need to use all our resources. So, tell the people close to you.' He glanced pointedly at Jack. 'Let your friends help. Trust me, they'll want to.'

* * *

Jack followed Meg into her house, tension tightening every muscle in his body as he locked the doors and secured the deadbolt. Meg's pale pink sundress swished around her fine legs as she placed her handbag on the table and scooped Lola into her arms. She kissed the fluffball's head while Jill bounced between him and Meg in her ridiculous bandana, unsure who she wanted to greet first. Swallowing the knot in his throat, Jack placed his hand on the kelpie's head and rubbed softly.

'Hey, girl.' He tried to draw comfort from the dog's happy eyes, but not even Jill's undying loyalty would ease his guilt and pain as he glanced at Meg. 'You should stay with your father tonight. We have to tell him what's going on anyway, but I don't want you to be alone.'

Meg's hand stilled in Lola's fluff. 'I won't be alone. I'll be with you.'

Everything inside Jack twisted and ached. 'Darlin'—'

'No, Jack.' Her voice hardened, ponytail swishing as she shook her head. 'Don't go getting any foolish ideas. You strode in here on Thursday determined and saying all the right things. You said you'll fight for us. Don't you dare take that back. We've lost too much time already because of this … this … person. I'm not giving into his demands, and neither are you.'

Jack resisted a wince as he straightened. Jill pawed at his knee, demanding more ears-rub, but he ignored her. He didn't want to retract what he'd said as he'd meant every word. 'Meg—'

'No!' She moved towards him, fire in her eyes. 'You promised, Jack. No more regrets. We're in this together. You and me. We love each other and it's about time we get what we want. Our dreams.' She clasped her hand around his forearm. 'Our future. This wanker has no business interfering in that.'

Jack's heart pounded at the determination in her eyes, the steel in her voice. Meg wouldn't let him go. He'd known that. And after everything he'd said when he'd come home on Thursday, he couldn't walk away from her now. These two weeks with her, most of which he hadn't even been home, would never be enough.

But he'd rather have only had two weeks than to find himself pinned beneath another tractor. Or have something happen to her.

'I don't want to put you at risk.'

Her eyes softened. 'I know you don't, but this isn't your fault. You know that.'

His jaw tensed. She was right, of course, but what could he do? He'd hoped they'd be safe. Been determined that he could overcome any hurdle and find happiness like Liam and Adam had. But he'd been in denial hoping the threat wouldn't rear its ugly head, and it'd only returned because he'd given into carnal desire during a moment of weakness. He'd been a fool and as Meg stood before him now, small, delicate, and precious, he knew the only sure-fire way to protect her was to walk away.

Meg lowered Lola onto the lounge and placed her hand on his chest. 'I know you're scared, Jack. I am too. But I'm also angry. I'm angry that someone would do this to us. Confused. Insulted. But I won't give up everything I've always wanted just because someone who's too cowardly to show his face tells me to. And you shouldn't either.'

Her hands brushed up to wrap around his neck. Keeping his gaze on hers, Jack tried to draw strength from Meg, to find the same confidence that radiated through her. It was there. He'd had it only this morning.

But his turmoil continued to rage. The scar on his leg burned. Panic rose in his throat. He'd almost lost his life to this man before. He wouldn't do so again.

He wouldn't lose Meg's life.

'Can we pretend we broke up?'

She rolled her eyes. 'No.'

Jack drew her close and breathed in her sweet, fruity scent. Meg's body curved against his, her arms lowering to his waist as she rested her head on his chest. Jack dropped his cheek onto her soft hair and closed his eyes.

He'd been determined. He'd been hopeful. He would marry this woman and build a future with her. They couldn't go back to being just friends and they couldn't secretly date. He couldn't run away and leave town. There was only one option. One thing they could do. The scariest option of all.

'I'm angry too,' he whispered. 'Angry that I let him get to me. That I sacrificed all those years with you. Time that was wasted.'

Her hands brushed up and down his back. 'We didn't waste them. We formed a friendship that I treasure, Jack. We got to know each other on the inside without the romance. Sometimes, that gets in the way.'

He'd never thought of it like that, but Meg was right. 'Built a foundation, did we, darlin'?'

'One that is unbreakable. One that we can stand on now and be strong. So, stand with me, Jack.' He lifted his head as she tilted hers and placed her chin on his chest. 'Fight with me. For me.'

The plea in her eyes crumbled his resolve. Jack's hands hardened against her back as he breathed out the anger. 'Darlin', I'd start a war for you.'

His lips found hers, igniting a fire inside him unlike any he'd ever known. Anger, frustration, and regret outweighed his fear unequivocally. Letting Meg go now was impossible. No matter how deeply he wished he could wrap her up and keep her safe, protect her to within an inch of his life, he couldn't.

He hadn't been strong before, but he would be strong now. Because strength wasn't sacrifice. Strength was courage. It was fighting for what you wanted. Liam and Ana had fought. His parents had fought. Both couples had won because they'd stood united. They'd been stronger together and hadn't let anything break them apart.

They were happy, and that's what Jack wanted. To be happy. To shake the surliness, the heartache, the regret, and the darkness he'd spent years suffocating in.

Drawing away from her kiss, he watched Meg's blue eyes flutter open. 'You and me. Together. That's all I want.'

Her mouth curved. 'Me too.'

'But we can't stick to a routine,' he said, protective instinct creeping up his spine. If they were going to do this, he wouldn't take any chances. 'We'll mix it up. Won't establish a pattern. So tonight, we'll go to my place because I want to cook you dinner.'

'Okay. I'll grab my things and you pack up the girls.' Reaching onto her toes, she kissed him. 'Thank you, Jack.'

'Always, Meg.'

She dashed up the hallway. 'Don't forget Jill's new bed!'

Jack glanced at the mini pink sofa in the corner, then looked at Jill. 'I'm not sure you really need that.'

Her head tilted and mouth closed as she sent him a look that clearly said, 'I'm pretty sure I do.'

Chapter Thirty

Meg spent the second week of school holidays among friends. Sitting outside The Bent Banana, she scribbled lyrics and hummed new tunes while Lola and Jill enjoyed the sunshine and peanut butter paw biscuits.

She and Jack had told Liam of their situation, and everyone had agreed that Meg couldn't be considered 'alone' when Liam, Isabella, and the other workers were inside. And she'd rather be there where she could spend time with her dogs and friends than locked up in the whirr and chaos of the Shadow Creek packing sheds.

Meg had coffee with Elanora on Monday as they discussed the trivia night, then on Wednesday, she and Ana had a late lunch after her friend returned from Mareeba with ultrasound photos. Meg's mummy hormones buzzed as she gazed upon the little bub's face and pressed her hand to her chest.

'Oh, Ana. She's beautiful. Or he. You must be so excited.'

'Yeah. Or terrified. I'm not sure which, but I am happy.' Ana beamed as Meg passed her back the phone. 'So, any plans for you and Jack bringing Sophie Maguire into this world any time soon?'

Longing filled Meg's heart as she covered her smile with a sip of Diet Coke. She'd confessed to Ana about wanting a daughter named Sophie during one of their girly chats last year.

'Who knows? But I doubt we'll rush into anything. Not until we sort out this stupid threat.'

'Fair enough. And I'm so sorry that's happened to you, Meg.' Ana reached across the table and grasped Meg's hand. 'I know what it's like to live in fear so if you ever need to talk, I'm here.'

'Thanks, Ana. But if anything, I'm angry. So bloody angry. Jack and I are finally together and now we have to deal with this crap.'

'I know. But I don't understand it. Everyone loves you.'

'I thought so,' she muttered, spinning the can on the table. 'I mean, I know not *everyone* likes me, but I didn't think someone would hate me enough to threaten me like this.'

'It makes no sense. But you're doing the right thing, Meg.' Ana squeezed her hand. 'You and Jack deserve to be together.'

The pressure in Meg's chest eased. 'Thank you, Ana.'

* * *

Jack clasped Meg's hand as they strode up the path towards Riley Manor. She looked adorable tonight with her blonde hair tumbling down the back of her blue dress decorated with white dots and yellow tulips. The skirt swished around her knees, nipped at her waist, and gave her a look so feminine he ached to toss her over his shoulder and cart her home. It wouldn't be hard when she weighed no more than a bunch of bananas. A thought that made his gut coil with dread.

Almost a week had gone by with no word from their

assailant, but Jack refused to take any chances. Meg might be strong-willed and toned, but she was a tiny woman, and that vulnerability fuelled his urge to protect her. His mind would ease when she returned to work and the safety of the school, but he trusted Liam to look out for her at The Bent Banana as if anyone understood his fear, it was his cousin. Brett and Cade were also keeping watch, and Ron Riley was making his own enquiries.

When Jack hadn't been at work, he'd been with Meg.

She opened the door and Jack glanced up as they stepped inside, always forgetting how grand Riley Manor was. The sweeping staircase, wide at the base, curved up towards the second floor on the right, while a sunken lounge opened to the left. Creamy walls set off the timber trims and plush carpet, all highlighted by crystal light fittings. A wooden table he suspected his brother had built stood by the staircase where fresh flowers sat in a porcelain vase.

'Hello!' Meg called.

'Hi, Meg!' Susan smiled as she strode out of the kitchen, her arms outstretched. 'Jack. How are you both?'

She hugged her daughter, then Jack.

'Good, Susan. Thank you for having us tonight.'

'It's my pleasure. Besides, now that you're dating my baby, I need to keep a closer eye on you.'

'Oh, Mum …'

'Shush. Now, go get your father from upstairs and I'll take Jack into the kitchen.'

'Please don't hurt him,' Meg said as Susan gently took his arm. Meg backed away with a twinkle in her eye, showing no guilt over leaving him as she dashed up the stairs in her white kitten heels.

Susan laughed. 'What? Does she think I'll scare you off?'

'I dunno.' Jack smiled in return as she led him into the kitchen. 'Adam was scared of you when you used to pester him about woodturning.'

'But he's a marvellous craftsman and he's doing so well now. You should help him more.'

'You know it's not my thing, Sue. I'm no good at woodturning.'

'But you're good at building things, and you helped Adam with those tables. Maybe you could find your own passion.'

She handed him a beer and he accepted it with thanks. 'Farming's my passion, Sue. I'll help Adam out when he needs a second set of hands, but that's his thing. And Michael's the builder.'

'You help him too, but I guess you're busy enough with the farm.'

'I am. I enjoy helping my brothers, but Shadow Creek is my life.'

Her eyes twinkled as she poured two glasses of Golden Drop mango wine. 'Do you still plan to expand?'

His throat tightened. 'One day. Diversifying Shadow Creek has been my focus these past few years as I like trying new things and the lychees have brought us good business.'

'What else would you like to grow?'

Jack shrugged, ignoring the unease niggling in his gut. 'My sister wants us to grow pineapples.'

'Oh, they'd do well up here.'

'What would?' Meg asked, and Jack's shoulders relaxed as she and Ron entered the kitchen.

'Pineapples. Jack wants to grow them.'

'Jack wants to grow lots of things.' Meg accepted the mango wine her mother handed her as Jack placed his beer down to shake Ron's hand.

'Nice to see you, Jack.'

'You, too.' He'd seen Ron a few times this week, once when he and Meg had visited after the phone call, and another time that Meg didn't need to know about.

Ron grabbed a beer while Susan resumed dinner preparations. Jack had always found them an odd-looking couple, Susan petite while Ron was tall and broad from his days of playing rugby league. Like everything else he did, Ron had once been the captain of the Elizadale football team and continued to live and breathe the sport. Even Jack's father and Uncle Cliff had played for Ron as no man could have said no. Like his daughter, Ron Riley considered himself a friend of most locals and there was a history between their families that had begun long before Jack had been born. It'd been no surprise when Meg and Lucy had become friends.

Ron uncapped his beer. 'Pineapples, hey?'

'Yeah. Lily's idea.'

'Then I'm sure you'll be clearing a field the moment she returns home.'

Jack smiled. It was true he had a soft spot where Lily was concerned and if she desperately wanted to grow pineapples, he'd let her. 'Yeah, but she'll have chosen a different fruit by then.'

'I thought you were interested in the exotic market. Your lychees do well and I hear breadfruit is on the rise.'

Jack smiled. 'Yes, but breadfruit wouldn't thrive on Shadow Creek. Wrong kind of climate.'

'Fair enough. Avocados do well, though.'

Jack paused with his beer halfway to his mouth while Meg blew out her breath.

'Dad ...'

Ron held up his hands. 'I'm just saying. The man wants to

expand the farm, Meg, and you know your grandparents are ready to sell. Ideally, they'd like you, Christina, or Chaz to have it.'

Meg's gaze flickered to Jack's, then back to her father. 'I know they do. But Jack and I have just started dating, Dad. Please don't pressure us.'

Jack's spine loosened. He understood her grandparents' motive as giving the farm to Meg would ease the burden from Victor and Carol's shoulders, and if it was as easy as bringing it under the Shadow Creek banner, then Jack would seize the opportunity to build his empire with both hands.

But someone was willing to kill them to stop it.

'Right.' Ron's gaze darted towards Jack before returning to his daughter. 'Sorry. Besides, Chaz might change his mind, hey?'

Meg laughed. 'I doubt that, Dad. Chaz wrote a whole album about how much he *doesn't* want to be a farmer.'

'One that won him a Golden Guitar,' Jack said, ironically finding those songs some of his favourite. *Fuck the farm, I'd rather be a plumber.*

'He might be on his way to winning another, if what Heather says is true,' Sue said from the stove. 'That new song "Not my Boots" is my new fav.'

'And I'm glad to see you're singing again too, Meg.' Ron smiled. 'Maybe you'll win your own Golden Guitar.'

Meg blushed. 'I don't need one. But I'm excited about the concert and I even have a new song.'

'Really?' Sue's eyebrows shot up, and Jack grinned.

'Meg hasn't been able to stop writing or singing,' he said, pride filling his chest. 'She's always waltzing around the house humming a new tune.'

'You should put out an album yourself,' Ron said, clapping

her on the shoulder. 'You'll have offers from all over after you launch this new song.'

'Yeah …' Meg's gaze met Jack's as she turned the wineglass in her hands. 'We'll see. Right now, I just want to get through show queen, the concert, and the show. It's all coming up so fast.'

* * *

Meg returned to work on Monday to prepare for the second semester while the children enjoyed a pupil free day. She worked on English lessons and recovered reading books from storage before joining Elanora and Ana in the staffroom for lunch.

'I'm thinking about bidding at your auction,' Elanora said, and Meg's eyebrows shot up.

'That's fantastic! Have you liked the Facebook event? Samantha's putting the men's bios on there, but I hope to get a couple more signed up before the day.' She had no one in mind to ask, but she wouldn't turn away anyone who offered.

'Yep. I've looked at the list.'

'Anyone you like?'

Elanora shrugged. 'I don't know. It doesn't have to be anything serious, right? All I want is to get that first date over with and spend time with someone who isn't Shane.'

'It doesn't have to be serious. We've listed that in the bios too, stating which men have said it's just for charity and which ones have expressed interest in finding a woman to date. Cade convinced Darren to do it, but I don't know why he's arranged for Lucy to buy him.' Meg rolled her eyes. 'Why isn't he open to dating?'

'I really thought he and Jessica were good together,' Elanora said.

'Yeah, but the spark went out. And you know Joe signed up, right?'

Meg glanced at the physical education teacher sitting at the other end of the table chatting with David Brennan. Joe Cooper had been in Elizadale for a few years now, was in his early thirties, and was seriously sexy with his athletic body and wide footy-player shoulders.

Elanora considered him as she sipped her water. 'Is he charity or open?'

'Charity.' Although again, Meg didn't know why. He was single and had hardly dated since arriving in town.

'Hmm … we'll see. I'd even go on a picnic with Darren or Cade, and I saw a few guys who work on Mum and Dad's farm are doing it.'

'A lot of the farm workers have signed up, and it spread like wildfire though Kelly Coffee. But either way, I'm glad you want to bid.'

It might be part of the conditions for fellow contestants and mentors to support each other's events, but Meg was pleased to see the light back in her friend's eyes.

Later that afternoon, Meg locked up her classroom and met Jack by the gate, where he waited for her with Jill and Lola on their sparkling pink leads. Grinning, Meg skipped down the path and kissed him.

'I could get used to this leaving work early thing,' he said, wrapping his arm around her waist. 'Even if you do call me overprotective.'

'You are.' She didn't see why she couldn't go home after work alone. 'But I like you picking me up and I'm glad you brought the girls. You even managed to catch Lola.'

'Didn't have to catch her. I didn't even plan to bring her. I said the W word and she went crazy dancing by the door. If I'd tried to leave without her, I reckon she'd have bitten my legs off.'

Meg laughed as she took Lola's lead. 'Is she wearing you down, Jack?'

His mouth thinned as he frowned at her precious little dog. 'She thinks she is. Thinks that she can rule the roost on the cute factor alone. But I'm still not feeding her part of my dinner.'

Meg smiled to herself as they strolled towards her car. At least he'd called Lola cute and while he might not admit it, he had softened. He allowed Jill to sit with them on the lounge and he'd absently rub Lola's head whenever she was secure in Meg's arms. Otherwise, her little munchkin still didn't go near him.

She clipped Lola into her car seat and rubbed her fluffy ears. 'You need to be nicer to Jack, Lola. Just because he doesn't feed you at the table doesn't mean you don't obey him.'

Lola's head flicked to Jack, then back to Meg. Clearly, she didn't agree.

Chapter Thirty-One

Thoroughly stretched out and relaxed after yoga on Thursday evening, Meg waved goodbye to her friends and slipped into her car to drive to Jack's house. Even though they'd heard nothing more from their tormentor, they continued to mix up their routine, so Jack had taken the girls to his place and had promised to have dinner ready.

Meg turned up the stereo, singing along to Carrie Underwood as she drove beneath the Shadow Creek sign and into the darkness of the bush. She'd enjoyed yoga this past year and tonight, Grace had announced she'd begin an advanced class, exciting both her and Natalia. Meg wasn't sure what it would entail, but she was keen to test her stronger body and longed to do a headstand. Natalia had demonstrated one once, looking the pinnacle of strength, and Meg had wanted to try it herself. But apparently, she needed to work on her dolphin pose before advancing to the headstand. Meg also wanted to try hand balances, but currently lacked the upper body strength. Natalia had been worth slapping when she'd lifted into a smooth crane pose.

But Meg shouldn't get too far ahead of herself as with any

luck, she too would soon be avoiding prone and inverted positions like Ana and Natalia when—

The car swerved, and Meg's grip tightened around the wheel. 'Shit!'

She regained control and pressed the brakes, her heart thumping as she slowed to a stop. Had she blown a tyre?

Great. Just what she needed. Unclipping her seatbelt, Meg climbed out of the car, leaving the door open for the light. Indeed, the back tyre lay flat on the dirt road. Meg planted her hands on her hips. 'Fantastic.'

She knew how to change a tyre. Her father had shown her when she'd got her licence ten years ago. But she'd never had to *do* it and right now, she wouldn't have a clue where to start.

Meg reached into the car, grabbed her phone, and called Jack. 'Hey. I just blew a tyre.'

'While you were driving? Are you okay? Where are you?'

'Yeah, all good. I'm a few minutes into Shadow Creek by the guava orchard.'

'Do you have a spare?'

'Yeah, but I don't have tools on me and it's dark and—'

'Darlin', I wasn't suggesting you do it,' he said with a laugh. 'I'm on my way.'

Switching the phone to her other ear, Meg sank onto the edge of the driver's seat, her belly fluttering as she kicked a loose pebble with her toe. 'I can change a tyre, you know.'

'I'm sure you can. But like you said, you don't have the tools.'

'Thanks, Jack. I'll just—' A crack sounded in the bush and Meg glanced up.

'What, darlin'?'

She stared into the scrub that separated the road from the guava trees, leaves rustling in the wind. Hairs prickled at the back of her neck. Goosebumps dotted her skin. 'Nothing. I was just …'

'Meg?'

She swallowed nervously and swung her legs into the car. 'It's just eerie out here, is all.'

'Shit,' he breathed, his tone darkening. 'Are you in the car?'

She shut the door and reached up to switch the light on. 'I am now.'

'Lock the doors,' he said, the rumble of the Raptor sounding through the phone. 'Stay in the car.'

'Jack—'

'I mean it, Meg. Get down and don't move.'

Ice ran through her veins. 'You don't think it blew spontaneously.'

'No. I don't.'

Heart hammering, Meg sank lower in her seat. He was right. Tyres rarely just blew, and she'd driven this road hundreds of times. The Maguires graded it regularly, and she doubted she'd caught an animal bone. The chances of this being an accident? Unlikely.

'Okay. I'm down and I'm not going anywhere.'

'I'm coming, darlin'. Stay on the line.'

She concentrated on her breathing. *In through the nose, out through the mouth. In … and out.*

A tree rustled and she jumped, gasping.

'Meg?'

She couldn't see past her reflection in the window with the light on. Hand shaking, she switched it off. It was too quiet.

'I'm okay. Just nature doing its thing. Making me nervous.' Someone, undoubtedly, was out there. She could feel it. Sense it. 'You're almost here, right?'

'Yes. Stay calm, darlin'.'

Was it her imagination or did she hear footsteps? Meg turned in her seat, her breath loud in her ears. She couldn't see the lights of town. If someone was out there …

She sank lower. This wasn't a coincidence. The voice that threatened her reverberated through her mind. *Or else …*

Meg rechecked the doors were locked and held her phone tight. She shivered. 'I'm scared, Jack.'

'Don't be, darlin'. I'm coming.'

His voice was soothing, calm, and she clung to it. Jack. Her love. The one person she could depend on. He wouldn't be far and would come as quickly as he could. Yet the seconds slowly ticked by into minutes. She longed to turn the music up as Carrie had always been of comfort to her, but Meg didn't want to distract herself from the sounds outside.

'Why is this happening, Jack?' she whispered. 'What will this person do to us? What does he plan to do to me?'

Was this a trap? Was he luring Jack to her? Would he kill them together? Better off dying together than losing him and being alone.

Meg squeezed her eyes shut and shook that thought away. No. That was ridiculous.

But this assailant would have known she'd have her phone. That she'd call Jack. That she wouldn't sit alone on this road and change her tyre just so that he could whack her over the head with a tyre iron.

'I don't know, darlin'. Just hold on. I'm almost there.'

Peeking up through the windscreen, she caught a flash of approaching headlights and breathed a sigh of relief. Yet at the same time, dread shivered up her spine. 'You don't think he's waiting for you? Will hurt you? Both of us?'

Jack's breath hissed through the phone. 'Let him try, Meg. Let him fucking try.'

She straightened, strength returning to her spine as the Raptor raced towards her.

'But we're not taking any chances, darlin'. Grab your things and get ready. I'll pull up and you jump straight into the back seat.'

'Okay.' Tossing her handbag over her shoulder, her headlights switched off as she took the keys from the ignition and unlocked the door. She didn't know who was waiting for them, or if they were, but he was right. They couldn't take any chances.

'Ready?' Jack asked in her ear.

'Ready.'

He slowed to a stop. Meg leapt out of her car and up into the back of his. Her hand fell to his shoulder as he reached back to grasp her fingers.

'I've got you, darlin'.'

'Thank you.' She sank back and clipped her seatbelt on as he took off again. 'You must think I'm so silly to—'

A bang echoed through the air. Meg gasped, head whipping to glance over her shoulder. 'Was that …'

'Gunshot.' Jack floored the engine. 'You weren't silly, darlin'. Call Brett now.'

* * *

Jack parked outside the shack, his body tight with barely controlled rage. Helping Meg out of the back seat, he held her in front of him as they hurried to the door. He doubted anyone was there ready to take another shot, but if they were, they wouldn't get Meg.

Jack bolted the deadlock, ignoring Jill as Meg scooped Lola into her arms and clutched the fluffball to her chest.

'Let's wait in the kitchen.' He placed his hand on the small of her back to guide her. 'Dinner will keep, unless you're hungry?'

She shook her head. Despite calmly relaying everything to Brett, her cheeks had drained of colour and her eyes barely blinked.

'All right. Sit on the floor, darlin'. I'll be right back.'

'Where are you going?'

'Locking up the house.'

Meg leaned against the pantry and sank to the floor. Jack secured the house before placing the salads he'd left out into the fridge and joining her. She stared into space with Lola tucked beneath her chin.

'I can't believe it ...' she breathed.

Jack wrapped his arm around her and pulled her close. 'We're all right.'

Physically maybe, but nothing was all right about the emotions surging through him. This bullshit was absurd. All he wanted was to love her, yet he was putting her in harm's way. Things had been easier when they'd just been friends.

Hadn't they?

Closing his eyes, Jack breathed her in, revelling in her fruity scent and the softness of her warm skin. Nothing about being just friends with Meg had been easy, and he fucking loved how he could hold her close and delight in their intimacy. Keeping his hands off her had been bloody torture. He'd hated not touching her, never having kissed her, and watching her date other men. He'd spent all those years miserable and being the butt of everyone's jokes. Jack had tolerated it for her sake, shrugged it off to protect her, yet it had killed him a little more each day.

Now, he was happy for the first time in years. Fucking

pissed off at this bastard, but the future was theirs for the taking. They would get everything they'd always wanted.

But that was the last time she went anywhere alone. From now on, she would remain guarded. He didn't care if he suffocated her or he gave up work. She was his every happiness and he would hide them away from the world if that meant they both kept breathing.

'Why didn't he shoot me? I was all alone outside looking at the tyre. Why am I still here?'

Jack's teeth clenched. 'I'm not complaining.'

'Do you think he'll come here?'

'No. He doesn't want to be discovered.'

'We didn't imagine that gunshot. And I know you didn't imagine the ones that rolled the tractor. So, what will stop him from shooting us while we're walking to our cars? Through the window of our houses?' Her head lifted. 'What are we going to do?'

Every muscle in his body tightened at the terror in her sapphire eyes. Jack wished he had words of comfort to offer her as she trembled in his arms, but he wasn't a great conversationalist at the best of times.

He pressed a kiss to her forehead. 'I don't know, darlin'. Let's just wait for the police.'

She snuggled in closer and drew her knees into her chest. Lola wriggled, but Meg clutched to the Pomeranian tight and Jack wrapped them both in his arms. Jill rested her head on his knee and they sat in silence.

Chapter Thirty-Two

It seemed like years but was only minutes until an engine approached. Meg's head snapped up, but her spine softened at the quick flash of red and blue lights on the wall. Jill scurried back as Jack stood and helped Meg to her feet.

'It's me!' Cade called as Jack strode across the living room to let him in. 'You guys okay?'

'Just shaken up,' Meg replied, squishing Lola to her chest.

Jack nodded. 'And pissed.'

'Understandable.' Cade gestured them onto the lounge. 'Dad and Jim stopped to look at your car, but they'll be here soon. How about you tell me what happened?'

Sitting beside Jack, Meg took comfort in stroking Lola's soft fur as she filled Cade in. He nodded along, taking notes until Brett and Jim arrived.

'We think he was about fifty metres away,' Brett said, crossing his arms over his chest and assuming the wide stance of formidable copper. 'The shot he fired was at a tree and he brought down the whole branch. Maybe he fired in anger, I don't know. But he wasn't firing at you.'

'We'll double check for casings in the daylight,' Jim added.

'We found nails dug into the road though. Quick examination of Meg's tyre shows she caught two and the tyre deflated quickly.'

'I almost lost control.'

'You were lucky,' Jim said. 'Your front passenger side caught one too, but it's a slower leak. It was flat by the time we got there.'

'I'll get Darren to tow it in and we'll have a better look at it,' Cade said.

'We cleared the nails, but we should let your family know,' Brett told Jack.

'I'll call Dad and he can do the ring around. We'll double check the road in the morning to make sure you didn't miss any.'

Brett nodded. 'Now, as for the shooter …'

'Do we have any leads?' Jack asked. 'Guns aren't very common around here, are they? I know some people have them on the farms—'

'And we have the gun club,' Cade said. 'Many farmers are part of that, but we have a few townies too.'

'I don't even know who's in it,' Jack muttered.

Sitting forward, Meg cleared her throat. 'Well, many are farmers. We've got the Mansfields, Charlie and Edward White are members, so are Bernie, Paul, and Harry. Joel Newman shoots ever since he married into the Taylor family, as do a few guys on Red Back Station. And my grandfather. I hope we can rule him out.'

'We could chat to Victor,' Cade said, glancing at Brett. 'See if he can think of anyone who might have something against his granddaughter. Or him giving his farm to her and Jack.'

'Good idea,' Jack said, but all Meg could do was frown.

'If he knew that, wouldn't he have told me?'

Cade shook his head. 'He might not have made the connection.'

'But what if it isn't a farming connection?' Meg asked.

'We believe it's the most likely link.' Cade sat forward to rest his elbows on his knees. 'But any idea which farm would lose the most when you two get hitched?'

Meg shook her head and glanced at Jack. He shrugged, the same helplessness that filled her soul flashing through his eyes. None of this made any sense. All her grandfather had was land, and it wasn't even that much. Not like Shadow Creek, Tropic Sun, or White Peaks. And it wasn't like avocados were a profitable industry now that everyone with a spare acre seemed to grow them.

But while her grandfather's farm seemed like a cause for harming her, part of her felt it had more to do with her father's influence. Ron Riley had been a prominent leader in Elizadale since his early twenties, when his father had died suddenly, and he'd inherited the family trust. He hadn't asked for it, but locals respected him, and he loved their town. He fought for their needs with the Mareeba Shire Council, generated ideas, and listened to the wishes of the people. Her father was their elected representative because he was easy-going, approachable, and he cared. She'd drawn her passion for Elizadale from him. This town was their legacy, love for it ran through their veins, and Meg would carry that dedication into the future. She might not run to be Elizadale's local representative, but she would cherish her town and her history until the day she died and passed that love on to her children.

Children who would be Maguires and inherit the massive spread of Shadow Creek. Meg wasn't naïve as the apparent motives made some sense. Her family had wealth, power, prestige, and influence.

But who had a problem with that?

'I have cousins on White Peaks and Tropic Sun,' Meg reminded them. Her Aunt Vicki's daughters, who were Rileys by blood, were married to Charlie White and Jason Taylor. 'Edward White's always been a recluse, but John and Millie Taylor are friends with Henry and Cliff, and Jason and Jack work together as advocates for tractor safety.'

'Jason would never have tried to kill me with one,' Jack agreed.

'And the Kellys certainly wouldn't hurt the Maguires either,' Meg said. 'Bernie, Liz, Henry, and Cliff are lifelong best friends.'

Silence fell, Meg's words ringing true as they all stared at each other.

Then Jack cleared his throat. 'Bernie and Liz wouldn't. But honestly, I've never understood why Paul hates us so much.'

Meg gasped. 'No …'

'I mean, I get the whole Adam and Jordan thing, but that's over.'

Heart pounding, Meg shook her head. 'He wouldn't.'

'Paul *did* ask you out,' Cade reminded her. 'And you said it yourself. You don't know his reasons.'

'But it wasn't like that! Paul isn't angry, he's in pain! Hurting. He doesn't want to kill me or Jack.'

Her gaze shot to Jack's as he rubbed her knee. 'Think about it, Meg. Paul never told you why he wanted to date you.'

'We didn't date! Yes, he had his reasons, but it had nothing to do with me. In fact, he said if I went out with him, it'd make you jealous enough to want me! He wanted us together, and I doubt it was to kill us!'

Jack frowned. 'He wanted us together?'

'Yes! As for him … I think he's lonely. He probably misses

his brother, or maybe he wants a girlfriend. I don't know. But he made it clear he wasn't interested in me.'

Jack paused, then glanced at Cade. 'You'll look into it?'

Cade nodded.

Meg blew out her breath. She couldn't believe this. 'Fine, but don't make out that we *actually* suspect him. Please?'

'All I'll do is check his alibi. Same as everyone else.'

'No one knows that someone's threatened you,' Brett said, 'so we can stay under the radar. We'll check out everyone we know who has a gun licence, although unlicenced weapons remain a problem despite the laws.'

Meg nodded as she glanced at Lola's little face. That's what scared her the most. Considering Australia's strict gun laws, they weren't something she ever thought about. Getting shot at was virtually unheard of, unless you were caught up with drug groups or a psycho.

'In the meantime,' Cade said, 'please stay safe. Stick together and keep the doors locked. We'll do what we can to catch this guy, but we don't have many leads. And I don't want to see either of you hurt. You're my friends.'

Wrapping up the conversation, they all stood. Cade hugged her tight, then the police left. After bolting the door, Jack turned to Meg and pulled her close.

She clung to him. 'I can't live like this. It's horrible. I want to be strong, but I can't bear the thought of being alone. I want to say "fuck you" to this person and walk down the street, but I know I won't make it a step outside the door.' Taking a deep breath, she tried to slow her racing heart. It didn't work. 'I'm scared, Jack.'

He pressed a kiss to her hair. 'We should break up,' he muttered. Meg stiffened, but before she could retort, his arms tightened around her. '*Should.* It's the smarter thing to do.'

Her fingers curled around his shirt. 'Or we could run away.'

'To Nashville,' he said, rocking her gently. 'You can sing and I'll farm something.'

Meg managed a small smile. 'What do they farm in Tennessee?'

Jack chuckled. 'Whiskey?'

Choking out a laugh, Meg lifted her head, the tension easing in her spine. 'I think you mean corn.'

He lifted his hands and tilted her head back. 'I'd learn to grow corn for you, darlin'. I'd do anything as long as you're safe.'

'Me too,' she breathed. 'But we're not running away.'

No matter how much she might want to, neither of them could live like that. They might have each other, but family meant everything to them.

Jack's jaw clenched. 'No. We will fight together, Meg. You and I. We're in this.'

Everything inside her loosened. 'I'm so proud to hear you say that.'

'And I'm glad you gave me the strength to believe in it.' His mouth brushed hers. 'Let's just hope that this bastard fucked up tonight so we can catch him.'

* * *

Jack joined Adam and Cade at first light in the guava orchard. After spending an hour soothing Meg to sleep, Jack's fury had continued to rage overnight and hadn't lessened when he'd left Meg in the safe hands of his parents this morning. His father would drive her to work, and Darren would arrive soon to tow her car to the workshop so that the police could take detailed photos of the nail trap. Jack hadn't wanted to miss checking out the vehicle or inspecting the area, so he followed Cade and his brother into the first row of shady guava trees.

'He was kneeling,' Adam said, pointing to the imprints in the dirt beneath the tree. 'Waiting for you.'

Jack stood a metre in front of the print, then knelt himself. The position brought Meg's car into perfect view while remaining beneath the cover of the bushy guavas. In the dark, he'd have been invisible. 'He had a good position.'

'Indeed,' Cade said.

Bile rose in Jack's throat as he imagined Meg outside her car, bending to check the tyre and unknowingly offering her body as a target. He stood. 'Why didn't he take the shot?'

Cade slipped his hands into his pockets. 'Maybe he wanted the two of you together? Have you as a witness? Or her? Or maybe the fact she was on the phone saved her. Hard to tell.'

'Here are tyre marks,' Adam called, and Jack and Cade moved through the next two rows of trees. 'Motorcycle. Thin, so a dirt bike.'

'Might need to ask people on Station Drive if they saw anyone riding—'

'Doubt it.' Adam shook his head and pointed. 'He went south. Probably rounded town back to the highway. The Mansfields live down there.'

'Meg dated Scott Mansfield …' Jack reminded them.

'And his father's a cruel bastard,' Adam muttered.

'With a record.' Cade crossed his arms over his chest. 'I'll talk to them, but …'

'Scott wouldn't have hurt me all those years ago,' Jack said, strangely sure of that. 'But as much as Meg defended Kelly, we can't wipe out a suspect just because we don't think them capable. We don't think anyone is capable.'

'I'll talk to Kevin Mansfield,' Cade said grimly. 'Don't like the idea as I can't stand the old bastard, but if he can hurt animals like he does, don't see why he can't hurt a human.' He'd charged the Mansfields with animal cruelty last year in a quite mysterious scandal. 'I'll also get a list of members from the gun club and chat with as many as possible.' Cade clapped his hand on Jack's shoulder. 'We'll get to the bottom of this.'

Jack's jaw tensed. 'Thanks, mate.'

Chapter Thirty-Three

He'd fucked up. He knew that, so wasn't surprised when he spotted the bloody police cruiser coming up his dusty driveway on Friday afternoon.

He shouldn't have discharged the weapon, but frustration at being thwarted had boiled over. He'd wanted Maguire there. He'd wanted to take them by surprise. Have the boy hero come to rescue his useless girlfriend and watch as she acted helpless. Maguire would be all macho, begin to change the tyre, then *bam*! He'd shoot him. Or her. He hadn't been sure who would go first, but someone would have experienced the grief of finding their bloodied bodies on the road that morning.

Except Maguire had never got out of the car. Fucking suspicious bastard.

The cruiser pulled up, and father and son alighted. He stood and offered them a smile, all of them exchanging pleasantries as though the Wilsons dropped by often.

He resisted a snort. As if. They were no friends of his.

'What brings you by?'

'There was a bit of trouble last night,' Brett said

conversationally. 'Were wondering where you might have been between eight and nine pm.'

'Why?'

'Answer the question.'

He'd love to give them the runaround, ask why they were interested, if he was a suspect, and act insulted. But the less he said, the more he co-operated, the better. He'd been in enough trouble with the police to know how to handle them.

'Here at home. With the wife. Where else would I be at that time of night? I have a farm to run and am up at sparrowfart.'

'Is your wife home?' Cade asked.

His heart lurched. 'In the kitchen.'

'Mind if I say hi?'

Question her more like, but what choice did he have? He nodded. The senior constable left, and he levelled his gaze with Brett.

'What was the trouble?'

'Shots were fired. No one was hurt, but we're following up with everyone who's licensed to carry firearms.'

'You have a whole gun club here.'

'And we'll talk to as many members as possible. What are you carrying these days?'

'I have a rifle and a shotgun. Both berettas. They do what I need them to do.'

The door opened behind them, and Cade exited. He nodded, and Brett nodded back.

'All right. Thanks for your time.'

He didn't reply. Bloody cops. He watched the pigs leave, then went inside to where his wife was preparing lunch.

'What'd you tell him?'

She turned. 'What do you think? I said you were home with

me. It's none of their business that you were at the pub. Last thing I need is for you to be done for another DUI.'

Snickering behind her, he snatched up a piece of beef and ripped off a bite with his teeth. But even though he might have got away with it this time, he needed a new tactic. He couldn't risk using his gun again now that the cops had come sniffing. And even though he'd always known Maguire and Riley were stupid, this was taking it to a whole new level.

What were they thinking? He'd warned them. He'd almost killed them and yet, they *still* didn't take him seriously. That just pissed him off. If they wanted to risk their lives, so be it. He didn't care. He just needed to remain in the shadows and not get caught. Like hell would he go to prison.

Chewing his beef, he considered Meg Riley. She was small. Tiny. Weak despite that crazy yoga shit she and the other bitches liked to do. She had a narrow waist, slender neck, and probably weighed no more than a sack of grain.

He was a big man. Strong. He didn't need a gun to take her out.

Chapter Thirty-Four

Meg forced a smile to her face and joy into her voice as she taught mathematics and launched her class's new science project. But despite her best efforts, her mind kept slipping back to last night and the danger that awaited her outside the sanctuary of her cheerful classroom. Her hands shook as she wrote on the whiteboard, and she made two embarrassing mistakes in subtraction. After a comforting hug from Ana at lunch and her friend's reassuring words, Meg hoped an afternoon of craft might ease her worries. Until a thud sounded on the window.

She squealed, colourful pop sticks flying into the air as her hands shot to her mouth. Bree and Holly also gasped, while Bryan laughed and pointed at the window.

'It was a bird!'

Meg watched as the magpie flapped onto the windowsill, ruffled his feathers, then took flight. Pressing her hand to her racing heart, she tried to catch her breath.

'Are you okay, Miss Riley?'

Lisa glanced up at her with round blue eyes, and Meg

placed her hand on her little cousin's shoulder. She didn't want to worry the children.

'Yes, darling.' Meg forced a smile. 'The bird just startled me, is all.'

'It scared me too!' Holly cried.

Bree nodded. 'I think he's okay though.'

'Yes, he is.' Meg knelt on to the floor and reached for the pop sticks. 'Would you girls like to help me? Then we'll get started on our clay pots for the show.'

She made it through the rest of the afternoon, but as she and Ana locked up their classrooms, the back of her neck prickled and Meg suppressed a shiver.

'I'll see you at the Royal shortly,' Ana said as they strode towards the lunch shelter. 'I'm looking forward to—oh, hi, Jack!'

Meg glanced up to find Jack striding towards them, dirty and sexy as hell in his farm clothes. And just like that, most of her tension eased.

'Hey, Ana.' He wrapped his arm around Meg. 'How are you, darlin'?'

'Better now.'

'Oh, you two are so cute. I'll catch you later!'

They waved Ana off, then headed to Riley Road where he'd parked the Raptor.

'Thank you for picking me up. I've been shaky all day.'

'No worries.' He kissed her before opening her door, helping her into the car, and rounding to his side. 'Cade wants us to come down to the station.'

She raised her eyebrows as he started the ute. 'Any leads?'

'He didn't say.'

Jack did a U-turn and headed for the highway. The police station was located almost in the centre of the town strip, a block down from the Royal Hotel. They stepped inside and Cade ushered them into his office.

'Everyone seems to have an alibi for last night, which isn't surprising. Even the culprit could have come up with a good lie.'

Meg's heart sank. 'Who have you struck off?'

'Nick Smithfield, for sure. He was working. And Joel Newman was drinking at Smithy's with Jason Taylor and some other friends. They were there all night, Luke verified that.'

'Wouldn't have suspected them anyway,' Jack said. 'They're all top blokes.'

'True. And the Kellys … well, Bernie was in a meeting with his head roaster until dinner, so he had no time. And Paul Kelly was having dinner with Elanora at the Royal.'

'El left yoga at the same time I did.'

'Georgina vouched for them. But other members of the gun club stated they were at home and while that might be true and their partners have said no different, it doesn't create a solid alibi.'

Meg swallowed. 'So, it could still be anyone?'

'The Mansfields, Whites, various farmers who have been in the area for years. Plus, we're not sure where Harrison Kelly is.'

'Did you speak with Victor O'Shea?' Jack asked.

'Yes, Ron and I spoke to him. Vic's just as shocked at the notion as he was five years ago and can't identify any potential enemies. I'm sorry, guys.' Cade smiled softly. 'Will I see you two in better circumstances at the pub later?'

Sighing, Meg nodded. Sure, someone had tried to kill them last night, but why not just go to the pub?

Slumping into the passenger seat, she rested her chin in her hand and stared out the window. 'Now I understand.'

'What, darlin'?'

'How you felt all these years. The utter hopelessness of our situation.'

Jack's hand fell to her thigh. 'It's not hopeless, Meg.'

'But I get it.' She straightened and glanced his way. 'The anger and betrayal you must have felt. I hate it. How dare someone try to control our lives? Our happiness?'

He squeezed her knee. 'I know.'

'What right do they have to manipulate and control other people?'

'They don't. And that's what you helped me realise, darlin'.' His dark eyes left the road and met hers. 'We can't give in. We can't let him win by bringing us down. Because I love you and we're in this together.'

His words warmed her chest, cooling a fraction of her anger as she took his hand from her knee and squeezed. 'I love you too, Jack.'

He had faith, and she couldn't lose hers now. She needed to remain positive. Stay strong. So, when they returned to his house, she showered and pulled on her favourite floral pink maxi dress.

When they arrived at the Royal, they strode in hand in hand.

* * *

She was ordering drinks when Paul Kelly leaned on the bar beside her. Meg jumped, but common sense shook her anxiety away. He may have had his fair share of punch-ups with Jack, but Paul was not a killer. Not if the polite concern in his grey eyes was any indication.

'Did I see your car being towed today?'

She nodded. 'Two punctured tyres.'

'That's unfortunate.'

'Yep. How was dinner with El last night?'

'Good. She seems to be getting better. I want to help her with the trivia thing because I heard show queen was raising money for cyclone relief. Thought it was the least I could do.'

Meg handed her card to Yasmine, the new barmaid. 'I thought it would be better to do that this year.'

'I heard Maguire went to Innisfail to help a mate.'

'Yeah, they got the farm back in order. I went down for the night and the damage …' Meg shook her head. 'It was devastating.'

'I know a horse breeder down that way who lost some infrastructure. Horses are okay, but it'll take some time to do repairs.' The barmaid asked him if he wanted a drink and Paul ordered a beer. 'Anyway, I'm glad you sorted things out with Maguire, Meg. That you got what you wanted.'

'Me too.' She smiled softly, reassured that she was right about him. 'Did our dinner work out for you?'

He gave a slight shake of his head. 'I think that's a lost cause. I'll just …' He paused, then straightened from the bar, the shutters coming down over his eyes. 'I'm glad things worked out for you.'

A strange tightness filled Meg's chest as he turned and walked away. She might never discover Paul's secret or what his motive had been for asking her out, but he was hurting and despite her own troubles, the longing to help still lingered. And maybe …

'Paul, would you like to be part of our bachelor auction this weekend?'

He turned, frowning. 'Your show queen thing at High Ridge?'

'Yeah. Plenty of guys are doing it and I don't know if you're looking for a date or anything, but it could be fun. No pressure, everyone just shares a picnic after the auction, which you supply. And Lucy said there's an equestrian club staying at the retreat, so there'll be plenty of horsie girls who might like to have lunch with you.' She smiled. 'You could meet someone nice.'

Paul slipped his hands into his pockets, his feet shuffling as his gaze drifted past her shoulder. She waited patiently, not wanting to hurry him as it was a big decision to put yourself out there like that, for charity or not.

Then he shrugged and even managed a small smile. 'What do I have to do?'

'Wear something nice, put together a tasty lunch, and give me your email so I can have Samantha send you questions to answer for your profile.'

'All right.' Paul gave his details, then thanked her and left. Grabbing the drinks from the bar, Meg almost skipped back to the booth.

'All good?' Jack asked as she handed him his beer. He raised his eyebrows, but there was no hint of jealousy or frustration in his eyes.

'Yep. I just signed Paul up for the bachelor auction.'

Adam chuckled. 'That's going to be fun.'

'It will be.' If she could ease Paul's troubles even a little, Meg would be happy. Because whether she liked it or not, his ill-thought-out scheme had worked. She and Jack had stopped tiptoeing around each other and were fighting for their happy ending.

Paul probably deserved whatever he was looking for too.

* * *

High Ridge buzzed as Elizadale gathered once again to support their beloved community. Meg's heart filled, impressed by the generosity of the people in her town. Last night's trivia had drawn a great crowd, and many had showed up today to support another young woman's effort to raise money for cyclone victims.

Then again, Meg had lined up Elizadale's finest single men, and the ladies didn't plan to miss their chance to win themselves a date, especially the equestrian club staying at High Ridge.

Leaving Samantha and her friend to conduct the proceedings, Meg sat on the crowded open deck beside Lucy. The first part of the auction went swimmingly as people paid a reasonable price for an hour of ironing, crochet lessons, and weekly car washing for two months. Jack's offer of 'an afternoon of odd jobs' went to an old widow from church and Jason and Rebecca Taylor won Lucy's horse-riding lesson for their daughter, Lisa. Then the teenage girls bid for their dates with enthusiasm only the youth exploring first love could possess.

'I still can't believe you signed Paul up for this,' Lucy said, shaking her head as the adult bachelors gathered side stage.

'Why not? He's young, single, and quite attractive, Luce. Especially in that red shirt. And it's nice to see him take part in something.'

'If you say so,' Lucy muttered. 'I just hope those wannabe show ponies don't raise the bid too high for Cade. It's going to be war.'

Meg frowned as she studied the women in the front row. 'You mean the equestrian girls? Are they the two you can't stand?'

Lucy no longer competed in show jumping since turning

her focus to running High Ridge and training horses for her trail riding business. At one stage, she'd even wanted to breed her mare Esme, but she'd put those plans on hold this past year. She still attended the occasional hacking or dressage competition and helped Lily on the show circuit though, so Lucy knew some competitors quite well.

'Yep. I was keen to host the retreat for the club until I realised Sarah and Tiffany would be part of it. Tiffany's too prissy to even brush down her own horse and Sarah's been jealous of me since I beat her in the supreme hack at the Mareeba Show a few years ago. Honestly, I just want them to leave.'

Meg nodded as Samantha, completely in her element, announced the first bachelor, a young farmhand from Tropic Sun. Claire Taylor helped up his bid, but let him go to another young lady. A few men later, Claire won herself a picnic with Darren Hudson.

'So unfair. He has his mother's chocolate cake.' Lucy slumped in her seat. 'I shouldn't have agreed to win Cade. Mrs Hudson's chocolate cake is to die for.'

Meg smirked. 'I'm glad you're bidding at all, even if it is for a platonic date with Cade.' She paused. 'It *is* platonic, right?'

'Of course.'

'Right … and you're sure it couldn't become anything more?'

'Meg!' Lucy jerked, her eyebrows lifting. 'What … what are you … it's *Cade*.'

'So?'

'He's Liam's best friend. And Adam and Jack and Michael's. Therefore, another big brother to me. I can't *date* Cade.'

'Why not? Yeah, the guys would give you both hell, but

they'll get over it. They like him, and Cade's nice. Not to mention hot.'

'He's flammable.'

Meg grinned. 'So, what's the problem?'

Lucy crossed her arms again and glanced towards the stage where Joe Cooper was being auctioned. 'Why are you so keen for me to date?'

'I want you to be happy.'

'I am happy. And so, it seems, is Elanora.'

Elanora won the picnic with Joe, and Meg joined in the applause. Perhaps if she wanted to match make, she should advocate for Elanora and Joe rather than her best friend who was hellbent against dating.

'Next we have Mr Michael Maguire,' Samantha announced, and Michael took centre stage in a pair of cut-off chinos and a white shirt that defined his upper body. 'Michael is a builder by trade and helps pick bananas on his family's farm Shadow Creek. He enjoys evening walks, kayaking in the creek, and even though he's only doing this for charity, he does want to find that one special lady. Today, he has a picnic of sweet chilli pesto sliders, rainbow salad, and mini banana muffins.'

'Oh yum. Can I bid on my cousin?' Lucy whispered.

'No. He might say it's for charity, but I think Michael's looking for a girl he'd like to get to know.'

'Well, as long as it's not *that* one,' Lucy muttered as one of the equestrian girls raised the bid. 'Tiffany will only be after his house.'

'Lucky for him, Jessica Smithfield seems keen.'

'Hmm … do you think they'd start things up again?'

Meg shook her head. 'They "dated" when they were thirteen. There's no spark there.'

'You never know,' Lucy said as Tiffany backed out and Michael found himself off on a picnic with his first ever girlfriend. 'Oh, God. It's Paul's turn.'

'Paul Kelly is a local coffee grower,' Samantha announced. 'His family produces some of the finest beans in the north, as well as breeds some excellent horses. In his spare time, Paul enjoys riding, cooking, and hiking with his dog Buster. Today he'd like to take a lady on a picnic of pumpkin and ricotta quesadillas with a side of mango and avocado salad, apple crumble coffee cake, and homemade lemonade.'

Lucy groaned. 'These picnics are making me hungry.'

Meg's stomach rumbled on cue. 'Me too.'

'Cade better have packed me something good.'

'The man who can't cook? Sure he did. Maybe you'll need to knock Paul over for his quesadilla.'

'I wish,' she muttered, slumping in her seat.

The bidding for Paul started and fired up quickly, until it became a war between the two equestrian girls. Sarah won.

Meg crossed her arms. 'Well, I hope she isn't as bad as you say she is.'

'Yeah …' Lucy worried her lower lip. 'She'll be going home on Tuesday though, so doesn't matter. Ooh, my turn!'

The ladies perked to attention when Samantha announced Cade. Suddenly, Meg was grateful that he had Lucy in his corner.

'Ham and cheese sandwich?' Lucy muttered. 'Really? Why didn't I pack his damn picnic? That carrot cake better be from Vicki's bakery, that's all I'm saying.'

She let someone else commence the bid, then raised. There was another shout. Then another. Lucy bid again.

It kept going.

Cursing, Lucy raised her hand. Two ladies dropped out. Meg watched in stunned silence.

'Ahh … Luce, that's an awful lot of money.'

'He's paying.'

Tiffany raised the bid, and Lucy swore again before lifting her hand. There was a pause.

'Going once … going twice … Congratulations, Lucy Maguire! Enjoy your lunch with our lovely senior constable.'

Lucy blew out her breath. 'Bloody ridiculous for a ham and cheese sandwich.'

With Cade the last man for the day, Meg helped Samantha complete the payments and wrap up the event.

'Congratulations, Samantha, that was fantastic,' Linda Wilson said as she collected her hour of ironing certificate.

Meg smiled as everyone continued to congratulate the warm, bubbly young woman. She'd outdone herself as not only had she hosted a wonderful event, but the community had become involved in so many ways. Kids would be washing cars and weeding gardens out of the goodness of their hearts, young people would help the older generation with tasks they could no longer do on their own, and the wiser folk would give back by sharing their skills in crafts and other talents. Not to mention the love that might bloom between those couples who were open to this picnic being the first of many. Hope rose in Meg's heart as she watched Cade and Lucy stride out into the sunshine. If nothing else, maybe today would inspire Lucy to open her heart. Love had lifted Meg up inside and she revelled in it, so she wished everyone would find that special person.

She just hoped that when Lucy found it, she wouldn't have shadows casting a gloom over her happiness.

'I think that was a success, darlin',' Jack said as he drove them away from High Ridge. 'It reminded me of your show queen events. Samantha has community spirit almost as passionate as yours.'

'She did a great job and is well on her way to winning, I think. And yeah … she reminds me of me a little. I loved show queen. Staging my concerts was the highlight of my year.'

'I enjoyed watching you too.' Reaching across the console, Jack squeezed her hand. 'And just think, next weekend, you'll sing to a crowd of thousands.'

Shivers raced up Meg's spine, nudging aside her nerves as her toes curled in excitement. 'It's going to be amazing.'

'It will be.' Jack's smile could have lit that stage.

Chapter Thirty-Five

Ana dropped Meg home from work on Monday and after bolting the doors, she fed Jill and Lola a banana bone she'd baked yesterday, wrapped matching pineapple bandanas around their necks, then settled in the living room with her guitar. This was her big chance, and she wouldn't slack off. Since tomorrow was Anzac Day and she had the day off work, she and The Charlie Boys planned to spend the afternoon rehearsing. After attending the official commemorative ceremony to remember their war heroes, of course.

She strummed the opening notes to 'Home Again' and moved about the room, making notes on stage direction as she put her heart into the performance. Jill and Lola watched from the lounge as darkness settled around her and she stopped dancing to switch on the lights. This weekend was going to be fabulous. She couldn't wait, nor stop thinking about possibilities for more concerts in the future. If she could make the right connections, she could get into concerts that would suit her. Mackay had a great festival, and it wasn't far away. And Mareeba was always an option. One day, she and

Jack might even visit Gympie and finally get their night camping under the stars.

Heart swelling, Meg set her guitar aside to get dressed for the Monday night catchup with her friends, which they'd switched from afternoon drinks to dinner on account of the public holiday tomorrow. She fed the girls, then headed for the shower. A chill had settled in the air tonight, so Meg pulled on her white jeans and a strapless blue top she would pair with a cardigan. Her phone beeped as she slipped on her white heels and Jill raced past the bedroom. Jack's name flashed on the screen.

Running late. Problem with the lychees. Be there soon.

Meg started tying a reply, then Jill's barks shrilled through the house. Her phone cluttered to the dresser as Meg raced out of the bedroom and down the hall. The kelpie stood at the front window, her body rigid and eyes focused outside as she expressed her alarm.

Meg's neck prickled. 'What is it, girl?'

She crept towards the window, then stilled. Her heart rose into her throat. Lola stood on the front lawn sniffing the mailbox. 'Lola!'

Meg ran. Hands shaking, she pulled at the chain, flipped the deadlock, and yanked open the door. How had Lola got out? She didn't know about road safety! Meg shouted her name and ran outside. Lola looked up. 'Lola, stay! Don't—'

Jill's barking grew deeper. Fiercer. But before Meg could step off the verandah and rescue her little dog, arms snatched her backwards. She stiffened as a hand pressed over her mouth. The other arm held her tight against a large, hard body. She tried to scream, but no sound came out. Wriggling was useless. Blood pounded in her ears as he dragged her along the verandah. She lost her footing.

Barking filled her ears and hot breath seared her neck as he leaned in close. 'I warned you, you bitch.'

The vice around her loosened. He grabbed her hair and shoved her forward. Blinding pain shot through her skull.

Everything went black.

* * *

Jack drummed his fingers on the steering wheel, eager to get going, but he'd stupidly answered a phone call from Charlie White regarding the stable roster for the show. And he didn't drive while talking on the phone.

'Yeah, no worries, mate. I'll be in and out checking on Lucy's horses anyway.' Plus, he'd entered Dante into the show, so he had to do his bit to help.

'Thanks, Jack. Much appreciated. We especially need someone at the end of the day to help clean up.'

'Sure. Anything else?'

'Nah. You doing all right?'

'Yeah, been busy. I guess you've got a lot going on with the show.'

'We're putting our bull in and organising the cattle comps.' As they usually did since White Peaks was one of the largest cattle stations neighbouring Elizadale, second only to their neighbour, Red Back. 'Can't judge, of course, but it's always a good time of year.'

'Yeah. Anyway, mate. Better get going as I'm running late. But always happy to help.'

'Thanks, Jack. Chat later.'

Charlie hung up, and Jack messaged Meg. **On my way.**

Shoving the ute into gear, he headed to town. The drive into Elizadale wasn't long, but tonight, the road seemed to stretch forever as dust swirled in his high beams. Finally, he arrived at the intersection that led to High Ridge, town, or Adam's house. He turned left and after another Lee Kernaghan song faded to an end, he drove beneath the overhanging sign and pulled onto Station Drive.

He accelerated just as a ball of caramel ran into his headlights. Jack's heart lurched as he slammed on the brakes. Squealing tyres echoed above the engine. Lola stared at him from the middle of the road.

Chest heaving, Jack blinked. What the—? 'Fuck!' He leapt out of the ute. 'Lola!'

The fluffball skittered backwards. She barked.

'Lola, don't do this shit. Come here.' Heart pounding, he approached the little dog. What was she doing out? Where was Meg? How—

Fuck! Meg.

'Lola!'

She cowered. Unable to think, unable to breathe, Jack strove for calm. Something was wrong. He needed to get to Meg. But he couldn't leave the fluffball on the street. Meg would be going out of her mind if she'd found Lola missing.

He knelt and forced cheer into his voice. 'Come on, Lols. It's okay.' He patted his knees and extended his arms. Smiled. 'Come here.'

She stood. Frozen. Jack bit back a curse. 'I'll give you a bickie.'

She took a tiny step towards him. He inched closer. 'Chicken?'

Her head tilted. His teeth clenched. *For fuck sake!* 'I have apple.'

Lola's eyes lit up, and she ran towards him. Jack held his breath until his hands closed around the fluffball. 'Bloody hell, dog.'

He had no time for relief. Leaping into the car, he dropped Lola onto the passenger seat and gunned it the hundred metres to Meg's house. Jill stood silhouetted in the screen door and his panic skyrocketed. He pulled on the handbrake, left Lola, and ran. 'Meg!'

Jill's incessant barking made his breath catch as he skidded to a halt on the verandah. But as he reached for the door, his gaze drifted sideways, and he froze.

She lay face down on the concrete, her limbs at odd angles. Even in the darkness, he couldn't mistake the blood pooling around her.

'Meg!' Jack leapt across the verandah and fell to her side. 'No! No, no, no …'

His hand fell to her shoulder. Her eyes were closed, and a lump formed around the cut on her head, seeping blood through her golden locks and onto the concrete.

Jack's breath caught. Hands shook. The warm, sticky sensation of blood oozing through the knees of his jeans jolted him back into action.

Phone. He needed the phone.

He'd left it in the ute. Shit.

'Hold on, darlin'.'

He scrambled to his feet and dashed to the ute. Grabbing the phone, he tucked Lola under his arm and ran back. He tossed—placed—her inside, where Jill's barks had reduced to whimpers, and dialled Natalia. It wasn't protocol in an emergency, but when his sister-in-law was the doctor, he reserved rights to that privilege.

The phone rang as he crumbled back beside Meg. She had

a pulse. She was breathing. She'd lost so much blood. Natalia was taking too fucking long to answer.

'Jack!' Cheer filled her voice, the music and chatter from the pub cutting through the horror surrounding him. 'Are you—'

'Meg's hurt. Come now. Her place. She's unconscious and bleeding and—'

'On my way. Don't panic. Adam—' Jack didn't catch the words she directed away from the phone. 'Jack, put pressure on the wound and I'll be right there. Adam's calling the police.'

'Okay.' He dropped the phone without bothering to hang up. Instinct had him tearing off his shirt and balling up the material to press against Meg's head. Only then did reality catch up. His shoulders slouched as he stroked the blonde locks off her forehead. She was so beautiful. Her cheekbones, long lashes, her pale lips. Jack took a deep breath. Then another.

But nothing suppressed the pain rising inside him. This was his fault. He'd let her down. She was hurt. Dying?

His breath caught. Shit, it was a lot of blood. Too much.

'Dammit, Meg.' The metallic stench clogged his senses as he lowered his head to hers. 'I've got you. Don't you dare go anywhere. Hold on, darlin'.'

An engine roared and tyres screeched. Jack lifted his head at the hurried footsteps as Natalia arrived with Ana and Lucy on her heels.

'Did you move her?'

Jack shook his head as Natalia crouched beside him. She lifted his shirt as the verandah light switched on, casting more horror over the scene. But Jack didn't register the blood streaking from the verandah railing. He saw only Meg.

'It's a slow ooze,' Natalia said calmly, placing the shirt back as another engine rumbled to a stop. She touched Jack's shoulder. 'Step back, Jack. She'll be okay.'

Adam and Liam arrived beside him with a stretcher, but Jack didn't move. Natalia gave instructions, but Jack paid them no attention until Adam knelt beside him.

'Mate, Cade's on his way. He said to take a photo before we move her. Step back, hey? Then we'll take her to the surgery.'

It took a firm hand on Adam's part for Jack to stand. Numb, shaking, he moved away as Liam took photos, then helped get Meg onto the stretcher. Grace White arrived and jumped into her nursing role as she spoke medical with Natalia. Cade and Brett pulled up just as rubbernecks started assembling on the footpath at the sight of Elizadale's community ambulance.

'We're ready to move,' Grace said.

'We've got the scene, you guys go.' Cade reached for Jack's arm. 'You all right, mate?'

Jack swallowed. 'No.'

'Adam, go with Jack.'

He didn't know how, but Jack found himself in the back of the ambulance beside Meg. Adam and Liam had gone to fetch it, but now Grace was driving. Two corners later, they were at Elizadale Medical. Jack followed Natalia and Grace on autopilot as they wheeled Meg in. The women worked efficiently, and Adam arrived in time to help move Meg onto a bed.

Jack sank against the wall and shoved his fingers through his hair. He didn't care about the blood. He needed Meg to wake up.

Would she?

Pain ripped through his chest. *Fuck!*

'Jack.' Adam appeared before him and gripped Jack's shoulder. 'Nat and Grace have her, mate. She'll be all right. Come with me and we'll get you cleaned up.'

'I'm not going anywhere.'

'Just over to the sink. Wash the blood off, then you can sit beside her.'

Exhaling, Jack let Adam steer him towards the sink. He needed to get a grip. Shake off the shock and regain some control, because when he found this bastard ...

Brown soapy water swirled down the drain as Jack scrubbed his hands. 'I knew this would fucking happen.'

'I know. I'm sorry, mate.'

'She doesn't deserve this.'

'No one does,' Adam said as Jack wrenched the paper towel out of the dispenser. 'But Nat's got her. Meg will be okay.'

Jack threw the towel into the bin, then crossed the room, grabbed a chair, and plonked down beside Meg. His fists curled at the sight of the neck brace and the blood matted in her fair hair. She lay flat while Natalia prodded her skull. He didn't like the look on his sister-in-law's face.

Natalia turned to Grace. 'I'll do her neuro exam if you could call Mareeba ED.'

Jack's pulse skyrocketed. 'What's wrong?'

'Stay calm, Jack.' Natalia leaned over Meg and shone a light in her eyes. 'This is a serious injury, so I'm going to ensure she's stable and then we'll get her to Mareeba for a head CT. We need to check that there's no brain bleed. Pupils are equal and reactive.'

Jack shuddered. 'Do you think she has one?'

'Her neuro exam is good. I'll give her some time to wake up as I'd rather her conscious for transport, and I'm just waiting for Joanne to—'

'Joanne? Shit, Nat!' She was calling in the whole cavalry. 'Just tell me—'

Natalia leaned across Meg and gripped his shoulder. Hard. 'Don't panic. I need x-rays and I can't do them because I'm pregnant.'

'Oh. Right.'

The doors opened and Elizadale's long-time local doctor Joanne Brennan strode in, holding a T-shirt out to Jack. 'Liam got this for you. How's her exam, Nat?'

Damn, his friends were good. Standing, Jack moved out of the way and pulled the T-shirt over his head, watching as the women worked around his beloved. His chest ached. Eyes prickled. Why wasn't Meg waking up?

Joanne and Grace wheeled Meg away, leaving him alone with Natalia tapping away on the computer. Sinking back into his chair, he dropped his head into his hands. He'd left her alone. Yes, she should have been safe locked up inside, but—

Lola. Shit. How had Lola got out?

He squeezed his eyes shut. 'Fuck, darlin' …'

'Don't blame yourself, Jack,' Natalia said softly.

'Who else am I supposed to blame?'

'The person who did this. He's cold and calculating, Jack. No matter what you did, he was going to get to her.'

His teeth clenched. 'Is that supposed to make me feel better?'

'No. But you can't be everywhere at once.'

'Someone threatened her, Nat! I knew this would happen and I left her alone!'

'You didn't know it would happen tonight. And you didn't mean for her to get hurt. I know it's hard, Jack, but we can only do our best.'

Shaking his head, he stared at the ground. 'She shouldn't have been outside. What was she …'

Lola. Had she escaped when Meg had been hurt? Or had she been outside? Had Meg gone out to—

His hands clenched, fury rising inside him as the doors opened and Grace wheeled Meg back in.

'Joanne's reviewing the scans, but they look fine. No obvious skull or cervical fractures. Mareeba said to bring her down when you can, no problem.'

She and Natalia continued to speak, but Jack tuned them out. He took Meg's hand between his, heart hammering against his ribs. That bastard had used her dog to lure her outside. Meg wouldn't have thought twice.

Jack pressed his forehead to their clenched hands and closed his eyes. She had to wake up. Nothing else would rid him of his despair.

Natalia bid Joanne goodbye, then gathered what she needed to suture Meg's head wound.

'When do we go to Mareeba?' he asked.

'I'll stop this bleeding first. It's not too bad, but I want to give her some time to wake up.'

'How much time?'

'You let me worry about that. Just hold her hand.'

That didn't answer his question, but before he could ask again, a knock sounded on the door.

'Can I come in?' Cade asked.

Natalia snapped on her gloves. 'Did you find anything?'

'Not much,' he said, glancing at Meg from the foot of the bed. 'Took photos of the scene, but there's no way of knowing what happened. From how she was lying and the location of the wound, it seems she was pushed forward, meaning someone had grabbed her from behind.' He lifted his gaze to Natalia. 'Any evidence of bruising or something to suggest a tight hold?'

Jack stiffened. He hadn't even considered other injuries.

'Red marks on her forearm could suggest a grab. But whatever happened, I'd say it was quick as there's no other sign of injury.'

'We'll just have to wait until she wakes up, then. Let me know. I'll be at the station.' He placed his hand on Jack's shoulder. 'Ana's fetching you both clean clothes and Liam called her parents. They're outside and to see her when you're ready.'

Guilt swirled in Jack's gut as he stared at his blood-soaked jeans. Fuck, now he'd have to face Ron and admit he'd failed. 'Okay.'

'We'll get his bastard. You hear me?'

Jack met Cade's dark, hard gaze. He'd never seen Cade more determined. More fired up. Swallowing, Jack nodded.

Cade glanced at Meg. 'No one gets away with doing this to my friends. My people. I don't want bastards like this in my town.'

Jack cleared his aching throat. 'Neither do I.'

Chapter Thirty-Six

Meg's head pounded as she squeezed her eyes tighter against the sharp, burning pain. Her mouth was dry, she could barely swallow, and strange sensations filled her hands. One had something stuck to it, the other hardly seemed like it was there.

Grimacing with effort, she forced her eyelids apart, squinting against the fluorescent lights. Her hand was there, just clutched between Jack's and buried beneath his head. Wriggling her fingers, she winced as pins and needles shot up her arm.

Jack's head snapped up. 'Meg? You're awake? Nat, she's awake!'

His shout ricocheted through her head, and she groaned. 'Wh-what happened?'

Jack didn't have time to answer as Natalia appeared. She studied the machine attached to Meg's finger and the cuff around her arm tightened. Natalia said something about a head injury and bleeding, and explained everything she did, but Meg barely registered any of it. Disorientated, she longed for water and squinted as Natalia shone a light in her eyes.

'Follow my finger.'

Meg did so. She pushed against Natalia's hands as instructed, up, down, and out. Eventually, the doctor sank onto the edge of the bed.

'You'll be okay.'

Jack let out a deep, shuddering breath.

'Do you remember what happened?' Natalia asked.

Meg tried to shake her head, but it hurt too much. 'No. I was—' Her heart lurched. 'Lola!'

'Shh.' Jack's hand pressed on her shoulder and Meg realised she'd tried to sit up. 'She's okay. I found her.'

Meg crumpled into the mattress. 'Good. I saw her outside and—'

'You rushed out to get her.'

Her cheeks heated. 'Yeah.'

'It's okay, Meg,' Natalia said gently. 'It was instinct, but it seems like someone might have lured you outside. They attacked you. Jack found you on the verandah bleeding.'

Meg's gaze shot to his, her chest constricting as Jack shook his head, squeezed his fingers around hers, and buried his face into their clasped hands. Deep breaths rasped from his throat. His shoulders shook. Meg tried to reach for him but didn't have the energy to lift her other hand.

Natalia muttered something about updating her friends and left the room. After one long exhale, Jack's gaze returned to hers, his eyes glistening. 'Dammit, darlin', I've never been so scared in my life.'

Guilt clogged her throat as she lifted her hand from his to caress his stubbly face. 'I'm sorry.'

'Don't you dare be sorry. This isn't your fault. Nat's right, you acted on instinct. I should have been the one to—'

'It's not your fault either. Come on, Jack. Let's not do this.'

Pain lined the corners of his mouth. 'I almost killed your dog.'

Her stomach clenched. 'Is she okay?'

'She's fine.' He lifted himself out of the chair and perched on the edge of her bed. Gathering her strength, Meg wrapped her arms around him as he touched his forehead to hers.

'It's okay, Jack. I'm okay.' Apart from the grogginess. Must be the blood loss. 'But I don't remember what happened.'

'He lured Lola outside. Cade looked around and found the padlock on your side gate cut. He must have planned it, Meg. Got Lola, you went outside, and he grabbed you from behind. Your head hit the railing. Your x-rays were clear, but now that you're awake, we're taking you to Mareeba for a head CT.' He drew away. 'Nat's not too worried since your blood pressure is stable, but she wants to make sure your brain's not bleeding.'

'Okay.'

'And I am *so* sorry that I wasn't there to prevent this. I would have been there sooner if …' Jack stilled, his eyes steeling over.

'What is it?'

He slipped out of whatever thought he'd had and shook his head. 'Nothing. But we need to find this bastard. I can't do this again. I can't see you hurt. Finding you there … shit, darlin'. I can't—'

Her eyes welled at the same time his did. 'It's okay, Jack. We've got this. The police will catch him.'

'What if they don't? Fuck, I'm so bloody angry.' He tried to pull away, but Meg held him still. 'I failed you and all these "what if" scenarios keep flashing through my head. He could have killed you. I could have run over your fucking dog.'

Heart racing, she studied his jaw, his tormented eyes. She knew how he felt. Meg had been through it herself the day the helicopter carrying him to Townsville had disappeared into the sky. She'd never been more terrified. She'd imagined the worst. But while she might not understand why this was happening to them now, she knew one thing. 'Please don't give up on us, Jack.'

Pulling back, he ran his hands down his face. 'It's so fucking hard, Meg.'

'You can't protect me all the time.'

'I can try.'

'Stop it.' She grabbed his hand and squeezed. 'We're in this together. And I'm fine.'

'There are stitches in your head,' he growled.

Meg bit down on her lower lip. He wanted to pull away. Any sane person would. It was the easier choice and God, she almost wanted to let him. She didn't want to be hurt, see Jack hurt, or get either of them killed. But if they gave up, then this crazy bastard won. He'd saunter back into the shadows and continue to play his role in her sunshine town while she spent her days in misery.

She wouldn't stand for it.

'We will both be fine, Jack. Don't break my heart now.'

Turning back to face her, his hand hardened over her hip. 'I'll never break your heart, darlin'. I love you. Something chronic. And I'm not going anywhere. I'll get this bastard if it's the last thing I do.'

* * *

Determination and doubt warred inside Jack as he held Meg close in the back seat of Natalia's Rav-4. The drive wasn't long, and Adam probably drove a little over the limit, but Jack didn't care. Adam pulled up outside emergency at Mareeba Hospital and Jack and Natalia helped Meg from the car before his sister-in-law strode inside and made things happen quickly. Jack waited with his head in his hands and Adam beside him, his brother's hand on his back. Neither of them said a word until Meg and Natalia returned, the on-call doctor and likely Natalia herself, having cleared Meg's head CT.

Jack's shoulders slumped as he drew his beloved into his arms.

'She'll have a repeat scan in a fortnight,' Natalia said, 'and you'll need to lookout for any neurological symptoms as brain bleeds can still occur weeks after a head injury.'

'Which is the last thing I need,' Meg said as they strolled outside and waited for Adam to bring the car around. 'I'm still singing on Saturday.'

Jack squeezed her shoulders. 'Of course you are. Like hell are we letting this bastard stop you from achieving your dreams.'

Natalia nodded. 'Take it easy between now and then, and you should be fine.'

They drove home with The Charlie Boys playing softly and minimal talking. Meg had almost dozed off in Jack's arms by the time Adam pulled up outside her house. Natalia gave him strict instructions, and Jack would follow them to a tee as he took Meg inside.

'Straight into the shower, darlin'. Then I'll dry off that wound and put you straight to bed.'

'Okay.' She reached for Jill's head as Lola danced around their feet. 'Hey, girls.'

Before the little dog could escape, Jack scooped her up and

held her out to Meg. She smiled softly and kissed Lola's head. 'Glad you're okay.'

Throat tightening, Jack placed Lola on the lounge and guided Meg to the bathroom. Her colour hadn't returned, and her eyes drooped with fatigue, so he wanted her horizontal as soon as possible. But he didn't hurry as he helped her undress, sat her in the shower with her head out of the spray, and then knelt to wash out the blood tarnishing her long golden locks. Fury continued to pound through his veins, but tension loosened from his shoulders when the water finally ran clean. He loaded her loofah with strawberry shower gel, helped her wash, then turned off the shower and wrapped her in a fluffy towel, letting her dry while he fetched her pyjamas.

Lola waited outside the bathroom. His gut clenched as he scooped her up and lifted her little face to his. Her tiny nose twitched, and she blinked her big black eyes. 'Thank fuck I didn't run you over. You are bloody lucky. But don't you dare scare your mummy and me like that again.'

Her mouth fell open in a happy pant. Cursing, Jack kissed her fluffy head, tucked her under his arm, and pulled open Meg's dresser. Returning to the bathroom, he helped Meg into the nightgown while still clutching the dog, then led her to bed.

'Just sleep now, okay, darlin'?'

'Yep. But I forgot to message Mum. About the CT.'

'I'll do it.' He tucked Lola into her arms, drew up the blankets, then kissed her forehead. 'I'll be right back.'

Her eyes fluttered closed and straightening, Jack retrieved Meg's phone. Ron and Sue had seen Meg before and after she'd woken up, then they'd gone to talk to Cade. Jack sent them a quick message before returning to the bathroom, hopping back into the shower, and scrubbing himself with a vengeance. He dried himself, pulled on his own pyjamas, and switched off the lights. Jill stood at the bedroom door, her tail wagging slowly from side to side. She tilted her head and quirked her ears.

Jack's shoulders slumped. 'Come on, then.'

Jill raced into the room and climbed onto the end of the bed where Meg had let her sleep while he'd been away. She circled a few times, then curled up, watching him as he slipped between the sheets. He rubbed her head, then wrapped his arm around Meg. Lola peeked up at him and he rubbed her tiny ears. What did it matter if he shared a bed with the dog? Meg loved her, he loved Meg, and he'd rather have the fluffball warm and snug with them than be digging a hole for her in the backyard.

Fuck, he was lucky. He could have lost Meg. And why hadn't he? What was this bastard's agenda? Did he want to kill them? Or just hurt and scare them? He'd had the opportunity, so why did Meg lie warm and safe in his arms?

Jack didn't know. Pressing his face into Meg's neck, he closed his eyes and settled his hand beneath her chest, comforted by the faint beat of her resting heart. The what ifs tortured him. He slept, but not well, and woke with the dawn. But unlike other Australians who were commemorating the wars and servicemen with the Anzac Day dawn service, Jack lay in bed with his racing thoughts until Meg stirred in his arms. She groaned softly and rolled over, her eyes blinking open to meet his.

He forced a smile. 'Morning, darlin'. Sleep well?'

'Yeah.' She arched her back, stretching. 'Tired though. And hungry.'

He kissed her softly, then sat up. 'I'll let the girls out and make you breakfast.'

She looked ready to argue, then sank against the pillows. Jill was already up, but he had to prise Lola out of bed to take her outside. Placing her on the grass, Jack inspected the gate where Cade had found and removed the sawed padlock.

Resting his hands on his hips, Jack let out a breath. On the odd occasion, he had doubted himself these past years. He'd wondered if Brett and his father had been right. The chances of wear, tear, sticks, or rocks blowing the tractor tyre had far outweighed the possibility of someone shooting it out from beneath him, despite what he'd heard.

But there was little satisfaction in being right, and he couldn't stop fighting. He would protect Meg.

He just wished he knew who he was protecting her from.

Chapter Thirty-Seven

Meg studied her man as he placed a pile of banana pancakes on the table, her heart warming at his unconditional support. Despite having been through a terrible ordeal last night, his strength hadn't wavered, and she couldn't be prouder.

Getting through the rest of the week would be a challenge though. She enjoyed her pancakes, but happily let Jack refuse her help in cleaning up the kitchen. Already, she was keen for a nap. But Meg was determined to keep her strength up, so on Natalia's advice, she and Jack took a short stroll along the creek, then she did some light yoga. She wanted to go to rehearsal with The Charlie Boys, but the band suggested they postpone, so Meg spent the afternoon curled up in front of the TV with Jack as she introduced him to the majestic world of Downton Abbey.

Work would be interesting tomorrow. Her hair covered the stitches, so at least she wouldn't frighten the children, but it didn't seem to matter anyway as this was Elizadale and news spread like wildfire. Which probably wasn't such a terrible thing when little Tommy entered the classroom with a posy of marigolds.

'These are for you, Miss Riley. I'm sad that you were hurt.'

An ache filled Meg's chest as she accepted the flowers. 'Thank you, Tommy. That is very thoughtful of you. And don't be sad, okay?' She placed her hand on his tiny shoulder. 'We all get hurt sometimes, but I'm all right.'

The little boy nodded, reassured. 'Mummy said you were, but I wanted to bring you flowers because that's what Daddy said to do.'

'And they are beautiful flowers. I will put them here on my desk so we can see them all day.'

Fetching a small pencil holder, Meg did just that as the children continued to arrive. Bree gave her a massive hug, and Holly brought her a handmade card. Bryan, of course, wanted to see her stitches.

'Wow! I had stitches in my head once. I fell running in the house and hit my head on the table.'

Meg joined Bryan in his laugh. Why wasn't she surprised? 'That must have hurt.'

Bryan shrugged. 'It bled a lot. My brother came off his skateboard once and sliced his arm right open. Down to the bone and everything. Doctor Brennan had to dig the road out of his muscle, and he had lots of stitches.'

That sounded like Bryan's brother too.

She made it through the day, although Ana took Meg's playground duty so she could relax in the staffroom. After work, Chaz picked her up and they drove to Chuck's for rehearsal. She didn't dance and they played without amps, but the music calmed her, focused her mind, and brought her satisfaction she'd almost forgotten about. She laughed, teased her cousin, and tapped her foot along to Chuck's beat. She'd almost forgotten about what ailed her, until Jack picked her up and the exhaustion returned.

Like always, he helped her step up into the ute and she slumped into the seat. 'I just want to go to bed.'

'You need dinner first,' Jack said, and Meg couldn't argue with that as he closed the door. She was hungry and food was the only thing that would replenish her energy.

They returned to her house, and Jack twisted the deadlocks and applied the chain. 'What would you like to eat?'

'Nat said I need grains and protein, so I want spaghetti.'

'All right. I'll start cooking while you shower.'

Wrapping her arms around his waist, she flashed him her best smile. 'You're not joining me?'

Chuckling, he brushed his lips over hers. 'You know I would. But I showered before I picked you up, and I think we both need food.'

'Yeah, okay.' Needing a touch of normalcy, she kissed him softly, then headed towards her bedroom. 'You know where everything is?'

'I'll be fine, darlin'.'

She showered and returned to the kitchen to find the spaghetti boiling and the rich aroma of bolognese simmering on the stove. Meg took the moment to revel in the domesticated bliss. Her man looked so sexy preparing dinner as he greeted her with a glass of fizzy Diet Coke. But as she sank onto a stool at the breakfast bar, gloom rose to replace her hunger.

'Do you have everything you need for work tomorrow?'

Jack nodded as he stirred the spaghetti. 'Don't really need much, but I have enough clothes to last the week. I just thought it'd be easier to commute from here.'

Meg twisted the glass around on the bench, staring at the ice cubes in the dark liquid. 'Chaz was like a guard dog when he picked me up.'

'He's just worried. We all are.'

Her shoulders slouched. They didn't want her to be alone. She couldn't drive so soon after her head injury and hated to be a burden, but Jack had insisted he didn't need to be at the farm as early as usual and that he could take her to work. It's not like they spent many nights apart anymore, and thankfully, he'd had no problem with Chaz picking her up for rehearsal. But the whole situation cast a shadow over an exciting time in her life and while Meg thought it ridiculous, she couldn't complain. Not when the constant itch of sutures in her head reminded her of just how close she'd come to losing her life.

Why hadn't she?

Shuddering, she forced the thought away and focused on Jack. 'I had a good time at rehearsal tonight, and I'm confident with my set list. I don't know if I'm more nervous or excited.'

'Go with excited. I see the joy in your eyes when you sing, darlin'. I want you to celebrate this weekend.'

Meg nodded. Yes, she should focus on the positives. After all, that's what she usually did. She might have had a recent blood loss, but this was her chance. Her moment. So when Cade called on Thursday to tell her he had no new information, Meg refused to allow her hopes to plummet. Jack was right. She'd lost her dreams to this monster before. She wouldn't let it happen again.

* * *

When Jack pulled up outside the Mareeba Showgrounds on Saturday, Meg held onto her joy as she undid her seatbelt and flashed him a grin. 'I don't know what I've been so afraid of.'

'You'll be fantastic.' Eyes shining, he leaned over to kiss her. 'Will I see you later?'

'Text me when you arrive and I'll see what I can do.' She climbed out of the ute. 'Have a good day.'

With a wave, she turned and joined The Charlie Boys, who were waiting for her by the gate. The concert wouldn't start for a few hours yet, but they had a morning of rehearsal and soundchecks to get through first.

'There she is!' Chuck wrapped his arm around Meg. 'Our amazing songwriter. Ready for a big night?'

'Yeah, guys.' She glanced at them all, her smile lingering on Chaz. 'Let's do this.'

They led her backstage where Chaz introduced her to the production team, including the guy who organised Savannah in the Round, Mareeba's annual country music festival.

'Pleasure to meet you,' he said. 'Chaz has said some great things about you, Megan. Make sure you apply for a spot in the festival early, and I'll look out for you.'

Meg smiled. Securing an hour singing on one of the small bar stages at Savannah in the Round would certainly help get her noticed. 'Thank you.'

Soon, other artists arrived.

'Oh, you're Chaz's cousin!' Andrew, one of Australia's newest solo stars, gripped Meg's hand in a firm shake. 'Nice to meet you. He talks about you all the time.'

'You're the one who wrote tonight's song, right?' Melanie asked, another singer Meg loved.

'Yes, I did.'

'Fabulous. It'll be a hit.'

Meg could only hope so as they prepared to run their feature song for the evening. The sound technicians wired them up, and they took to the stage of the empty arena. She couldn't wait to see it full later, but for now, she soaked in the atmosphere and enjoyed the experience as she sang the words she'd written as per Chaz's arrangement. When everyone's voices blended at the end to belt out the anthem, shivers coursed through her body. They sounded amazing. The song was everything she'd hoped it would be and more. Tonight, they'd capture the live recording and money would pour in for the cyclone victims as it played over the radio and received downloads. A half hour of scribbling lyrics had led to something beyond her wildest dreams. But more than that, she had her spark back. Her creative juices flowed. She was writing, and she wanted to sing.

Meg's heart filled as they called it a wrap on the group rehearsal. The future held so many possibilities. She had her second chance with Jack, and she'd get that chance with music too. Dreams didn't have to die.

Meg skipped up to Chaz backstage and threw her arm around him. 'Thank you for making me do this.'

He squeezed her tight. 'It took me a few years, but you're welcome. You deserve this, Megan.'

'I'm starting to see that. Today's been fun and the show hasn't even started yet.'

'There's a lot of behind-the-scenes work, but yes. These events are fun. Music festivals are even better. You could always come with us later in the year for Groundwater or the Denny Ute Muster or Gympie. I know they're the big ones, but duet with us and you'll get noticed.'

His eyes filled with cheek, and she shook her head. 'Don't tempt me.'

'Oh, but I will. And remember, Tamworth is always during school holidays.'

'Don't you worry. I know that.'

'Good. But are you happy with your song?'

She nodded. 'It sounds great. And do you know what else?'

'What?'

'I'll record it with you.'

Chaz's eyebrows shot up. 'Yeah?'

Meg would have said the blood loss had gone to her head, but she'd never wanted anything more. She nodded and with a whoop, Chaz lifted her off her feet and spun her around. Meg ignored the dizziness and let herself laugh.

'Bloody excellent! Hey guys! We have ourselves a duet to record!'

Chuck fist pumped the air. 'Fuck yeah!'

They all leapt in to hug her, and she relished it. There was no use clinging to pride. She wasn't using them or their fame to get ahead. These guys loved her and if they wanted to record a duet with her, then who was she to say no?

* * *

The weight inside Jack's chest eased as he strolled out of the jewellery store in Mareeba. Grinning like a loon, he climbed into his ute, slipped his package securely away, and cranked up Kenny Chesney as he returned to the showgrounds to join his family. And Meg's. Everyone was there for her big night and to support the cause, including her paternal grandmother Margaret Riley, and maternal grandparents Victor and Carol O'Shea.

Ron shook Jack's hand, Sue and Heather hugged him, and everyone else greeted each other as they found a spot close enough to the stage for a good view, but far enough to avoid mosh-pitting. Music pumped through the speakers and excitement filled the cooling air, but no one's heart raced faster than Jack's. Especially when Victor came and stood beside him.

'It's been a while, Jack. Carol and I have been meaning to have you and Meg over for dinner now that you're dating my girl. What do you think?'

'We'd be happy to, Vic.' Jack swallowed the ball in his throat as he met the older man's gaze. 'How's the farm?'

'Thriving.' Victor grinned, his blue eyes sparkling. 'Just getting a bit much for me, you know?'

Jack slipped his hands into his pockets. 'You've got good staff though, right?'

'Oh yeah. Don't do much of the work myself anymore. But Carol and I really want to retire. So, are you serious about my granddaughter?'

The old man raised a bushy grey eyebrow. Jack let out a deep breath and nodded. 'Yeah.'

Victor clapped him on the shoulder. 'You come for dinner next week. Okay?'

'All right,' Jack said, forcing the tension out of his spine.

'Good. Now, do you know much about this song these grandkids of mine have put together?'

Jack smiled as the older man settled into his camp chair. 'Nope. Meg hasn't sung it for me, but she and Chaz have been working all week.'

Pride shone in Victor's eyes. 'They make a good pair, don't they?'

'Yep. I've always believed that.'

It might be five years later than planned, but his girl was finally taking her shot. She might have claimed to no longer be interested in music these past few years, and it killed Jack to know that his rejection of their relationship had sent her muse running for the hills. If heartache and fear hadn't plagued his soul, he might have realised that and pushed harder. But he would live by their new motto—no regrets.

They had come full circle. Meg was singing. They were in love, and Victor wanted to talk to him about the farm.

Jack had never been happier, and when Meg walked onto the stage as the third warm-up act, his heart swelled until he feared it would burst out of his chest. Everyone around him cheered, Adam probably the loudest of them all, but Jack simply stood and watched, smiling softly at the beautiful woman on stage.

'Hello, Mareeba! And to everyone who has come here tonight from across North Queensland.' Joy filled her voice, her eyes sparkling on the big screens. 'Thank you for supporting this amazing event. I'm Megan Riley. I grew up in Elizadale and attended Mareeba High, so I'm honoured to be singing here today for this wonderful cause. I'm going to play some songs from an EP I released five years ago. This one's called "Men in Boots."'

She tossed her golden hair back as she adjusted her guitar. The shimmery material of her black dress sparkled beneath the stage lights while she tapped her foot in her pink cowgirl boots. Jack's breath caught as the backup band launched into the song and Meg strung a chord.

There she was. The girl he'd watched sing in Elizadale all those years ago. The girl he'd fallen in love with. All grown up.

And his.

Adam sang along, but thankfully, Meg's voice drowned his brother out as she enveloped the showgrounds in her sweet, upbeat music.

Ana cheered, applauding when Meg finished. 'That's a fun song.'

'She needs to release more of them.' Liam glanced at Jack. 'You reckon she will?'

Jack shrugged. But these past few weeks had brought him more hope than he'd had in years. She'd drafted catchy tunes, sweet ballads, and even though she'd kept tonight's anthem under wraps, he knew it would be brilliant. Meg would have a music career. No one and nothing would hold her back again.

She moved into the love song 'Can I have this Dance?', then sang 'Home Again'. Everyone else sang along, but even though he knew every word, Jack remained silent and absorbed the moment, revelling in the image of her shining on stage. Only when she finished with 'Country Girls Gone Wild' did he release a cheer, applauding and bursting with pride.

He met her side stage and swept her warm, sweaty body into his arms. 'You were fantastic, darlin'!'

Her hands hardened on his back as she snuggled against his chest. 'It was amazing up there, Jack. So much fun. And everyone here is so nice. They don't care that I'm Chaz's cousin or think I'm riding in his wake. They love my song and it sounded awesome in soundcheck. So, guess what?' Her eyes lit up. 'I'm going to record it with him.'

Jack's mouth widened into a grin to match hers. 'Bloody brilliant. I'm so proud of you.'

It was hard to let her go after that, but he kissed her goodbye, and slipped back into the crowd.

* * *

Meg watched from the wings as The Charlie Boys opened the main event. Her hips grooved and she broke into a grin when the opening chords of 'Life in the North' roared through the speakers. It was certainly a crowd pleaser in this part of the world and still the best song she'd written.

Well, it had been.

Wringing her fingers, Meg reminded herself to breathe. But her nerves refused to fade as she paced by the sound booth. Andrew began his set and continued to rock the crowd with his catchy tunes. To make the show run smoothly, The Charlie Boys were the leading band for everyone tonight, so they never left the stage.

Then before Meg knew it, the music stopped and Chaz took the microphone to thank everyone for coming again before inviting the headliners back onstage as he spoke about the disaster relief effort. Taking a deep breath, Meg slipped her equalisers into her ears and followed Melanie out underneath the hot, bright lights. A massive crowd filled Mareeba Park, but her gaze automatically shot out to the left where she could just make out her family and friends.

'So, before we each give you one last song, we have something very special for you. This is a new song, written by our very talented Megan Riley. And lucky me, she's going to record it with us for our upcoming album!'

Meg couldn't help the grin that broke free as she saw her mother and Aunt Heather shoot their arms into the air, while everyone else applauded and Chuck let out a 'whoop' from behind the drums. It was going to happen, and she couldn't wait to visit Tamworth and hit the recording studio with Chaz and his team.

'But tonight, we're all going to sing it together for a live recording, and all proceeds will go to cyclone relief. So be sure to download and share when it's released on Wednesday. So, North Queensland! Stand with me as we tell the world that "Our Spirit Can't Blow Away!"'

The crowd roared and, knees shaking, Meg gripped the microphone as the lights dimmed. Her heart pounded, spine tingled, but as the slow beat of Chuck's drums, Eric's bass rhythm, and Chaz's chords filled the air, her confidence rose, the spotlight shone, and she opened her song.

'*You and I. Live in this town. And every day. I see you around.*'

Chaz joined in. '*When you need help, I lend you a hand. 'Cause in our town, together we stand.*'

Meg smiled, her tension easing as everyone launched into the bridge. '*Now when a threat arrives. We stand, help, and survive. Together. Forever.*'

'*Gather friends and all your family,*
And protect the one you love.
When the clouds deliver darkness,
We search for the sun above.
Then a new day dawns to show us,
All we've lost, we stand and say.
You may have knocked us down.
Our spirit can't blow away.'

Meg drew away from the microphone, her heel tapping and eyes glistening as Andrew and Melanie sang the second verse. She'd been too scared to look towards her family while she'd been singing, but as her gaze met Jack's, her heart filled and she flashed him a grin. He smiled back and even though he was a little too far away to tell, she knew pride filled his eyes. It might be five years later, but they were there. They'd made it. He would always be there for her, and she him. The words she wrote reverberated through the speakers, captured her heart, and caused her breath to catch in her throat.

'*Deep inside,*
My soul I know,
You'll never reap,
More than I can sow.
With every beat,

Of my heart,
I'll never stop,
Until we make a fresh start.'

She hadn't recognised the subtext before, but gazing into Jack's eyes over the distance, she sang the bridge with all her heart.

'So when a threat arrives,
I know we will survive.
Together. Forever.'

Chapter Thirty-Eight

Elizadale buzzed as locals gathered in James Abbot Park, but not because they were excited about the fun run. Meg heard her name spoken in many conversations while friends and acquaintances stopped to congratulate her on her performance last night.

'You were spectacular,' her colleague, Vivian, said.

'You sang so beautifully,' Lizzie from church told her.

'I couldn't make it down there,' Samantha Hudson said, 'but I heard your song was amazing.'

'I've already pre-ordered the recording.'

'When's the album coming out?'

Meg accepted everyone's compliments, thanked them for their support, and chatted cheerfully before finding security among her friends.

'They're not wrong though,' Adam said, stretching out his deltoids while stepping from side to side and kicking his heels to his butt. 'I want a signed copy of the album.'

'Would you produce a CD?' Natalia asked, jogging on the spot. 'I thought most artists just rely on downloads.'

'Of course, she needs a CD!' Adam cried. 'What else will she sign for me?'

Meg pulled her foot to her bum in a quad stretch. 'Nat's right. Record labels still produce CDs, but I'll likely go down the indie track, so it might not be worth my time.'

'But you'll produce a small batch, right?' Liam asked. 'I'll need to sell them at The Bent Banana.'

Meg swapped legs and resisted a wince. Since Liam had sold hundreds of copies of her EP through the Tourist Centre, she could hardly say no. 'Fine. It'll be a Bent Banana exclusive.'

'Yes!' Adam grinned at Jack. 'You've got a star there, mate.'

Jack's eyes shone. 'Always knew that.'

They were called to assemble and those serious about the race hurried to the front of the group. Lucy planned to do her best, but Meg didn't know why Adam thought he would beat Natalia as she stood with Jack, Isabella, and Michael in the middle of the pack. Liam and Ana lingered at the back with the rest of the walkers.

'I'll see you at the finish line, hey?' Meg said with a laugh.

Jack shrugged. 'I don't plan to be far behind you.'

'Why? Want to appreciate the view?'

'No.' Jack's eyes darkened. 'Want to make sure nothing happens to you.'

She stilled. 'Of course. Silly me. We'll run it together.'

'*Go!*' The crowd began moving and Meg started off at a light jog as they crossed the highway, Brett on momentary traffic control, and into the parkland running alongside Shadow Creek—the actual water, not the farm. Isabella broke away from them, but Jack and Michael flanked Meg, keeping pace together as they descended into the bush.

'You reckon Adam will keep up with Nat?' Michael asked.

Meg giggled. 'No. She's probably left him in her dust. They may have been running together, but Nat does ten k's every morning and has been training for a marathon.'

'I kinda wish we could watch them battle it out,' Jack said.

'I should run more,' Michael mused as the three of them rounded a pair of older ladies.

'No harm in it, mate,' Jack said. 'Izzy's sure taken off.'

'That's 'cause she's a fit little thing.'

They emerged from the trees, passed the caravan park, and crossed Jim's traffic-controlled highway when they caught sight of a familiar red shirt with a sweaty V ahead.

Jack chuckled. 'Oi, slowpoke!'

Adam glared at them over his shoulder.

'Can't keep up with the misses?'

'Did for a while.' Adam slowed until they caught up. 'Bloody woman isn't human. She took off at a sprint.'

'I'm sure you tried,' Meg said, barely holding her smile back as she patted his shoulder.

The four of them crossed the finish line together in just under forty minutes to the sound of cheering from Lucy, Isabella and Natalia. Meg slowed into a walk, exhaling in relief.

'Good job, guys!' Natalia called.

Jack wiped sweat from his forehead with the back of his arm, far too sexy in his black muscle shirt. 'We did it.'

'Did you have fun?' Lucy asked, biting into a banana.

Meg nodded. 'I feel great.'

Natalia wrapped her arm around Adam's shoulders. 'How'd you go?'

'You've been taking it easy on me on our runs, haven't you?'

'Of course. You've only been running for a few months. You need to work your way up.'

He rolled his eyes. 'Did you at least win?'

'Sure did!'

They moved towards the tent where Brittany and her friends had set up bottled water and fresh fruit, Natalia reminding them to keep moving to aid their post-race recovery. Meg and Jack fetched water and oranges before standing beneath the trees to wait for Ana and Liam.

'That's it for the show queen events,' Isabella said, biting into an apple. 'I think everyone did well.'

'They always do,' Lucy agreed. 'All the girls deserve to win.'

Meg nodded. 'They've done an amazing job of bringing the community together, which is the main thing.'

'Now we just need to get our entries ready,' Lucy said. 'I have a big week of baking ahead of me.'

'So do I,' Meg muttered, groaning as she remembered the number of competitions she'd foolishly entered. What had she been thinking?

* * *

'There's my favourite big brother!'

Jack stepped off the verandah as Lily leapt out of the ute, meeting him halfway across the yard in a bone-crushing hug.

He chuckled. 'You say that to all of us.'

'You say I'm your favourite little sis.'

'You're my only little sis.'

'Which makes you lucky.' She stepped back and lifted her sunglasses. 'But you are my favourite because the others aren't here. Where are they?'

Lily popped her hand on her hip and glanced behind her as though expecting Adam and Michael to leap out of nowhere. Honestly, Jack didn't blame her.

'They're coming. Adam's probably caught up woodturning and Mike said he'd be here, but you're early.' He narrowed his eyes. 'Were you speeding again?'

She averted her eyes. 'No …'

'Lily.'

'I looked down once and was five over the limit! I slowed down.'

Jack crossed his arms over his chest. 'Cade will catch you.'

'Please, like I'm scared of Cade. He'd probably—hey, Mum!'

The screen door crashed open as Wendy rushed towards them with her arms outstretched. 'Oh, my baby is home! How was the drive? Are you hungry? Why are you early?'

'I *wasn't* speeding.' Lily glared at Jack.

'You didn't text me when you were in Mareeba.'

'I didn't stop! Do you want me to text and drive?'

'Absolutely not,' Wendy said, drawing away.

'I bet Jack doesn't have to text you at every town when he's driving.'

Jack resisted a grimace. That might be true, but he'd admit, he too was guilty of protecting and coddling Lily. She was nine years younger than him and it was hard to think of her as a young woman of twenty-two when she would always be his baby sister.

'We worry about you—everyone really—on the roads, Lil,' Jack said. 'But to make it up to you, I have the jumps set up and—'

Lily pivoted and ran, sprinting beneath the jacaranda tree towards the stables.

Sighing, Wendy shook her head. 'Already, Jack? You couldn't have let me have her for five minutes?'

Grinning, he swooped down to kiss his mum's cheek, then

backed towards the stables. 'Hey, I'm her favourite big brother.'

Her shoulders dropped. 'I'll be over soon.'

Knowing full well he'd been lucky to receive the first hug, Jack strode after Lily. He might be her favourite brother, but Lily had been known to bypass her human family entirely and visit her true love first upon returning home. Sure enough, he found her in the paddock with her arms around Lightning's neck.

'I've missed you, girl. Has Uncle Jack been taking good care of you? Lucy sent me videos of you training. You've been so good, haven't you?'

Lightning whickered in agreement, her head draped across Lily's back.

'Lightning's done well. She's been spending most of her days in the paddock and I've kept her rugged up so that she doesn't get too fluffy.'

Lily ran her hand down Lightning's shoulder. 'She looks beautiful. No one will beat us in the hacking.'

Jack smirked. 'Or the jumping. I assumed you'd want to start practising right away.'

'You assumed right.' Lily scratched the white diamond on the palomino's golden forehead. 'You ready, girl? You want to do some jumps?'

They had the mare saddled by the time Adam and Michael arrived. Lily ran to them, commencing the battle over who got to hug her first with many calls of favourite sis and favourite bro.

'Jack's my favourite. You two weren't even here to meet me.'

'I was woodturning. Lost track of time. Baby furniture is tricky, you know?'

Lily shook her head. 'I still can't believe you're going to be a dad.'

Adam rubbed his jaw. 'Neither can I. Don't know what I was bloody thinking.'

'Cold feet, mate?' Jack called.

'Nah, I'll be right. But do you know how many bars need to be on a damn crib?'

'You're turning all the bars?' Lily asked.

'Of course!'

'But that's like—'

'Fifty!' Adam cried. 'It's insane.'

Michael cleared his throat. 'You know … you can *buy* a crib.'

Adam baulked. 'My kid won't sleep in some commercial junk!'

'Then stop complaining! You've got plenty of time.'

'I guess … But you should see the bowl I've made for the show. Best piece yet.'

Jack and his brothers moved Lightning into the jumping ring while Lily raced into the homestead to get changed, returning in her boots, jodhpurs, and a rainbow T-shirt in record time. She readjusted her dark ponytail to fit her helmet and, despite her short stature, leapt nimbly astride Lightning. Adam and Michael perched on the fence and their mum arrived with fruit and hibiscus tea as Lily ran Lightning through a warmup.

Assuming his role as timekeeper, Jack opened the stopwatch on his phone and leaned back against the fence. With his sister home, his family was whole again, filling the yard with the sound of bickering and cheer that Shadow Creek should always harness. And it would. Adam had a baby on the way and Jack would be damned if he and Meg didn't marry and start a family soon. She wanted it, he wanted it, and he was done with some unknown villain dictating his life.

But he needed Adam's help, so once Lily had finished training, Jack pulled his brother aside and shared his plan. The jackass couldn't help but throw his head back and laugh.

'Mate, that's just insane.'

Jack gritted his teeth. 'It might be over the top, but we're talking about Meg, remember? She likes all that romantic bullshit.'

'True.' Adam pulled Jack into a hug and slapped him on the back. 'Of course, I'll help you out. It's about fucking time.'

Chapter Thirty-Nine

Washing his hands of the animal's blood, he wished it had been Meg Riley's. He should have killed her. He'd had the chance, and killing her was what he had intended to do. Except …

'Fuck!' Heat surged through his veins as he scrubbed beneath his nails. He'd screwed up. Again. He'd held her. Smelled her fear. He'd heard her head crash against the wooden railing. He knew she hadn't been dead. Not yet. He should have got it over and done with. Put everyone out of their misery. There was no use dragging it out.

But as he'd reached down to grab her neck, he'd frozen. Her blonde hair had tumbled over her soft creamy face and memory had overcome him.

She looked so much like *her*.

Susan.

He'd lost momentum, and with that fucking dog barking, he'd needed to get out of there before someone came, so he'd run with the feisty fluffball chasing him down the street. Bloody pathetic excuse for a dog. The least he could have done was kill it. Might have made him feel better. But instead, he'd placated his frustrations with endless rum and had taken it out on the chicken today. Now, his wife was plucking the bird and he'd munch on some juicy legs while he plotted how he would end this.

It needed to be soon.

Chapter Forty

Show Day arrived, spreading organised chaos beneath the shadow of the massive Ferris wheel on Saturday afternoon. Locals and visitors parked their utes, trucks, and trailers in designated zones while everyone bustled about with boxes of food, craft, produce, and farm animals of every kind. Excitement shimmied through Meg's veins as she and Jack arrived at the Maguires' campsite. Since the animals stayed overnight, so did most of the owners, and as always, Henry and Cliff had set up beside the Kellys.

'Wow.' Meg blinked at the sleek silver horse truck featuring the blue logos of Kelly Stud that took up half the campground. 'That's new.'

'Hmm …' Lucy's mouth thinned as she glared at the impressive transport. 'They're certainly flashing with the cash. What does that hold, like six horses? Don't know why I bother bringing mine when I have to compete against *that*.'

'Yeah, but Liz works hard. She deserves it.'

'And you do well, Luce,' Jack said. 'Are you still interested in breeding?'

Lucy shrugged. 'Esme has some good breeding years in

her, but who knows? Let's go to the hall, Meg, and get ourselves set up.'

Jack accompanied Meg and Lucy to the hall, still unwilling to let her out of his sight. Not that she minded when the thought of being alone rendered her frozen with fear. It had been almost two weeks since her attack, but while she felt stronger every day and hadn't experienced any of the neurological symptoms Natalia had warned her about, there was still no lead on who wanted her dead. And she couldn't shake the constant feeling that she was being watched.

They arrived at the exhibition halls where the committee members and locals rushed about setting up the displays. People greeted Meg with a mixture of excitement and concern as while they longed to talk about her music and pester her about an album, the attack still lurked in everyone's minds.

Meg was pinning her students' photos to a display board when her cousins Rebecca and Zoe found her.

'Aww, look at Banjo,' Rebecca said, tapping her finger on the photo of her kelpie smiling at the camera. 'Lisa took so many pictures to get that one right. Banjo's not usually photogenic.'

'She's done a good job,' Meg agreed. 'And I've been meaning to call you. We should get Jill and Banjo together for a playdate.'

Rebecca laughed good-naturedly. 'Why not? Banjo and Maggie see each other often and would love to play with Jill. We can meet at the park one weekend.'

'Excellent.' Excited to get the kelpie siblings together, Meg stuck another photo to the board.

'How are you anyway?' Rebecca asked, placing her hand on Meg's shoulder. 'Is your head okay?'

Meg nodded. 'Stitches came out this week. I've been feeling fine, but I have a repeat CT on Tuesday.'

'I still can't believe someone hurt you,' Zoe said, shaking her head.

'I was speaking to Mum and she said Uncle Ron thinks someone has a problem with *us*? The Riley family?'

'Which is absurd,' Zoe added.

'I know. It's ridiculous.' Even though Meg understood the motive. Jack wouldn't hold back when he expanded, and her grandparents would certainly discuss business at dinner later this week. One day, Meg would be the landlord of various tenants and businesses while holding Riley House and all its history in trust. But for someone to kill them over that? Who would carry such a nasty grudge?

Exhaling, Meg stuck another photo to the board. She didn't want to think about it right now. It was show weekend, her favourite time of the year, so she chatted to Zoe and Rebecca for a while longer and focused on enjoying herself.

By five o'clock, the halls had turned into an extravaganza of displays. Photographs and paintings showcased gorgeous local images along one wall while crochet and knitting hung on another. Isabella's quilted blanket was certainly a winner with the stunning mix of greens and blues surrounding brown pawprints and two border collie faces.

Meg wrapped her arm around her friend. 'It's gorgeous, Iz. I bet Ana and Liam love it.'

'I showed them yesterday and Ana cried.'

'I'm not surprised. Come on, let's look around.'

They wandered into the next hall where fruits and vegetables lined the tables and a sweet aroma lifted from the displays of freshly cut flowers. Natalia dragged them around the room, bouncing with excitement as she pointed out her various vegetable entries. Meg had to admit, her capsicum looked splendid.

She caught up with Lucy at the cooking display where dozens of biscuits and cakes proudly awaited tasting. Meg didn't envy those judging that competition. She'd get a stomach-ache.

'Everything looks fantastic,' Lucy said as they exited the hall. Jack and Adam stood from where they'd been waiting outside.

'It always does,' Meg agreed. 'I think we had more entries than usual in most competitions.'

'I entered a lot, although I don't know about my cauliflower anymore.' Natalia bit down on her lower lip. 'Leanne Newman's looked so much better.'

Meg patted her friend's shoulder. 'You can't win them all, Nat.'

'That's what I keep telling her,' Adam said, wrapping his arm around his wife's waist. 'Now, let's go watch this show queen thing.'

Jack took Meg's hand as they crossed the park to watch the announcement of the show queen. The young ladies shone in their final interviews as they spoke passionately about their love for Elizadale and what they hoped to achieve during their reign. When Deborah announced the whopping amount of money they'd raised for disaster relief, Meg almost fell off her chair before joining in the crowd's heartfelt cheers. They couldn't have asked for more.

Then, to her delight, Deborah announced Samantha as the winner. Meg stood and cheered as Samantha accepted her sash and crown before giving a beautiful speech and officially opening the Elizadale Show.

'And once again, you help another young woman become a star of the community,' Jack said as they broke away from their friends and made a beeline for the Ferris wheel. 'Samantha did well.'

'I know to some people it seems like a silly competition, but she worked hard. It builds confidence to win something like that. I know it helped build mine.'

'You've always been confident, darlin'.'

Not always, but she let that thought go when she spotted Chaz and Eric striding towards them. 'Hey! Do you have some news?'

Chaz's grin told her all she needed to know. 'We killed it, Megan!'

Squealing, Meg threw her arms around her cousin. 'Really?'

'Thousands of downloads. Radio stations are playing our song, and not only the country ones.'

Meg bounced on her toes, floating on air as she stepped back. Jack wrapped his arm around her waist and squeezed. 'That's amazing, Chaz. I'm so glad.'

'The label's happy to keep the live charity version running, but they want to release it as the next single. So, what do you say?'

Meg hadn't changed her mind about the recording. Every time she thought about standing on that stage, the lights, the atmosphere, she wanted to do it again. The concert had been the ultimate high, a success, and everyone had been so supportive. Chaz might have helped her reach this point, but together, they'd achieved something wonderful.

'I'm in, Chaz. Let's do it.'

'Excellent!' He grinned. 'I've got the studio booked for the next school holidays. You ready for Tamworth, Meg?'

'Bring it!'

Meg was a wriggling bundle of beans when she settled beside Jack on the Ferris wheel. He squeezed her hand as the attendant secured the bar across their waists and she gazed up into his warm, dark eyes.

'I'm so proud of you, darlin'.'

She smiled. It was because of him she had found the heart to give her dreams a second chance. And she was grateful more than anything that they'd knocked down their barriers.

'Thank you, Jack.' She gripped the bar as the Ferris wheel lifted them into the sky. 'I'm excited.'

'You should be. I was wondering though …' He brushed his thumb over her fingers, drawing Meg's gaze from the view of her beloved town below and back to his. 'Do you want to go on a date with me tomorrow?'

Her eyebrows shot up. 'What?'

'If you think about it, we've never been on one. I want to take you to dinner.'

Her heart fluttered. Gosh, he was right. They'd grabbed ice cream and had spent a copious amount of time together but hadn't done anything that would constitute as a 'date.'

'I'd love to go to dinner with you, Jack.'

He smiled softly. 'Excellent. But we'll have to leave straight after the show tomorrow, so we'll get changed here. Okay?'

'Why can't we just dash back to my place?'

Jack shook his head. 'No time. I … I have a surprise for you.'

His eyes heated, joy lingered, and not wanting to spoil his surprise, Meg didn't argue. 'Okay. It's a date.'

BANANA SURPRISE

Chapter Forty-One

Meg gasped when she was announced the winner of the apple pie competition on Sunday morning, unable to suppress her smile at the sight of the blue ribbon. Perhaps there was a certain satisfaction in gaining the title of Best Something in Town, but Millie Taylor could keep her reputation of having the best banana cake. She and Jack needed to keep their special traditions to themselves and even though the apple pie wasn't the most popular competition, Meg wasn't any less proud of her prize.

Lucy, however, won four biscuit competitions while Natalia bested her in the Anzac biscuits and was announced to grow the best capsicum and spinach in town. Isabella won Supreme Show Champion with her quilted blanket, and no one came close to touching Adam in the woodturning. Ana won a prize for her chocolate muffins and her marigolds, but Elanora's flowers remained the star of the show.

'We sure produce some beautiful things around here,' Jack said as they admired the arts and crafts. 'Your mum sure is talented.'

As always, Sue Riley had won prizes for knitting, sewing, and embroidery.

'I wish I shared half her skill. Maybe I could learn to knit,' Meg mused as she admired the knitted booties. Then again, why would she need to knit her own baby clothes? Her mother had probably started filling a closet full of the cutest little garments the moment she'd learned Meg and Jack were dating. Chuckling to herself, she shoved the thought aside and admired the artwork before they left the hall to see how Samantha was doing assisting with the pony rides.

They were lining up at the CWA tent for drinks when Meg heard her name called. She turned, her shoulders relaxing as Paul Kelly approached them.

'Hi, Paul.' Seeing him hand in hand with the brunette from the bachelor auction, Meg smiled softly. Perhaps love had bloomed after all?

'Hey.' He nodded quickly at Jack. 'Maguire.'

'Kelly.'

Paul's gaze returned to Meg. 'I haven't seen you in a while, so I just wanted to say I'm sorry to hear you were hurt.'

'Thank you, Paul.'

Jack touched her shoulder. 'I'll grab our drinks, darlin'.'

She nodded as he moved a few paces away.

'They haven't caught who did it?' Paul asked.

'No, not yet.'

'It's fucked up, for sure,' he said, equal amounts of anger and sincerity in his tone. 'Maguire taking good care of you?'

'He is.'

'Glad to hear it, Meg.' Paul smiled, genuine joy for her overshadowing the sadness that continued to linger in his eyes. 'I'm happy for you.'

'Thanks.'

'And I also wanted to thank you for getting me into that auction.'

'It seemed like it worked out well.' She glanced at the woman. What was her name again? 'You two hit it off, did you?'

'Sort of,' Paul said.

The woman's high-pitched laughter pierced Meg's eardrums as she wrapped her arm around Paul and nestled her head on his shoulder. 'Sort of? He means, *absolutely*.'

Meg held her smile in place. Sarah, that was her name, and according to Lucy, she wasn't very nice. Hopefully, Paul liked her more than Lucy did. Although judging by the strain in his eyes, Meg doubted it.

'Are you two enjoying the show?'

'Yeah, it's been good. Diego won the blue ribbon.'

'Who would have doubted it?' She recalled discussing Diego and his many virtues over dinner.

Jack returned to her side and handed her a can of Diet Coke.

'Anyway, we best be off,' Paul said, slipping out of Sarah's hold and taking her hand. 'See you in the woodchop this afternoon, Maguire.'

'Sure thing, Kelly.'

Paul and Sarah left, and Jack wrapped his arm around Meg. 'I need to check on the horses. You want to come or hang with Lucy?'

'I'll catch up with Luce and steal a bickie.'

Jack dropped her off at Lucy's bake stall before heading to the stables.

'Having fun?' Meg asked.

'Sure.' Lucy rolled her eyes as she lounged in her camp chair and nursed a thermos of coffee. 'A blast.'

Meg frowned. 'What's wrong? You love the show. And Esme got second place in her competition.'

'Yeah, losing to Faith.'

'I know. But Faith's a beautiful mare and it's hard to beat the Kellys.'

'Tell me about it,' she muttered, biting into her blue ribbon winning iced vovo. 'Not that I should complain since Liz has beautiful horses. I just hope she doesn't let that bloody Sarah anywhere near them.'

Meg sighed as she stretched out in the spare chair beside Lucy. 'Is she really so bad?'

'Yes,' Lucy muttered as she sipped her coffee. 'She's never been kind. Always wants the best and is a sore loser.'

'It doesn't look like she's competing today.'

Lucy scoffed. 'She'd think the Elizadale Show is beneath her.'

'Oh.' Meg helped herself to a jam drop. 'Well, it might not be the biggest event on the circuit, but I look forward to seeing Lily jump later. And did I tell you Jack and I are going on a date tonight?'

Lucy raised her eyebrows. 'Really?'

'Yep. We haven't really been on one, which is fine considering how we just fell into this relationship. But it'll be nice to dress up, go out, and have dinner. Just the two of us.'

Lucy smiled softly, though it didn't quite reach her eyes. 'I'm happy for you, Meg. It's what you've always wanted.'

'Yeah ...' Meg's heart fluttered. 'Despite everything that's been going on, I'm happy that we're together.'

'Me too. But please, I beg you. Don't make me wear pink at the wedding.'

Laughing, Meg stole another jam drop. 'I make no promises.'

* * *

Taking advantage of a moment alone, Jack met up with Adam to make final arrangements for tonight's date with Meg, then headed to the stables. He cleaned their horses' stalls, checked their water, then snuck them each a piece of liquorice.

'Don't tell Lucy and she'll give you more later,' he told Dante, rubbing his ears. 'And don't let this red ribbon get you down. You're still my best gelding.'

His family had done well with a few second and third places, but the Kellys were renowned in the horse business and had taken a clean sweep of blue ribbons. Losing to them in the horses was the one competition he would accept.

'You have a nice horse there, Maguire,' Charlie White said. He came up alongside Jack and slipped his hands into his pockets. His father, Edward, lingered a few paces away.

'Yeah, he's a good boy.'

'Saw your sister in the jumping. She sure knows how to ride.'

'Sure does.' Jack stepped away from Dante and turned to Charlie. He didn't associate with Charlie much, but since the man was married to Meg's cousin Zoe, they could very well see more of each other in the future. 'How are you, anyway?'

'Been busy getting the cattle ready.'

'Haven't been down that way yet. How'd you do?'

'Red Back Station beat us, of course,' Charlie said with an easy shrug. Behind him, Edward grunted. Jack heard the faint whisper of 'bastards' beneath the older man's breath but didn't comment. The results weren't surprising.

'There's always next year,' he said politely.

'Sure is.' Charlie clapped him on the shoulder. 'Good seeing you, Jack.'

'Yeah, catch you later.' Charlie strode past him. Jack nodded at the older man. 'Edward.'

He didn't reply, but Jack didn't take it personally. He rubbed Dante one more time, then cast a good look at the Kellys' prize-winning stallion before strolling out of the stables. He'd been away from Meg for too long and while he nodded briefly at a few people who called hello, he didn't stop until he reached the market stalls. Spotting Meg exactly where he left her, his breath escaped in a whoosh.

Her eyes brightened. 'Hey! Ready for the woodchop?'

Jack nodded. 'Let's go.'

* * *

Meg watched Jack's muscles bunch as he swung the axe into the log. He wasn't by any means a pro or one to follow the circuit, but the sheer masculinity of his powerful body had all her happy places warming. Crossing her legs, she squeezed her thighs and sat forward, cheering him on. Natalia did the same beside her while Lucy sat back with her arms crossed and an unusual scowl on her face.

'My man's going to beat your man,' Natalia said, jiggling in her seat.

Meg scoffed. 'Doubt it. Come on, Jack!'

'Come on, come on …'

'Whoohoo!' Meg threw her arms in the air as the top of Jack's log fell to the ground and he lowered his axe. A moment later, Adam did the same, followed by a Tropic Sun farmhand, followed by Paul.

'Adam might be good at turning wood, Nat,' Lucy said, 'but Jack's always been able to chop it faster.'

'Well, he can't be good at everything. His head's big

enough already. Though I guess I can't blame him after winning the grand prize in the woodturning. My man beat them all.'

Meg beamed at the pride in Natalia's voice. 'That's because he's an amazing woodworker.'

'They all have their skills,' Lucy said, standing. 'I'll catch you guys later for the last of Lily's jumping, but I better go relieve Aunt Wendy from my stall.'

Lucy left, hands in her pockets, while Meg and Natalia went to congratulate their men.

'Got a blue ribbon myself, darlin',' Jack said, holding it up.

'Yes, I saw …' Running her hands down his sweaty chest, she shivered and curved her body into his. 'And you looked damn good getting it.'

His eyes darkened. 'Is that so?'

'Yep.'

'I'll keep that in mind for later.' He kissed her. 'But for now, do you want to look at the stalls with me before we watch Lily in the six bar?'

They did a final lap of the showgrounds, stopping to chat and admire people's work. There were more congratulations about the charity concert and concerns about her attack, to which Meg simply nodded and smiled politely. She didn't want to talk about it and even though she'd tried to ignore the tingle in her spine, she couldn't shake that feeling of being watched.

She almost asked Jack if he felt it too but decided against it. She was just being paranoid. Besides, how could anyone hurt them in the middle of a crowd like this?

They found a seat around the equestrian ring, and Meg shifted her worries from one concern to another as she focused on the final show jump of the day—the six bar.

Jack shook his head. 'I don't know why she does this.'

'Because it's a test of skill and guts. And Lightning enjoys it.'

'But it stresses me out.'

'Me too,' Lucy muttered on Meg's other side. 'It's like watching a car crash in slow motion as she races towards death.'

Meg squeezed her friend's hand. Lucy was not wrong. The six bar was the ultimate test of a horse's and rider's skill and resilience, and it was bloody terrifying. Six jumps were set up only a stride apart with the heights gradually increasing. Every round, the height increased. It was nerve-wracking to watch, let alone compete in. Lucy's worst riding accident had occurred during the six bar.

Lily, however, was fearless.

There were only four competitors today, and each sailed through the first round. The bars rose and Tiffany from the bachelor auction, who Lucy had little tolerance for, jumped the course clear. The second jumper failed on the final jump. Then Lily and Lightning approached the course and sailed over one, two … six jumps.

'Damn, she has excellent form,' Lucy muttered.

'Plenty of height between Lightning and those jumps,' Meg agreed.

After the third round, it was only Lily and Tiffany. Meg pressed her hands to her mouth, her foot jiggling as Lily approached … and leapt over the jumps with what appeared such ease. And true skill. Tiffany failed on the fifth jump. Meg, Jack, and Lucy stood and cheered.

They went to meet Lily, and Jack swept his sister into his arms. 'Well done, Lil.'

'Thanks. But seriously, bro.' She pushed him away and wrinkled her nose. 'You're all sweaty.'

He laughed. 'That's because I have a blue ribbon in the woodchop.'

'And I have four for four.' Beaming, Lily lifted her helmet off her neatly braided hair. 'Definitely worth the trip home. So glad I beat that Tiffany in the supreme hack.'

'Me too,' Lucy said. 'I told Lightning not to let her win when the club was staying at the retreat.'

Lily smiled and wrapped her arm around Lucy. 'Thank you for getting her ready.'

'No worries. I had fun. But I'll catch you all later as I need to pack up my stall.' Lucy waved, then hurried away.

'I'll take Lightning and hose her down,' Jack said, glancing at Meg. 'You coming, darlin'?'

'I need to collect my entries first.'

'Right.' Jack handed Lightning back to Lily. 'We'll meet you at the stables.'

Meg would have protested, but she bit her tongue as Jack took her hand. It didn't make her less of a woman to prefer having Jack by her side. She felt safe with him. Secure. And that feeling of a target on her back just wouldn't go away.

Chapter Forty-Two

Meg collected her entries and her beautiful blue ribbon, as well as Lucy's horde, then left the hall to find Jack ending a phone call.

'All good?' she asked.

'Yeah, just Adam. Got everything?'

'Yep. I'm glad I entered as it was fun taking part in the show and not just running it.'

'You did well, Meg.' Jack kissed her on the forehead. 'And I'm glad that you won something.'

They returned to the chaos of the stables with the whinnies, shouts, and gushing of hoses as people cleaned out the stalls and owners loaded horses into floats. Those with only one were out in a flash, including Charlie White. But the Maguires and Kellys both had some work to do. Meg helped by gathering buckets and throwing them into the back of the ute, then she and Lily headed for the shower block while Jack finished in the stables. She still didn't know why they couldn't go home before dinner, but she changed out of her jeans and into one of her favourite maxi-dresses for her first date with Jack. Orange blossoms that she liked to pretend were golden wattle decorated the creamy material that gathered tight around her ribs before flowing to her ankles, the shoestring straps and sweetheart neckline leaving her shoulders bare.

'You look nice,' Lily said, dumping her riding gear by the basins as she untied her braids.

Meg finished applying her mascara and smiled. 'Thanks.'

'I'm glad Jack came to his senses and that you're together. He's been pissing me off for years mucking you about.'

Meg glanced sideways at the younger woman. 'Did Jack tell—'

'Oh, he told me what's been going on. Tried not to, of course, thinking I can't handle the horrors of this world, but I got it out of him. And I'm glad you did too.' Lily flashed her a smile. 'It's been a long time coming, Meg, and I'm glad to see that he's happy.'

Lily opened her arms and Meg's spine softened as they embraced. 'Me too, Lily. And it has been good, being together.'

'Nat's awesome, but I've always looked forward to having you as a sister. I just hope Michael gives me one I love as much as you two.'

Laughing, they left the shower block to find even more floats had gone.

'Where's Dad?' Lily asked Jack. 'I thought he was driving the truck home?'

'Lucy said she would,' he said, tethering Dante to the truck. 'She'll be down once she's packed up her stall.'

Lily and Jack retrieved the rest of the horses and Meg opted to stay with them while Jack finished cleaning and Lily left to help Liz Kelly in the jumping ring. Paul strode past with his mares and gave her a small nod. Rubbing Esme's neck, Meg smiled in reply, though her heart sank when she remembered what Lucy had said about Sarah. Paul deserved to be happy, and he hadn't looked all that comfortable earlier when that woman had been hanging off him.

'All right.' Jack returned and grabbed his shower things from the Raptor. 'Come on, darlin'. I'll rinse off this stink, then we'll go to dinner.'

He grabbed soap, a towel, and she strolled with him towards the shower block. As he headed into a stall, she waited in the doorway and kept an eye on the horses while galahs squawked overhead. Meg smiled as she glanced up at her favourite pink-and-grey birds.

The shower turned on and sighing, Meg rested back against the wall. It'd been a long day and even though she didn't feel like cooking, she'd rather go straight home and put her feet up than out for dinner. But she couldn't deny she wanted this date and that she looked forward to trying Smithy's renowned chocolate fondue. What said romantic more than shared dessert?

A high-pitched whinny cut through the air, and Meg glanced up as Esme reared. But being tethered to the float, she didn't get far. The other horses snickered and stamped their hooves. Meg rushed towards them.

'Hey, what is it? Is—'

A slither flashed in the grass, and Meg stilled. A snake? Shit! She stumbled back, turned, and collied with a solid body.

'Sorry, I was—'

Arms came around her as cold, sharp metal pressed against her throat. Meg froze. Blinked. And glanced up into the cold, angry eyes of Edward White.

Meg opened her mouth to yell. Gasp or scream. But fear rendered her vocal cords useless as Edward pressed the knife harder against her skin.

'Scream and I'll slit your fucking throat, bitch. And since I don't plan to do that here, you will do what I fucking say.'

Meg didn't comprehend his words, but some part of her brain managed to make sense of them. She couldn't make a scene, but co-operation would buy her time. Jack would be out of the shower any minute. Someone else might stumble along.

'Good girl.' Edward lowered the knife, spun her around, and held her against his body. Pressing the steel to her ribs, he urged her forward. 'Now move.'

It took her a few steps on shaking feet for Meg to gather her wits. Grasping her long skirt, she shot a look over her shoulder to where Esme continued to stamp her hooves. 'The horses—'

'Forget the horses.'

'There was a snake.'

'Python. Won't hurt them.'

Her gaze shot to the older man. 'You put the snake there?'

'Yep. Just like I let that mutt of yours into the front yard.'

Meg's hands clenched around her dress. 'How dare you! Lola could have been killed! Jack almost ran her over!'

'Shut up!'

Meg winced as pain shot through her side. She glanced down at the knife pressing against her torso. It was no ordinary kitchen knife. It was sharp, powerful, and strong enough to pierce leather. Or a calf. Or her.

Lifting her gaze, she strove for calm. What was she going to do? She tried to slow his hurried pace, but Edward continued to push her forward. Meg shot another glance over her shoulder, but no one was there. What was Jack doing in that damn shower?

Her foot found a divot and Meg almost tripped. She

gasped and Edward pulled her upright, the knife scraping her dress as she tore her gaze from the campground. Dammit, she needed to focus. They were heading for the trees lining Shadow Creek and even if she did scream, she doubted anyone would hear her. They'd all gone home.

Meg swallowed. She would get out of this. Keep him talking. Cause a distraction. Wait for rescue. Run.

'Why are you doing this?'

'It's too late for questions. I gave you a simple request and you ignored it. You only have yourself to blame.'

Meg dug her heels into the ground. She probably shouldn't. With one drive of his fist, Edward could stab that knife through her, but like hell was she going with this crazy bastard willingly.

With a surge of courage, Meg shoved her elbow into his gut, but her angle gave her little power behind the hit. Edward tightened his grip around her waist and shoulders. She wriggled, but to no avail. The old man might be crazy, but he was twice her size and bloody strong. He pressed the knife in deeper until the cold blade stung across her flesh. Meg stifled a cry.

'Don't be stupid. I'm the one with the fucking knife.'

'You won't get away with this. Jack will find you. Find me.'

'I'm counting on it. Because not only will they find you in the creek, but him as well.'

Meg's breath escaped in short, sharp bursts as she clutched at his forearm banded around her chest. She could fight him, but he was right. He had a weapon and she couldn't think straight. She'd never get away. But if she could buy time, Jack would find her and she could stand a chance. So, the words kept coming.

'What are you so worried about? What is it about me and Jack that intimidates you so much? Why do you want us dead?'

Edward snorted, his footsteps hurrying as the trees grew closer. 'You have no idea. This fight goes back well before your time. Those Maguires got everything they ever wanted, but I won't let them get their hands on Jade Farm.'

'Why do you care?' she cried, only to find the knife prick her again. 'It's just land, Edward!'

'Land that should have been mine! Your father and the Maguires screwed me over and I'm damn well not going to let it happen again.'

Her eyebrows shot up. '*That's* what this is about? That was years ago! The Maguires didn't—'

'Shut up!' He pushed her forward and Meg stumbled over the hem of her dress. 'They profited and I lost everything! And your mongrel of a father made sure it all happened. If it wasn't for him, you would never have been born and I wouldn't have lost Susie!'

Meg gasped. 'My mother? You … and my mother?' How did she not know about *that*?

Edward sneered. 'Left me for that bloody town hero, didn't she?'

Shock rendered Meg speechless as Edward dragged her towards the creek. The man was crazy. His motives were ill-founded and based on events that had occurred years before she'd even been born. She knew what had happened back then, and Edward was right. Her father *had* been a hero. And dammit, so was she. She would *not* let him take her life.

'Can't say I blame Mum.' And with all her strength, Meg spun and lunged away. Freedom found her and she stumbled towards the campground. But she only made it a couple of steps before Edward's arm snatched her around her waist and dragged her backwards. Her legs flailed.

Then his hand pressed against her mouth and the blade sliced across her ribs.

Meg screamed.

Chapter Forty-Three

The bloody water took forever to heat as Jack kicked his sweat-stained, dirty clothes aside and gave himself a quick rinse. The sooner he got Meg to the pub for dinner, the sooner he could take her home and do the one thing he'd wanted to do for so many years. Adam might have given him all sorts of shit about his plan, but beneath his tough exterior, his brother had grown into a romantic and would no doubt take great pride in setting up Meg's house for his surprise this evening.

Grinning, Jack scrubbed his hands through his hair. He'd wasted no time once he'd returned from Innisfail and after his sneaky visits to Ron Riley and Mareeba, he couldn't wait to see the look on Meg's face when he officially asked her to be with him for the rest of their lives. He had everything planned down to a tee and yes, it was over the top, cheesy, and involved too many roses. Adam had every right to laugh and tease him, but Meg would love it and that's all that mattered. The dread in his gut could just fuck off because even though it might not be the right time, he didn't want to waste any more of their life together. The past six weeks had almost made up for the five miserable years of living without Meg, and he wanted those weeks for the rest of time.

Rinsing off the soap, Jack shivered as a draught drifted through the shower block. He didn't want to turn off the hot water, but he needed to get back to her.

Shutting off the taps, he grabbed the towel. 'All good, darlin'?'

She didn't answer. Frowning, Jack dried his hair. She must be with the horses. They'd made quite a fuss a moment ago.

Tying the towel around his waist, he unlocked the cubicle. 'Meg?'

Barefoot, he strode through the shower block to the doorway. The horses stood by the trailer. Alone. Jack's gaze darted left and right as he walked outside. Where the hell was she?

'Maguire!'

Paul Kelly's shout echoed through the coolabah trees. Groaning, Jack turned as the man ran into the campground.

'Edward White has Meg! They just disappeared into the trees along Shadow Creek!'

Jack stilled, his blood turning to ice as everything around him vanished. Edward White had Meg? Why? How?

Paul leapt into the back seat of his ute and emerged a moment later with a rifle. Jack didn't know whether to be surprised or relieved as Kelly untethered and mounted the stallion. His eyes connected with Jack's. 'Are you just going to fucking stand there?'

'Fuck!' Jack ran towards Dante before realising he had no saddle. Or clothes. He glanced down at the towel around his waist. His bare feet. 'Fuck!'

Paul turned Diego away from the truck. 'I'll go after them. You want me to wait or—'

'Are you fucking kidding me, Kelly?' Jack raced back to the shower block. 'Go!'

***

Blood ran hot down her body, the wound parting with every rasped breath as Meg stumbled through the thicket along Shadow Creek. Pain and fear left her gasping and her pulse refused to slow. Reaching the edge of the water, Edward pushed her to the ground. The impact ricocheted up her arms as rocks scraped her hands and knees, unwillingly bringing tears to her eyes. What was taking Jack so long? Surely he would have realised she was gone by now. He'd raise the alarm. He wouldn't come alone and fall into Edward's trap. Everything would be okay. She just needed to keep away from that knife.

'Why are you doing this? What happens on Shadow Creek doesn't concern you, Edward.'

His laughter echoed along the banks, mean and dangerous. 'Billy helped the Maguires turn a profit this year, but with their tourism and all that fucking land, I can't let Jack Maguire spread his wings and build a fucking empire. He can't have Jade Farm.'

'Then we won't take it!'

Edward snorted. 'Yeah, right. Old Vic won't settle for that. It and the rest of your inheritance will all become part of Shadow Creek.'

Meg spun around, fury surging through her as she sat back on her haunches and looked up at the older man. 'I can't help it if my grandfather wants to give me a farm! Or that my father is rich! I might have money in my own right, but that doesn't make us bad people. You're just jealous because you can't make ends meet. It's sick! What good is Jade Farm to you when you're in prison?'

'I'm not going to prison.'

'My father will make sure of it. Your DNA is under my fingernails.'

Snarling, Edward grabbed her by the hair and pulled her to her feet. Meg yelled, her hands grasping his wrists as the tender spot on her head pulled. She wanted to struggle, but it only hurt more as he spun her back to his front and pressed the knife to her throat.

Meg's cries ceased.

'Any evidence will wash away after I spill your blood right here in Shadow Creek.'

Real, unadulterated fear rose inside Meg as her eyes darted to the glistening water. A whimper caught in her throat. Edward wouldn't wait for Jack. He'd kill her and let Jack live his worst nightmare when he arrived too late.

'You won't get away with this.'

'Oh, I think I will,' he said, manic laughter rumbling through her ears as he pressed the knife closer. 'And I doubt that—'

Hooves thundered and Meg's eyes flew open. Oh God, he'd come.

Except it wasn't Jack who charged in on the back of the stallion, and Meg wasn't disappointed to see Paul Kelly astride Diego with a rifle in his hands.

'Let her go or I'll blow your fucking head off.'

'No!' Edward screamed, his grip tightening as he yanked Meg around to position her between himself and the gun. 'It wasn't meant to be you! You're not supposed to come after her!'

If she could, Meg would have smiled. Edward would never get away with it now. He'd have to kill Paul too.

'Yeah, that's me. Always fucking things up. Now drop the knife!'

'You can't shoot a man, Kelly. You don't have the balls.'

'Try me.' Venom filled Paul's voice as he eased Diego forward. Edward pressed the knife closer until Meg squealed in pain. 'I mean it, White! You know I can shoot you past her ear. Don't fucking test me!'

Edward's chest heaved. Meg didn't move. She'd heard Paul was a good shot, but she didn't want him aiming the gun anywhere near her.

Then more hooves thundered. Edward's arm shook and with an all-mighty cry, he dropped the knife and shoved her away. Meg gasped, clutching her throat as she struggled to stay on her feet.

Warm arms gathered her close. 'I've got you, darlin'.'

Crumbling, Meg buried her face into Jack's bare chest and wept.

Chapter Forty-Four

Jack squeezed Meg into his body as Edward White in all his madness jumped into the creek. Paul leapt off his horse, eyes blazing as he tossed the gun aside and ran after the bastard.

Breath heaving, Jack watched in disbelief as the two men splashed through the water. It wasn't deep along the banks, but Edward didn't get a chance to leap into the flowing current before Paul grabbed him in a headlock. Edward thrashed, kicked, and yelled, but Paul was stronger as he dragged the old man back. Meg lifted her head from his chest, gasping for breath as she glanced over her shoulder. Jack longed to help, but he couldn't let her go. Not until she stopped shaking and his heart ceased galloping a million miles an hour.

Edward slammed his elbow into Paul. Paul grunted, losing his grip as he doubled over. Edward made another break for freedom, but Paul grabbed him by the leg, and they fell face first into the water.

Jack's teeth clenched. Edward surfaced and splashed back towards the bank. Meg whipped her head around. 'The gun.'

Jack's gaze followed hers. 'Fuck. Hold on, darlin'.'

He eased her out of his arms and scrambled to his feet, racing towards the weapon. He couldn't let Edward get his hands on the rifle and while he'd fucking hate firing it, a man had to do what he had to do. Checking it over—

'Maguire, don't!'

Jack stilled, then glanced at Paul struggling with Edward in the creek. Fucking idiot. Tossing the gun aside, Jack raced into the water as all the rage that had been simmering these past weeks—years—erupted. He grabbed Edward by the cuff of his shirt and hauled him towards the bank.

'Get the fuck off me!'

'You tried to kill me, you bastard!' Jack shook Edward, barely resisting the urge to drown the fucker. 'You're not going anywhere.'

Edward's fist ploughed into Jack's gut, but Jack didn't budge. Edward could hit him as hard as he wanted, Jack wasn't letting him go.

Then a tree root snagged his foot. Jack fell, his arse hitting solid ground as he landed on his back. Edward fell on top of Jack, knocking the wind out of him. The other man rolled and struggled to his feet. Paul leapt out the water to tackle him.

'Let me go!' Edward yelled.

Paul got another elbow for his efforts. Jack sat up, his chest heaving. This man wasn't going down without a fight. He kneed Paul, sending him onto his back. Edward scraped to his feet.

A glint of silver caught Jack's eye and instinct took over. Reaching for the knife, he grabbed Edward by the ankle and slammed the blade through his foot, boot and all. 'Run now, you fucker.'

An almighty howl echoed along the creek, rippling the water as Edward crumbled to the ground, clutching his foot.

Jack fell back onto his hands and fought for breath. Meg sat on her haunches, hands pressed to her mouth and eyes wide in horror. Paul lay on his back and spread his arms wide. Jack half crawled, half stumbled to Meg and cupped her delicate face in his hands.

'I've got you, darlin'.' He pressed his lips to her forehead. 'I'm so sorry.'

He repeated the words over and over as he pulled her into his arms. She clung to him, sobs ricocheting through her tiny body.

'It's okay, Jack. I'm okay.'

'You're not. You're bleeding.' He hadn't failed to notice the stain marring her floral dress. 'We need to get you to Nat.'

But Jack didn't move. He couldn't. He'd come so close to losing her and right now, he just wanted to thank his lucky stars that she was still breathing.

'You crazy fuckers!' Edward shouted, finding words after his hideous wailing. 'I should have killed her. Should have killed you too. Who survives a fucking tractor rollover?'

Jack stilled, his teeth grinding as he glared at the whimpering old man. He'd known he hadn't imagined it, known he'd been right, yet the confession had his rage surging all over again. Edward had blown out his tyre, made it look like an accident, threatened him against loving Meg and tried to lure them into traps all for what? Because White Peaks was a struggling shithole that couldn't wrangle its way out of debt?

'You really are a crazy old bastard,' Jack snarled. 'Your father stole from mine, yet you continue to blame us for your mistakes. Ron Riley helped put your father in prison, and you tried to kill his daughter.'

'You're all sorts of fucked up, White,' Paul growled. 'Were you going to kill us next? My parents were part of that too.'

Edward didn't respond as he lowered his head to the ground and clutched his foot.

'Crazy,' Paul muttered, pushing to his feet.

'Crazy?' Jack raised his eyebrows as Paul snatched the gun off the ground. 'You know what's crazy? What mad fucker rides into a fight with an unloaded rifle?'

Resting the weapon on his shoulder, Paul grinned. 'A mad fucker who doesn't keep a loaded rifle in his car.'

* * *

Paul remained behind with the weeping, wounded man while Jack and Meg returned to the campground. Riding in around the Kellys' monstrous truck, they found Lucy pacing with her phone to her ear.

'Dante! There you are!' She abandoned the phone call. 'I— Oh my God, what happened?'

Jack helped Meg off Dante, leaving her to explain while Lucy grabbed the first aid kit. Jack found his phone, which had many missed calls from Lucy, and dialled Cade. The cut on Meg's side wasn't bleeding too badly after they'd applied pressure and she'd stopped shaking, but Jack didn't dare let her out of arm's reach.

'Paul did *what*?' Lucy's eyes widened as Meg explained Kelly's actions. Jack hung up with Cade and called Natalia. 'Are you serious?'

Bernie and Liz hadn't left yet and were quick to arrive and ask what had happened. Meg reassured them she was fine while Jack left them in charge of calling his and Meg's parents. Cade soon arrived, informing them that Brett and Jim had arrested Edward. Paul returned with Diego as the Rav-4 drove in, and Adam and Natalia leapt out.

'Fucking hell, mate.' Adam gathered Jack in a tight hug. 'Here I was sprinkling fucking rose petals and you—'

'I know.' Jack squeezed his brother. 'But we're okay. She's okay.'

And that's all that mattered as he tuned into Natalia's assessment of Meg.

'That cut doesn't look too deep, but I'll take you in for stitches and you'll need antibiotics.' Natalia wrapped her arms around Meg. 'I'm so glad they caught him.'

Adam shoved his hand through his hair. 'I can't believe it was Edward.'

Nodding, Jack glanced past Adam to where Liz Kelly fussed over Paul. An engine roared around the corner and Bernie met Jack's parents as they drove into the campground, Ron and Sue Riley pulling up just behind them.

'Meg!' Sue ran towards them and gathered Meg close, her eyes squeezing shut to fight the tears streaming down her white face as she rocked her daughter from side to side. 'Thank God you're all right.'

A sob escaped Meg as she clutched to her mother. Jack placed his hand on her back, rubbing softly as his parents joined their huddle.

'I'm so sorry, baby girl,' Ron said, wrapping his arms around his wife and daughter. 'So, so sorry.'

'I can't believe Edward would do such a thing,' Sue said. 'Why? I just—'

'He has a thirty-year-old grudge,' Jack said, glancing at Ron and then Henry. 'From when you guys sent his father to prison.'

Henry blew out his breath. 'Unbelievable. Ian White stole from us and almost ruined Shadow Creek, but Edward still blames us for charging the bastard.'

Wendy crossed her arms over her chest. 'Ian was a horrid, despicable man.'

'He was.' Sue's eyes darkened. 'And Edward is no better. He can't take responsibility for anything and it's always someone else's fault.'

The Rileys separated but didn't let each other go.

Ron cleared his throat and brushed Meg's hair off her face. 'I suppose he said some things about your mother.'

Meg nodded. 'He wanted Jade Farm, so the thought of it going to me and Jack sent him a little crazy.'

Sue shook her head. 'I should have known.'

'No, I should have.' Ron placed a kiss on Meg's forehead and met Jack's gaze. 'Didn't we suspect Edward when we were investigating the tractor accident?'

Jack nodded. 'He must have faked that alibi of being at that cattle convention in Mareeba.'

'Yet after striking him off, the case had gone cold.'

'Yep.' Exhaling, Henry clapped his hand on Jack's shoulder before drawing him into a hug. 'I'm sorry, son.'

'Don't be, Dad.'

'No, I talked myself into believing it had been an accident. It was easier for me. But now …' Henry drew back, his eyes blazing. 'That bastard tried to kill you. Both of you.' He touched Meg's arm. 'And I'm sorry we didn't try harder to catch him years ago.'

'I'm sure you did all you could,' Meg said, smiling softly between Ron and Henry. 'But Jack and I are both okay. We need to focus on that.'

'True. It's over now.' Henry smiled at Jack. 'You and Meg can live your lives. Be happy.'

Nodding, Jack embraced his father again, the weight lifting from his shoulders. 'Thanks, Dad.'

'And I'm glad you're okay, Meg,' Henry said, brushing her cheek. Then he glanced at Ron. 'You want to go talk to Brett?'

'Absolutely.' Ron pressed another kiss to Meg's forehead. 'Jack will take you to the surgery, and I'll call you later.'

Jack nodded and glanced at Cade. 'We good to leave?'

'Yep. I need to see what Dad wants to do, as someone needs to take Edward to Mareeba to get his foot looked at. Come and give me a statement tomorrow and I'll make sure you can't be charged for that.'

'Thanks.' He slapped Cade on the shoulder, though he'd have accepted the charges for stabbing Edward if that had meant saving Meg's life.

'No worries. Nat, send me photos of Meg's wounds.'

She nodded and Cade left. Their parents made a bit of a fuss with their farewells, then left too, Meg and Jack promising they'd see them all tomorrow.

Lucy wrapped her arm around Meg. 'I'll get you some clothes and meet you at the surgery, okay?'

'Thanks, Luce,' Meg said as Lucy helped her towards the car. Jack started to follow, then shot his gaze over his shoulder. He halted.

'Hold on, darlin'.'

Jack strode over to Paul, who stood by his ute and, without hesitation, extended his hand. 'Thanks for your help.'

With an odd smile, Paul accepted Jack's hand. 'Only did what had to be done.'

'Yeah, but if you hadn't seen her …' Jack trailed off before he shuddered. 'Anyway. Don't want to go there.'

'Let's not.'

'So, thanks. For everything.'

'No worries.'

Jack stepped away and nodded. 'See you around, Paul.'

'Sure, Jack. Take care of her now.'

'He will,' Meg said, arriving at Jack's side. Smiling softly, she wrapped her arms around Paul. 'Thank you.'

He didn't smile, but Jack didn't miss the glisten in Paul's eyes. 'You're welcome, Meg.'

She stepped back and Jack wrapped his arm around her. Then, with a final nod to Paul, they returned to the Raptor where Lucy stood holding the door open.

'That's something I never thought I'd see,' she said as Jack helped Meg into the passenger seat. 'You and Paul shaking hands.'

'Paul was amazing tonight.' Meg smiled at Jack. 'And so were you.'

He lifted her hand and kissed it. 'I'm sorry we didn't get our date. But ...' It wasn't the right time and not at all like he'd imagined this moment would be, but what the hell? He'd waited long enough. 'I still have a surprise planned for you at home.'

* * *

Meg's cuts had been photographed, cleaned, stitched, and dressed, then Natalia sent her home with antibiotics. Adam had dashed to the roadhouse to grab them all food and while it hadn't been the date Meg had imagined, she'd eaten the stir-fry without complaint. Her father called to tell her Brett had handed Edward over to the Mareeba police and he would face court later that week, where Ron would do his best to ensure the court denied Edward bail. It wouldn't be hard considering his reputation as a solicitor in Mareeba and that he played golf with the local magistrates, but Meg was relieved to hear it anyway as the more tonight's events played over in her head, the crazier they seemed. She could hardly fathom Edward's madness. Because that's what it'd been. Madness.

But as Jack pulled up outside her house, she forced the trauma from her mind. She didn't want to think about Edward's motives, the history, or anything else that had happened in the past. Now that the nightmare was over, she just wanted to spend time with Jack.

She took his hand, and he helped her from the ute.

'This isn't how I meant to do this tonight,' he said as he unlocked her front door.

'Do what?'

'I had a romantic evening planned. I just hope the girls haven't destroyed everything in the rush Adam had leaving.'

Jack gestured her inside and Meg gasped as she gazed around her living room. Rose petals littered the floor, leading a path to her lounge where two glasses sat with a bottle of probably no-longer-chilled mango wine on the decorated coffee table. Fresh candles spread around the room, never having been lit, while Jill and Lola greeted her wearing matching heart-printed bandanas.

Meg bit down on her lip. 'Adam did this?'

'With Nat.'

She turned towards him, her heart pounding. This was why he hadn't wanted to get ready for dinner at home. He'd sent his brother to set up her living room so that he could … 'Oh, God. Jack …' Meg pressed her hands to her mouth as tears filled her eyes.

He smiled softly. 'Come and sit down, darlin'.'

He guided her to the lounge. Meg's knees shook, her hand squeezing his as they sat. Lola jumped up beside him while Jill sat and panted happily.

'Show weekend is your favourite time of year, so I planned

to do this tonight and despite the events earlier this evening, I won't let that crazy bastard delay us any longer.'

She laughed, but it came out more like a hiccup. Then Jack reached beneath the cushion and produced a little red box. Meg's heart stuttered inside her chest. Oh, no! He'd bought her a ring and she'd never mentioned—

He flipped the lid. Meg froze, her breath catching. She blinked and lifted her gaze to Jack's. 'It's my diamond.'

His mouth curved. 'Of course it is.'

'But …' She shook her head. 'How did you know?'

Jack plucked the pink diamond ring from the box, the jewel glittering beneath the lights. 'I remember once, you were still in high school, when you told Lucy it was yours. The Rileys' argyle pink diamond. You were sitting beneath the jacaranda tree and you said that you hoped it'd be your engagement ring. I never forgot that, so when I returned from Innisfail, I went to your father and asked if I could have it.'

Everything inside Meg numbed. Tears continued to fill her eyes. 'You did?'

His grin widened. 'Your dad had it in a box with my name on it. Then I took it to Mareeba and had it fashioned into this ring.'

Speechless, Meg brushed the tears from her cheeks. She couldn't believe it. Her grandmother had promised her that one day, her father would give the diamond to a lucky man worthy of marrying her and Meg had had her heart set on having the pink argyle on her finger ever since. She would have suggested to Jack that he visit her father for ring advice after they'd silenced the threat, as she'd thought he would only consider marriage once they were safe. But her man hadn't been prepared to wait, and she loved him for that.

A sob broke free. 'Oh, Jack …'

Wrapping his arm around her, he drew her against his chest. Meg breathed him in and held him tight. He was everything she'd ever wanted. All her dreams rolled into one. For a moment tonight, she'd feared it would all be over. But it wasn't. She had him. Her best friend. Her one love. Her future.

His hand rubbed up and down her arm as his lips brushed her hairline. 'So, darlin', what do you say? Will you marry me?'

'It's all I've ever wanted,' she said, pressing her lips to the centre of his chest before lifting her gaze. 'So yes, Jack Maguire. I will marry you.'

'It's all I've ever wanted too, my darlin'.' His lips captured hers and her breath hitched, but she kissed him back with everything left inside her before he drew away. Jack wiped her tears, then grinning, he twirled the ring. 'Can I put this on now?'

Her hand snapped up. 'Not a moment too soon.'

Jack's large hand clasped hers and he brushed his thumb over her fingers before sliding the pink diamond into its rightful place. Meg's heart swelled until she couldn't breathe.

'Perfect,' he whispered, and she nodded mutely. 'Meg?'

Somehow, she dragged her gaze from her engagement ring and glanced into his eyes. 'Yeah?'

'We've waited too long to be together, so let's get married soon.'

Grinning, she wrapped her arms around his neck as excitement replaced her disbelief. 'I can do that. I already have the wedding planned.'

He chuckled. 'I knew you would. And what do you say we commission Adam to build us our own crib?'

Meg squealed and squeezed him tight as her mummy hormones ricocheted through her body. 'He is *not* going to be happy! But yes. I want to have a baby with you, Jack. Lots of them.'

'There are *four* bedrooms in the homestead, Meg. And trust me, filling them is enough.'

'All right.' He probably had a point. 'I can't have a baby before the wedding though, so I'll talk to Mum and the minister and get everything sorted. And do you know what else this means?'

'What, darlin'?'

'You can farm avocados and start building your empire.'

'Yeah, I'm sure Victor will bring it up at dinner this week.' Grinning, he kissed her longingly. 'With no more threats, Meg, we can both have our dreams.'

'We can. Shadow Creek will expand across the region, and I will record with Chaz, release an album, and sing.'

'And I'll be there to support you. To love you and cheer you on.'

'I'm just glad to have my muse back.' Smiling, Meg placed her hand on his chest as she gazed into his glittering dark eyes. 'And that you're happy.'

Jack touched his mouth to hers. 'I'll always be happy as long as you're with me.'

Tropical cyclones are an infrequent part of life in North Queensland, but a detrimental threat to the horticultural industry. When I visited Gaia Farm prior to releasing this series, I discovered that the destruction to Innisfail banana farms caused by Cyclone Larry was the catalyst for boosting production of bananas in Mareeba and Lakeland, of which Elizadale is located between. Inspired, I knew I had to use this history in the Shadow Creek books, especially I needed to replace the cattle muster plot in Meg and Jack's original story, and I am thrilled with how this novel was transformed. Although, I do apologise for destroying the beautiful town of Innisfail with another devastating cyclone.

Cyclone Billy was inspired by Cyclone Larry and Cyclone Yasi. Cyclone Larry struck Innisfail on March 20, 2006, as a category 5 storm and at the time, he became the costliest cyclone to ever strike Australia. I lived in Mackay, 650km south of Innisfail, and there are two things I remember most about Larry. Firstly, the widespread support and fundraising for the victims across the state and school hosted many events, particularly to aid the recovery of Innisfail High. And secondly, the significant banana shortage that resulted in prices hiking to almost $20 a kilo. Since Australia doesn't import bananas due to risk of disease, the country relied on the remaining 10-20% of banana farms to produce the fruit. As the farmer in Innisfail told me, that is when Mareeba and Lakeland flourished. In my world, Shadow Creek would have flourished too. Elevated and inland, these towns aren't generally affected by coastal storms, and this continency plan saved the banana industry only five years later.

In 2011, Cyclone Yasi became the largest cyclone to ever hit Australia. At 650km wide, she was a monster threatening Cairns and Townsville, the two major cities in the north, and the rural towns and farmland in between, where the bananas grow. In comparison, Cyclone Larry was 50km wide.

Yasi crossed the coast on February 3, 2011, at Mission Beach, destroying the neighbouring banana regions in Tully and Innisfail. The cost of her damage was triple to that of Larry. 30% of houses in Tully were destroyed, and at least 75% of the banana crop, as deleafing helped. Damaged powerlines left 150000 homes without electricity, and 600km of power line and 2500 power poles were replaced. Some rural areas weren't reconnected until a month or more after the cyclone. Townsville's water supply system failed and was saved by running water out of Magnetic Island, and severe rain cut the highway between Townsville and Ingham, creating a 10km backup of traffic. Due to Yasi's size and power, she continued to leave destruction and rain halfway across the country until dissipating around Alice Springs in central Australia.

I was in Townsville for Cyclone Yasi. Our power was cut at 5pm and I spent the night inside the closed hot house with no fans or breeze while the winds howled around us. Come morning, a large tree had fallen through our back retaining wall, and we were without power for 48 hours. Damage in Townsville was minor in comparison to up north, and life went back to normal relatively quickly.

Then as fate would have it, this book was in final proofs when Cyclone Jasper crossed the coast north of Port Douglas on December 13, 2023, making direct contact with my fictional town of Elizadale. Jasper made landfall with lighter winds as a category 2 cyclone, but heavy rainfall and the flooding in the north has been catastrophic. Thousands of properties lost power and people were left stranded in the remote towns. By my best estimation, Elizadale would have been left without power for five days, but it was during this time that the final detail of Billy's destruction was added when I saw how rain and landslides snapped the Palmerston Highway in half. As the recovery from Jasper is ongoing, I cannot comment on the damage. However, I have been humbled by the amazing show of mateship and community spirit displayed by North Queenslanders as everyone knuckles down to help their communities recover and demonstrates the heart of what *Waltzing Maguire* is about. North Queensland's spirit can't be blown away.

Acknowledgements

Once again, I wrote this book alone tucked away in my little unit, but I couldn't have done it without the amazing help of all my favourite people who continue along on this journey with me.

A big thank you goes to my friends. Deeanna West, thank you for attending local shows with me and for sharing your knowledge and experience as a regular show-goer. It is thanks to you and Bridgette for teaching me about show jumping, the six bar, and inadvertently inspiring part of the next book…no hints allowed. I'm grateful for your ongoing support and to have you as a friend. Thank you to my local writing friends Linda Wright, Barbara Strickland, and Jill Staunton, for always being there for me to turn to. I always appreciate your wonderful advice. Jill, once again, you encouraged some final touches that authenticated the story, so thank you.

To my editor Nicola, I thoroughly enjoy working with you and am deeply grateful for your feedback. Your thoughts thoroughly polished this manuscript and helped tighten the places that needed tightening. Thank you also to my awesome cover designer Danielle, who does such a wonderful job. You nailed it with this cover and I'm still in love—it's pink!

But the biggest thank you goes to my parents for all your ongoing support and encouragement. 2023 was a massive year for us. Mum, you have been with me and the Maguires since day one, and I'm so glad you loved how Meg and Jack turned out. I really couldn't have done it without you. And to my stepfather Ian, thank you for jumping on the Shadow Creek bandwagon and for your support with this book. I loved working out the mechanics of the prologue and accident with you and I'm thrilled to have you on my production team. Thank you both for your notes, feedback, and bickering in the margins of this manuscript during proofreading. I am deeply grateful to you both and thank you for your assistance at markets and joining me on research trips. Our time in Mareeba added those final flourishes to this story and those to come. I love sharing my writing journey with you both.

Last of all, thank you to my wonderful readers. Without you enjoying the previous Shadow Creek books, bringing you the next wouldn't be half as fun, so I hope you liked Meg and Jack's story. More Maguire books are to come, and the next one is going to be awesome! I can't wait to share it with you, and I hope you stick with me along the way.

The *Shadow Creek* series

The Pub with No Food
Grace and Luke
A spinoff prequel

Home Among the Palm Trees
Ana and Liam

The Man from Shadow Creek
Natalia and Adam

Waltzing Maguire
Meg and Jack